The Horus Heresy series

Book 1 – HORUS RISING
Dan Abnett

Book 2 – FALSE GODS
Graham McNeill

Book 3 – GALAXY IN FLAMES
Ben Counter

Book 4 – THE FLIGHT OF THE EISENSTEIN
James Swallow

Book 5 – FULGRIM
Graham McNeill

Book 6 – DESCENT OF ANGELS
Mitchel Scanlon

Book 7 – LEGION
Dan Abnett

Book 8 – BATTLE FOR THE ABYSS
Ben Counter

Book 9 – MECHANICUM
Graham McNeill

Book 10 – TALES OF HERESY
edited by Nick Kyme and Lindsey Priestley

Book 11 – FALLEN ANGELS
Mike Lee

Book 12 – A THOUSAND SONS
Graham McNeill

Book 13 – NEMESIS
James Swallow

Book 14 – THE FIRST HERETIC
Aaron Dembski-Bowden

Book 15 – PROSPERO BURNS
Dan Abnett

THE HORUS HERESY

Dan Abnett

PROSPERO BURNS

The Wolves unleashed

BLACK LIBRARY

Belatedly, for Evan McNeill

A BLACK LIBRARY PUBLICATION

First published in Great Britain in 2011 by
The Black Library,
Games Workshop Ltd.,
Willow Road, Nottingham,
NG7 2WS, UK.

10 9 8 7 6 5 4 3

Cover and page 1 illustration by Neil Roberts.

A CIP record for this book is available from the British Library.

UK ISBN13: 978 1 84416 776 0
US ISBN13: 978 1 84416 777 7

See the Black Library on the internet at
www.blacklibrary.com

Find out more about Games Workshop
and the world of Warhammer 40,000 at
www.games-workshop.com

Printed and bound by CPI Group (UK) Ltd, Croydon, CR0 4YY

THE HORUS HERESY

It is a time of legend.

Mighty heroes battle for the right to rule the galaxy. The vast armies of the Emperor of Earth have conquered the galaxy in a Great Crusade – the myriad alien races have been smashed by the Emperor's elite warriors and wiped from the face of history.

The dawn of a new age of supremacy for humanity beckons.

Gleaming citadels of marble and gold celebrate the many victories of the Emperor. Triumphs are raised on a million worlds to record the epic deeds of his most powerful and deadly warriors.

First and foremost amongst these are the primarchs, superheroic beings who have led the Emperor's armies of Space Marines in victory after victory. They are unstoppable and magnificent, the pinnacle of the Emperor's genetic experimentation. The Space Marines are the mightiest human warriors the galaxy has ever known, each capable of besting a hundred normal men or more in combat.

Organised into vast armies of tens of thousands called Legions, the Space Marines and their primarch leaders conquer the galaxy in the name of the Emperor.

Chief amongst the primarchs is Horus, called the Glorious, the Brightest Star, favourite of the Emperor, and like a son unto him. He is the Warmaster, the commander-in-chief of the Emperor's military might, subjugator of a thousand thousand worlds and conqueror of the galaxy. He is a warrior without peer, a diplomat supreme.

As the flames of war spread through the Imperium, mankind's champions will all be put to the ultimate test.

~ DRAMATIS PERSONAE ~

Primarchs

Russ	The Wolf King
Magnus	The Crimson King

The Rout

Onn

Gunnar Gunnhilt	Called *Lord Gunn*, jarl

Tra

Ogvai Ogvai Helmschrot	Jarl
Ulvurul Heoroth	Called *Longfang*, rune priest
Bear	
Aeska	Called *Brokenlip*
Godsmote	
Galeg	
Aun Helwintr	
Orcir	
Jormungndr	Called *Two-blade*
Ullste	
Erthung Redhand	
Oje	
Svessl	
Emrah	
Horune	
Najot Threader	Wolf priest

Fyf

AMLODHI SKARSSEN   Jarl
SKARSSENSSON

VARANGR   Herald to Lord Skarssensson

OHTHERE WYRDMAKE Rune priest

TRUNC

BITUR BERCAW

Imperial Personae

GIRO EMANTINE   prefect-secretary to the
                        Unification Council

KASPER HAWSER   Conservator, also known as
                        Ahmad Ibn Rustah

NAVID MURZA   Conservator

Non-Imperial Personae

FITH OF THE ASCOMMANI

GUTHOX OF THE ASCOMMANI

BROM OF THE ASCOMMANI

LERN OF THE ASCOMMANI

In the Past

RECTOR UWE

'If I am guilty of anything, it is the
simple pursuit of knowledge.'

– The Primarch Magnus, at Nikaea

'Take but degree away, untune that string,
And, hark! what discord follows; each
thing meets
In mere oppugnancy: the bounded waters
Should lift their bosoms higher than the shores
And make a sop of all this solid globe:
Strength should become the lord of imbecility,
And the rude son should strike his father dead:
Force should be right; or rather
right and wrong
(Between whose endless jar justice resides)
Should lose their names, and so should
justice too.
Then every thing, includes itself in power,
Power into will, will into appetite.
And appetite, a universal wolf,
So doubly seconded with will and power,
Must make perforce a universal prey, and last eat up
himself.'

– attributed to the dramaturge Shakespire (fl. M2),
cited in the Prophecy of Amon of the
Thousand Sons (chp III verse 230)

'Those who cannot remember the past are
condemned to repeat it.'

– unattributable (circa M2)

PART ONE

THE UPPLANDER

ONE

At the Turning of Spring

DEATH HAD THEM surrounded.

It had come to cut threads, and today it wore four faces.

A burning death for those too hurt or too afraid to flee the settlement as the firestorm swept through it. A freezing death for those who ran away up the scarp to escape the murder-make. Even in spring, the wind came in off the ice flats with a death-edge that sucked an exposed man's life-heat out through his lungs, and rotted his hands and feet into black twigs, and left him as a stiff, stone-hard bundle covered in rime.

For others, a drowning death, if they attempted to flee across the blue-ice around the spit. Spring's touch was already working the sea ice loose against the shore, like a tooth in a gum. The ice would no longer take a man's weight, not reliably. If the ice broke under you, down you went: fast and straight if you plunged through, slow and screaming if an ice plate tipped and slid you in. Either way, the water was oil black, and so cold it would

11

freeze the thoughts in your brain before your lungs were even empty.

For the rest, for those who had remained to fight, a bloody death, the death of the murder-make. This was the death that knocked you down hard onto the ice with an axe or a maul, so you felt nothing except the cold burn of the ice, and the hot burn of your own blood, and the pain-scream of your crippling wound. This was the death that stood over you and knocked you again, and again, and as many times as necessary until you would not rise again, or until you were so disfigured that death could no longer bear to look at you, and moved off in disgust to find another soul to knock.

Any of those four faces would cut your thread as soon as look at you. And those were the faces the Balt were wearing.

The Balt. The Balt had brought the murder-make down on the Ascommani aett. Twenty boat. It was early in the season for a raid. A man had to be desperate to go out making red snow when he could wait for the first grasses and milder weather.

Twenty boat, and all of them still rigged for ice-running under their sea-sails.

If there had been time, the Ascomani might have wondered why their doom had come so early. Ironland, where the Balt had settled, had persisted twenty great years, but many now said its roots were soft. Many now said it would only be one more summer, two at the most, before the ocean sucked it down again into the world-forge.

Ascomani land ran from the spithead to the ice shelf, and was poor for farming and lacked natural defences, but it was yet just one great year old, and the dowsers had proclaimed it strong land, with many years left in it.

So land-thirst. Perhaps it was that.

Fith knew better. Nothing got the murder-urge pumping like fear, and nothing stoked up fear like a bad omen. A broom star. A day star. Colour in the ice. Bloom in the sea. Smoke out on the ice shelf where no settlement was. Some dead thing washed up that should not be. Something born to livestock or to a woman that should not be. Something with birth defects.

Sometimes a bad dream would be enough to do it, a bad dream that told you the tribe down the coast or around the headland was *maleficarum*. You let land-thirst be your excuse as you reached for your shirt and your blade, but you made sure the gothi marked your face in soot-glue with good cast-out marks like the sun-disk and the warding eye before you opened out your sails.

And there had been a bad omen, all right. Fith had seen it.

Fith had seen the make coming too. He'd seen the sails approaching along the in-shore early enough to blow the scream-horn, but too late for it to do any good. He had merely enabled his kinfolk to die awake.

The Balt main force had come up around the spit in their wyrmboats in the sightless pre-dawn grey, sailing black sails straight out of the water and onto the shore-ice on their rigs, translating from water-craft to ice-craft with barely a jolt. Their skirmishers had put ashore on the far side of the headland, and come romping in over the high back of the snow dunes to fall on the Ascommani settlement from the hind side.

After that, it had been fire and knocking. The Balt were mongrel-big, men with long faces and beards waxed into sun rays under their spectacle-face helms. They were horribly able with axe and maul, and the occasional high-status sword that some carried.

But they brought with them none of the screaming

vigour of a normal Balt raid or murder-make. They were silent, terrified of what they had come to kill, terrified of its sky magic. They were silent and grim, and set to murder everything to wipe the magic away. Men, women, the young, livestock, nothing was spared a knock. There was not a shred of mercy. There was not a moment's thought to claim prisoners or take slaves. Ascommani girls were famously fine-looking, and there were plenty of healthy girl-children too, who would make valuable breeding slaves in time, but the Balt had put away all appetites except for a fierce desire to be cleansed of fear.

The sound of an axe knocking-in is a wet smack of slicing meat and shattering bone, like sap-wood being cut. A maul makes a fat, bruising sound like a mattock driving pegs into marsh loam or wet ice. Worse than both are the after-sounds. The screaming of the agonised, the ruined and the dying. The begging shrieks of the hurt and maimed. The hacking impacts of death knocking until the fallen stop being alive, or stop trying to rise, or stop screaming, or stop being in once piece.

Fith had just enough time to get his shirt on and loft his axe. Several other hersirs fell to arms with him, and they met the first skirmishers coming in through the walls and window-slits of the settlement head on. The panic was up already. It was blind blundering in the dark, a reek of urine, the first noseful of smoke.

Fith's axe was balanced for a single hand. It was a piece of proper craft, with a high-carbon head that weighed as much as a decent newborn boy. From the toe of the blade to the heel of the beard, it had a smile on it wider than a man's hand-span, and it had kissed a whetstone just the night before.

The axe is a simple machine, a lever that multiplies the force from your arm into the force delivered by the blade. The rudiments apply whether you're splitting wood or men.

Fith's axe was a bone-cutter, a shield-breaker, a helm-cleaver, a death-edge, a cutter of threads. He was a hersir of the Ascommani aett, and he knew how to stand his ground.

It was a throttle-fight in the settlement itself. Fith knocked two Balts back out of the tent wall, but the tight confines were choking his swing. He knew he needed to get out. He yelled to the hersirs with him and they pulled back.

They got out of the tents into the settlement yard, wrapped in swirling black smoke, and went eye to eye with the Balts in their spectacle-helms. It was mayhem. A free-for-all. Blades swung like windmills in a storm.

Fenk went down as a Balt axe split his left calf lengthwise. He bawled in rage as his leg gave out, useless. Seconds later, a maul knocked his head sidelong, snapping his neck and his thread. He flopped down on the earth, his shattered skull-bag leaking blood.

Fith drove off a Balt with a mattock, scared him back with the whistling circles of his swinging axe.

Ghejj tried to cover Fith's flank, using the basics of shield-wall tactics. But Ghejj had not had time to collect a decent shield from the stack, just a tattered practice square from the training field. A Balt spear punctured him right through, and tore him open so thoroughly, his guts spilled out onto the snow like ropes of sausage. Ghejj tried to catch them, as though he could gather them up and put them back inside himself and everything would be all right again. They steamed in the spring air. He squealed in dismayed pain. He couldn't help himself. He knew he was ruined unto death.

He looked at Fith as he squealed again. It wasn't the pain. He was so angry that he was irreparably dead.

Fith put mercy into his stroke.

FITH TURNED AWAY from his last picture of Ghejj and saw
that there were fingers scattered on the snow, on the
snow that had been churned up by scrambling and sliding feet, along with blood by the bowl-full. They were
the fingers of women and children, from hands held up
to protect themselves. Defensive wounds.

There on the snow, a complete hand, the tiny hand of
a child, perfect and whole. Fith recognised the mark on
the ring. He knew the child the hand had once belonged
to. He knew the father the child had once belonged to.

Fith felt the red smoke blow up in his head.

A Balt came at him, silent and intent. Fith flexed the
lever of his axe, hooked it in, and made a ravine of the
Balt's face.

Four hersirs left. Fith, Guthox, Lern and Brom. No
sign of the aett-chief. The chief was probably dead and
face down in the red snow with his huscarls.

Fith could smell blood. It was overpoweringly strong,
a hot copper reek spicing the freezing dawn air. He
could smell Ghejj's insides too. He could smell the
inner parts of him, the ruptured stomach, the yellow fat
of his belly meat, the heat of his life.

Fith knew it was time to go.

The Upplander was in the furthest shelter. Even the
Ascommani knew to keep him away from people.

The Upplander was propped up against cushions.

'Listen to me,' Fith hissed. 'Do you understand me?'

'I understand you. My translator is working,' the Upplander replied, looking pale.

'The Balt are here. Twenty boat. They will knock you
dead. Tell me, do you want the mercy of my axe now?'

'No, I want to live.'

'Then can you walk?'

'Perhaps,' the Upplander replied. 'Just don't leave me
here. I am afraid of wolves.'

✠

THERE ARE NO wolves on Fenris.

When the Upplander had been told this, years before, he'd laughed.

He had heard it from a venerated scholar and conservator, later celebrated iterator, called Kyril Sindermann. The Upplander, not long graduated with distinction from the Universitariate of Sardis, had won a coveted place on an eight-month field mission to audit and preserve some of the arcane datacores of NeoAleksandrya, before sandstorms and scorching radiation squalls erased the precious ruins into the melancholy emptiness of the Nordafrik zone forever. This was many decades before the Upplander decided to go to Fenris, or call himself Ahmad Ibn Rustah. Back then he was twenty-five years old, and known to his friends as Kasper.

Sindermann learned his name early on. Sindermann wasn't the project head. He had been sent in for a three-week consult, but he was not afraid to get his hands dirty or to mix with the junior team members. He had an easy way with people. Names were important.

One evening, the team had fallen, according to their habit, into discussion over supper in the project's base, a modular station overlooking the library ruins.

They were all exhausted. Everyone had been working inadvisably long shifts to get the mission accomplished. No one wanted to see the precious digital memories that lingered in the ruins lost for all time.

So, everybody was sand-burned, and everybody was sleep deprived, and everybody had lost significant body mass to water debt. The nights should have been time for restorative rest, but they had found their dreams populated by the data-ghosts of NeoAleksandrya, talkative phantoms that would not let the living slumber undisturbed. So they stayed up to keep the phantoms out, and the nights became time for tired companionship and reflection as the ablative winds howled in over the radgrave of NeoAleksandrya and assaulted the station's bolted storm shutters.

They talked about everything, just to stay awake. Sindermann, perhaps the greatest polymath the Upplander would ever have the honour of knowing in his long life, had a tireless tongue.

The older team members talked about the various places they had visited in the courses of their careers, and the younger members talked of places they still wanted or hoped to visit. This led, inevitably, to the concoction of an ultimate wish list, a dream itinerary of the places in creation that any scholar, historian or remembrancer would give great wealth or a body part just to glimpse. It was a list of the universe's secret places, its remote wonders, its enigmatic corners, its rumoured sites and mythical locales. Fenris was one such. Ironically, given what the Upplander would witness towards the end of one of his lives, Tizca was another.

Sindermann, though even then a man of great age and experience, had not been to Fenris himself. The number of outsiders who had ever gone to Fenris was alarmingly small. But then, as Sindermann put it, Fenris did not welcome visitors, nor was it a gracious host. Thanks to its extreme conditions, even a well prepared man might be lucky to survive a few hours on its open surface.

'Still,' he had said to them, 'think of all that ice.'

It had sometimes reached forty degrees in the station at night, at least that when the climate control centre packed up. They had all groaned at Sindermann's tormenting words.

Then, apropos of nothing in particular, Sindermann made the remark about the wolves, a remark that had been passed to him down such a long relay of other travellers and historians, its provenance was obscure.

'There are no wolves on Fenris,' he had said.

The Upplander had smiled, expecting some droll wit-
ticism to follow. His smile had covered the shiver he
had felt.

'Except, of course... for the wolves, ser?' he had
replied.

'Exactly, Kasper,' the old man said.

Shortly afterwards, the subject had changed, and the
remark had been forgotten.

FITH DIDN'T MUCH want to touch the Upplander, but he
wasn't going to walk far without an arm around his ribs.
He hoisted the man up, and the Upplander groaned at
the jolt.

'What are you doing?' Brom yelled. 'Leave him!'

Fith scowled. Brom knew better than that. It wasn't
that Fith wanted to drag the Upplander around, but that
was the thing with omens. You didn't invite them into
your aett, but once they were in, you couldn't ignore
them.

Fith could no more leave the Upplander lying there
than the Balt could have refused to set out on the
murder-make that midnight.

Lern stepped up and helped Fith handle the injured
man. The shelters of the aett were ablaze, and choking
the pale dawn sky with fat rivers of black smoke. The
Balt hadn't finished cutting threads. Sharp screams of
anguish and pain split the air like arrows.

They ran along the edge of the scarp, stumbling with
the burden of the injured man. Guthox and Brom followed them, snow-running with wide, splayed steps.
Brom had got a spear from somewhere. A gang of Balt
took off after them, chasing like hunting dogs across the
snow, hunched and loping.

Guthox and Brom turned to meet them. Guthox's axe

knocked the first one onto his back, and a jet of blood squirted out in a five-metre arc across the snow. Brom's spear-tip found the cheek of another Balt, and tore it like cloth, digging out teeth that popped free like kernels of corn. Brom clubbed his victim dead with the butt of his spear-shaft as the man fell down holding his face.

The Balt circled and danced away from Brom's jabbing spear. Fith left Lern with the Upplander's weight and turned back. He came past Brom in a screaming charge, and lopped off the top of a Balt's skull with his circling axe. That shook things up. Spear or no spear, the Balt went for them. They tried to use their shields to get the spear out of their faces. One of them immediately took the spear in the breastbone. It made a dry-branch crack as the iron head went in, and the man puked blood. But the spear was wedged, and the Balt's dead weight wrenched it out of Brom's hands. He scrambled back with nothing but a long knife to guard himself.

Guthox used his axe to break a shield, and the arm holding it, then felled the Balt with a neck wound. He turned to fend off a bearded Balt axe with the cheek of his own, but the Balt was big and strong, and drove Guthox onto his heels with a series of relentless knocks.

Fith still had momentum. His charge ran down two more Balt, one of which he left bleeding to death, the other dazed, and he turned in time to rescue Guthox by burying the toe-point of his axe through the spine of the big Balt hacking at him.

Fith jerked the axe out with a snarl, and the Balt collapsed on his face. Brom was finishing another with angry, repeated stabs. The Balt had wounded Brom on his first pass, but had then made the mistake of getting too close to the hersir's long knife.

They ran back to where Lern was toiling with the Upplander. Brom had recovered his spear, but he was leaving red snow behind him.

The Upplander was panting with effort. Heat was steaming out of his loose, gasping mouth. Under his storm cloak, the Upplander wore garments made from fabrics unfamiliar to Fith or his kinsmen. The sky-fall had hurt the Upplander, broken some bones was Fith's guess, though Fith had never seen an Upplander opened up to know if they worked the same way inside as Ascommani, or Balt, or any other aettkind.

Fith had never seen an Upplander before. He'd never been tied up in an omen this bad. He wondered what had become of the aett's gothi. The gothi was supposed to be wise, and he was supposed to use that wisdom to steer and safeguard the wyrd of the aett.

Fine job he'd done. The gothi had not known what to make of the Upplander when the hersirs had first brought him in from the crash site, and he hadn't known what to do after that, except shake his bone jangles and his rattle full of fish teeth, and beseech the spirits with the same old tired chants, pleading with them to come down from Uppland and take back their lost kinsman.

Fith believed in the spirits. He firmly believed. He believed in Uppland above where the spirits lived, and the Underverse below, where the wights went. They were the only thing a man had to cling to in the changing landscape of the mortal world. But he was also a pragmatist. He knew there were times, especially when a man's thread was pulled so thin it might snap, that you had to make your own wyrd.

Three bow shots away from the aett, the Ascommani kept a basin for their boats. It was a little ice crater open to the sea on the north head, and they had better than ten boat in it. Most were up on blocks, hoisted from the ice, so the men could labour in daylight hours to remove the rigs ready for the spring waters. But one was the aett-chief's boat, ready to run at a moment's nod. It

was called 'keeping it nocked'. You nocked the cleft of
an arrow against a bowstring ready for tension, ready to
fly. The chief's wyrmboat stood on its runners on the
hard ice, its sails ready to drop and fill, checked only by
the anchor lines.

'Into the boat!' Fith ordered as they scrambled down
the slope to the basin edge.

'Which boat?' asked Lern.

'The chief's boat!' Fith snapped.

'But it's the chief's boat…' Guthox said, wary.

'He's not going to be needing it,' said Fith. 'Not as
much as we do, anyway.'

Guthox looked at him blankly.

'The chief's sleeping on the red snow, you arsehole,'
said Fith. 'Now get in the boat.'

They got into the boat, and laid the Upplander
down in the bow. The Balt began to appear at the crest
of the slope. The hersirs heard the air-buzz of the first
arrows.

Fith dropped the sea sails, and they filled in an
instant. The canvas cracked like thunder as it took the
world's breath. There was a hard snow-wind that morning, and he'd barely noticed it. The anchor lines creaked
and strained as the wyrmboat mithered on the ice,
impatient to slip.

'Cut the lines!' Fith yelled out.

Guthox looked at him from the stern, where the
wind-pull was chaffing the taut lines against the rail.

'He's really not coming?' he asked.

'Who?'

'The chief. You saw his thread cut?'

'He'd be here if he was coming,' said Fith.

They heard cracking sounds like green wood spitting
in a fire. The iron heads of arrows were smacking into
the ice around them, drilling up puffs of ice dust or
cracking punctures into the blue-black glass of the crust.

Two arrows hit the boat. One went into the main mast as deep as the length of a man's forearm.

'Cut the lines!' Fith yelled.

Guthox and Lern cut the lines with their axes. The wyrmboat took off like an escaping animal, its sails bellied out full and as rigid as iron. The lurch shook them on their feet. The bladed runners of the ice rig shrieked as they scratched across the marble ice of the basin.

Lern took the helm. He was the best steersman of them. He draped his armpit over the tiller, loading it with his weight to drive the blade of the sternpost rudder into the ice, and balanced the tension of the ropes coming from the quarter rudders, one in each fist. Steering a rigger was a battle of muscle and wit. One bad judgement, one over-light feathering of the quarters, one heavy-handed dig of the main blade, and the combination of polished ice and raw wind shear could tumble even the biggest wyrmboat, and knock it into kindling.

They left the basin. They went through the sea-cut in the granite lip that let out onto the open water. But it wasn't water. It was long past the great year's glacial maximum, and time was turning, but this stretch of sea along the shadowed inlet remained the sky's looking glass. In some places it was grey-green like an old mirror, in others blue like uncut sapphire, in others bright and clear like fine crystal, but everywhere it was thick to a depth two or three times the height of a man.

As soon as they were clear of the basin, and the boat's runners were shrieking across the surface of the mirror sea like the baleful voices of the wights of the Underverse, the cold hit them. It was the open cold, the cold of the dull, iron-hard end of winter, the blunt cold of the open ice range. All of them gasped at the shock of it, and immediately laced up their collars or wrapped up scarf bindings to protect their mouths and noses.

Fith looked at the Upplander sprawled in the bow. He

was panting from a combination of pain and exertion, and the breath heat was steaming out of him in great spectral clouds that the wind was stripping away.

Fith moved down the vibrating wyrmboat towards him, walking with the practised, rolling gait of an experienced ice-mariner.

'Cover up your mouth!' he shouted.

The Upplander looked up at him blankly.

'Cover up your mouth! Breathe through your nose!'

'What?'

Fith knelt down beside him.

'The heat'll bleed right out of you, with your mouth open like that. Breathe through your nose. Conserve it.'

He opened one of the woven-grass coffers tucked in under the boat's rail, and pulled out a blanket and some furs. They were all stiff with cold, but he shook them out and swaddled the Upplander in them.

'Through your nose,' he reminded. 'Don't you know that? Don't you know the cold?'

'No.'

'Then why the hell would you come to this land, if you didn't know all the ways it would try to kill you?'

⟡

THE UPPLANDER HAD no answer. He couldn't summon the effort. Renewed pain was gripping him, and it was extraordinarily comprehensive. It pinned his thoughts, and refused to allow him even a small reserve of mental power to use for other things. He'd never known pain like it, except perhaps once.

He could hear a clavier playing. The keys were ringing out a cheerful music hall melody that he could just pick out above the screaming of the runners and the roaring of the brutish crew.

He could hear a clavier playing, and he knew he ought to know why.

⟡

THE BALT CAME after them. Lern shouted out as soon as he spotted them, and pointed astern. Wyrmboats were skating out from around the spithead. They were black-sail boats, rigged for a murder-make by night. The Balt were resolved to see the make through to its bloody end. Fith had hoped the Balt might give up once the main raid on the aett was over.

But no. The Balt had to be terrified to keep up the pursuit. They weren't going to rest until everyone was dead.

What had their gothi told them, Fith wondered? What interpretation had he spouted that night when the broom star had sliced the sky, a ribbon of light that had left an accusatory glowing scar directly over Ascommani territory. How had he explained the land fall, the noise-shock of the star hitting ice?

What had he told his wide-eyed hersirs, his chief, the Balt womenfolk, the children woken up and crying because of the noise?

Fith had seen the Balt gothi once, three great years back, at a time when the Balt and the Ascommani had been on trading terms, when they could visit aett to aett for a barter-make with cargoes of pelts and grass-weave and smoked meat, and exchange them for preserved herbs, lamp-oil, whale-fat candles and ingots of pig iron.

There had been a formal meeting of the chiefs, with an exchange of gifts, a lot of bowing, a lot of long-winded rehearsal of lineage and bloodline from the skjalds, and a lot of blowing of the Balt's bronze horns, which made a sound half like a sea-cave echo and half like a muffled fart.

The Balt gothi had been skinny, 'taller than a warbow and twice as thin' as the saying went, with a heavy jaw like that of a mule-horse or a simpleton. There were so many metal piercings in his lips and nose and ears, he looked as if he had been plagued with boils and cold sores.

He had a wand made of a bear's arm blade, and a silver torc. Someone had braided seabird feathers into his long, lank hair, so that they made a white mantle around his bony shoulders. His voice was thin and reedy.

His name was Hunur.

He spoke sense, though. During the barter-make, Fith had come to the gothi's shelter, joined the listeners sharing the fire, and listened to him talk. The Balt gothi knew how the world worked. He talked plainly about the Verse and the Underverse, as if he had been told their secrets by the wights themselves.

The Ascommani gothi was a crazy brute. He had fits, and he smelled like a sea-cow, both of which factors had probably led to his election as gothi. He was good with stars, Fith had to give him that. It was as if he could hear the noise their rigs made as they skated around the glass of the sky. But the rest of the time he was foul-tempered and raving.

His name was Iolo.

At the barter-make, Iolo and Hunur had squared up to one another, sniffed and growled like rutting bull seals, and then spent the whole time trying to steal one another's secrets.

But it had also been as if they were afraid of one another. It was as if, in trying to steal one another's secrets, they were afraid that they were risking infection.

That was how it went with magic. Magic had an underside. Magic could transform a man's life, but it could corrupt it too, especially if you weren't careful, if you didn't watch it and soothe it and keep it sweet. Magic had a nasty undercurrent that could infect a man if he wasn't paying attention.

Magic could turn nasty. Magic could turn on you, even if you were the most exact and painstaking practitioner or gothi.

The worst magic of all, that was sky magic, and it was sky magic that was riding in the bow of their wyrmboat.

Fith wondered what the Balt gothi had said to his people to get them so fired up.

✥

LERN SWUNG THEM west, down the mirror-throat of the inlet, under the shadows of the spithead cliffs and out onto the ice field, the apron of the great glacier.

Ice was better than water; the same area of sail could invest you with ten times the speed. But the effort was mighty. Fith knew they'd have to change steersman in another hour, or stop to let Lern rest, because the concentration was so intense. Already, Lern's eyes looked drawn, what Fith could see of them over the lip of his collar.

They cut up across a long *strayke* of ice field the colour of grey fish-scales, and passed through the collar ridges where glacial moraines of broken rock pushed up through the ice of the glass like extrusions of deformed bone.

The Balt boats were steadily falling behind. A good Balt boat was one thing, axe-carved from ocean-wood and whale bones, but a good Ascommani boat was quite another, especially a fine rig built for an aett's chief.

They might live yet.

It was a fragile thought, and Fith hated himself for even thinking it and thus jinxing it. But it was real. They might yet outrun the Balts' murder-make and find sanctuary.

The Hradcana, they were the best hope. The Hradcana were a major power in the west, with several aetts along the jagged backbone of the ice field, less than a day away. More important, a peace-make understanding had endured between the Hradcana and the Ascommani for the lifetimes of the last six chiefs. Most

important of all, the Hradcana and the Balt had quar-
relled and made red snow on and off for ten
generations.

When Guthox saw the first Hradcana sails ahead,
Fith's spirit lifted. Some beacon look-out had seen them
raking in across the ice field and sent a horn-blast down
the chain, and the Hradcana chief had ordered out his
wyrmboats to greet and assist the Ascommani visitor.

Then he realised, with a sinking feeling, that the
explanation didn't fit the facts.

'We're too far out,' he murmured.

'What?' Brom asked. He was trying to sew his cut up
with fishing wire and a bone needle. The work was too
fussy for gloves, but the windchill was too severe for
bare hands to function with any finesse. He was making
a mess of himself.

'We're too far out for any Hradcana lookout to have
spotted us yet,' Fith said. 'They're coming out because
they knew we were coming.'

'Crap!' Brom snorted.

Fith looked at the sails of the Hradcana boats. Sails
were the most distance-visible aspect of a boat, so they
were often used to declare intention. A straw-yellow sail
invited trade and barter. A purple sail indicated aett-
mourning, the cut thread of a chief or a queen. A white
sail, like the one dragging Fith's wyrmboat, proclaimed
open approach and embassy. A black sail, like the ones
the Balt had come in under, was a treacherous sail,
because it hid its declaration in the night, and thus
defied the convention.

A red sail was an open announcement of the intention to murder.

The Hradcana sails were red.

✧

FITH SETTLED DOWN in the rattling bow of the wyrmboat
beside the Upplander.

'What are you?' he asked.

'What?'

'What have you done? Why have you brought this on us?'

'I did nothing.'

Fith shook his head. 'Red sails. Red sails. Gothi has spoken to gothi through the Underverse. The Balt came at us, now the Hradcana come at us too. Who else? Have you turned the whole Verse against us, or just against you?'

'I don't know what you mean,' the Upplander said.

'Did you make it your destiny to die here?' asked Fith.

'No!'

'Well,' the hersir replied, 'you certainly seem to have put some effort into making it happen.'

IT WAS AN exalted place.

Even on that pestilential day, with the tail-end of the six-week campaign to take the Boeotian citadel chattering and booming in the distance, there was an odd stillness in the shrine.

Kasper Hawser had felt it before, in other places where mankind had focussed its worship for unnumbered generations. A cathedral in Silesia, just the shell of it, brittle as paper, rising above the fuming, white rubble and slag of the atomic dustbowl. The deep, painted caves in Baluchistan where a closed priesthood had concealed precious cellulose scrolls inscribed with their sacred mysteries, and thus preserved the essence of their faith through the Age of Strife. The high, monastic refuges in the Caucasus where scholars and savants fleeing Narthan Dume's pogroms had hidden in exile, forlorn, ascetic outposts perched at such an altitude, you could see the expanding hive zones of the Caspian Bloc to the east and the nano-toxic waters of the Pontus Euxinus to the west, and the voice of some forgotten god lingered in the wind and the thin air and the bright sky.

The scholars had come out of Dume's Panpacific realm with a priceless cargo of data that they had painstakingly liberated from the Tyrant's library prior to one of his data purges. Some of that material, rumour suggested, dated from before the Golden Age of Technology.

When Hawser and his fellow conservators finally located the refuges, they found them long-since extinct. The cargo of data, the books and digital records, had degraded to powder.

The more man masters, the more man finds there is to be mastered; the more man learns, the more he remembers he has forgotten.

Navid Murza had said that. Hawser had never seen eye to eye with Navid Murza, and the various associations they'd been forced to make during their careers had fostered a sour and immotile disdain between them.

But there was no faulting Murza's passionate intent. The strength of his calling matched Hawser's.

'We have lost more than we know,' he said, 'and we are losing more all the time. How can we take any pride in our development as a species when we excel at annihilation and fail to maintain even the most rudimentary continuity of knowledge with our ancestors?'

Murza had been with him that day, in Boeotia. Both of them had been awarded places on the conservator team by the Unification Council. Neither of them had yet seen their thirtieth birthday. They were both still young and idealistic in the most vacuous and misguided ways. It rankled with both of them that they had tied in the appointment rather than one winning and one losing.

Nevertheless, they were professionals.

The vast refinery eight kilometres away had been mined by the retreating Yeselti forces, and the resulting fires had blanketed that corner of Terra in lethal black smoke, a roiling, carcinogenic soup of soot-black petro-carbon filth as thick as oceanic fog and as noxious as a plague pit. The conservators wore sealed bodygloves and masks to go in, shambling through the murk with their heavy, wheezing aug-lung packs in their hands, like suitcases. The packs were linked to the snouts of their masks by wrinkled, pachydermic tubes.

The grave gods loomed to meet them through the smoke. The gods wore masks too.

They stood for a while, looking up at the grave gods, as immobile as the ancient statues. Divine masks of jade and gold, and staring moonstone eyes looked down on haz-guard masks of plastek and ceramite, and lidless photo-mech goggles.

Murza said something, just a wet sputter behind his visor.

Hawser had never seen anything like the gods in the Boeotian shrine. None of them had. He could hear the visor displays of several team members clicking and humming as they accessed the memories of their data-packs for comparative images.

You won't find anything, Hawser thought. He could barely breathe, and it wasn't the tightness of the mask or the spit-stale taste of the aug-lung's air flow. He'd scanned the grapheme inscriptions on the shrine wall, and even that quick glance had told him there was nothing there that they'd expected to find. No Altaic root form, no Turcic or Tungusic or Mongolic.

The picters they carried were beginning to gum up in the sooty air, and battery packs were failing left and right. Hawser told two of the juniors to take rubbings of the inscriptions instead. They turned their goggles towards him, blank. He had to show them. He cut sheets of wrapping plastek into small squares and used the side of the wax marker-brick to scrub over the faint relief of the mural marks.

'Like at school,' one of the juniors said.

'Get on with it,' Hawser snapped.

He began an examination of his own, adjusting the macular intensity of his goggles. Without laboratory testing, it was impossible to know how long the shrine had stood there. A thousand years? Ten thousand? Exposed to the air, it was degrading fast, and the pervasive petrochemical smog was destroying surface detail before his very eyes.

He had a desire to be alone for a minute.

He went outside, back up the throat of the entrance-way. The Boeotian Conflict had uncovered this treasure. The site had been exposed by a parcel of wayward sub-munitions rather than the diligent hand of an archaeologist. But for the war, this treasure would never have been found, and because of the war, it was perishing.

Hawser stood at the entrance and put his aug-lung on the ground beside him. He took a sip of nutrient drink from his mask feeder, and cleaned his fogging goggles with hand spray.

To the north of his position, the conflict in the Boeotian citadel underlit the horrendous black roof of the sky, a bonfire shaped like a city. The blackness of the vast smoke canopy was all around, as dense as Old Night itself. Gusting pillars of bright flame came and went in the distance as the smoke shifted.

This, he remarked to himself with leaden irony, was what the great era of Unification looked like.

According to history tracts that were already published and in circulation, that were already *being taught in scholams*, for goodness sake, the glorious Unification

Wars had brought the Age of Strife to an end over a century and a half earlier. Since then, there had been more than one hundred and fifty years of peace and renewal as the Emperor led the Great Crusade outwards from Terra, and courageously reconnected the lost and scattered diaspora of mankind.

That's what the history tracts said. Reality was far less tidy. History only recorded broad strokes and general phases of development, and assigned almost arbitrary dates to human accomplishments that had been made in far less definitive instalments. The aftershocks of the Unification War still rolled across the face of the planet. Unification had been triumphantly declared at a point when no power or potentate could hope to vanquish the awesome Imperial machine, but that hadn't prevented various feudal states, religious adherents, remote nations or stubborn autocrats from holding out and trying to ring-fence and preserve their own little pockets of independence. Many, like the Boeotian Yeselti family, had held out for decades, negotiating and conniving their way around treaties and rapprochements and every other diplomatic effort designed to bring them under Imperial sway.

Their story demonstrated that the Emperor, or his advisors at least, possessed extraordinary patience. In the wake of the Unification War, there had been a strenuous and high-profile effort to resolve conflicts through non-violent means, and the Yeselti were not tyrants or despots. They were simply an ancient royal house eager to maintain their autonomous existence. The Emperor allowed them a twilight grace of a century and a half to come to terms, longer than the lifespan of many Terran empires.

The story also demonstrated that the Emperor's patience was finite, and that when it was exhausted, so was his mercy and restraint.

The Imperial Army had advanced into Boeotia to arrest the Yeselti and annex the territory. Hawser's accredited conservator team was one of hundreds assigned to follow the army in, along with flocks of medicae, aid workers, renovators, engineers and iterators.

To pick up the pieces.

Hawser's mask-mic clicked.

'Yes?'

It was one of the juniors. 'Come inside, Hawser. Murza's got a theory.'

In the shrine, Murza was shining his lamp pack up angled stone flues cut in the walls. Motes of soot tumbled in the beam, revealing, by their motion, a flow of circulation.

'Airways. This is in use,' he said.

'What?'

'This isn't a relic. It's old, yes, but it's been in use until very recently.'

Hawser watched Murza as he prowled around the shrine. 'Evidence?'

Murza gestured to the faience bowls of various sizes dotted along the lip of the altar step.

'There are offerings of fish and grain here, also copal resins, myrrh I believe. Scanners show carbon counts that indicate they're no more than a week old.'

'Any carbon count is compromised in this atmosphere,' Hawser replied. 'The machine's wrong. Besides, look at the state of them. Calcified.'

'The samples have degraded because of the atmosphere,' Murza insisted.

'Oh, have it both ways, why not?' said Hawser.

'Just look at this place!' Murza shot back, gesturing with his gloved hands in exasperation.

'Exactly what are you proposing, then?' asked Hawser. 'An occulted religious observance conducted outside the fringe of Boeotian society, or a private order of tradition sanctioned by the Yeselti?'

'I don't know,' Murza replied, 'but this whole site is guarding something, isn't it? We need to get an excavator in here. We need to get into the recess behind the statues.'

'We need to examine, record and remove the statues methodically,' Hawser said. 'It will take weeks just to begin the preservation treatments before we can lift them, piece by–'

'I can't wait that long.'

'Well, sorry, Navid, but that's the way it is,' said Hawser. 'The statues are priceless. They're our first concern for conservation.'

'Yes, they are priceless,' Murza said. He stepped towards the solemn, silent grave gods. The juniors were watching him. A few took sharp breaths as he actually stepped up onto the base of the altar, gingerly placing his foot so as not to dislodge any of the offertory bowls.

'Get down, Murza,' said one of the seniors.

Murza edged up onto the second step, so he was almost at eye level with some of the gazing gods.

'They are priceless,' he repeated. He raised his right hand and gently indicated the blazing moonstone eyes of the nearest effigy. 'Look at the eyes. The eyes are so important, don't you think? So telling?'

He glanced over his shoulder at his anxious audience. Hawser could tell Murza was smiling, despite the hazmask.

'Get down, Navid,' he said.

'Look at the eyes,' Murza said, ignoring the instruction. 'Down through time, they've always meant the same thing to us, haven't they? Come on, it's basic! Someone!'

'Protection,' mumbled one of the juniors awkwardly.

'I can't hear you, Jena. Speak up!'

'The eye is the oldest and most culturally diverse apotropaic symbol,' said Hawser, hoping to cut to the chase and end Murza's showboating.

'Yes, it is,' said Murza. 'Kas knows. Thank you, Kas. The eye *guards* things. You put it up for protection. You put it up to ward off evil and harm, and to keep safe the things you hold most precious.' His fingertip traced the outline of the unblinking eye again. 'We've seen this so many times, just variations of the same design. Look at the proportional values! The eye shape, the brow line, this could have been stylised from a *nazar boncugu* or a *wedjat*, and it's not a million kilometres away from the Eye of Providence that is so proudly displayed in such places as the Great Seal of the Unification Council. These are gods of aversion, there's no doubt about it.'

He jumped down from the steps. Some of the party gasped in alarm, but Murza did not disturb or break any of the precariously placed bowls.

'Gods of aversion,' he said. 'Keep out. Stay away.'

'Have you finished?' Hawser asked.

'The pupils are pieces of obsidian, Kas,' Murza said eagerly as he came towards Hawser. 'You get as close as I did, get your photo-mech to decent resolution, you can see that they're carved. A circle around the edge, a dot in the middle. And you know what that is.'

'The circumpunct,' Hawser replied quietly.

'Which represents?' Murza pressed.

'Just about anything you want it to,' said Hawser. 'The solar disc. Gold. Circumference. Monad. A diacritical mark. The hydrogen atom.'

'Oh, help him out, Jena, please,' Murza cried. 'He's just being awkward!'

'The eye of god,' said the female junior nervously. 'The all-seeing singularity.'

'Thank you,' Murza said. He looked directly at Hawser. His eyes, behind the tinted lenses of the goggles, were fierce. 'It says keep out. Stay away. I can see you. I can see right into your soul. I can reflect your harm back at you, and I can know what you know. I can read your heart. I can keep you at bay, because I am power and I am knowledge, and I am protection. The statues are priceless, Hawser, but they are gods of aversion. They're guarding something. How valuable is something, do you suppose, that someone would protect with *priceless statues*?'

There was silence for a moment. Most of the team shifted uncomfortably.

'They're a family group,' said Hawser quietly. 'They are a representation of a dynastic line. A portrait in statue form. You can see the gender dimorphism, the height differentials, and the placements, thus determining familial relationships, hierarchies and obligations. The tallest figures on the highest step, a man and a woman, lofty and most exalted. Below them, children, perhaps two generations, with their own extended families and retainers. The first son and first daughter have promi- nence. It's a record of lineage and descent. They're a family group.'

'But the eyes, Kas! So help me!'

'They are apotropaic, I agree,' said Hawser. 'What could they be guarding? What could be more priceless than a gold and jade effigy of a god-king, and his queen, and his divine sons and daughters?'

Hawser stepped past Murza and faced the altar.

'I'll tell you. The *physical remains* of a god-king, and his queen, and his divine sons and daughters. It's a tomb. That's what's in the recess. A tomb.'

Murza sighed, as if deflated.

'Oh, Kas,' he said. 'You think so small.'

Hawser sighed, knowing they were about to go around again, but they turned as they heard noises from the entrance.

Five soldiers clattered into the shrine, spearing the
gloom with the lamps strapped to their weapons. They
were Imperial Army, hussars from the Tupelov Lancers,
one of the very oldest regiments. They had left their
cybernetic steeds outside the shrine and dismounted to
enter.

'Clear this site,' one of them said. They were in full
war-armour, combat visors down, frosty green photo-
mech cursors bouncing to and fro along their optical
slits.

'We've got permission to be here,' said one of the
seniors.

'Like crap you have,' said the hussar. 'Gather your stuff
and get out.'

'Who the hell do you think you're talking to?' Murza
exclaimed, pushing forwards. 'Who's your commander?'

'The Emperor of Mankind,' replied the hussar. 'Who's
yours, arsewipe?'

'There's been a mistake,' said Hawser. He reached for
his belt pack. Five saddle carbines slapped up to target
him. Five lamp beams pinned him like a specimen.

'Whoa! Whoa!' Hawser cried. 'I'm just reaching for
my accreditation!'

He took out the pass-pad and flicked it on. The holographic credentials issued by the Unification Council
Office of Conservation billowed up into the smoky air,
slightly blurred and malformed by the edges of the
smoke. Hawser couldn't help but notice the Eye of Providence on the Council seal that flashed up before the
data unfurled.

'That's all very well,' said one of the hussars.

'This is all current. It's valid,' said Hawser.

'Things change,' said the hussar.

'This was personally ratified by Commander Selud,'
said one of the seniors. 'He is primary commander
and–'

'At oh-six thirty-five today, Commander Selud was relieved of command by Imperial decree. All permits and authorities are therefore rescinded. Get your stuff, get moving, and live with your disappointment.'

'Why was Selud removed?' asked Murza.

'Are you High Command? Do you need to know?' sneered one of the hussars.

'Just unofficially?' Murza pleaded.

'Unofficially, Selud's made a total clusterfug of the whole show,' said the hussar. 'Six weeks, and he still manages to let the refinery fields catch fire? The Emperor's sent someone in to tidy the whole mess up and draw a line under it.'

'Who?' asked Hawser.

'Why are these civilians still here?' a voice asked. It was deep and penetrating, and it had the hard edges of vox amplification. A figure had entered the chamber behind the Tupelov Lancers. Hawser wasn't sure how it could have possibly walked in without anyone noticing.

It was an Astartes warrior.

By the pillars of Earth, an Astartes! The Emperor has sent the Astartes to finish this!

Hawser felt his chest tighten and his pulse sprint. He had never seen an Astartes in the flesh before. He hadn't realised they were so big. The curvature of the armour plating was immense, oversized like the grave god statues behind him. The combination of the gloom and his goggles made it hard to resolve colour properly. The armour looked red: a bright, almost pale red, the colour of watered wine or oxygenated blood. A cloak of fine metal mesh shrouded the warrior's left shoulder and torso. The helmet had a snout like a raven's beak.

Hawser wondered what Legion the warrior belonged to. He couldn't see any insignia properly. What was it that people were calling them these days, now that the bulk of all Astartes forces had deployed off Terra to spearhead the Great Crusade?

Space Marines. That was it. Space Marines. Like the square-jawed heroes of ha'penny picture books.

This was no square-jawed hero. This wasn't even human. It was just an implacable thing, a giant twice the size of anybody else in the chamber. Hawser felt he ought to have been able to smell it: the soot on its plating, the machine oil in its complex joints, the perspiration trickling between its skin and its suit-liner.

But there was nothing. No trace, not even a hint of body heat. It was like the cold but immense blank of the void.

Hawser could not imagine anything that could stop it, let alone kill it.

'I asked a question,' the Astartes said.

'We're clearing them now, ser,' stammered one of the Lancers.

'Hurry,' the Astartes replied.

The hussars started to herd the team towards the entrance. There were a few mumbles of protest, but nothing defiant. Everyone was too cowed by the appearance of the Astartes. The aug-lungs were wheezing and pumping more rapidly than before.

'Please,' said Hawser. He took a step towards the Astartes and held out the pass-pad. 'Please, we're licensed conservators. See?'

The hologram re-lit. The Astartes didn't move.

'Ser, this is a profound discovery. It is beyond value. It should be preserved for the benefit of future generations. My team has the expertise. The right equipment too. Please, ser.'

'This area is not safe,' said the Astartes. 'You will remove yourselves.'

'But ser–'

'I have given you an order, civilian.'

'Ser, which Legion do I have the honour of being protected by?'

'The Fifteenth.'

The Fifteenth. So, the Thousand Sons.

'What is your name?'

Hawser turned. The Tupelov Lancers had led most of
the team out of the shrine, leaving only him behind.
Two more Astartes, each as immense as the first, had
manifested behind him. *How could something that big
move so stealthily?*

'What is your name?' the new arrival repeated.

'Hawser, ser. Kasper Hawser, conservator, assigned
to–'

'Is that a joke?'

'What?' asked Hawser. The other Astartes had spoken.

'Is that supposed to be a joke?'

'I don't understand, ser.'

'You told us your name. Was it supposed to be a joke?
Is it some nickname?'

'I don't understand. That's my name. Why would you
think it's a joke?'

'Kasper Hawser? You don't understand the reference?'

Hawser shook his head. 'No one's ever…'

The Astartes turned his beaked visor and glanced at
his companions. Then he looked back down at Hawser.

'Clear the area.'

Hawser nodded.

'Once the security of this area can be guaranteed,' said
the Astartes, 'your team may be permitted to resume its
duties. You will evacuate to the safe zone and await
notification.'

NO NOTIFICATION EVER came. Boeotia fell, and the Yeselti
line came to an end. Sixteen months later, by then
working on another project in Transcyberia, Hawser

heard that conservator teams had finally been let into the Boeotian Lowlands.

There was no trace that any shrine had ever existed.

FITH WONDERED WHAT kind of wight he would come back as. The kind that flashed and flickered under the pack ice? The kind you could sometimes see from a boat's rail, running along in the shadow of the hull? The kind that mumbled and jittered outside an aett's walls at night, lonely and friendless in the dark? The kind that sang a wailing windsong between the high ice peaks of a scarp on a late winter day?

Fith hoped it would be the darkest kind. The kind with the oil-black eyes and the slack-hanging mouth, the kind with rust and mould clogging the links of its shirt. The kind that clawed its way up from the Underverse using its fleshless hands as shovels, gnawed its way through the rock waste and permafrost, and then went walking at night.

Yes.

Walking until it reached Ironland and the hearth-aetts of the shit-breath Balt. Walking with a special axe in its hand, an axe forged in the Underverse from the bitter wrath of the restless and murdered, hammered out on god's own anvil, and quenched in the bile and blood of the wronged and the unavenged. It would have a smile on it, a smile sparked on wyrd's grindstone to a death-edge so keen it would slice a man's soul from his flesh.

Then threads would be cut. Balt threads.

Fith hoped that would be the way. He wouldn't mind leaving the Verse so much if there was an expectation of returning. He hoped the wights would let him do that. They could carry him away to the Underverse for all he cared, knocked down by a Balt maul or a Balt arrow, his own cut thread flapping after him in the gales of Hel, just so long as they let him return. Once he reached that unfamiliar shore, they had to remake him, build him back up out of his own raw pain, until he looked like a man, but was nothing more than an instrument, like an axe or a good blade, forged for one pure, singular purpose.

It wouldn't be long before he found out.

Guthox had taken the tiller so that Lern could bind his rope-sawn fingers. The red sails were gaining on them, faster than the black sails of the Balt.

They had one chance left, in Fith's opinion. A half-chance. One last arrow in wyrd's quiver. If they cut north slightly, and ran through the top of Hradcana territory, they might make it to the ice desert beyond. The desert, well, that was death too, because it was a fatal place that no man or beast could live in, but that was a worry for later. They would make their own wyrd.

If they went to the desert, neither the Hradcana nor the Balt would follow. If they could get through a cut in the rock rampart the Hradcana called *The Devil's Tail*, they'd be free and clear, free to die on their own terms, not hounded and knocked to Hel by a pack of soul-cursed murder-makers.

But it was a long run to The Devil's Tail. Brom was too messed up to take a turn at the tiller, and even in rotation, the rest of them would be hard pressed to keep going. It was a run you'd break into four or five shorter runs, maybe sleeping out on the ice and cooking some food to rebuild your strength. To make it non-stop, that would be a feat of endurance, a labour so mighty the skjalds should sing about it.

If there were any Ascommani skjalds left alive.

Braced against the rail, Fith talked it over with Lern and Brom. All three of them were hoarse from the fight, from yelling hate back into the Balts' faces.

Brom was in poor shape. There was no blood in his face, and his eyes had gone dim like dirty ice, as if his thread was fraying.

'Do it,' he said. 'The Devil's Tail. Do it. Let's not give these bastards the satisfaction.'

Fith made his way to the bow, and knelt down beside the swaddled Upplander.

The Upplander was speaking.

'What?' asked Fith, leaning close. 'What are you saying?'

'Then he said,' the Upplander hissed, 'then he said I can see you. I can see right into your soul. That's what he said. I can reflect your harm back at you and I can know what you know. Oh god, he was so arrogant. Typical Murza. Typical. The statues are priceless, Hawser, he said, but how valuable is something, do you suppose, that someone would protect with *priceless statues*?'

'I don't know what you're telling me,' said Fith. 'Is it a story? Is it something that happened in the past?'

Fith was afraid. He was afraid he was hearing sky magic, and he didn't want any part of it.

The Upplander suddenly started and opened his eyes. He stared up at Fith in sheer terror for a second.

'I was dreaming!' he cried. 'I was dreaming, and they were standing looking down at me.'

He blinked, and the reality of his situation flooded back and washed the nonsense of his fever dream away, and he sank and groaned.

'It was so real,' he whispered, mainly to himself. 'Fifty fugging years ago if it was a day, and it felt like I was right back there. Do you ever have dreams like that? Dreams that unwrap fresh memories of things you'd forgotten you'd ever done? I was really there.'

Fith grunted.

'And not here,' the Upplander added dismally.

'I've come to ask you, one last time, do you want the mercy of my axe?' asked Fith.

'What? No! I don't want to die.'

'Well, first thing, we all die. Second thing, you're not going to get much say in the matter.'

'Help me up,' said the Upplander. Fith got him to his feet and propped him against the bow rail. The first pricking gobs of sleet were hitting their faces. Up ahead, the sky had risen up in a great, dark summit of cloud, a bruised stain like the colour of a throttled man's face, and it was rolling in on the ice field.

It was a storm, coming in hard, flinging ice around the sky. Late in the winter for a storm that dark. Bad news, whichever way you looked at it. The rate it was coming, they weren't going to get anywhere much before it blew in across them.

'Where are we?' the Upplander asked, squinting into the dazzle of the ice field rushing by.

'We're somewhere near the middle of shit-goes-our-luck,' said Fith.

The Upplander clung onto the rail as the wyrmboat quaked across a rough strayke.

'What's that?' he asked, pointing.

They were coming up fast on one of the Hradcana's remote northern aetts. It was just an outpost, a few shelters built on some crags that rose above the ice plain. The Hradcana used it to resupply and safe-harbour their fisher boats when the sea thawed out. It was uninhabited for months at a time.

A row of spears had been set tip-down in the sheet ice in front of the aett. They stood like a row of fence posts, six or seven of them. On the raised end of each spearhaft, a human head had been impaled.

The heads were turned to look out onto the ice field at them. Their eyes had been pinned open.

They were most likely the heads of criminals, or enemy captives, ritually decapitated for the purpose, but it was possible they were Hradcana, sacrificed in desperation because of the extremity of the maleficarum. Their eyes were open so they could see the evil coming and ward it off.

Fith spat and cursed. He dearly wished Iolo had been able to badge their faces with cast-out marks, to bounce the warding magic back. The wyrmboat had eyes on its prow, of course: the all-seeing sun-disc eyes of the sky god, painted bold and bright, and decorated with precious stones. All wyrmboats had them, so they could find their way, see off danger, and reflect an enemy's magic.

Fith hoped it would be enough. The boat was a strong boat, an aett-chief's boat, but it had run hard and it was tired, and Fith was worried that its eyes might not be powerful enough to turn the magic back anymore.

'Gods of Aversion,' the Upplander murmured, gazing at the staked heads. 'Keep out. Stay away. I can see you.'

Fith wasn't listening to him. He yelled back down the long, narrow deck at Guthox, signalling him to turn wide. The aett was inhabited. A second later, the spiked heads flashed by, and they were skating the inshore ice under the shadow of the crag.

Guthox cried out. They were still two or three decent bow shots from the islet, but someone was either gifted or favoured by the Underverse. An arrow had gone into him.

Now more struck, *thakking* into the hull or falling short and skipping across the ice. Fith could see archers on the rim of the islet crag, and others on the beach.

He raced back down the boat to Guthox. Lern and Brom were moving too.

It was a monstrously lucky shot, except for Guthox. The arrow had gone through the tight-ringed sleeve of his shirt, the meat of his left tricep, shaving the bone, and then through the sleeve again, and then the shirt proper, before punching into the hersir's side between his ribs, effectively pinning his arm against his body. Guthox had immediately lost control of one of the quarter rudder ropes. The pain was immense. He had bitten through his tongue in an effort not to scream.

Two arrows were embedded in the deck boards beside them. Fith saw they had fish-scale tips: each head shaped and finished from a single, iron-hard scale from a deep water monster. They were barbed, like a backwards-slanted comb.

That was what had gone into Guthox. It would never come out.

Guthox spat blood and tried to turn the tiller. Brom and Lern were shouting at him, trying to take over, trying to snap the arrow shaft so they could free Guthox's arm. Guthox was slipping away.

Another wave of arrows hit. One, perhaps, came straight from the same gifted or favoured archer. It hit Guthox in the side of the head, and ended his pain by cutting his thread.

Blood droplets and sleet stung their faces. Guthox fell away from the tiller and, though Brom and Lern sprang in, the wind became their steersman for a split-second.

That was all the time the wind needed, and it had no interest in sparing their lives.

TWO

Dis-aster

THE WIND FLUNG them into the rocks abutting the beach, and the wyrmboat shattered like a crockery jar. The impact was sustained, like a relentless series of hammer blows. The world vibrated and up-ended, and the shivering air filled with rock-grit and out-flung stones, along with sleet, with slivers of ice, and with raked splinters of deck-wood as sharp as darning needles. The maniacal wind tore the sails away, like a vicious child plucking the wings off a long-legged fly. The sail-cloth, so full of hard air that it was splitting, cracked as it flew free, and the halyards screamed as they fled through the blocks and sawed into the pins. There was a brief, sharp reek of smoke from unwetted wood as the rigging lines friction-burned their way through and away. Under tension, the escaping lines whirred and buzzed like bees.

Fith smelled the wood-burn in the last instant of the wyrmboat's life. The deck broke under him, and flipped him into the sleeting sky. Then he hit the ice with his face.

The wyrmboat had gone right over, and folded up into the rocks where the wind had driven it. Thrown clear, Fith slid face-down across the glazed sea, his throat full of ice and blood. He rotated, head and toe, as he slowly came to rest.

He raised his head. The ice beneath him was as dull and cold as the flat of a sword. His chest and face were one big aching bruise, and it felt like he had taken the smile of an axe in his breastbone, and another in his cheek.

He tried to get up. He felt as if he was too cracked to even breathe. Sucking air into his chest was like swallowing broken glass. Part of the wyrmboat's mainsail, full of wind and trailing its lines, danced away along the shore of the islet like a gleeful phantom, like a capering wight with its arms out-flung.

Fith began to limp towards the ruin of the boat. A few arrows hissed overhead. Hradcana bowmen were scrambling down the rocks to reach the wreck. Hradcana red sails were closing in across the ice. Fith could hear the shriek of their bladed runners.

The ice in his path was scattered with debris. Here was a piece of mast, sheared off. There was part of the starboard rigger, torn off, its iron-shod skate stuck in the crazed ice like a giant's arrow. Here was a section of spar. Fith picked it up, and hefted it as a weapon.

There was Guthox's body. The wyrmboat had spilled it as it tumbled, and one of the riggers had sliced right over it, mashing it flat at the waist.

A Hradcana arrow whipped past Fith's face. He didn't flinch. He saw his axe lying near Guthox, and discarded the spar.

He picked up his axe.

Close beside the mangled ruin of the wyrmboat, Lern was dragging the Upplander's corpse onto the shoreline rocks. Blood was streaming down one half of Lern's face and soaking his whiskers. Fith began to limp faster to reach them.

When he left the ice and set foot on the ice-fused shingle, the Hradcana had come close enough for him to see their wild eyes and the white ash-glue coating their faces. They were so close that he could smell the stink of their ritual ointments. These were foul-smelling pastes their gothi had made, aversion remedies to keep the maleficarum at bay. The warriors had put aside their bows and taken up their axes and their swords. A bad omen had to be more than just killed. It had to be cut apart, hacked apart, dismembered and un-remembered. That was how you got magic to leave you alone.

Brom had got up to face them with his axe. Fith wondered how he was even standing any more. He limped to stand at Brom's side.

One of the Hradcana was shouting out at them. It wasn't a challenge or a threat, it was a ritual thing, a statement of intent, a declaration of what they were doing and why they were doing it. Fith knew that from the singsong cadence of the words, rather than the words themselves. The warrior was using the Hradcana's private tribal tongue, their wyrd-cant, which Fith did not speak.

'This is onto you and onto your heads, in the day and the night, in the time of the moving sea and in the time of the still sea,' the Upplander suddenly said out loud as Fith stepped past him. He wasn't dead after all, though both of his legs had undoubtedly been broken in the crash. Lern, blood still pouring from his scalp, was trying to make him secure, but the Upplander was pushing away and trying to pull himself up onto a rock.

'This is the wyrd that you have written for yourself by taking the disaster into your aett and deciding to protect it,' the Upplander continued. He looked at Fith. 'That's what they're saying. My translator is reading it. Do you understand them?'

Fith shook his head.

'Why do they call me a disaster? What did I ever do?'

Fith shrugged.

A look of realisation suddenly crossed the Upplander's drawn face. 'Oh, it's just the translator! It's literal, just literal... "dis-aster"... *bad star*. They're calling me *Bad Star*.'

Fith stood beside Brom and faced the Hradcana. The Hradcana warrior was finishing his declaration. Behind him, Fith could hear the Upplander translating the last of it.

The Hradcana rushed them.

Without shields, the two Ascommani took the charge. They put over-swings into the first row of faces, and under-swings into the second. Like the surge of the sea when the sea was wet, the Hradcana slipped back and came in again across the shingle. Brom split a man's shoulder. Fith smashed a man's jaw into mammocks and managed to wrest the man's shield away from him. He punched the iron boss of it into the face of the next Hradcana who came looking for an opening, and broke the man's nose-bone up into his skull. A big axe, a two-hander, swept at Brom, but Fith knocked it away with his captured shield, and Brom tore out the owner's belly while his arms were still pushed up.

The next wave came, breaking on their shield. They had to take a few steps back each time. Red-sailed wyrmboats were grounding on the beach, and men were disembarking.

'Do you think they've brought enough bodies?' Brom asked. He was panting hard, and his face was bloodless with pain and effort, but there was still a laugh in his voice.

'Nothing like enough,' said Fith. 'And nothing like enough threads, either.'

⚜

LERN LEFT THE Upplander in the rocks and came to stand beside them. He took a sword out of a dead man's hand, thanked him for it, and hunched his back to face the surge.

The storm was behind them. It was shrieking in across the ice field, across the stilled sea, wailing like an Underverse chorus. Everything in the world that was loose was beginning to shake. The three Ascommani felt the grit of sleet hitting their necks and the backs of their heads. They heard the prickle of it pelting off their mail shirts.

The storm of men was in front of them. They were Hradcana, most of them, three or four score painted for murder, but there were Balt too, just arriving in their slower boats, slithering up the ice-cake beach in their eagerness.

It was a strange eagerness. It was born of desperation, the frantic wish to be free of a burden or a curse, to discharge an onerous duty and be done with it. There was no yelling, no war-shouts, no rousing bellow of comradeship and common purpose. They had no taste for it, or else fear had soured the words in their mouths.

They were chanting instead, steady and slow. They were reciting the rhymes of banishment and aversion they had learned around the aett hearth as children, the sharpened words, the strong words, the power words, the words with enough of a death-edge on them to keep bad stars at bay.

But the bad star was keeping them at bay too.

They were a great gang of men: hersirs, mostly, veterans, riggers, strong men with arms made thick from axe-work and backs made broad from the long oar. They crowded the beach: an army, bigger than any decent raiding party, as many faces as Fith had ever seen in one place. With a host like that, you could take a kingdom. You could conquer a chief's whole territory.

All they had to do, these men, was kill three hersirs and a cripple. Three hersirs and a cripple with but one shield between them, stuck on a shingle spit in the cold empty, with nowhere left to run and nothing at their backs except the approaching enmity of the winter's last, psychopathic storm.

Yet they were faltering. They were wary. There was no conviction in their surges. When they rushed in, they rushed in with fear in their eyes and hesitation in their blades. Each surge drove the Ascommani back closer to the ice, where standing steady and meeting a push would be impossible. But after half a dozen surges, Fith, Brom and Lern had knocked ten men down with red snow under them.

Then Fith saw the Balt gothi, Hunur. A wyrmboat had just brought him in, and hersirs were carrying him to the beach. He stood up tall on their cupped palms, such a tall skinny bastard, waving his bear's arm blade at Uppland above. The storm light, yellow and frosty as the sky closed down, glinted off the gothi's piercings and silver torc. His mantle of seabird feathers streamed out in the air behind him, white like early snow.

He was screaming. He was howling toxic curses into the thundering wind, calling on the spirits of the air and the wights of the Underverse and all the daemons of Hel to come forth and extinguish the bad star. Fith felt a prickle on his skin that was more than the battering sleet.

The sight of the gothi spurred the Hradcana on, that and the sound of his screams. They surged again, and Fith knew this would be the worst rush yet. The shock of impact drove the three Ascommani back a step. Two axes hooked into Fith's shield and dragged it down. A third broke its rim. Fith hacked his own axe into a Hradcana skull, then levered it out of the collapsing dead weight and swung it again. The poll of it broke a helmet's cheek guard and cracked the rim of an eye socket. Fith could no longer cover Brom's flank.

Brom was mindless with fatigue and pain. He was jeering and lunging with his axe, but there was no strength or skill left in his arm.

Fith heard Lern shouting at Brom to keep his eyes up. Lern was laying in with his wight-loaned sword. He knew to use the tip and not the edge in a crush-fight, jabbing it in at belt height, skinning ribs and gouging hips and rupturing bellies. The blade was good, with a keen point that pinged through the rings of a man's shirt and speared the meat beneath.

Then one of the Hradcana got a shield in the way, and Lern's sword punched clean through it, almost to the length of a man's forearm. It punched clean through and the blade stuck fast in the tight-grained wood. Lern tried to pull it out, but the shield man pulled back and dragged Lern out of line. The Hradcana took him and cut his thread: four or five enemy swords stabbing into him repeatedly, rehearsing the lesson in sword-work that Lern had delivered.

He disappeared under their feet, and the surge rolled over him. Brom was on his knees. He wasn't really aware of where he was any more. Fith had both hands clamped around the throat of his axe, and both sets of knuckles were dripping red.

The surge rolled back and parted, and the Balt gothi approached. Balt hersirs were still carrying him in a cradle of hands. He aimed the bear blade-bone at Fith and for a moment it felt like the two of them were alone on the sleet-battered beach.

The gothi started speaking. He started speaking magic words to forge a spell that would blast Fith off the beach. The men around him, Hradcana and Balt alike, covered their eyes or ears. The hersirs holding Hunur up began to weep, because their hands were busy and they could not block his words out.

Fith didn't know the meaning of the words, and didn't want to. He tightened his grip around the throat of his axe. He wondered if he could reach the gothi and bury the smile of it in his pierced face before the Hradcana and the Balt cut him down, or the gothi's magic turned his bones to melt-water.

'Enough.'

Fith glanced over his shoulder. The Upplander, crumpled in the lee of a wet-black boulder, his mangled legs twisted under him, had spoken. He was looking up at Fith.

Fith could see he was trembling. His heat was pouring out of his mouth in steaming clouds. Sleet pelted them both, and settled in small white clumps in the Upplander's matted hair.

'What?' Fith asked.

'I've heard enough,' the Upplander said.

Fith sighed. 'Have you? Have you, indeed? So now you want the mercy of my axe, now we've come to this? You couldn't have asked the favour earlier, before–'

'No, no!' the Upplander snapped. Every word was an effort, and he was clearly frustrated to have to say anything more than was absolutely necessary.

'I said,' he replied, 'I've heard enough. I've heard enough of that shaman's ravings. My translator's sampled enough, and it's built a workable grammatical base.'

Fith shook his head, not understanding.

'Help me up,' the Upplander ordered.

Fith hoisted the Upplander a little more upright. The barest movement caused the Upplander to grimace in pain. The pulverised bones in his legs ground together. Tears welled in his eyes and froze on his lower lashes.

'All right, all right,' he said. He adjusted the little translator device woven into his quilted collar.

He began to speak. A huge voice, tinny and harsh,

boomed out of the device in his collar. Fith recoiled at the sound of it. The voice boomed out words just like the words the gothi was yelling at them.

The gothi scrambled down out of his hersirs' hands and stopped shouting. He stared at Fith and the Upplander. There was terror on his twitching face. The Hradcana and the Balt edged backwards, uneasy and unsettled.

'What did you say?' Fith asked in the silence as the sleet billowed around them.

'I used his words back at him,' said the Upplander. 'I told him I'd bring a daemon out of the storm if they didn't back off. If they're afraid of me because they think I'm a bad star, I might as well act like one.'

The gothi was gabbling at his warriors, trying to spur them in again to finish the matter, but they were really reluctant to move. The gothi was losing his temper. He kept staring at Fith and the Upplander with the same, terrified look as before. So were a lot of the men.

Then Fith realised that none of them were looking at him or the Upplander after all.

They were looking past him. They were looking out at the ice field, out at the still sea, out at the Hel-storm that was screaming in and staining the sky black. Fith turned, the wind in his hair and the sleet in his face, to see the storm approaching. It was a low, racing blackness, like blood swirling through water. The snow and sleet that formed its bow-wave hazed the air like dust. Ice splintered up from the surface of the frozen sea, whirling away like petals in its vortex. Bars of lightning stabbed from the skirts and the belly of the storm like jagged, blinding lances, and smote the sea crust.

There was something in the storm. There was something just ahead of it, staying ahead of it, pounding out of the sleet-blur towards them.

It was a man. It was a huge man, a shadow on the ice,

running towards them, running across the sea, out-running the storm.

The Upplander's bad star magic had brought a dae-mon down to punish them all.

HUNUR SCREAMED. HIS hersirs had been bewildered for a moment, but they snapped to attention at the squeal of his voice, and loaded their bows. Fith threw himself flat as the first salvo of arrows loosed at the approaching daemon. The men were firing at will, spitting iron-head darts into the air as though they hoped to pin the storm to the sky.

The daemon struck. He came in off the sea at the tip of the storm in great bounding strides. Fith could hear the ice crunch under each pounding step. Furs and a ragged robe fluttered out behind him. He leapt up into the beach rocks, turned the bound into a sure-footed hop that propelled him off one of the largest boulders and up into the air, arms outstretched. This soaring leap took him clean over Fith and the Upplander. Fith ducked again. He saw the great axe uplifted in the dae-mon's right hand. The air was thatched with black arrows.

The daemon hung for a second in the mayhem of sleet, arms wide against the black sky like wings, robes trailing like torn sails. The host of Balt and Hradcana below him tilted back from him in fear, like corn stalks sloped by the wind.

Then he smashed down into them. The impact threw men into the air on either side. Shields, raised in haste at the last moment, fractured and splintered. Blades shattered. Bows broke. Arms snapped.

The daemon howled. He had landed in a crouch, at least two men crushed beneath his feet. He rose, hunched over in a fighter's stance. He swung his broad upper body, and put the full force of his vast shoulders behind his axe. Its death-edge went through three men. Arterial blood, black in the foul light, jetted into the air, and drops of it rained down in the sleet. Men were screaming. Hradcana voices, Balt voices, all screaming.

The daemon drove into the enemy mass, breaking wood and bone. He seemed blade-proof, as if he was made of iron. The tongues of swords cracked as they rebounded off him, the handles of axes snapped. There were two or three black-fletched arrows buried in the daemon's bulk, but he didn't appear to even feel them, let alone be slowed down by them.

The daemon let out another roar. It was an animal sound, the deep, reverberative throat-roar of a leopard. The sound penetrated. It cut through the booming swirl of the storm, and through the frenetic din of steel and sleet and voices. It cut like the keenest death-edge. Fith felt it in his gut. He felt it shiver his heart, colder than ice, worse than fear.

He watched the slaughter unfolding in front of him.

The hulking daemon drove into the great gang of killers. He pushed them against the wind and down the beach. They mobbed around him and onto him, like dogs on a bear, trying to out-man him, trying to smother his blows and choke his swing, trying to ring him and pull him down. They were terrified of him, but they were even more terrified of letting him live.

Their efforts were nothing. It was as if the Hradcana and the Balt were made of straw, cloth dummies stuffed with dry grass, like they were empty vessels with no weight. The daemon broke them and knocked them down. He swung and sent them flying. Men took off from each ploughing impact. They left the ground, flung into the sleet, limbs pinwheeling, a boot flying off, a shield in tatters. They flew out sideways, tumbling over the ice-caked shingle and ending up in still death-heaps. They lofted up from an axe-whack, split asunder, squirting blood from their cleaved bodies, raining broken rings from their shredded shirts, chainmail rings that pinged like handfuls of coins as they scattered across the beach. They cartwheeled over his shoulders, pitched like forked bales.

They littered the shingle. Most times, they were no longer in one piece once he'd done with them. Some lay as if they were sleeping. Others were crumpled in limp, slack poses that the living could not mimic. Some were split and steaming in the sleet. Some were just portions and pieces scattered by the relentless axe. Blood ran between the ice-black beach stones, coiling, trickling, deep and glossy, thick red, meat red, or cooling into slicks of rusty brown and faded purple.

The daemon's axe was a massive thing, a two-hander with a long, balanced handle. Both grip and blade were engraved with complex, weaving patterns and etched chequers. It sang to itself. Fith could hear it. The axe hummed and purred, as though the death-edge was privately chortling with delight at the rising tally of threads. A drizzle of blood droplets was flying off it, as if the blade was licking its lips clean.

Nothing stopped it. It was unimaginably sharp, and it was either as light as a gull's bone, or the daemon was as strong as a storm giant. It carved through everything it encountered. It went through shields, whether they were cured leather or hardwood or beaten copper. It went through armour, through padded plates, through iron scales, through chain. It went through the hafts of spears, through the handles of good axes, through the blades of swords that had been passed down for generations. It went through meat and muscle and bone.

It went through men effortlessly. Fith saw several men remain on their feet after the axe had sheared off their heads, or half of their heads, or their bodies from the shoulders. They stayed standing, their truncated figures swaying slightly with the pulse of the blood spurting from the stump or cross-sectioned portion. Only then would they collapse, soft and boneless, like falling cloaks.

The murder-makers were close to breaking. The daemon had cut so many of their threads, and left so many of them scattered on the blood-drenched beach, their resolve had thawed like ice in springtime. The storm was right above the islet now, enfolding the beach and the crag in its sharp, screaming embrace. The wind had been put to a whetstone. The air was shot through with bullets of hail. Where the demented sleet hit the hard stones of the beach, it scoured the blood away, and turned the dead into puffy, bleached, white things that looked like they had been waterlogged for a month.

A fire was driving the gothi Hunur. A fire had been lit in his blood. He had seen the evil of the bad star hanging in the future, and he had raised the murder-make to exterminate it. Now the evil was manifesting, driven into the open, he was all the more determined to end it.

He scrambled back to some higher rocks above the beach, and yelled down at the last of the Balt wyrmboats, where men had yet to disembark. They got out their bows, and Fith saw a glimpse of tallow flame in the stormy gloom.

The bowmen started to loose pitch-arrows.

The arrows were longer than regular man-stoppers, with simple iron spike tips and knobs of pitch-soaked rag knotted around the shafts behind the head. The rags caught as soon as flame was applied. Burning arrows ripped into the lightning-split sky.

Other men were spinning bottles on leather cords, letting them fly under their own weight. The bottles were filled with liquid pitch and other volatiles. Their contents sprayed out as they struck the beach and shattered. The burning arrows quickly ignited the spreading slicks.

Bright flames leapt up with a plosive *woof* like the sound of wind biting sailcloth. A great thicket of fire spread along the beach, fed by the blazing arrows. The flames were painfully bright, almost greenish and incandescent. The daemon, and the press of murder-makers around him, were swept up in the flames within seconds.

A burning man's screams are unlike the screams of a cut or knocked man. They are shrill and frantic. Engulfed, wrapped up in flames they could not shrug off or outrun, men stumbled out of the fight, mouths stretched wide, breathing fire. In the driving wind, the flames and the rank, black fat-smoke poured off them, like the burning tails of falling stars.

Their flaming arms milled in the air. Their hair and beards burned. Their undershirts ignited and cooked the rings of their shirts into their flesh. They ran into the sea, but the sea was just hard ice and couldn't quench their agonies, so they fell down onto it instead, and burned to death with the ice crust sizzling under them. They were gaunt black shapes in clothes of fire, like the effigies that burned at Helwinter. They were human tinder, crackling and sparking and fizzling in the sleet, hearth-brush kindling blown on by the storm until it flared white-hot.

The daemon came through the flames. He was singed black, like a coal carving. His furs and ragged robe were alive with little blue flames. His eyes were like polished moonstones in his soot-black face. He roared again, the throat-thunder of a hunting cat. It wasn't just his eyes that lit a wild white against his blackened flesh. His teeth glinted too: white bone, long canines no human mouth should possess.

The daemon buried the smile of his axe in the beach ice, and left it sticking fast with its handle pointing at the sky. Two more flaming arrows hit him. He tore one out of his cloak, flames licking around his fingers.

He brought something up from his side, something metal and heavy that had been strapped there. It was a box with a handle. Fith didn't know what it was for. All he knew was it was some daemonic device. The daemon pointed it at the Balt wyrmboats.

The box made a noise like a hundred thunderbolts overlapping. The sound was so loud, so sudden, so alien, it made Fith jerk in surprise. Gouting flashes of fire bearded the front of the daemon's curious box, blinking and flickering as fast as the rattling thunder-roar.

The nearest Balt wyrmboat shivered, and then disintegrated. Its hull shredded and flew apart, reduced to wood chips and pulp and spinning nails. The mast and the quarter rigs exploded. The figurehead splintered. The men on board atomised in puffs of red drizzle.

The wyrmboat behind it began to shred too, and then the boat beyond that. The daemon kept his roaring lightning-box aimed at the boats, and invisible hands of annihilation demolished the craft drawn up along the ice-line. A thick brume of wood-fibre and blood-mist boiled off the destruction into the wind. Then the pitch bottles that had yet to be thrown exploded.

The inferno was intense. Despite the storm, Fith could feel the heat of it on his face. The line of boats lit off, like the fire graves of great heroes at a boat burial. Ash and sparks zoomed crazily like fireflies. The wind took hold of the thick black smoke coming off the burning, and carried it out across the sea almost horizontally like a bar of rolling fog.

The daemon's lightning-box stopped roaring. He lowered it and looked up the beach at the gothi. Hunur was a shrunken, defeated figure, his shoulders slack, his arms down. A few Hradcana and Balt were fleeing past him up the rock slope, seeking the far side of the islet.

The daemon raised his lightning-box and pointed it at the gothi. He made it flash and bark just once, and the gothi's head and shoulders vanished in an abrupt pink cloud. What remained of Hunur snapped back off the rock, as if snatched from behind.

The daemon walked down to the ice-line. The intense heat of the burning boats had liquefied the sea ice along the shore, creating a molten pool of viscous water that was greedily swallowing the boat wrecks down into the darkness in a veil of angry steam. The iron-edged smell of the ocean was released to the air for the first time that year.

The daemon knelt down, scooped water up in the cup of his massive right hand, and splashed it over his face. The soot streaked on his cheeks and brow. He rose again, and began to walk back up the beach towards Fith.

The *hrosshvalur* rose without much warning: just a blow of sour bubbles in the turbulent melt-pool and a sudden froth of red algae. Like all of the great sea things, its diet had been constrained by the ice all winter long, and it was rapaciously hungry. The burning boats had opened the sea to the air, and their cloudy ruins had brought down quantities of meat and blood to flavour the frigid water with an intoxicating allure. The hrosshvalur may have been leagues away when it got the taste; one particle of human blood in a trillion cubic litres of salt water. Its massive tail flukes had closed the distance in a few beats.

The daemon heard the liquid rush of its emergence, and turned to look. The melt-pool was barely big enough to fit the sea thing. Its scaled flanks and claw-toed flippers broke the ice wider, and it bellied up onto the beach, jaws wide and eager at the scent of blood. The flesh inside its mouth was gleaming white, like mother of pearl, and there was a painful stink of ammonia. Its teeth were like spears of ragged yellow coral. It brought its shuddering, snorting bulk up onto the shingle, and boomed out its brash, bass cry, the sound you sometimes heard at night, on the open water, through the planks of the hull. Smaller *mushveli*, yapping and writhing like worms, followed it up out of the melt-hole, equally agitated by the promise of meat. The hrosshvalur drove them aside, snapping the neck of one that got too close, and then wolfing it down whole in two or three jerking gulps. It levered its body across the shingle on its massive, wrinkled flippers.

The daemon crossed in front of the giant killer. He knew that its appetite was as bottomless as the North Ocean, especially since the turning of spring. It would not stop until it had picked the aett islet clean of anything remotely edible.

The daemon plucked his axe out of the ice-cake shingle. He pulled it up with his hand clasped high under the shoulder, and then he let the handle slip down through his loose grip, pulled by the head weight, until he had it by the optimum lever point between belly and throat. He ran at the ocean monster.

It blew its jaws out at him in a blast of rancid ammonia. The jaws hinged out so wide they formed a tooth-fringed opening like a chapel cave. The maw was so big that a full crew of men could have carried a wyrmboat into it on their shoulders. Then its secondary jaws extended too, driven by the undulating elastic of the throat muscles, bristling with spine teeth made of translucent cartilage. The spine teeth, some longer than a grown man's leg, flipped up out of the gum recesses like the blades of a folding knife, each one as transparent as glacial ice and dewed with drops of mucus. The hrosshvalur lunged at the charging daemon, the vast tonnage of its bulk grinding and scraping off the beach stones.

The daemon brought his axe down and cut through the lower, primary jaw between the biter-teeth at the front, splitting the jaw like a hull split along its keel. Noxious white froth boiled out of the wound, as if the hrosshvalur had steam for blood. Whooping, it tried to turn its injured head away. The daemon knocked his axe into the side of its skull, so that the blade went through the thick scale plate to its entire depth. Then he put it in again, directly below one of the glassy, staring eyes that were the size of a chieftain's shield.

The ocean monster boomed, and spewed out a great torrent of rank effluvium. The daemon kept hacking until there was a bubbling pink slit where the hrosshvalur's head met its neck. The beach underneath them was awash with stinking milky fluid. The slit puckered and dribbled as air gusted out of it. The beast wasn't dead, but it was mortally stricken. The yapping mushveli began to eat it alive. The daemon left it to die, and walked towards Fith.

The Upplander had been awake to see most of the spectacle. He watched the daemon's approach. Close to, they could see the plated form of the daemon's decorated grey armour under his scorched robes and furs. They could see the corded brown lines tattooed into his face, down the line of his nose, across the planes of the cheek and around the eyes. They could smell him, a scent like an animal, but clean, the heady pheromone musk of an alpha dog.

They could see his fangs.

'You are Ahmad Ibn Rustah?' the daemon said.

The Upplander paused while his translator dealt with the words.

'Yes,' the Upplander replied. He shuddered with cold and pain. It was a miracle he was still conscious.

'And you are?' he asked.

The daemon said his name. The translator worked quickly.

'Bear?' asked the Upplander. 'You're called Bear?'

The daemon shrugged.

'Why are you here?' asked the Upplander.

'There was an error,' said the daemon. The purring growl was never far from the edges of his voice. 'An oversight. I made the error, so now I make amends. I will take you out of this place.'

'These men too,' said the Upplander.

The daemon looked at Fith and Brom. Brom was unconscious against a rock, dusted with pellets of hail. The blood seeping from his wounds had frozen. Fith was just staring at the daemon. There was still blood on the handle of his axe.

'Is he dead?' the daemon asked Fith, nodding at Brom.

'We're both dead,' Fith replied. That was all that was left for him now; the voyage to the Underverse to be remade.

'I haven't got time,' the daemon said to the Upplander. 'Just you.'

'You'll take them. After what they gave today, keeping me alive, you'll take them.'

The daemon let out a soft, throbbing growl. He stepped back and took some sort of tool or wand from his belt. When he adjusted it, it made small, musical noises.

The daemon looked out to sea, out into the storm in the direction he had come from. Fith followed his gaze. Driving sleet flecked his face and made him blink and wince. He could hear a noise like a storm inside the storm.

The daemon's boat appeared. Fith had never seen its like before, but he recognised the smooth boat-lines of the hull, and fins like rudders. It was not an ice rig or a

water boat: it was an air boat, a boat for riding the wind
and the storm. It came slowly towards them across the
ice, hanging in the sky at mast-top height. Screaming air
blasted down from it, keeping it up. The air flung ice
chips up off the sea. Small green candles lit on and off
at the corners of its wind rigs.

It came closer, until Fith had to shield his face from
the blitzing air and the ice chips. Then it settled down
on the sea crust with a crunch and opened a set of jaws
as large as the hrosshvalur's.

The daemon scooped up the Upplander in his arms.
The Upplander shrieked as his broken leg bones ground
and rubbed. The daemon didn't seem particularly bothered. He looked at Fith.

'Bring him,' he said, nodding at Brom again. 'Follow.
Don't touch anything.'

⚜

HAWSER HAD BEEN working in the upper strata of Karelia
Hive for over eight months when someone from the
Council legation finally agreed to see him.

'You work in the library, don't you?' the man asked.
His name was Bakunin, and he was an understaffer for
Emantine, whose adjunct had repeatedly refused
Hawser's written approaches for an interview or assessment. Indirectly, this meant that Bakunin reported to
the municipal and clerical authorities, and was therefore part of the greater administrative mechanism that
eventually came to the attention of Jaffed Kelpanton in
the Ministry of the Sigillite.

'Yes, the Library of the Universitariate. But I'm not
attached to the Universitariate. It's a temporary position.'

'Oh,' said Bakunin, as if Hawser had said something
interesting. The man had one eye on his appointment
slate and could not disguise his eagerness to be elsewhere.

They'd met in the culinahalle on Aleksanterinkatu 66106. It was a high-spar place, with a good reputation and great views down over the summitstratum commercias. Acrobats and wire artists were performing over the drop in the late afternoon sun that flooded through the solar frames.

'So, your position?' Bakunin inquired. Elegant transhuman waiters with elective augmetic modifications had brought them a kettle of *whurpu* leaf and a silver tray of snow pastries.

'I'm contracted to supervise the renovation. I'm a data archaeologist.'

'Ah yes. I remember. The library was bombed, wasn't it?'

'Pro-Panpacifists detonated two wipe devices during the insurrection.'

Bakunin nodded. 'There can be nothing whatsoever to recover.'

'The Hive Council certainly didn't believe so. They passed the area for demolition.'

'But you disagreed?'

Hawser smiled. 'I persuaded the Universitariate Board to hire me on a trial basis. So far, I've recovered seven thousand texts from an archive that had been deemed worthless.'

'Good for you,' said Bakunin. 'Good for you.'

'Good for all of us,' said Hawser. 'Which brings me to the purpose of this meeting. Have you had a chance to read my petition?'

Bakunin smiled thinly. 'I confess, no. Not cover to cover. Things are very busy at the moment. I have reviewed it quickly, however. As far as the general thrust of your position goes, I am with you all the way. All the way. But I can't see how it isn't already covered under the terms of the Enactment of Remembrance and–'

Hawser raised his hand gently. 'Please, don't point me

to the Offices of the Remembrancers. My requests keep
getting channelled in that direction.'

'But surely you're talking about commemoration,
about the systematic accumulation of data to document
the liberation and unification of human civilisation. We
are blessed to be living through the greatest moment in
the history of our species, and it is only right that we
memorialise it. The Sigillite himself supports and pro-
motes the notion. You know he was a direct signatory of
the Enactment?'

'I know. I am aware of his support. I celebrate it. So
often, at the great moments in history, the historian is
forgotten.'

'From my review of your statements and personal history,' said Bakunin, 'I am in no doubt that I can secure
you a high-profile position in the Remembrance order.
I can recommend you, and I'm confident I can do the
same for several other names on the list you submitted.'

'I'm grateful,' said Hawser, 'truly, I am. But that's not
why I requested this meeting. The remembrancers perform a vital function. Of course we must record, in great
detail, the events that are surrounding us. Of course we
must, for the public good, for the greater glory, for pos-
terity, but I am proposing a rather more subtle
endeavour, one that I fear is being overlooked. I'm not
talking about writing down what we're doing. I'm talking about writing down what we know. I'm talking
about preserving human knowledge, systemising it,
working out what we know and what we've forgotten.'

The understaffer blinked, and his smile became rather
vacuous. 'That's surely… pardon me, ser… but that's
surely an organic process of the Imperium. We do that
as we go along, don't we? I mean, we must. We accu-
mulate knowledge.'

'Yes, but not rigorously, not methodically. And when
a resource is lost, like the library here in Karelia, we

shrug and say oh dear. But that data wasn't lost, not all of it. I ask the question – did we even know what we had lost when the wipe devices detonated? Did we have any idea of the holes it was eating in the collective knowledge of our species?'

Bakunin looked uncomfortable.

'I need someone to champion this, ser,' Hawser said. He knew he was getting bright-eyed and eager, and he knew that people often found that enthusiasm off-putting. Bakunin looked uneasy but Hawser couldn't help himself. 'We… and by we I mean all the academics who have put their names to my petition… we need someone to take this up the line in the Administratum. To get it noticed. To get it to the attention of somebody who has the position and influence to action it.'

'With respect–'

'With respect, ser, I do not want to spend the remainder of my career following the various Crusade forces around like a loyal dog, dutifully recording every last detail of their meritorious actions. I want to see a greater process at work, an audit of human knowledge. We must find out the limits of what we know. We must identify the blanks, and then strive to fill those blanks or renovate missing data.'

Bakunin let out a nervous little laugh.

'It's no secret that we used to know how to do things that we can't do anymore,' said Hawser, 'great feats of technology, and constructions, miracles of physics. We've forgotten how to do things that our ancestors five thousand years ago considered rudimentary. Five thousand years is nothing. It was a golden age, and look at us now, picking through the ashes to put it back together. Everyone knows that the Age of Strife was a dark age during which mankind lost countless treasures. But really, ser, do you know what we lost exactly?'

'No,' replied Bakunin.

'Neither do I,' Hawser replied. 'I cannot even tell you something as basic as what we lost. I wouldn't know where to start.'

'Please,' said Bakunin. He shivered as though he was sitting in a draught. 'Caches of data are being recovered all the time. Why, just the other day, I heard that we now had complete texts for all three of Shakespire's plays!'

Hawser looked the understaffer in the eye.

'Answer me this,' he said. 'Does anyone even know why the Age of Strife happened? How did we end up in the great darkness of Old Night to begin with?'

HAWSER WOKE UP. He could still smell the whurpu leaf and hear the background chatter of the culinahalle.

Except he couldn't.

Those things were years ago and far away. He'd blacked out and been dreaming for a second. He could smell blood and lubrication oil. He could smell body odours, scents of dirt and pain.

The pain of his own injuries was incandescent. He wondered if the Astartes – Bear – would give him a shot of something. It didn't seem likely. Bear's attitude towards suffering appeared to be fixed to a different scale. It was more probable that the Upplander's mind would, at some point, cease registering the extremes of pain in a desperate effort to protect itself.

The cabin space was dark around the metal stretcher he had been laid out on. His limbs had been strapped down. They were in the air still. Everything was vibrating. There was a constant howl from the drop-ship's engines. Every so often, turbulence jolted them.

Bear appeared. He loomed up over the stretcher, looking down. He'd sheared off the burnt ends of his mane of hair, and tied the rest back with a loop of leather. His face was long and noble, with high cheek ridges, a long nose and a prominent mouth, like a snout almost. No, not a snout, a muzzle. The intricate lines of the brown tattoos followed the geometry of Bear's face, and accented the planes of the cheek and nose, and the angles of the cheeks and brows. His skin was wind-burned and tanned. It looked as if his face had been carved out of hardwood, like the figure post of a wyrm-boat.

He stared down at the Upplander. The Upplander realised the Astartes was scanning him with a handheld device.

He clicked it off and put it away.

'We're coming in now,' he said. The Upplander's translator raced to keep up. 'There'll be a surgeon waiting to tend you, but this is a special place. You know that. So let's start as we mean to go on.'

He reached down, and with the fingers of his left hand, he gouged out the Upplander's right eye.

THREE

Aett

IF THE DAEMON, Bear, represented salvation, then he also represented a final submission. The Upplander no longer needed to fight the cold to stay awake, or the pain to stay alive. He let go, and sank like a rock into the glassy silence of a freezing sea. Pain devoured him. It beset him like a blizzard, so violent and furious that he could see it, even with his blinded eye.

The blizzard continued long after the pain blew out.

THEY WERE APPROACHING the special place that Bear had promised to take him to. They were arriving in a snow storm. It was a terrible snow storm.

Or was it white noise? Flecks of static instead of particles of snow? A faulty pict-feed? The signal trash of a damaged augmetic optic? Just fuzz, just buzzing white speckles against–

Against blackness. The blackness, now that had to be real. It was so solid. Solid blackness.

Unless it was blindness. His eye hurt. The absence of it hurt. The socket where his eye had been hurt.

Snow and static, blackness and blindness; the values interchanged. He couldn't tell them apart. His core temperature was plummeting. Pain was being diluted with numbness. The Upplander knew he had long since ceased to be a reliable witness of events. Consciousness refused to reignite in any stable fashion. He was caught in an ugly cleft of half-awareness, a pitiful fox-hole in the lee-side of a snow-bank of insensibility. It was unbearably hard to distinguish between memories and pain-dreams. Was he seeing white noise on a blacked-out display screen, or blizzarding snow against solid black rock? It was impossible to tell.

He fancied the blackness was a mountain beyond the snow, a mountain that was too big to be a mountain, a black tooth of rock that loomed out of the blizzard, broader and taller than could be taken in at a single glance. It was so big that it had already filled his field of vision, up and down and side to side, before he even realised it was there. At first, he thought it was the blackness of the polar sky, but no, it was a solid wall of rock, rushing towards him.

He sighed, reassured, able at last to comfort himself by definitively separating one memory-fact from dream-fiction. The mountain, that was *definitely* a dream.

No mountain could be *that* big.

⚜

HE WAS CARRIED in out of the storm, down into the warm and muffled blackness of a deep cave. He lay there and dreamed some more.

The Upplander dreamed for a long time.

The dreams started out as pain-dreams, sharpened by the pangs of his injuries, distorted by opiates flooding into his bloodstream. They were fragments, sharp and imperfect, like segments of a puzzle, or pieces of a broken mirror, interspersed with deadened periods of unconsciousness. They reminded him of the moves of a regicide game, a match between two experienced players. Slow, considered moves, strategically deep, separated by long stretches of contemplative inaction. The regicide board was old and inlaid with ivory. He could smell the lint that had collected in the corners of the board's case. Nearby, there was a small toy horse, made of wood. He was drinking radapple juice. Someone was playing the clavier.

The sharp edges of his mental fragments dulled, and the dreams became longer and more complex. He began to dream his way through epic cycles of dreams. They lasted years, they enumerated generations, they saw the ice encroach and thaw away again, the ocean harden and return to motion, the sun rush across the cloud-barred sky like a disc of beaten copper, winking, glittering, growing bright like a nova and then dull like a dead stellar ember. Day, night, day, night…

Inside the dreams, men came to him and sat by him in the secret gloom of the cave. They talked. A fire was burning. He could smell the copal resin smoking into the air. He could not see the men, but he could see their shadows, cast up the cave wall by the spitting fire. They were not human. The shadow shapes had animal heads, or antlers, or horns sometimes. Man-shapes sat and panted through dog-snouts. Spiked branches of horn-crest nodded as others spoke. Some were hunched with the weighty shoulder hump of winter-fat cattle. After a while, he became uncertain if he was seeing shadows on the cave wall, or ancient parietal art, smudged lines of ochre and charcoal, that had been lent the illusion of movement by the inconstant flames.

He tried to listen to what was being said by the men during the long, mumbling conversations, but he couldn't concentrate. He thought that if he was able to focus, he would hear all the secrets of the world come tumbling out in a murmured river, and learn every story from the very first to the very last.

Sometimes the Upplander's dreams picked him up and carried him outside the cave. They took him up to some high vantage where there were only stars overhead, in a roof of velvet blue, and sunlit lands below, a tapestry of worlds, all sewn together, all the worlds in creation, like the inlaid board of a great game. And on that board, epic histories played out for him. Nations and empires, creeds and races, rising and falling, bonding and fighting, forming alliances, making war. He witnessed unifications, annihilations, reformations, annexations, invasions, expansions, enlightenments. He saw it all from his lofty vantage, a seat so high and precarious that sometimes he had to cling on to the throne's golden arms for fear of falling.

Sometimes his dreams swept him back inside himself, into his own flesh, into his own blood, and there, at a microscopic level, he observed the universe of his own body as it disassembled atom from atom, his essence sampled down to the smallest genetic packet, like light sifted and split into its component colours by a subtle lens. He felt he was being dismantled, working part from working part, like an old timepiece, and every last piece of the damaskeened movement laid out for repair. He felt like a biological sample: a laboratory animal, belly slit and pegged open, its organs removed one by one like the gears of a pocket watch; like an insect, pinned and minutely sectioned for a glass slide to learn what made it tick.

When his dreams took him back to the cave, where the therianthrope shadows sat muttering in the firelight, he often felt as if he had been put back together in an altogether different order. If he was an old timepiece, then his dismantled movement had been rearranged, and some parts cleaned or modified, or replaced, and then his mainspring and his escapement, his going train and his balance wheel, and all his tiny levers and pins had been put back together in some inventive new sequence, and his cover screwed shut so that no one could see how he had been re-engineered.

And when he was back in the cave, he thought about the cave itself. Warm, secure, deep in the black rock, out of the storm. But had he been taken back there for his own protection? Or had he been taken back there for safe-keeping until the man-shapes around the fire got hungry?

⟡

THE STRANGEST AND most infrequent dreams of all were of the coldest, deepest part of the cave, where a voice spoke to him.

In this place, there was only blackness cut by a cold, blue glow. The air smelled sterile, like rock in a dry polar highland that lacked any water to form ice. It was far away from the soft warmth and the firelight of the cave, far away from the fraternity of murmuring voices and the smell of smouldering resin. The Upplander's limbs felt leaden there, as though he had swallowed ice, as though cold liquid metal ran in his veins and weighed him down. Even his thoughts were slow and viscous.

He fought against the arctic slowness, afraid to let it pull him down into dreamless sleep and death. The best he could muster felt like a feeble twitch of his heavy limbs.

'Be still!'

That was the first thing the voice said to him. It was so sudden and unexpected, he froze.

'Be still!' the voice repeated. It was a deep, hollow voice, a whisper that carried the force of thunder. It wasn't particularly human. It sounded as if it had been fashioned out of the bleating, droning notes of an old signal horn. Each syllable and vowel sound was simply the same low, reverberative noise sampled and tonally adjusted.

'Be still. Stop your twitching and your wriggling.'

'Where am I?' the Upplander asked.

'In the dark,' the voice replied. It sounded further away, a ram's horn braying on a lonely cliff.

'I don't understand,' he said.

There was a silence. Then the voice came again, directly behind the Upplander's right ear, as if the speaker had circled him.

'You don't have to understand the dark. That's the thing about the dark, it doesn't need to be understood. It's just the dark. It is what it is.'

'But what am I doing here?' he asked.

When the voice answered, it had receded. It came as a rumble from somewhere ahead of him, like the sound of a wind moaning through empty caves. It said, 'You're here to be. You're here to dream the dreams, that's all. So just dream the dreams. They'll help pass the time. Dream the dreams. Stop your twitching and your wriggling. It's disturbing me.'

The Upplander hesitated. He didn't like the threat of anger in the voice.

'I don't like it here,' he ventured at length.

'None of us like it here!' the voice boomed, right in the Upplander's left ear. He let out an involuntary squeak of terror. Not only was the voice loud and close and angry, but there was a wet leopard-growl in its thunder.

'None of us like it here,' the voice repeated, calmer now, circling him in the darkness. 'None of us chose to be here. We miss the firelight. We miss the sunlight. We've dreamed all the dreams they give us a hundred times over, a thousand times. We know them off by heart. We don't choose the dark.'

There was a long pause.

'The dark chooses us.'

'Who are you?' the Upplander asked.

'I was called Cormek,' the voice said. 'Cormek Dod.'

'How long have you been here, Cormek Dod?'

Pause, then a rumble. 'I forget.'

'How long have I been here?'

'I don't even know who you are,' the voice replied. 'Just be still, and shut up your racket, and stop disturbing me.'

THEN THE UPPLANDER woke up, and he was still on the metal stretcher Bear had strapped him to.

The stretcher was swaying slightly, suspended. The Upplander's vision swam into focus and he looked up, up at the chains rising from the four corners of the stretcher. They all met at a central ring, and became a single, thicker length of chain. The main chain, dark and oiled, extended up and away, into the oppressive twilight of the vast roof space above him. It felt like a cave, an enormous cave, but it wasn't the dream-cave where the animal-men had murmured by the firelight, and it wasn't the deep, cold cave with the blue glow either.

Everything was in shadow, in a twilight of a greenish cast. From what he could make out in the half-light, the cave was a vast space, like the nave of a cathedral, or the belly-hold of a voidship. And it wasn't actually a cave, because the structural angles and edges were too straight and regular.

The Upplander couldn't turn his head or move his limbs, but he was relieved to find that he was no longer in pain. There was not even a vestigial nag of discomfort from his torso or his shattered legs.

His relief was rather eclipsed by the anxiety he felt at his new situation: trapped and pinned, strapped down,

unable to twist his head to see anything but the black
roof space above. A dull, drowsy weight on his heart
made him feel sluggish and leaden, as if he'd taken a
tranquiliser or a sleeping draught. He blinked, wishing
he could rub the grit out of his eyes, wishing the
stretcher would stop swinging.

A swaying length of thick chain ran back down out of
the darkness at an oblique angle to the central chain
supporting him, and from its rhythmic jolts, it seemed
clear that he was being hoisted up into the vaulted roof
of the cathedral. The links clattered through an invisible
block high above him.

He stopped ascending. The stretcher wobbled for a
moment, and then swung hard to his left, out across the
room, drawn with such force it started to rotate. Then
the chain began to rattle back up in fits and starts, and
the stretcher began to descend. The taut chains securing
the four corners of the stretcher shuddered with every
downward jerk.

He began to panic. He strained at the buckled canvas
restraints. They wouldn't give, and he didn't want to tear
or strain any of his wounds.

He came down lower, in a series of jolting drops, onto
some sort of deck area or platform. Men moved in
quickly from either side to take hold of the stretcher
and steady it.

The Upplander looked up at their faces, and his anxiety transmuted into fear.

The men wore robes of simple, poor-quality cloth
over tight body-suits of intricately fashioned brown
leather. Each leather suit was constructed in artful panels, some shaped, some decorated with piercing or
knotwork or furrowed lines, so that the whole resembled an anatomist's diagram of human musculature:
the wall of muscle around the ribs, the tendons of the
arms, the sinews of the throat.

Their faces were animal skulls, masks fashioned from bone. Stub horns curled from discoloured skull brows. Branching antler tines rose from unicorn centre-burrs.

The eyes staring out of the mask slits at the Upplander were inhuman. They were the black-pinned yellow eyes of wolves. They shone with their own light.

Get off me! he shouted, but his voice was dust-dry in his throat, as though he hadn't spoken for centuries. He coughed, panic rising in his chest. The bone faces crowded in around him, puzzled at his antics. All of them smiled the simpleton smile of skulls, the idiot grin of death's face, but the eyes in the sockets and slits put the lie to that glee. The fire in the yellow eyes was predatory, a fierce intellect, an intent to do harm.

'Get away from me!' he cried, finding his voice at last, dragging it out, old and rusty, from the parched creek bed of his throat. 'Get back!'

The skulls did nothing of the kind. They came closer. Hands sheathed in intricate brown leather gauntlets reached towards his face to clamp his mouth. Some of them had only two or three fingers. Some had dew-claws.

The Upplander began to thrash in his restraints, pulling and twisting in a frenzied effort born of panic. He no longer cared if he tore sutures, or reopened a healing gash, or jarred a mending bone fracture.

Something broke. He felt it snap, thought it was a rib or a hamstring, braced himself for the searing pain.

It was the canvas cuff on his right arm. He'd torn it clean off the metal boss that anchored it to the stretcher's frame.

He lashed out with his freed arm and felt his knuckles connect with the hard ridges of a skull mask. Something let out a guttural bark of distress. The Upplander punched again, yelling, then he scrabbled at the buckles girthed around his throat, and undid the neck straps. With his throat free, he could lift his shoulders off the hard bed of the stretcher, and raise his head clear of the leather brace that was preventing all lateral movement. He bent up, leaning over to unfasten the canvas cuff holding his left wrist. The right-hand strap was still buckled around his right forearm with a frayed tuft sprouting from its underside where he'd torn it off the steel boss.

The skulls came at him, grabbing him and trying to press him back down. Unbraced, the stretcher swung wildly. The Upplander fought them off. His legs were still strapped in. He punched and twisted, and cursed at them in Low Gothic, Turcic, Croat and Syblemic. They gibbered at him, in commotion, trying to pin him and restrain him.

The Upplander's right leg came free. He bent it, and then lashed out a kick with as much force as he could muster. He caught one of the skulls full in the chest, and rejoiced to see the figure recoil with enough violence to tumble at least another two of its robed companions backwards.

Then his left leg tore free too. As his weight shifted suddenly, the stretcher tipped and he spilled off, falling into half a dozen of the skulls trying to keep him in place. His fists were flying. The Upplander had never been taught to fight, and he'd never had to, but terror and a frantic survival instinct impelled him, and there didn't appear to be any huge mystery to it. You swung your fists. If your fists connected with things, you hurt them. The things jerked backwards. They uttered growls of pain or barks of breath. If you were lucky, they fell down. The Upplander milled his arms like a madman. He kicked out. He drove them back. He kicked one of them so hard that it sprawled and broke its skull mask against the smooth granite of the platform.

The Upplander found his feet. The skulls were circling

him, but they had become wary. Some of them had
been bruised by his slugging fists. He snarled at them,
stamping his feet and gesticulating wildly with his fists,
as though he was trying to scare off a flock of birds. The
skulls drew back a little.

The Upplander took a second to get his bearings.

He was standing on a platform of dark granite, a shelf
that had been cut, sharp and square-edged, from the
rock around it. Behind him, the stretcher was swinging
on its chains. To his left, a row of oblong granite blocks
lined one side of the platform, permanent catafalques
onto which stretchers like his own could be lowered
and rested. Above him dangled four or five more chain
pulleys of various gauges and sizes.

To his right, the platform overhung a gulf. It went
straight down into darkness, and smelled of wet minerals and the centre of the world. The gulf was a shaft,
rectangular in cross-section, and the sides of the shaft
had been cut, like the platform, out of the living rock.
The shaft dropped into the darkness below him in
square-cut, oblong bites, like the layers of a cake, or the
cubic levels of a monolithic quarry. They looked like
they had been cut with sideways slices of a giant chisel.

All around him, the chamber rose in majesty, its
cyclopean walls rock-hewn like the shaft, too regular
and rectilinear to be a natural cave, too make-shift and
imperfect to have been planned in one piece. Monumental stonemasons and mining engineers had opened
this cavity over a period of decades or centuries, excising
one or two levels of oblong blocks at a time, increasing
the space in rectilinear levels, quarrying each layer of
stone away and leaving artificial lines of division and
stratification in the gigantic walls. Each phase must
have been a monstrous effort, from the sheer tonnage of
rock alone. The square-cut bites showed how huge and
unwieldy each removed block of stone must have been.

The cubic mass of a mountain had been hollowed out of the heart of a bigger mountain.

The platform and the shaft top were lit by the frosty green twilight. Watermarks streaked the horizontally scored, stratified walls, leaving downstrokes of emerald minerals and algae stain. The Upplander could not see how far up the ceiling was, because it was lost in the cavity's darkness.

He edged backwards, the skulls around him. He became conscious of the way that every sound they made became a deep bell-echo in the vast chamber. He tried to move to keep the catafalques between him and the skulls. They circled in between the biers, trying to outflank him. He noticed that, although they looked solid-hewn, the catafalques had metal plates set in their sides. The plates incorporated vent caps, indicator lights and recognisably Terran control pads. Stout, reinforced metal ducting sprouted like drainpipes from the plates and disappeared flush into the platform. There was tech in this primordially quarried chamber, a lot of tech, and it was largely concealed.

The skulls attempted to rush him. The Upplander darted backwards and reached the pendulating stretcher. He grabbed its metal frame and steered it at the skulls, ramming it at them. They jumped back out of its way, and he rammed it again to keep them at bay. He saw the buckled canvas cuffs anchored to the stretcher's bed. He had assumed he'd simply pulled them all off their pins, like the right-hand cuff that was still fastened around his forearm. But both leg straps and the left-hand cuff had been ripped. The waxed canvas and leather trusses had torn open along their stitching. He'd as good as wrenched himself free of his bonds.

The thought disturbed him. He was sick and injured, surely? He didn't feel sick and injured. The Upplander looked down at himself. He was whole. His feet were bare. They were pink and clean. The still-buckled canvas cuff hung around his right wrist. His body was cased in a dark grey bodyglove with reinforced panels at the major joints like the undersuit of some void-armour. It was tight and form-fitting. It revealed a figure that looked remarkably lean and strong, with surprising muscle definition. It did not look like the well-worn, over-taxed eighty-three year-old body he had last looked down at. No thickness at the hips, no incipient paunch from too many amasecs over too many years.

No augmetic implant from that day in Ossetia.

'What the *hell*...?' the Upplander breathed.

Sensing his sudden disconcertion, the skulls came at him.

⍟

HE SWUNG THE stretcher into them with all the force he could muster. Its metal nose caught one in the breast-bone, and almost flipped it onto its back. He glimpsed a cracked dog-skull mask, strap broken, sliding away across the platform. Another skull grabbed the opposite end of the stretcher and tried to wrench it out of his hands. The Upplander uttered a despairing, denying cry that echoed around the vast chamber, and hauled the stretcher out of the skull's grip. The skull's feet left the ground for a moment as it tried to cling on.

The Upplander pulled the stretcher right back and let it fly. It swung like a wrecking ball. It struck one skull down and slammed into a second, knocking it off the edge of the platform into the gulf.

The skull managed to catch the lip of the platform as it went over. Its hands clawed frantically at the granite surfaces. The weight of its legs and body slid it backwards. The other skulls rushed forwards and grabbed it by the hands and sleeves.

While they were occupied pulling their kin to safety, the Upplander ran.

He left the chamber, his bare feet slapping against the cool stone floor. He passed under a broad lintel, and down the throat of an entrance hall big enough to fly a cargo spinner through. The permeating green dusk cast a confused light. His shadow ran away from him in different directions.

The grand entrance hall, and the rock-cut tunnel that lay beyond it, were more finished than the vast chamber behind him. The rock walls had been planed or polished to a dull shine, like dark water ice in the middle of a hard winter. The floor was stone. The ceiling, and the edges of the floor where it met the wall, along with the interspersed archways, ribs and regular wall panels, were dressed in beams and fittings of gleaming off-white, like varnished blond wood. Most of the white wood finishings were massive, as thick as tree boles, and hard-edged, although some were expertly curved to form arches, or chamfered to make wall ribs.

The gloomy place made memories fire in his head, sudden and sharp. The halls reminded him of ikon caskets he had once recovered from atomic bunkers under the nanotic ground zero outside Zincirli, in Federated Islahiye. They reminded him of Gaduarene reliquaries with their engravings of lightning stones, and the case of Rector Uwe's treasured old regicide set. They reminded him of the elegant, silk-lined boxes of the Daumarl Medal. They reminded him of Ossetian prayer boxes, the ones made of grey slate set into frames of expertly worked ivory. Yes, that was it. Gold sheets, hammered around carcasses of wood and pin-screwed bone, so old, so precious. The white posts and pillars finishing his surroundings looked like they were made of bone. They had an unmistakable, slightly golden, cast, a warmth. He felt as if he were inside a box of Ossetian slate lined with ivory, as if he were the ancient treasure, the rusted nail, the lock of saintly hair, the flaking parchment, the keepsake.

He kept running, straining to hear whether he was being followed. The only sounds were the slaps of his soles and the faraway sigh of wind gusting along empty hallways. The draught made it feel as though he were in some high castle, where a casement shutter had been left open somewhere, allowing air to stir through unpopulated chambers.

He stopped for a moment. Turning to his left, he could feel the breath of the wind against his face, a faint positive pressure from one direction.

Then he heard something else, a ticking sound. A clicking. He couldn't tell where it was coming from. It was ticking like a clock, but faster, like an urgent heartbeat.

He slowly made sense of what he was hearing.

Something was padding along the stone floor of the tunnel, somewhere close by, a quadruped, soft-footed, moving with purpose, but not running. It had claws, not the retractable claws of a feline, but the claws of a dog, prominent and unconcealed, the wear-blunted tips tap-tap-tapping on the stone floor with every step.

He was being stalked. He was being hunted.

He started to run again. The tunnel broadened out, under a fine, spandrelled arch of blond wood, and revealed a great flight of stairs up ahead. The steps were cut from the native rock, square and plain. They became winders after the first ten steps where the flight turned away. The depth of the tread and the height of the risers were two or three times the normal dimensions. It was a giant's staircase.

He heard the claw-clicks closing in behind him, and began to bound up the steps. The lustrous green twilight threw strange shadows. His own shadow loomed alarmingly at his side, staining the wall like the therianthropic shapes in his dream-cave. His shadow-head looked more like an animal's on the curving wall, so much so that he had to stop for a moment and feel at his face to check that he had not woken in possession of a snout or muzzle.

His fingers found the lean flesh of his face, human and familiar, with a trace of moustache and a patch of beard on the chin.

Then he realised he could only see out of one eye.

The last breathing memory he had was of Bear taking his right eye out with his fingers. The pain had been dull, but enough to shock him into unconsciousness.

Yet it was his right eye he could see out of. It was his right eye that was showing him the frosty green twilight around him. His left eye registered only blackness.

The claw-taps approached behind him, louder, nearly at the bullnose step at the foot of the flight. He resumed his escape. Looking down, he watched the shadows on the winding steps move and alter behind him. The edge-step shadows fanned out into a radiating geometric diagram, like the delicate compartments of a giant spiral seashell, or the partitioned divisions of some intricate brass astrolabe or timepiece.

Tick, tick, tick – each second, each step, each stair, each turn, each division.

A new shadow loomed below him. It spread up across the outside wall of the giant staircase, cast by something on the stairs but out of sight around the turn.

It was canine. Its head was down, and its ears were forward and alert. Its back, thickly furred, was arched and tensed. Its forepaws rose and took each step with mesmeric precision and grace. The ticking had slowed down.

'I'm not afraid of you!' he cried. 'There are no wolves on Fenris!'

He was answered by a wet throat-growl that touched some infrasonic pitch of terror. He turned and ran, but his foot caught a step wrong, and he tripped and fell hard. Something seized him from behind, something powerful. He cried out, imagining jaws closing on his back.

A tight grip rolled him onto his back on the steps. There was a giant standing over him, but it was a man, not a wolf.

The face was all he saw. It was sheathed in a tight mask of lacquered brown leather, part man, part daemon-wolf, as intricately made as the body-suits of the skulls. Knotted and straked, the leather pieces circled the eye sockets and made heavy lids. They barred the cheek like exposed sinew, and buffered the chin. They wrapped the throat, and were shaped to mimic a long moustache and a bound-up tusk of chin-beard. The eyes revealed through the mask slits were the colour of spun gold with black pinprick pupils.

The mouth held bright fangs.

'What are you doing here?' the giant rumbled. It bent down and sniffed at him. 'You're not meant to be here. Why are you here?'

'I don't understand!' the Upplander quailed.

'What are you called?' the giant asked.

Some shred of wit remained in the Upplander's head. 'Ahmad Ibn Rustah,' he replied.

THE GIANT GRASPED him by the upper arm and dragged him the rest of the way up the stairs. The Upplander scrambled to keep up, his feet slipping and milling, like a child pulled along by an adult. The giant had a lush black pelt around one shoulder and his immense, corded physique was packed into a leatherwork body-glove. The build, the scope of the giant's physicality, was unmistakable.

'You're Astartes...' the Upplander ventured, half-running, half-slithering in response to the dragging grip.

'What?'

'Astartes. I said, you're–'

'Of course I'm Astartes!' the giant rumbled.

'Do you have a name?'

'Of course I have a name!'

'W-what is it?'

'It's shut up or I'll slit your bloody throat! That's what it is! All right?'

They had reached a landing, and then the doorway of a massive but low-ceilinged chamber. The Upplander felt heat, the warmth of flame. Vision was suddenly, curiously, returning to his dead left eye. He could see a dull, fiery glow ahead. It was enough to catch the shape of things in the dark, the shape of things his right eye saw in hard, cold, green relief.

The giant dragged him in through the stone archway.

The chamber was circular, at least thirty metres across. The floor was a great disk of polished bone or pale wood, laid in almost seamless sections. There were three plinths in the room, each one a broad, circular platform of grey stone about five metres in diameter rising about a metre off the bone floor. Each plinth was simply cut and worked smooth. In the centre of each was a firepit, crackling with well-fed flames, oozing a blush of heat into the air. Conical iron hoods hung down over each fire from the low, domed ceiling to vent the smoke.

Through his right eye, the chamber was a bright place of spectral green light. The licking flames were blooming white in their brightness. To his left, it was a dark, ruddy cave suffused by an uneven golden glow from the fires. The expanse of bone floor and brushed pale stone reflected the firelight's radiance. Opposite the chamber

door, where the low wall met the down-curved edge of
the domed roof, there were shallow, horizontal window
slits, like the ports of a gun emplacement. The depth of
the angled recesses around the slits spoke of the extraordinary thickness of the walls.

Four men occupied the room, all seated on the flat
top of the furthest plinth. All of them were giants in furs
and leather like the one who clasped his arm.

They were relaxed, sipping from silver drinking bowls,
playing games with bone counters on wooden boards
laid out on the plinth between them. It looked like one
of the men, cross-legged and nearest the firepit, was
playing all of the other three, simultaneously running
three boards.

They looked from their games, four more daemon
faces cased in tight leather masks, four more sets of yellow eyes, catching the lamplight like mirrors. The flash
was brightest in the green-cast view of the Upplander's
right eye.

'What have you found now, Trunc?' asked one.

'I've found Ahmad Ibn Rustah on the Chapter stairs is
what I've found,' replied the giant holding him.

Two of the men by the fire snorted, and one tapped a
finger to his crown to imply a touch of simple-
headedness.

'And what's an Ahmad Ibn Rustah, then?' asked the
first one again. The pelt he was wearing was red-brown,
and his hair, long and braided stiff with wax or lacquer,
projected out of the back of his full-head mask in an S-
curve like a striking serpent.

'Don't you remember?' the giant replied. 'Don't you
remember, Var?' The giant let go of the Upplander's arm
and shoved him down onto the bone floor until he was
kneeling. The floor was warm to the touch, like fine
ivory.

'I remember you talking shit yesterday, Trunc,'

returned Var of the serpent-crest. 'And the day before that, and the day before that. It all blurs into one to me.'

'Yes? Bite my hairy arse.'

The men lounging on the plinth burst out laughing, all except the one sitting cross-legged.

'I remember,' he said. His voice was like good steel drawing across an oiled whetstone. The others fell silent.

'You do?' asked Trunc.

The one sitting cross-legged nodded. His mask was the most intricate of all. The cheeks and brow were seething with interlocking figures and spiralling ribbon-shapes. His wide shoulders were draped with two pelts, one coal-black, the other white.

'Yes. And you'd remember him too, Varangr, if you only thought about it for a bloody minute.'

'I would?' asked Var of the serpent-crest uncertainly.

'Yes, you would. It was Gedrath. It was the old Jarl of Tra. Remember now?'

Var nodded. The crest of bound hair went up and down like the arm of a hand pump. 'Oh, yes, Skarsi, I do. I do!'

'Good,' said the man in the black and white pelts, and casually fetched Var an open-handed clip around the side of the head that seemed to deliver the same playful force of a mallet seating a fence-post.

'I recognise my failing and will be sure to correct it,' Var mumbled.

The man in the black and white pelts uncrossed his legs, slipped to the edge of the plinth, and stood up.

'What do we do with him, Skarsi?' Trunc asked.

'Well,' the man said, 'I suppose we could eat him.'

He stared down at the kneeling Upplander.

'That was a joke,' he said.

'I don't think he's laughing, Skarsi,' said one of the others.

The man in the black and white pelts aimed an index finger at Trunc.

'You go down and find out why he's awake.'

'Yes, Skarsi,' Trunc nodded.

Skarsi turned the finger towards Varangr.

'Var? You go and find the gothi. Bring him here. He'll know what's to be done.'

Var nodded his serpent-crest again.

Skarsi pointed at the other two men. 'You two, go and… just go. We'll finish the game-circle later.'

The two men got off the plinth and followed Var and Trunc towards the chamber door. 'Just because you were losing, Skarsi,' laughed one of them as he went by.

'You'll look pretty funny with a *hneftafl* board jammed up your arse,' Skarsi replied. The men laughed again.

When the four of them had passed through the arched doorway and out of sight, Skarsi turned back to the Upplander and hunkered down to face him with his hands clasped and his elbows resting on his knees. He cocked his huge, masked head on one side, studying the man kneeling on the floor in front of him.

'So, you're Ibn Rustah, then?'

The Upplander didn't reply at first.

'You got a voice in you?' Skarsi asked, 'or is it just the words I'm using?' He tapped the lips of his tight leather mask. 'Words? Yes? You need a translator? A *translator*?'

The Upplander put his hand to his chest, and then remembered that his environment suit was long gone.

'I've lost my translator unit,' he replied. 'I don't know where it went. But I understand you. I'm not sure how. What are you speaking?'

Skarsi shrugged. 'Words?'

'What language?'

'Uh, *Juvjk*, we call it. Hearth-cant. If I speak Low Gothic like this, is it any better?'

'Did you switch just then?' asked the Upplander.

'Between Juvjk and Low? Yes.'

The Upplander shook his head, slightly mystified.

'I heard a sort of accent shift,' he replied, 'but the words stayed the same. It was all just the same.'

'You know you're speaking Juvjk back to me, don't you?' Skarsi said.

The Upplander hesitated. He swallowed.

'I couldn't speak Juvjk yesterday,' he confessed.

'That's what a good night's sleep'll do for you,' said Skarsi. He rose. 'Get up and come sit over here,' he said, pointing at the plinth where the four Astartes had been gaming. The Upplander got up and followed him.

'You're Space Wolves, aren't you?'

Skarsi found that amusing. 'Oh, now *those* words aren't Juvjk. *Space Wolves*? Ha ha. We don't use that term.'

'What do you use, then?'

'The *Vlka Fenryka*, if we're being formal. Just *the Rout*, otherwise.'

He beckoned the Upplander to sit on the broad stone plinth, sliding one of the wooden game-boards out of his way. In the firepit, kindling spat and cracked, and the Upplander could feel the fierce press of heat against his left side.

'You're Skarsi?' he asked. 'Your name?'

Skarsi nodded, taking a sip of dark liquid from a silver bowl.

'That's so. Amlodhi Skarssen Skarssensson, Jarl of Fyf.'

'You're some kind of lord?'

'Yes. Some kind.' Skarsi appeared to smile behind his mask.

'What does Jarl of Fyf mean, then? What language is that?'

Skarsi picked up one of the bone-disc counters from the game boards and started to play with it absent-mindedly.

'It's *Wurgen*.'

'Wurgen?'

'You ask a lot of questions.'

'I do,' said the Upplander. 'It's what I do. It's why I came here.'

Skarsi nodded. He flipped the counter back onto the board. 'It's why you came here, eh? To ask questions? I can think of plenty of better reasons for going to a place.' He looked at the Upplander. 'And where is here, Ahmad Ibn Rustah?'

'Fenris. The fortress of the Sixth Legion Astartes, called – forgive me – the Space Wolves. The fortress is known as the Fang. Am I right?'

'Yes. Except only an idiot calls it the Fang.'

'What does a man call it if he isn't an idiot?' the Upplander asked.

'The Aett,' said Skarsi.

'The Aett? Just *the Aett*?'

'Yes.'

'Literally *clan-home*, or *fireplace*? Or… *den*?'

'Yes, yes, yes.'

'Am I annoying you with my questions, Amlodhi Skarssen Skarssensson?'

Skarsi grunted. 'You are.'

The Upplander nodded. 'Useful to know.'

'Why?' asked Skarsi.

'Because if I'm going to be here, and I'm going to ask my questions, I'd best be aware of how many I can get away with at a time. I wouldn't want to piss the *Vlka Fenryka* off so much they decide to eat me.'

Skarsi shrugged and crossed his legs.

'No one's going to eat you for that,' he said.

'I know. I was joking,' said the Upplander.

'I wasn't,' replied Skarsi. 'You're under Ogvai's protection, so only he can decide who gets to eat you.'

The Upplander paused. The heat of the firepit against

the side of his face and neck suddenly felt unpleasantly intense. He swallowed.

'The *Vlka Fenryka*… they're capable of cannibalism then, are they?'

'We're capable of anything,' replied Skarsi. 'That's the whole point of us.'

The Upplander slid off the plinth and stood up. He wasn't sure if he was moving away from the Astartes lord or the disagreeable heat. He just wanted to move away, to walk around.

'So who… so who's this Ogvai who has power over my life?'

Skarsi took another sip from his bowl.

'Ogvai Ogvai Helmschrot, Jarl of Tra.'

'Earlier, I heard you say someone called Gedrath was Jarl of Tra.'

'He was,' said Skarsi. 'Gedrath's sleeping on the red snow now, so Og's jarl. But Og has to honour any of Gedrath's decisions. Like bringing you here under protection.'

The Upplander moved around the room, his arms folded against his chest.

'So *jarl*. That's *lord*, we've established. And *tra* and *fyf*? They're numbers?'

'Uh huh,' nodded Skarsi. 'Three and five. *Onn, twa, tra, for, fyf, sesc, sepp, for-twa, tra-tra, dekk.*'

'So you're lord of *five*, and this Ogvai is lord of *three*? Fifth and third… what? Warbands? Divisions? Regiments?'

'Companies. We call them companies.'

'And that's in… *Wurgen*?'

'Yes, Wurgen. Juvjk is hearth-cant, Wurgen is warcant.'

'A specialised combat language? A battle tongue?'

Skarsi waved his hand in a distracted manner. 'Whatever you want to call it.'

'You have a language for fighting and a language for when you're not fighting?'

'*Fenrys hjolda*! The questions never end!'

'There's always something else to know,' said the Upplander. 'There's always more to know.'

'Not true. There's such a thing as too much.'

This last comment had been made by a new voice. Another Astartes had entered the chamber behind the Upplander, silent as the first snow. Varangr lurked at his heels in the doorway.

The newcomer had the stature of all of his breed, and was dressed in a knotwork leather suit like the others the Upplander had encountered. But he was not masked.

His head was shaved, apart from a stiffly waxed and braided beard that curled like a horn from his chin. There was a cap of soft leather on his scalp, and a faded tracery of tattooed lines and dots on the weather-beaten flesh of his face. In common with all of the *Vlka Fenryka* the Upplander had seen, the newcomer's eyes were black-centred gold, and his lean, craggy face was noticeably elongated around the nose and mouth, as if he had the hint of a snout. When he opened his mouth to speak, the Upplander saw what the extended jaw was made to conceal. The newcomer's dentition resembled that of a mature forest wolf. The canines in particular were the longest the Upplander had seen.

'There's such a thing as too much,' the newcomer repeated.

'Exactly!' Skarsi exclaimed, getting up. 'Too much! That's exactly what I was saying! You explain it to him, gothi! Better still, you try answering his endless questions!'

'If I can,' said the newcomer. He gazed at the Upplander. 'What is the next question?'

The Upplander tried to return the stare without flinching.

'What did that remark mean? Too much?' he asked.

'Even knowledge has its limits. There is a place where it becomes unsafe.'

'You can know too much?' asked the Upplander.

'That's what I said.'

'I disagree.'

The newcomer smiled slightly. 'Of course you do. I am not at all surprised.'

'Do you have a name?' the Upplander asked him.

'We all have names. Some of us have more than one. Mine is Ohthere Wyrdmake. I am rune priest to Amlodhi Skarssen Skarssensson. What is your next question?'

'What is a rune priest?'

'What do you suppose it is?'

'A shaman. A practitioner of ritual.'

'A rattler of bones. A pagan wizard. You can barely disguise the superior tone in your voice.'

'No, I meant no affront,' the Upplander said quickly. The priest's lips had curled into an unpleasant snarl.

'What is your next question?'

The Upplander hesitated again.

'How did Gedrath, Jarl of Tra, die?'

'He died the way we all die,' said Skarsi, 'with red snow under him.'

'It must have been sudden. In the last few days.'

Skarsi looked at the rune priest.

'It was a time ago,' the priest told the Upplander.

'But Gedrath gave me his protection, and that has passed to Ogvai. Ogvai must have replaced him in the last week. What? Why are you looking at me like that?'

'You are basing your assumptions on a false premise,' said Ohthere Wyrdmake.

'Really?' asked the Upplander.

'Yes,' said the priest. 'You've been here for nineteen years.'

FOUR

Skjald

THEY GAVE HAWSER the Prix Daumarl. When he was told of the decision, he felt flattered and nonplussed. 'I've done nothing,' he said to his colleagues.

There had been a shortlist of notable candidates, but in the end it had come down to Hawser, and a neuro-plasticist who had eradicated the three strands of nanomnemonic plague devastating Iberolatinate Sud Merica. 'He's done something, a considerable some-thing, and I've done nothing,' Hawser complained when he found out.

'Don't you want the prize?' Vasiliy asked. 'I hear the medal is very pretty.'

It was very pretty. It was gold, about the size of a pocket watch, and it came mounted in a Vitrian frame in an elegant casket lined with shot purple silk. The cita-tion bore the hololithic crests of the Atlantic legislature and the Hegemon, and carried the gene-seals of three members of the Unification Council. It began, 'Kasper Ansbach Hawser, for steadfast contributions towards

the definition and accomplishment of Terran Unification...'

Soon after the presentation, Hawser learned that the
whole thing was politicking, which he generally
detested, though he did not speak up as the politicking
in this instance served the cause of the Conservatory.

The award was presented at a dinner held in Karcom
on the Atlantic platforms, just after the midsummer of
Hawser's seventy-fifth year. The dinner was arranged to
coincide with the Midlantik Conclave, and thus served
as an opportunity to celebrate the Conservatory's thirtieth anniversary.

Hawser found it all rather dreadful. He spent the
evening with the elegant little purple box clutched to
his chest and a sick smile on his face waiting for the
interminable speeches to conclude. Of the many
dignitaries and men of influence attending the dinner
that midsummer night, no one was paid more
deference than Giro Emantine. By then, Emantine was
prefect-secretary to one of the Unification Council's
most senior members, and the common understanding
was that Emantine would be given the next seat that
came vacant. He was an old man, rumoured to be on
his third juvenat. He was accompanied by a remarkably
young, remarkably beautiful and remarkably silent
woman. Hawser couldn't decide if she was Emantine's
daughter, a vulgar trophy wife, or a nurse.

Emantine's status placed him directly at the right hand
of the Atlantic Chancellor (though nominally the guest
of honour, Hawser was three seats down to the left,
between an industrial cyberneticist and the chairman of
one of the orbital banking houses). When it was
Emantine's turn to speak, he appeared to have great
difficulty in remembering who Hawser was, because he
spoke fondly of their 'long friendship' and 'close working
association' down the 'many years since Kas first spoke

to me about the notion of founding the Conservatory.'

'I've met him three times in thirty years,' Hawser whispered to Vasiliy.

'Shut up and keep smiling,' Vasiliy hissed back.

'None of this actually occurred.'

'Shut up.'

'Do you suppose he's on some kind of strong medication?'

'Oh, Kas! Shut up!' Vasiliy bent close to Hawser's ear. 'This is just the way things are done. Besides, it makes the Conservatory look good. Oh, and his adjunct has informed me that he'll want to see you afterwards.'

After the dinner, Vasiliy escorted Hawser up to the Chancellor's Residence on Marianas Derrick.

'It's a beautiful city,' Hawser remarked as they walked up the terrace. He had drunk a couple of amasecs at the end of the meal to settle himself for the acceptance speech, and then there had been the toasting, so he was in a wistful mood.

Vasiliy waited patiently for a moment as Hawser stopped to admire the view. From the terrace they could see out across the plated scape of Karcom and beyond. It glittered in the late sun, the surface of a metropolitan skin nine kilometres thick that capped and encased the ancient dead ocean like an ice-pack. Shoals of aircraft, silver in the sunlight like reef-fish, flitted and drifted over the scape.

'Amazing enough that man could build this,' said Hawser, 'let alone build it three times.'

'Man probably shouldn't have kept nuking it, then, should he?' said Vasiliy.

Hawser looked at his mediary. Vasiliy was terribly young, little more than twenty-five. 'Isak Vasiliy, you have no soul,' he pronounced.

'Ah, but that's why you hired me,' Vasiliy replied. 'I don't let sentiment get in the way of efficiency.'

'There is that.'

'Besides, to me the very fact that the Atlantic platforms have been obliterated and re-built twice is symbolic of the Conservatory's work. Nothing is so great that it cannot be recovered and restored. Nothing is impossible.'

They went into the Residence. Ridiculously ornate robotic servitors imported from Mars were attending the select group of guests. The Chancellor had commissioned the machines directly from the Mondus Gamma Forge of Lukas Chrom, an ostentatious show of status.

The windows of the Residence had been dimmed against the glare of the setting sun. A pair of servitors in the shape of humming birds brought Hawser a glass of amasec.

'Drink it slowly,' Vasiliy advised discreetly. 'When you speak to Emantine, you need to be coherent.'

'I doubt I'll drink it at all,' Hawser said. He'd taken a sip. The amasec served by the Atlantic Chancellor was of such a fine and extravagantly expensive vintage, it didn't really taste like amasec anymore.

Emantine approached after a few minutes, his silent female companion in tow. He shed his previous conversational partners behind him like a snake sloughing skin; they knew when their brief allotted audiences with the prefect-secretary were done.

'Kasper,' Emanantine said.

'Ser.'

'Congratulations on the prize. A worthy award.'

'Thank you. I… Thank you, ser. This is my mediary, Isak Vasiliy.'

Emantine did not register anyone as lowly as Vasiliy. Hawser felt the prefect-secretary was only registering him because he had to. Emantine drew Hawser away towards the windows.

'Thirty years,' Emantine said. 'Can it really be thirty years since all this began?'

Hawser assumed the prefect-secretary meant the Conservatory. 'Nearly fifty, actually.'

'Really?'

'We measure the life of the Conservatory from its first charter at the Conclave of Lutetia, which was thirty years ago this summer, but it took nearly twenty years to get the movement to that place. It must be fifty years ago I first contacted your office to discuss the very basic first steps. That would have been in Karelia. Karelia Hive. You were with the legation back then, and I dealt, for a long time, with several of your understaffers. I had a dialogue with them for a number of years, actually, before I met you for the first time and–'

'Fifty years, eh? My my. Karelia, you say? Another life.'

'Yes, it feels like that, doesn't it? So, yes, I worked with a number of adjuncts to get some awareness. Made a bit of a nuisance of myself, I'm sure. Doling was one. Barantz, I remember. Bakunin.'

'I don't remember them,' the prefect-secretary said. His smile had become rather fixed. Hawser took a sip of his amasec. He felt slightly invigorated, slightly warm. He had become fixated upon Emantine's hand, which was holding a crystal thimble of some green digestif. The hand was perfect. It was clean and manicured, scented, graceful. The skin was white and unblemished and uncreased, and the flesh plump and supple. There were no signs at all of the consequences of age, no wrinkles, no liver spots, no discolourations. The nails were clean. It wasn't the gnarled, sunken, prominently-veined claw of a hundred and ninety year-old man, and prefect-secretary Giro Emantine was at least that. It was the hand of a young man. Hawser wondered if the young man was missing it. The thought made him snigger.

Of course, the prefect-secretary had access to the best juvenat refinements Terran science could afford. The treatments were so good, they didn't even look like juvenat treatments, not like the work Hawser had had done at sixty, plumping his flesh with collagenics, and filling his creases and wrinkles with dermics, and perma-staining his skin a 'healthy' tanned colour with nanotic pigments, and cleaning his eyes and his organs, and resculpting his chin, and pinching his cheeks until he looked like a re-touched hololith portrait of himself. Emantine probably had gene therapies and skeleto-muscular grafts, implants, underweaves, transfixes, stem-splices...

Maybe it *was* a young man's hand. Maybe the skin-weaves were why the prefect-secretary's smile looked so fixed.

'You don't remember Doling or Bakunin?' Hawser asked.

'They were understaffers, you say? It was a long time ago,' Emantine replied. 'They've all climbed the ladders of advancement, been posted and promoted and trans-ferred. One doesn't keep track. One can't, not when one runs a staff of eighty thousand. I have no doubt they're all governing their own ecumenopolises by now.'

There was a slightly awkward pause.

'Anyway,' said Hawser, 'I should like to thank you for getting behind the idea of the Conservatory all those years ago, be it thirty or fifty.'

'Ha ha,' said Emantine.

'I appreciate it. We all do.'

'I can't take the credit,' said Emantine.

Of course you damn well can't, Hawser thought.

'But the idea always had merit,' Emantine went on, as if he was content to take the credit anyway. 'I always said it had merit. Too easily overlooked in the headlong rush to build a better world. Not a priority, some said. The needs – and they're budgetary often – of Unification and consolidation far exceed conservation. But, we stuck to it. What is it now, thirty thousand officers worldwide?'

'That's just direct. It's closer to a quarter of a million counting freelance associates and archaeologists, and the off-world numbers.'

'Superb,' said Emantine. Hawser continued to stare at his hand. 'Then of course, there's the renewal of the charter, which is never opposed. Everyone now understands the importance of the Conservatory.'

'Not quite everyone,' said Hawser.

'Everyone who matters, Kasper. You know the Sigillite himself is keenly interested in the Conservatory's work?'

'I had heard that,' Hawser replied.

'Keenly interested,' Emantine repeated. 'Every time I meet with him, he asks for the latest transcripts and reports. Do you know him at all?'

'The Sigillite? No, I've never met him.'

'Extraordinary man,' said Emantine. 'I've heard he even discusses the Conservatory's work with the Emperor on occasion.'

'Really?' said Hawser. 'Do you know him?'

'The Emperor?'

'Yes.'

A slightly glassy expression flickered across the prefect-secretary's face, as if he wasn't sure if he was being mocked.

'No, I… I've never met him.'

'Ah.'

Emantine nodded at the purple box still clamped under Hawser's arm. 'You deserve that, Kasper. And so does the Conservatory. It's part of the recognition we were talking about. It's high-profile, and it'll bring around those few closed minds.'

'Bring them around to what?' asked Hawser.

'Well, support. Support is vital, particularly in the current climate.'

'What current climate?'

'You should cherish that award, Kaspar. To me, it says that the Conservatory has matured into a global force for Unification…'

And it doesn't hurt at all that your name is forever attached to it by the simple accident that you were at the top of the bureaucratic chain I first approached, Hawser thought. This has done your career no harm, Giro Emantine. To recognise the importance of the Conservatory project, to give it your support and backing when others scorned it. Why, what a wise, humanitarian and selfless man you must be! Not like all those other politicians.

The prefect-secretary was still speaking. 'So we need to be ready for changes in the next decade,' he was saying.

'Uhm, changes?'

'The Conservatory has become a victim of its own success!' Emantine laughed.

'It has?'

'Whether we like it or not, it's time to consider legitimacy. I can't nursemaid the Conservatory forever. My future is beckoning in different ways. A seneschalship to Luna or Mars, maybe.'

'A seat on the Council, I was told.'

Emantine pulled a modest face. 'Oh, I don't know.'

'It's what I heard.'

'The point is, I can't protect you forever,' said Emantine.

'I wasn't aware the Conservatory was being protected at all.'

'Its resource and personnel budget has become quite considerable.'

'And is scrupulously policed.'

'Of course. But it's the mandate that bothers some. It's

having what is essentially a vital organ of government, a key and growing human resource, functioning separately from the Hegemonic Administration.'

'That's just the way it is,' replied Hawser. 'That's just the way it's evolved. We're transparent and open to all. We're a public office.'

'It might be time to consider bringing the Conservatory in under the umbrella of the Administration,' said Emantine. 'It might be better that way. Centralised, which would help with the bureaucratic management, and with archiving and access, not to mention funding.'

'We'd become part of the Administratum?'

'Really just for book-keeping purposes,' replied the prefect-secretary.

'I... well, I think I'd be a little hesitant. Resistant, in fact. I think we all would.'

The prefect-secretary put his digestif down and reached out his hand to clasp it around Hawser's. His young man's fingers enclosed Hawser's grandfather hand.

'We must all move with a fluid, common purpose towards Unification, that's what the Sigillite says,' said Emantine.

'The Unification of Terra and the Imperium,' replied Hawser. 'Not the literal union of the intellectual branches of mankind that–'

'Doctor Hawser, they may refuse to renew the charter if you resist. You've spent thirty years showing them that the systematic conservation of knowledge is important. Now the feeling is – and it's shared by many on the Council – conservation of knowledge is so important, it's time it was conducted by the Administration of the Hegemony. It needs to be official and sanctioned and central.'

'I see.'

'Over the next few months, I'm going to be handing

off a lot of responsibilities to my undersecretary, Henrik Slussen. Did you meet him earlier?'

'No.'

'I'll see to it you meet him tomorrow at the manufactory visit. Get to know him. He's extremely able, and he'll steward this situation in directions that will reassure you.'

'I see.'

'Good. And once again, congratulations. A deserving winner. Fifty years, eh? My my.'

Hawser realised his audience had concluded. His glass was empty too.

✥

'How CAN IT be so long?' he asked, as the Astartes took him from the firepit chamber and out along the dark, breathing halls of the Aett. The wind gusted around them. Away from the firelight, his left eye lost its sight again.

'You've been asleep,' the rune priest replied.

'You say nineteen years, but you mean Fenrisian years, don't you? You mean great years?'

'Yes.'

'That's three, four, times as long in Terran years!'

'You've been asleep,' the rune priest said.

The Upplander felt light-headed. The sense of personal dislocation was intense and nauseating. He was afraid he might be sick, or pass out, and he was afraid of doing anything so frail in front of the Astartes. He was afraid of the Astartes. The fear added to his sense of personal dislocation, and made him feel sicker.

There were three of them with him, walking behind him: the rune priest, Varangr, and another whose name the Upplander did not know. Skarsi had shown no particular interest in coming with them. He had turned back to his playing boards, as though the Upplander was a mild diversion that was now finished with, and more important things, like bone counter discs on an inlaid board, had become more significant.

As they walked, the Astartes directed him with the occasional tap on the shoulder to turn him left and right. They walked him through great rock crypts and chambers of basalt, sulking voids of granite, and mournful hollowed halls panelled in bone. He saw all of these places through the green glare of his right eye, with only impenetrable darkness in his left. All of them were empty, except for the plaintive lament of the respiring wind. They were like tombs, tombs waiting to be filled, great sepulchres carved out in the expectation of an immense death toll, in anticipation of the corpses of a million warriors, carried in on their shields and laid to rest. A million. A million million. Legions of the fallen.

The wind was just rehearsing for its role as chief mourner.

'Where are we going?' the Upplander asked.

'To see the priests,' said Varangr.

'But you're a priest,' the Upplander said to Ohthere, half-turning. Varangr gave him a little push to encourage him forwards.

'Different priests,' said Varangr. 'The other kind.'

'What other kind?'

'You know, the other kind,' said the nameless Astartes.

'I don't know. I don't understand,' said the Upplander. 'I don't understand and I'm cold.'

'Cold?' echoed Varangr. 'He shouldn't feel the cold, not where he's been.'

'It's a good sign,' said the other.

'Give him a pelt,' said the rune priest.

'Do what?' retorted Varangr.

'Give him a pelt,' the rune priest repeated.

'Give him my pelt?' Varangr asked, looking down at the red-brown skin around his shoulders. The S-curve of his lacquered hair rose like a spear-casting arm as his chin dipped. 'But it's my pelt.'

The other Astartes snorted and pulled off his own fur, a grey wolfskin. He held it out to the Upplander.

'Here,' he said. 'Take it. A gift from Bitur Bercaw to Ahmad Ibn Rustah.'

'Is this some kind of compact?' the Upplander asked warily. He didn't want to accidentally become beholden to a wolf Astartes on top of everything else.

Bercaw shook his head. 'No, not anything with blood mixed in it. Maybe when you tell my account, you'll remember this kindness, and make it part of the story.'

'When I tell your account?'

Bercaw nodded. 'Yes, because you will. When you tell it, you make me look good, sharing the pelt with you. And you make Var look like a selfish hog.'

The Upplander looked at Varangr. His eyes shone like lamps in the frosty dark. He looked as if he was going to strike Bercaw. Then he saw the rune priest watching him. He sagged a little.

'I recognise my failing and will be sure to correct it,' he mumbled.

The Upplander pulled Bercaw's gift around his shoulders. He looked up at Ohthere Wyrdmake.

'I still don't understand.'

'I know,' said the priest.

'No, no,' the Upplander replied in frustration. 'This is where you reassure me. This is where you tell me that everything will be explained.'

'But I can't,' replied the priest, 'because it won't. Some things will be explained. Enough things, probably. But not everything, because explaining everything is never a good idea.'

They arrived at the drop.

The long, draughty hall came to an end and they were standing on the lip of a great cliff. A chasm plunged away beneath them, dropping sheer into total blackness. On the far side of the great drop, the Upplander could see the ghost-green ragged wall of the shaft. The sepulchral hall had brought them to an enormous flue, rising vertically through the rock in the heart of the mountain. The shaft vanished into darkness high above them. The winter gale gusted up from far below.

'Which way now?' asked the Upplander.

Varangr gripped him firmly by the upper arm.

'Down,' he said, and he stepped off the cliff and took the Upplander with him.

⚜

HE WAS TOO shocked to scream out the terror that exploded his chest and burst his brain. They fell. They fell. They fell.

But not hard, and not to their deaths. They fell softly, like flecks of down from a torn sleeping roll, caught by the breeze, like papery flecks of ash, like a pair of humming bird servitors defying gravity with wings so fast they seemed still.

The wind of Fenris was everywhere inside the Aett, gusting in halls, breathing through crypts and vaults and chambers, but in the great vertical flue it blew with enough upward force to catch falling objects and cushion their descent. The rising gale lowered them slowly, dragging against their flapping pelts, and flapping the beads and straps of the Astartes.

Varangr stuck out an arm, the one that wasn't gripping the Upplander's limp frame. He stuck it out like an eagle's wing into the updraught, and steered them. He turned them slowly, at an angle in the fierce blast. The Upplander's tear-shot eyes, blinking furiously in the wind and out of gutting fear, saw another cliff-lip below, another shelf opening into the flue. They came into it at a perfect angle. Varangr landed on his feet, and turned the landing into a couple of quick steps that bled off his speed. The Upplander's feet scrambled and kicked, and he fell on his face. The pelt flopped forwards over his head like a hood.

'You'll learn the knack,' said Varangr.

'How?' asked the Upplander.

'By doing it more,' replied the Astartes.

On his hands and knees, the Upplander convulsed violently and retched. Nothing but spittle and mucus came up out of a gut that had been empty for nineteen years, but his body wrenched and wrung itself in a brutal effort to find something.

Bercaw and the rune priest landed on the lip behind them.

'Pick him up,' said the priest.

They carried him forwards, away from the cliff edge. His head lolled, but his left eye woke up. He saw a chamber up ahead, well lit with biolumin lamps and electric filaments in glass tubes. The sudden illumination was painful. He had a hot, orange version of the scene in his left eye, full of fire shadows and the warm yellow glow of tube lights and ivory flooring. In the other eye, the scene was an incandescent green, violently bright. The lamps and other light sources were so intense to his right eye, they had almost scorched out of vision entirely and become white-hot spots and afterimage blooms. There were very few shadows in his right eye, and the focus was shot.

The Astartes put him down.

The Upplander could smell blood, salt water and the bleachy reek of counterseptic. The chamber was either a medical facility or an abattoir. Or perhaps it was both, or had been one and was now the other. There was also a hint of laboratory, and a smack of kitchen. There were metal benches and adjustable cots. There were clusters of overhead focus lights, and branches of automated servitor arms and manipulators sprouting from the ceiling like willow trees. There were stone slabs, like butcher blocks or altars. Hidden machinery hummed and whirred, and electronic notes sounded a constant background chorus like a digital rainforest. Archways led through to other kitchen-morgues. The complex was vast. He glimpsed the frosty doors of cryogenic units and the glass-lidded tanks of organic repair vats. Library shelves stretched off into the distance, lined with heavy glass bottles and canisters, like giant jars of pickled and preserved fruit in a winter root cellar. But the flasks did not contain vegetables or radapples in their dark, syrupy suspensions, and they were slotted into the shelves to connect with the facility's vital support system.

Horned skulls appeared, robed men with animal skull heads like the ones who had surrounded him when he first woke up. The rune priest sensed his alarm.

'They are just thralls. Servants and grooms. They will not hurt you.'

Other figures appeared from invisible corners of the rambling laboratory. These were Astartes, from the build of them. Horned skulls of significantly greater scale and threat than the ones worn by the thralls covered their faces. Their robes were floor length and had a quilted look, stitched together from sections of soft, napped leather. When they reached out their hands to greet or grasp the Upplander, he saw that their hands were covered in gloves patched together from the same material, and that the gloves were sewn into the enveloping cloaks, as if they were inside patchwork bags of skin with integral glove extensions that allowed them to work. The stitching on the patchwork seams, though expertly neat, reminded the Upplander far too much of surgical sutures.

They were sinister figures, and their presence was not helped by the fact that even Ohthere Wyrdmake showed deference to them.

'Who are you?' the Upplander asked.

'They are the wolf priests,' said Ohthere softly at his shoulder, 'the geneweavers, the fleshmakers. They will examine you.'

'Why?'

'To make sure you're healthy. To check their workmanship.'

The Upplander shot a quick glance at the rune priest.

'Their what?'

'You came to the Aett broken and old, Ahmad Ibn Rustah,' said one of the wolf priests in a voice that creaked like floe-ice, 'too broken to live, and too old to heal. The only way to save you was to remake you.'

One of the horned giants took his right hand, another his left. He let them lead him into the slaughterhouse chapel like parents leading a child. He took off the pelt and settled on the black glass bed of a body scanner. There were a lot of wolf priests around him now, shamanic shadows with feral horns and guttural voices. Some were intent on adjusting the backlit wall plates of the control panels. Others were occupied with the elaborate tapping and shaking of rattlebags and bone wands. Both tasks seemed to carry equal significance.

The scanner bed elevated him and tilted him backwards. Manipulator arms, some of them fitted with sensors, others with the finest micrometre tool-heads, clicked down around him in a cage, like a crouching spider. They started working, twitching and brushing and scurrying. He felt the tickle of scan-beams, the nip of pinpricks, the sting of diagnostic light beams penetrating his held-open eyes.

He looked up, past the surgical lights, and saw himself, full length, reflected in the tinted canopy of the body scanner.

He had the fit, athletic body of a thirty year-old. Fitter and more athletic, in fact, than the thirty year-old body he had once possessed. The muscle definition was impressive. There was not an ounce of fat on him. Nor was there any sign of the old augmetic. He had the makings of a moustache and beard, a fuzz of growth a few weeks thick. His hair was shorter than he chose to wear it, as if it was growing back in after being shaved. It was darker than it had been since his fiftieth birthday.

Behind the beard growth, his face was still his own: younger, but still his own. This fact filled him with greater relief and confidence than anything else that had happened since he had woken.

It was the face of Kasper Ansbach Hawser, twenty-five years old, back when he was headstrong and arrogant and knew nothing about anything. This latter detail seemed more than a little appropriate.

In the reflection, dozens of hands in gloves of patchwork skin worked on him.

'You refashioned me,' he said.

'There was significant damage to your limbs and to your internal organs,' said the ice-creak voice. 'You would not have survived. Over a period of nine months, we used mineral bonding and bone grafts to reconstitute your skeletal mass, and then resleeved it in musculature gene-copied from your own coding, though reinforced with plastek weaves and polymers. Your organs are primarily gene-copied transplants. Your skin is your own.'

'My own?'

'Removed, replenished, rejuvenated, retailored.'

'You skinned me.'

They did not reply.

'You worked on my mind too,' he said. 'I know things. I know a language I didn't know before.'

'We did not teach you anything. We did not touch your mind.'

'And yet here we are conversing, without a translator.'

Again, they did not reply.

'What about the eye? Why did you take my eye? Why do I keep going blind in my left eye?'

'You do not keep going blind in your left eye. The sight in your left eye is human-normal. It is your eye.'

'Why did the warrior take my right eye?'

'You know why. It was an implant. It was not your eye. It was an optical recording device. It was not permitted. Therefore, it was detected and removed.'

'But I can see,' the Upplander said.

'We would not blind you and leave you blind,' said the ice-creak voice.

He looked up at his reflection. His left eye was the eye that he remembered.

His right eye, gold and black-pinned, was the eye of an adult wolf.

✣

RECTOR UWE CALLED them in, just as the moon rose. All the children had spent the day outside, because the weather was clement and the grids had forecast no rad clouds or pollution fogs on the desert highland.

The children had worked outdoors, especially the older ones. That, the rector taught, was the purpose of community. The parents, all the adults, they were rais-ing the city, the great city of Ur. They were gone for months at a time, away in the sprawling work camps that surrounded the vast street plan that the Architect had marked out on the chosen earth. Rector Uwe showed the children scenes from Faeronik Aegypt in old picture books. Gangs of industrious labourers with uni-form asymmetric haircuts pulled ropes to raise the travertine blocks that made the monuments of Aegypt. This, he explained, was very much the way their parents were working, pulling together with a single purpose to build a city. The difference, he added, was that in old Aegypt, the builders were slaves, and in Ur, the workers were freemen, come willingly to the task, and all according to Catheric teachings.

Though they could not work on the city itself, the children still worked. They harvested fruit and vegetables from the tented fields, and washed them and packed them to be shipped to the work camps. They patched and mended worn clothes sent back from the labour site in yellow sacks, and wrote messages of encouragement and salvation on slips of paper that they tucked into pockets to be discovered at random.

In the afternoons, the rector gave the children instruction. He taught lessons in language, history and Catheric lore in the long room of the commune, or out under the trees of the tent fields, or even out in the actual open, in fair weather. The children learned their letters and their numbers, and the basic elements of salvation. They learned about the world as well: the name of the desert highlands, and the long valley, and the site chosen for Ur. They learned the names of all the other communes, just like their own, where other rectors looked after other student bodies, all part of the greater community. Rector Uwe had no staff, except for Niina the nurse-cook, so as the older children learned, they took charge of the younger ones' instruction. The rector let the brightest of all use the half-dozen teaching desks in the annex beside the commune's library.

Kas was only a little boy, four or five, but he was already one of the brightest. Like a lot of the children in the rector's care, Kas was an orphan as far as the rector could determine. One of the Architect's surveyor troops had found him in the cot-box of an overturned track-wagon out on the radland flats, a year back. The wagon had tipped on a salt depression, with no hope of righting. Its cells were flat dead, and there was no sign of any adults, except for a few bones and hanks of clothing about a kilometre further on.

'Figure predators got them,' said the surveyor troop leader when he brought Kas in. 'The ride went over, so they walked to find water and help, and preds found them first. The boy's lucky.'

Rector Uwe nodded, and touched the little gold crux around his neck. It was an odd definition of the word.

'Lucky we found him,' the leader clarified. 'Lucky the predators didn't.'

'You see any preds?' the rector asked.

'The usual meat birds,' the leader replied. 'Plus dog tracks. A lot of dog tracks. Big, maybe even wolves. They're getting bolder. Coming closer, every year.'

'They know we're here,' replied the rector, meaning mankind, back to his old tricks, with all the bonus scraps and left-overs that entails.

There were a lot of orphans in the commune, because building a city was hard, but most came with names. The boy didn't have one, so Rector Uwe chose one for him. A suitable name. The troops had found a little toy horse made of wood, like the Horse of Ilios, in the trackwagon with the child, so that made the choice easier.

He called them in at moonrise. After work and lessons, they had run out into the open woods and the meadow beyond the stream that moved their wheel. The meadow grass was the last, long straw from summer, bleached by sun and rads. The sky was wort-blue. Stars prickled the early evening. The children chased along the avenues of trees, under the tunnels of their rad-blacked leaves. They swung and played shouting games. Thunder warriors was popular with the boys. They made guns from fingers and death noises with their mouths, and came back in for supper with skinned knees.

There were always stragglers at supper call. Niina used the threat of wolves to bring the laggards in.

'The wolves are out there! The wolves will get you, now the moon's up!' she'd call from the back door of the kitchen.

When he came in that night, red-faced and out of breath, Kas looked at Rector Uwe.

'Are the wolves here?' he asked.

The boy was flushed and sweating. He'd probably been playing thunder warriors with the older boys, running to keep up and shout as loud. But he also appeared scared.

'Wolves? No, that's just what Niina says,' Rector Uwe replied. 'There are preds, so we must be careful. Dogs, most likely. A lot of wild dogs, living in packs. They're scavengers. Sometimes they come down off the high desert and raid our midden. But only if they're bold, only if the winter's been bleak. They're more scared of us than we are of them.'

'Dogs?' Kas asked.

'Just dogs. Dogs used to live with men, as their companions. Some communes still keep them as guards and to mind livestock.'

'I don't like dogs,' the boy replied, 'and I am afraid of wolves.'

He ran off to join the end of the noisy game. He ran with a little boy's acceleration, from nothing to maximum speed in a blink. Rector Uwe smiled, but his heart was heavy. He wondered what it had been like in the cabin of that overturned trackwagon. He wondered how much a three year-old could remember. He wondered how close the preds had got, how close they had got to breaking into the wagon body, how terrifying they would have been.

The clement weather stayed with them for several weeks. Autumn was late. In the evenings, the light spun out, long and golden, and stretched the shadows of the raddled trees. The sky was like the glass of a blue bottle.

Occasional little clouds dotted the horizon, cotton-white, like smoke signals lost for words. The children played out late. It was good to get open air into them, not recyc.

After supper, most nights, Rector Uwe liked to take out his regicide set and play a game or three with the smartest kids. He liked to teach them (he even had a few old books of instruction that he was prepared to lend) but he also enjoyed the challenge of a live player, how-ever unschooled they might be, because it was an improvement over the programmed opposition pro-vided by the teaching desks.

The rector's regicide set was very old and very worn. The case was something he called shagreen, framed with discoloured ivory and lined with blue velvet. The board, unfolded, was made of inlaid walnut (it was slightly warped), and the pieces were made of bone and stained hoganny.

Kas was a quick learner, quicker even than some of the older clever boys. He had the wit for it. Uwe taught him what he could, knowing it would take a long time to season him and show him a decent range of opening schemes and ending-outs.

As they played that night, a game that Rector Uwe eas-ily won, Kas mentioned the name of one of the other boys, and said that the boy had heard dogs barking ear-lier that day.

'Dogs? Where?'

'Up on the western slopes,' Kas replied, considering his next move with his chin on his fist, the way he had seen the rector do it.

'Probably crows cawing,' said the rector.

'No, it was dogs. Did you know that all dogs, every-where in our world, all of them descended from a pack of wolves tamed on the shores of the Youngsea River?'

'I did not know that.'

'It was fifty-five thousand years ago.'

'Where did you learn this?'

'I asked the teaching desks about dogs and wolves.'

'You are properly afraid of them, aren't you?'

Kas nodded. 'It is sensible. They are predators and they devour.'

'Are you afraid of meat-birds?'

Kas shook his head. 'Not really, though they are ugly and they can hurt you.'

'What about eater-pigs and wild swine?'

'They are dangerous,' the boy nodded.

'But you're not afraid of them?'

'I would be careful if I saw one.'

'Are you afraid of snakes?'

'No.'

'Of bears?'

'What is a bear?'

Rector Uwe smiled. 'Make your move.'

'They are all animals besides,' the boy said, moving his piece.

'What are?'

'The things you're asking me about, the snakes and the pigs. Are bears animals? I think they are all animals, and some of them are dangerous. I don't like spiders. Or scorpions. Or big scorpions, the red ones, but I am not afraid of them.'

'No?'

'Yaena has a red scorpion in a jar in his foot locker, and when he shows it to us, I am not afraid of it.'

'I will be talking to Yaena about that.'

'I am not afraid of it, though. Not like Simial and the others. But I am afraid of wolves, because they are not animals.'

'Oh? What are they then?'

The boy scrunched up his face, as if determining the best way of explaining it.

'They are… well, they are like ghosts. They are devils, like scripture tells us about.'

'They are supernatural, you mean?'

'Yes. They come to destroy and devour, because that is their nature, their only nature. And they can be wolves, that is dog-shape, or they can walk about in the shape of men.'

'How do you know this, Kasper?'

'Everyone knows it. It is common knowledge.'

'It may not be correct. Wolves are just dogs. They are canine animals.'

The boy shook his head fiercely. He leaned forwards and dropped his voice very low.

'I have seen them,' he whispered. 'I have seen them walk about on two feet.'

HE WAS GIVEN some food, a basic nutrient broth and some dry biscuits, and then he was left on his own in a draughty room near the kitchen-morgue. The room was panelled in white bone, and it had a small firepit and a bench cot. It also had a lamp, a small metal-bodied bio-lumin unit of the type stamped out in their millions for the Imperial Army. Light from the lamp let him see the room around him with both eyes. He was getting used to the discrepancy between vision types.

The food had come on a brushed metal tray. It made a poor hand mirror, but a mirror nonetheless. He looked at his new eye in its rubbed surface.

His new eye had extraordinary night and low-light response. He had spent a great deal of his time, since waking, moving around in pitch darkness without even realising it. That was why his real eye had seemed blind. It was also why the world looked spectral green, and why actual light sources flared to white blooms of painful radiance. The Wolves of Fenris lived in darkness most of the time. They hadn't much need for artificial light.

His new eye lacked good, defined distance vision. Everything became slightly unfocussed at distances of more than thirty metres, like looking through an extremely wide-angle optical lens, the sort he had often used on good quality picter units for architectural recording. But the peripheral vision and the sensitivity to movement were astonishing.

Exactly what you'd expect from a predator's eye.

He held the tray up in front of his face, and closed one eye, then the other, back and forth. When he switched back to his wolf eye for the fifth time, he noticed, in the battered reflection, the half-shadow in the doorway behind him.

'You'd better come in,' he said, without looking around.

The Astartes came into the room.

The Upplander put the tray down, and turned to look at him. The Astartes was as big as all his kind, wrapped in a slate-grey pelt. His fur and his armour looked wet, as if he had been outside. He had removed his leather mask, to show his face, weathered and tattooed. The Upplander knew the face.

'Bear,' he said.

The Astartes grunted.

'You're Bear,' the Upplander said.

'No.'

'Yes. I don't know many Astartes, I don't know many Space Wolves–'

He saw the Astartes's lip curl at the use of the term.

'But I know your face. I remember your face. You're Bear.'

'No,' the warrior said. 'But you might remember my face. I'm known as Godsmote now, of Tra. But nineteen winters ago I was called Fith.'

The Upplander blinked.

'Fith? You're Fith? The Ascommani?'

The Astartes nodded. 'Yes.'

'Your name was Fith?'

'My name's still Fith. They call me Godsmote or Godsmack in the Rout, because I've got a good swing on me, a swing like an angry god, and I once buried the smile of a blade in the forehead of a warboss...'

His voice trailed off.

'That's another story. Why are you looking at me like that?'

'They... they made you into a Wolf,' said the Upplander.

'I wanted it. I wanted them to take me. My aett was gone, and my folk. I barely had my thread left. I wanted them to take me.'

'I told them. I told Bear to take you. You and the other one.'

'Brom.'

'Brom, yes. I told Bear to take the both of you. I told him to make bloody sure he took the both of you, after all you did for me.'

Fith nodded. 'They changed you too. They changed us both. Made us both sons of Fenris. It's what Fenris always does. Changes things.'

The Upplander shook his head in slow disbelief. 'I can't believe it's you. I'm glad it is. I'm happy to see you alive. But I can't believe... *look* at you!'

He glanced down at the brushed steel tray.

'Come to that, look at me. I can't believe this is me either.'

He stood up and held out his hand to the Astartes.

'I want to thank you,' he said.

Fith Godsmote shook his head. 'No need to thank me.'

'Yes, there is. You saved my life, and it cost you everything.'

'I don't see it like that.'

The Upplander shrugged, and lowered his hand.

'And you don't look too happy I saved your life,' the Astartes added.

'I was then,' the Upplander replied. 'Nineteen winters ago. Now, well, everything's a little strange to me. I'm adjusting.'

'We all adjust,' said Fith. 'It's part of changing.'

'Bear, he's still alive, is he?' the Upplander asked.

'Yes. Bear's running a thread still.'

'Good. He didn't think to come and see me now I'm awake?'

'I don't see he's got much reason to,' replied the Astartes. 'I mean, his debt to you is long since done. He made an error, and he atoned for it.'

'Yes, about that,' the Upplander said, sitting down again and leaning back. 'What was his error? His oversight, that he had to make amends for?'

'It was his fault you were out there. It was his fault you fell as a bad star.'

'Was it?'

Fith nodded.

'Was it really?'

Fith nodded again. 'You'll see Bear, I should think, when Ogvai calls you to Tra. You'll probably see him then.'

'So why's Ogvai going to call me to Tra?'

'He'll decide what we should do with you.'

'Ah,' said the Upplander.

Fith reached under his pelt and produced a limp plastek sack, tied shut. It was a miserable bundle, and the skin of the bag was wet with droplets of ice mush and meltwater.

'When I heard you had come back awake, I fetched this. It's the bits you were carrying with you when you came to Fenris. All that I could find, anyway. I thought you might want them.'

The Upplander took the cold, wet sack and began to unpick the knot.

'So where is Brom?' he asked.

'Brom never made it,' Fith replied.

The Upplander stopped picking at the knot and looked at the Astartes.

'Oh. I'm sorry.'

'No need to be. There is a place for all things, and Brom is in Uppland now.'

'That word,' the Upplander said, 'I remember that word. When I got here, when the Ascommani pulled me from the crash site, that's what you called me. An Upplander.'

'Yes.'

'It meant heaven, didn't it? It meant the places up there, above the world?' The Upplander pointed at the chamber's ceiling. 'Upplander is someone who comes down to the land, to the mortal Verse. The stars, other planets, heaven, they're all the same thing, aren't they? You thought I was some sort of god, fallen out of heaven.'

'Or a daemon,' Fith suggested.

'I suppose. Anyway, my point is… you know about space and the stars now. You know about other planets. You must have been to some. Now you've become an Astartes, you've learned about the universe and your place in it.'

'Yes.'

'But you still use a word like Uppland. You said Brom is in Uppland. Heaven and hell are primitive concepts, aren't they? Is it just the reassurance of old names?'

Fith didn't reply for a moment. Then he said, 'There's still an Uppland, as far as I'm concerned. Just like there's a Verse and an Underverse. And as for Hel, I know there's a Hel. I've seen it several times.'

※

When they came to take him to see the Jarl of Tra, he was in fear for his life. This was an unnecessary fear, he reasoned, because the Wolves had put significant effort into preserving and maintaining his existence. It seemed unlikely that they would expend that effort only to dispose of him.

But the fear clawed him and would not go away. It hung around him like a pelt. Whatever they were, the Wolves showed absolutely not a scrap of sentiment. They arbitrated decisions, right or wrong, on what seemed like whims, though were probably the blink-fast instincts of accelerated warriors. He was, to them, a curiosity at best. The work they had put into saving his life must have been a considerable effort. To them, with their halfway-immortal lives, it might just have been a way of fending off boredom through a long winter.

Fith Godsmote came to fetch him, along with others from Tra whose names the Upplander would only learn later. Fith was junior to them all, and from a different company. They were hulking, longtooth monsters with shadowed eyes. The Upplander realised that Fith's inclusion in the honour guard was a mark of respect shown to a novitiate by his elders. Fith had saved the Upplander and brought him to the Aett, so it was only right that he should be part of an escort, even if the escort duty would normally fall to the company veterans.

That made logical sense. It made logical sense when they first came to his white bone room and summoned him with a gesture. By the time they had ascended to the Hall of Tra, a climb that had taken an hour, and had woven up deep staircases and rock chutes and one, stomach-wrenching ascent on the wind itself, fear had mutated the logic, and the only sense the Upplander could see was that Fith Godsmote had to be present at his death as some form of punishment duty.

The Hall of Tra was cold and lightless. His wolf-eye caught the ghost radiation of barely smouldering firepits. In terms of heat and light, the Wolves were making no allowances for human tolerances of comfort. They had given him a pelt and an eye to see through the dark with. What more could he want?

He realised he wasn't alone. The company was all around him. Their body heat was barely detectable, dimmer than the dull firepits. The Hall was a massive natural cavern, ragged and irregular, and the Astartes were ranged around it, huddled and coiled in their furs, as immobile as a sibling pack of predators, gone to ground overnight, dormant and pressed close for warmth. Faces cowled by animal skin hoods were watching his approach. There were occasional grumbles and murmurs, like animals growling in their sleep or tussling over bones. As his eye resolved the scene better, the Upplander saw some evidence of movement. He saw hands casually raise silver bowls and dishes so that men could sip black liquid from them. He saw hunched shapes engaged in the counter game, hneftafl, that the Upplander had seen Skarsi playing.

Little heed was paid to him. Tra Company was resting. They had not assembled to give him audience. He was just something being brought through their hall so that business could be settled. He was a minor distraction.

At the back of the hall, at the highest point of the cavern, was Ogvai Ogvai Helmschrot. High Wolf. Pack master. *Jarl of Tra*. Just from his bearing, his authority was beyond question. He was big, long-boned, a runner who would make pursuit relentlessly across waste and tundra with immeasurable stamina. His hair was long and straight, centre-parted, black, and his head was tilted back to invest his black-circled eyes and clean-shaven jaw with a commanding arrogance. The centre of his lower lip was tagged with a fat steel piercing that gave him a petulance that seemed childish and dangerous.

He slid forwards off a mound of battered old skins to get a look at the Upplander.

'So this is what a bad omen looks like when it stands up in your face?' he asked no one. The Upplander's breath was steaming the frigid air, but barely a curl escaped Ogvai's mouth alongside his words. Astartes biology was marvellously adapted for heat retention.

The jarl was wearing a laced leather jacket with no sleeves. His arms were long and his skin was sun-starved white. There were dark tattoos on the albino flesh there. He stretched one arm out and took up a silver bowl. It was full of a liquid so dark it looked like ink. The jarl's fingers, curled around the lip of the silver lanx, were armoured with dirty rings. The Upplander imagined the jarl wore them less for decoration and more for the damage they would do to the things that he hit.

Ogvai took a sip, and then offered the lanx to the Upplander. He held it out.

'He can't drink that,' said one of the escort. '*Mjod* will go though his innards like acid.'

Ogvai sniffed.

'Sorry,' he said to the Upplander. 'Wouldn't want to kill you with a toast to your health.'

The Upplander could smell the petroleum reek of the drink. There was blood in it too, he guessed. Liquid food, fermented, chemically distilled, extremely high calorific content... more akin to aviation fuel than a beverage.

'It keeps the cold out,' Ogvai remarked as he set the bowl down. He looked at the Upplander.

'Tell me why you're here.'

'I'm here at the continuing discretion of the Rout,' the Upplander replied in Juvjk.

Ogvai curled his lip.

'No, that's why you're still breathing,' he said. 'I asked why you're here.'

'I was invited.'

'Tell me about this invitation.'

'I sent a number of messages to the Fenris beacon, requesting permission to enter Fenrisian world-space. I wished to meet with and study the Fenrisian Astartes.'

One of the escort standing behind the Upplander snorted.

'That doesn't sound like a request that we would say yes to,' said Ogvai. 'Were you persistent?'

'I think I sent the request, with various elaborations, about a thousand times.'

'You think?'

'I can't be sure. I had a log of the precise number, with transmission dates. My effects were returned to me, but all my data-slates and notebooks were missing.'

'Written words,' said Ogvai. 'Written words and word storage devices. We don't permit them here.'

'At all?'

'No.'

'So all my notes and drafts, all my work, you destroyed it?'

'I would think so. If that's what you were idiot enough to bring with you. Don't you have back-up off-world?'

'Nineteen great years ago, I did. How do you record information here on Fenris?'

'That's what memories are for,' said Ogvai. 'So you sent this message a lot. Then what?'

'I got permission. Permission to set down. Coordinates were given. The permit was verified as Astartes. But during planetfall, my lander suffered a serious malfunction and crashed.'

'It didn't crash,' said Ogvai. He took another sip of his ink-black drink. 'It was shot out of the sky. Wasn't it, Bear?'

Nearby, at the foot of the jarl's seating mound, one of the dark masses of huddled furs stirred.

'You shot him down, didn't you, Bear?'

There was a grumble of reply.

Ogvai grinned. 'That was why he had to come out and rescue you. Because he shot you down. It was a mistake, wasn't it, Bear?'

'I recognised my failing, jarl, and I was sure to correct it,' Bear replied.

'If you knew all this, why did you ask me?' asked the Upplander.

'Just wanted to see if you remembered the story as well as I did.' Ogvai frowned. 'Your telling's not up to much, though. I'll put that down to the fact that you've been in the icebox a long time and your brain's probably still frosty. But as a skjald, you're not really what I expected.'

'As a skjald?'

Ogvai leaned forwards and rested the elbows of his long, white arms on his knees. His pale skin glowed in the gloom, like glacier ice.

'Yes, as a skjald. I'll tell it now, then. I'll tell the account. Gedrath, who came before me, he warmed to your messages. He talked to us in Tra, and to me, who was his right hand, and to the other jarls, and to the Wolf King too. A skjald, he said. That would be amusing. Diverting. A skjald could bring new accounts from Upp and out, and he could learn ours too. Learn them, and tell them back to us.'

'This is what you thought I'd be?' asked the Upplander.

'Is it what *you* thought you'd be?' asked the jarl. 'You wanted to learn about us, didn't you? Well, we don't give our stories cheaply. We don't give them to just anybody. You sounded promising, and eager.'

'Then there was the name,' said one of the escort

behind the Upplander. Ogvai nodded, and the Tra veteran stepped forwards. He was lanky and grey-haired, with blue tattooing writhing up and out from the edges of his leather face mask and across his deep brow. Plaited grey beard tails sprouted from the mask's lower rim.

'What's that, Aeska?' asked Ogvai.

'The name he gave us,' said Aeska. 'Ahmad Ibn Rustah.'

'Oh yes,' said Ogvai.

'Jarl Gedrath, rest his thread, had a romantic soul,' said the warrior.

Ogvai grinned. 'Yes. It appealed to him. To me too. I was his right hand, and he looked to me. He didn't want to appear whimsical or weak, but a man's heart can be touched by an old memory or the smell of history. That's what you intended, wasn't it?'

He was looking directly at the Upplander.

'Yes,' said the Upplander. 'To be honest, after a thousand or so messages, I was willing to try anything. I didn't know if you'd know the significance.'

'Because we're stupid barbarians?' asked Ogvai, still smiling.

The Upplander wanted to say *yes*. Instead, he said, 'Because it's old and obscure data by any standard, and that was before I knew you kept no written or stored records. Long ago, before Old Night, before even the rise of man from Terra, and the Outward Urge, and the Golden Era of Technology, there was a man called Ahmad Ibn Rustah, or ebn Roste Esfahani. He was a learned man, a conservator who went out into the world to discover and preserve knowledge, learning it first-hand so he knew it to be accurate, to be the truth. He went from Isfahan in what we know as the Persian region, and travelled as far as Novgorod, where he encountered the Rus. These were the peoples of the Kievan Rus Khaganate, part of the vast and mobile genetic group that encompassed the Slav, the Svedd, the Norsca and the Varangaria. He was the first outsider to integrate with them, to appreciate their culture and to report them to be far more than the stupid barbarians they were thought to be.'

'You see a parallel here?' asked Ogvai.

'Don't you?'

Ogvai sniffed and rubbed the end of his nose with the pad of his thumb. His finger nails were thick and black, like chips of ebony. They each had deep and complex patterns embossed or drilled into them. 'Gedrath did. You used the name as a shibboleth.'

'That's right.'

There was silence.

'I understand I've been brought here so you can decide what to do with me,' said the Upplander.

'Yes, that's about it. It falls to me to decide, now I'm jarl and Gedrath is gone.'

'Not to… your primarch?' asked the Upplander.

'The Wolf King? That's not the kind of decision he bothers himself with,' replied Ogvai. 'Tra had seneschal-ship of the Aett the season you came along, so Gedrath was the lord in charge. This is down to his whimsy. Now I find out if Tra comes to regret it. Do you really want to learn about us?'

'Yes.'

'That means learning about survival. About killing.'

'You mean war? I have lived most of my life on Terra, a world that is still riven by conflict as it restores itself. I've seen my fair share of war.'

'I don't mean war so much,' said Ogvai doubtfully. 'War's just an elaboration and codification of a much purer activity, which is being alive. Sometimes, at the most basic level, to be alive you must stop other people being alive. This is what we do. We are extremely good at it.'

'I have no doubt of that, ser,' the Upplander replied.

Ogvai picked up his lanx and held it pensively in front of his mouth in both hands, ready to sip.

'Life and death,' he said softly. 'That's what we're about, *Upplander*.' He said the name scornfully, as if mocking. 'Life and death, and the place where they meet up. That place, that's where we do business. That's the space we inhabit. That's the place where wyrd gets decided. You want to come with us, you'll have to learn about both of them. You'll have to get close to both. Tell me, you ever been close to *either*? You ever been to the place where they meet?'

HE COULD HEAR music. Someone was playing the clavier.

'Why can I hear music?' he asked.

'I don't know,' Murza replied. He clearly didn't care either. A fat pile of manuscripts and maps was spread out over the battered desktop, and he was picking over them.

'It's a clavier,' said Hawser, cocking his head.

The day was fine, sunny. The white dust kicking up from the Army shelling seemed to have dried out the previous day's rain and left the sky a deep, dark blue, like the lid of a box lined with velvet. Sunlight sloped in off the street through the blown-out window and doorway, and brought the distant music with it.

The building had once been a clerical office, perhaps for patents or legal work, and a penetrator shell had gone through its upper storeys like a round through a brainpan. The floor of the front office they were standing in was stained navy blue from the hundreds of bottles of ink that had been blown off the shelves and shattered. The ink had soaked in and dried months before. The blue floor matched the sky outside. Hawser stood in the patch of sunlight and listened to the music. He hadn't heard a clavier playing in years.

'Look at this, will you?' Murza said. He passed a hand-held picter unit to Hawser. Hawser looked at the image displayed on the back-plate screen.

'This has just come through from our contact,' he said. 'Do you think it's a match?'

'The image quality is poor–' Hawser began.

'But your mind isn't,' snapped Murza.

Hawser smiled. 'Navid, that's probably the nicest thing you've ever said to me.'

'Get over it, Kas. Look at the pict. Is it the box?'

Hawser studied the image again, and compared it to the various antique archive picts and reference drawings that Murza had arranged in a line across the desk.

'It looks genuine,' he said.

'It looks beautiful is what it looks,' smiled Murza. 'But I do not want to get bitten like we did at Langdok. We have to be sure this is genuine. The bribes we've paid, the finder's fees. There'll be more, you can count on it. The local priesthood will have to be financially persuaded to look the other way.'

'Really? You'd think they'd be grateful. We're attempting to salvage their heritage before this war obliterates it. They must realise we're attempting to save something they can't?'

'You know that this is much more complicated than that,' replied Murza. 'It's a matter of faith. That much should be obvious to a good Catheric boy like you.'

Hawser didn't rise to the bait. He'd never made an attempt to hide the tradition of belief he'd been raised to. All teaching at the commune that had been his first home had been Catheric, as had all the communes and camps serving the Ur project. A city built by and for the faithful. It was an appealing idea, one of an infinite number that had tried and failed to make sense of mankind's lot after Old Night. Hawser had never been much of a believer himself, but he'd had great patience

and respect for the ideas of men like Rector Uwe. In
turn, Uwe had never presumed to impose his beliefs on
Hawser. He'd supported Hawser's ambition to attend a
universitariate. Almost accidentally, in conversation
with a faculty senior many years later, Hawser had discovered that he had been awarded his scholarship to
Sardis principally on the basis of the letter Uwe had sent
to the master of admissions.

Without Rector Uwe, Hawser would never have left
the commune and Ur, and entered academia. But for his
place at Sardis, Hawser would still have been at the
commune when the predators, the human predators,
had stolen in off the western slope radlands and put an
end to the dream of Ur.

It was a salvation he still found uncomfortable, two
decades later.

Hawser was interested in the tradition and histories of
faith and religion, but it was hard in the modern age to
believe in any god who had never bothered to prove his
existence, when there was one who most profoundly
had. It was said that the Emperor denied all efforts to
label Him a god, or entitle Him with divinity, but there
was no getting around the fact that, as He had risen to
prominence on Terra, all the extant creeds and religions
of the world had correspondingly dried up like parched
watercourses in summer.

Murza now, he hid his beliefs. Hawser knew for a fact
that Murza had also been raised Catheric. They'd discussed it sometimes. Catheric had a strand of
Millenarianism in it. The proto-creeds that had given
rise to it had believed in an end time, an apocalypse,
during which a saviour would come to escort the right-
eous to safety. An apocalypse had come all right. It had
been called Strife and Old Night. There had been no
saviour. Some philosophers reasoned that mankind's
crimes and sins had been so great, redemption had

been withheld. Salvation had been postponed indefi-
nitely until mankind had atoned sufficiently, and only
once that had happened would the prophecy be revis-
ited.

That didn't satisfy Hawser especially. No one knew, or
could remember, what the human race might have
done to displease god so spectacularly. It was, Hawser
reasoned, hard to atone if you didn't know what you
were atoning for.

The other thing that made him uneasy was that the
rise of the Emperor was seen by an increasing number
of people as evidence that the postponement was over.

'I'm sorry. It's easy to mock religion,' Murza said.

'It is,' Hawser agreed.

'It's easy to scorn it for being old-fashioned and inad-
equate. A heap of superstitious rubbish. We have
science.'

'We do.'

'Science, and technology. We are so advanced, we
have no need of spiritual faith.'

'Are you going somewhere with this?' Hawser asked.

'We forget what religion offered us.'

'Which is?'

'Mystery.'

That was his argument. Mystery. All religions required
a believer to have faith in something inexpressible. You
had to be prepared to accept that there were things you
could never know or understand, things you had to take
on trust. The mystery at the heart of religion was not a
mystery to be understood, it was a mystery to be cher-
ished, because it was there to remind you of your scale
in the cosmos. Science deplored such a view, because
everything should be explicable, and that which was not
was simply beneath contempt.

'It's no coincidence that so many old religions contained myths of forbidden truth, of dangerous

knowledge. Things that man was not meant to know.'

Murza had a way of putting things. Hawser believed that Murza was considerably more scornful of the faith that had raised him than Hawser was, even though Murza believed and Hawser didn't. At least Hawser had respect for Catherisism's morality. Murza made a great show of treating anyone who professed a faith as an irredeemable idiot.

But he cared. Hawser knew that. Murza believed. The little sign of the crux he wore under his shirt, the genuflection he sometimes made when he thought no one was looking. There was an inkling of the spiritual about the sardonic Navid Murza, and he kept it alive to preserve his sense of mystery.

It was mystery that propelled Murza and Hawser on their expeditions to recover priceless relics of data from the world's shattered corners. Rescued data unlocked the mysteries that Old Night had burned into the tissue of mankind's collective knowledge like lesions.

Sometimes it was mystery that sent them after spiritual relics too. Prayer boxes in Ossetia, for example. Neither of them believed in the faith that had constructed the boxes, or the sacred virtue of the things they were supposed to contain. But they both believed in the importance of the mystery the items had represented to past generations, and thus their value to human culture.

The prayer boxes had kept faith alive in this cindered part of Terra through the Age of Strife. There was very little chance they contained any data of actual, practical value. But a study of their nature and the way they had been crafted and preserved could reveal a great deal about human thought, and human codes, and the way man thought about his place in a cosmos where science was increasingly proving to be inimical.

There was a noise outside in the street, and Vasiliy stepped in out of the sunlight.

'Ah, captain,' said Murza. 'We were about to send for you.'

'Ready to advance?' Vasiliy asked.

'Yes, up through Old Town to a rendezvous point,' said Hawser.

'Our contact has come up with the goods,' Murza added.

The captain looked reluctant. 'I'm concerned about your welfare. In the last hour, this whole region has become very active. I'm getting reports of actions with N Brigade forces all down the valley as far as Hive-Roznyka. Moving through Old Town will make you very exposed.'

'My dear Captain Vasiliy, Kas and I have absolute faith in you and your troops.'

Vasiliy grinned and shrugged. She was a good looking woman in her mid-thirties, and the plating and ballistic padding of the Lombardi Hort battlegear did not entirely disguise the more feminine highlights of her form. Her right elbow was leaning on the chrome 'chetter strap hung from her shoulder. Sunlight glinted off the armoured links of the ammo feed that ran between weapon and backpack. A giant slide-visor of tinted yellow plastek came down over her eyes like an aviator's headcan. Hawser knew its inner surface was flickering with eyeline displays and target graphics. He knew it because he'd asked her to let him try it on once. She'd grinned, and buckled the strap tight under his chin, and explained what all the cursors and tags meant. In truth, he'd only done it so he could see her whole face. She had great eyes.

In the street, the Hort forces were moving up. Vox officers scurried like beetles with their heavy carapace sets and long, swaying antennae. Troopers prepped 'chetters and melters, and set off in fire-teams. The sunlight winked off their yellow slide-visors.

A modest sub-hive dominated the hill's summit, punctured and dilapidated by fighting. In its foothills, the outskirts known as Old Town, much more ancient street patterns and urban growths fanned out like root mass from a tree trunk. Hawser could hear shelling away to the south, and rockets occasionally whooped and squealed as they spat off overhead.

Hawser and Murza had spent three months in the region, tracking down the prayer boxes through a long and complex series of contacts and intermediaries. The boxes were said to contain the relics of venerated individuals from the Pre-Strife Era, part of a local tradition of Proto-Cruxic worship. Some contained old packets of scripture on paper or old-format disk too. Murza was especially excited about the translation possibilities.

So far, they'd recovered two boxes. Today, they hoped, they'd get the third and best example before the brutal inter-hive warfare finally forced them to quit the region. The item was owned and guarded by a small, underground coven of believers, who had kept it safe for six centuries, but picture records made by an antiquarian ninety years earlier attested to its outstanding significance. The antiquarian's records also spoke of considerable scriptural material.

'You do as I say,' Vasiliy told them, as she did every morning when she led them out into the open.

They moved through the town under escort.

'Can you hear music?' Hawser asked.

'No, but I do hear it's your birthday,' said Vasiliy, by way of reply.

Hawser blushed. 'I don't have a birthday. I mean, I only have a rough idea what day I was born on.'

'It says it's your birthday on your bio-file.'

'You looked me up,' said Hawser.

She feigned disinterest. 'I'm in charge. I need to know these things.'

'Well, captain, the date on my bio-file is the birthday I was given by the man who raised me. I was a foundling. It's as good a birthday as any.'

'Uh huh.'

'So why do you need to know?' he asked.

'It just occurred to me that tonight, when this business is done, we could raise a glass to celebrate.'

'What a fine idea,' said Hawser.

'I thought so,' she agreed. 'Forty, huh?'

'Happy birthday me.'

'You don't look a day over thirty-nine.'

Hawser laughed.

'When you two have stopped flirting,' said Murza. His link had just received a pict-message from their contact. It was another image of the prayer box, its lid open. The image was of better quality than the previous one.

'It's as though he's teasing us, tempting us,' said Hawser.

'He says the box is safe in the basement of a public hall about half a kilometre from here. It's waiting for us. He's agreed terms and a fee with the cult elders. They're just glad the box can be removed to safety before war tears the city down.'

'But they still want a fee,' said Vasiliy.

'That's really for the contact, not the elders,' said Hawser. 'One hand washes the other.'

'Can we move ahead?' asked Murza sharply. 'If we're not outside in twenty minutes, they're going to call the whole thing off.'

Vasiliy signalled the troop forwards again.

'He's impatient, isn't he?' she said to Hawser quietly, nodding at Murza up ahead.

'He can be. He worries about missed opportunities.'

'You don't?'

'That's the difference between us,' said Hawser. 'I want to preserve knowledge – any knowledge – because any knowledge is better than none. Navid, well I think he's hungry to find the knowledge that matters. The knowledge that will change the world.'

'Change the world? How?'

'I don't know… by revealing some scientific truth we'd forgotten. By showing us some technological art we'd lost. By telling us the name of god.'

'I'll tell you how you change the world,' she said. She fetched a creased pict-print out of her thigh pouch. A sunny day, a grinning teenager.

'That's my sister's boy. Isak. Every male in my family gets the name Isak. It's a tradition. She got to marry, and raise the kids. I got to have a career. Apart from living expenses, every penny I earn goes back to her, to the family. To Isak.'

Hawser looked at the picture and then handed it back to her.

'Yes,' he said. 'I like your way more.'

They came around a street corner and saw the clavier.

It was sitting in the middle of the street, an upright model, missing its side panel. Someone had wheeled it out of one of the bombed-out buildings for no readily apparent reason other than that it had survived. An old man was standing at its keyboard, playing it. He had to hunch slightly to accommodate the length of his limbs and the lack of a stool. He'd been good once. His fingers were still nimble. Hawser tried to recognise the tune.

'I told you I could hear music,' he said.

'Clear the street,' Vasiliy voxed to her men.

'Is that necessary?' asked Hawser. 'He's not doing any harm.'

'N Brigade members strap toxin bombs to children,' she snapped back. 'I am not going to take chances with an old man and a wooden box large enough to take a mini-nuke.'

'Fair enough.'

The old man looked up and smiled as the troops approached him. He called out a greeting, and changed what he was playing mid-bar. The tune became, unmistakably, the *March of Unity*.

'Cheeky old bastard,' muttered Murza. Vasiliy's men surrounded the old man and began to gently persuade him away from his music-making. The march missed a few notes, added a few dud ones. The old man was laughing. The *March of Unity* became a jaunty music hall melody

'So, your birthday,' said Murza, turning to Hawser.

'You've never remembered before.'

'You've never been forty before,' said Murza. He reached into his coat. 'I got you this. It's just a trinket.'

The music stopped. The Hort troopers had finally got the old man to step away from the clavier. His foot came off the *forte* pedal. There was a metallic whir, like the counterweight wind of a clock movement, as the firing plate of the nano-mine inside the clavier engaged.

In less time than it takes a man's heart to beat its final beat, the clavier vanished, and the old man disappeared, and the troopers surrounding him puffed into vapour like cotton seed heads, and the surface of the street peeled away in a blizzard of cobblestones, and the buildings on either side of the road shredded, and Murza left the ground in the arms of the shockwave, and his blood got in Hawser's eyes, and Hawser started to fly too, and all the secrets of the cosmos were illuminated for one brief moment as life and death converged.

✧

OGVAI SENT THE Upplander away while he thought about his decision. Eventually, after what the Upplander calculated to be about forty or fifty hours, during which time he saw no one except the thrall who brought him a bowl of food, the warrior called Aeska appeared in his doorway, sent by the jarl.

'Og says you can stay,' he remarked, casually.

'Will I… I mean, how does this work? Are there formalities? Are their patterns or style conventions for the stories I record?'

Aeska shrugged. 'You've got eyes, haven't you? Eyes, and a voice, and a memory? Then you've got everything you need.'

PART TWO

WOLF TALES

FIVE

At the Gates of the Olamic Quietude

HE ASKED THEM if, under the circumstances, he ought to be armed. The thralls and grooms who were preparing and anointing the company for drop cackled behind their skull masks and animal faces.

Bear said it wouldn't be necessary.

THE QUIETUDE HAD placed a division of their *robusts* on the principal levels of the graving dock. The dock was an immense spherical structure comparable to a small lunar mass. It consisted of a void-armoured shell encasing a massive honeycomb of alloy girderwork in which the almost completed Instrument sat, embedded at the core, like a stone in a soft fruit.

Deep range scanning had revealed very little about the Instrument, except that it was a toroid two kilometres in diameter. There were no significant cavity echoes, so it was not designed to be crewed. An unmanned vehicle could only be a kill vehicle in the opinion of the commander of the 40th Imperial

Expedition Fleet, and Ogvai Ogvai Helmschrot tended to agree.

Tra made entry via the polar cap of the graving dock megastructure. The company then moved down into the dock interior, descending via the colossal lattice of girderwork that cradled the Instrument. The Wolves came down, hand over hand, swinging from fingertips and toe holds, gripping struts with their knees, sliding, dropping, leaping from one support to another beneath. Hawser imagined that this process would look crude and ape-like; that the Astartes, bulked out even more than usual in their wargear, would appear clumsy and primitive, like primates swinging down through the canopy of a metal forest.

They did not. There was nothing remotely simian about their motion or their advance. They poured down through the interlocking ribs and spans like a fluid, something dark and glossy, like mjod, or blood. Something that ran and dripped, swelled and flowed again, a dark something that found in every angle, strut and spar the quickest unbroken route by which to follow gravity's bidding.

✠

LATER, THIS OBSERVATION was the first to earn Hawser any compliments as a skjald.

✠

THE WOLVES DESCENDED and they did so silently. Not a grunt of effort, not a gasp of labour, not a click or crackle from a vox device, not a clink or chime from an uncased weapon or an unlagged armour piece. Hair was tied back and lacquered or braided. Gloves and boot-treads were dusted with ground hrosshvalur scales for grip. The hard edges of armour sections were blunted with pelts and fur wrappings. Behind tight leather masks, mouths were shut.

The Quietude's robusts matched the Astartes in bulk and strength. They had been engineered that way. Each one was hardwired with remarkable sensitivity to motion, to light, to heat and to pheromonal scent. Somehow, they still didn't see the Wolves coming.

Why don't the men of Tra draw their weapons, Hawser wondered? His panic began to escalate. Great Terra above, they've all forgotten to draw their weapons! The words almost flew out of him as the Wolves began to drop out of the girderwork and onto the heads of the robusts patrolling below them.

Most went for the neck. A robust was big, but the weight of a fully armoured Astartes dropping on it from above was enough to bring it down onto the deck, hard. With open hands, unencumbered by weapons, the Astartes gripped their targets' heads, and twisted them against the direction of fall, snapping the cervical process.

It was an economical and ruthless execution. The Wolves were using their own bodies as counterweights to clean-break steelweave spinal columns. The first audible traces of the fight were the rapid-fire cracks of fifty or more necks breaking. The sounds overlapped, almost simultaneous, like firecrackers kicking off across the vast, polished deckspace. Like knuckles cracking.

Distress and medical attention signals began to bleat and shrill. Few of the robusts who had been brought down were actually dead, as they did not enjoy life in the same way that conventional humans did. The robusts were simply disabled, helpless, the command transmissions between their brains and their combat-wired bodies broken. An odd chorus of information alerts began to sound throughout the dock's megastructure. Layer added upon layer incrementally, as different bands of the Quietude's social networks became aware of what was happening.

Stealth ceased to be a commodity of any value.

Having made their first kills, the Wolves rose to their feet. They were all, very suddenly, aiming guns. The fastest way to arm themselves had been to appropriate the weapons that were ready-drawn and clutched in the paralysed hands of their robust victims. The Wolves came up raising streamlined chrome heat-beamers and gravity rifles. It was really not Hawser's place, then or later, to remark how sleek and unlikely these weapons looked in the hands of Rout members. It was like seeing pieces of glass sculpture or stainless surgical tools gripped in the mouths of wild dogs.

Instead, Hawser's account reflected the following point. It is, the Wolf King teaches, good practice to use an enemy's weapon against him. An enemy may fabricate wonderful armour, but the Wolves of Fenris have learned through experience that the effectiveness of an enemy's protection is proportionate to the efficacy of his weapons. This may be a deliberate design philosophy, but it is more usually a simple, instinctive consequence. An enemy may think 'I know it is possible for armour to be strong to X degree, because I am able to forge armour that strong; therefore I need to develop a weapon that can split armour of X degree, in case I ever encounter an opponent as well-armoured as I know I can be.'

The heat-beamers emitted thin streaks of sizzling white light that hurt the eyes. They made no dramatic noises except for the sharp explosions that occurred when the beams struck a target.

The gravity rifles launched pellets of ultra-dense metal that laced the dock's warm air with quick smudges like greasy finger marks on glass. These weapons were louder. They made noises like whips cracking, underscored by oddly modulated burps of power. Unlike the heat beams, which split robust armour open in messy

eruptions of cooking innards and superhot plate fragments, the gravity rifle pellets were penetrators that
made tiny, pin-prick entry marks and extravagantly
gigantic exit wounds. Stricken robusts faltered as their
chests caved in under scorching heat-beam assault, or
lurched as their backs blew out in sprays of spalling,
shattered plastics, liquidised internals and bone shards.

It was almost pathetic. The Quietude had a martial
reputation that was measured in centuries and light
years, and the robusts were their battlefield elite. Here,
they were falling down like clumsy idiots on an icy day,
like clowns in a pantomime, a dozen of them, two
dozen, three, smack on their faces or slam on their
backs, legs out from under them, not a single one of
them even managing to return fire, *not a single one*.

When the robusts finally began to rally, the Wolves
played the next card in their hand. They tossed away the
captured guns and switched to their own weapons,
principally their bolters. The Quietude's social networks
had frantically analysed the nature of the threat, and
processed an immediate response. This took the networks less than eight seconds. The robusts were
armoured with interlocking, overlapping skins of
woven steel as their principal layer of protection, but
each one also possessed a variable force field as an outer
defensive sheath. After only eight seconds of shooting,
the social networks of the Olamic Quietude successfully
and precisely identified the nature of the weapons being
used against its robusts. They instantly adjusted the
composition of the individual force fields to compen-
sate.

As a result, the robusts were effectively proofed
against heat-beams and gravitic pellets at exactly the
same moment as they started to take Imperial bolter
fire.

Further humiliation was heaped upon the Quietude's

reputation. The men of Tra spread out, firing from the chest, mowing down the robusts as they attempted to compose themselves.

For this, thought Hawser, for this work, for these deeds: this is why the companies of Wolves are kept.

He had never seen a boltgun live-fired before. All his eight-and-the-rest decades of experience, all the conflict he'd witnessed, and he'd never seen a boltgun shot. Boltguns were the symbol of Imperial superiority and Terran unification, emphatically potent and reductively simple. They were Astartes weapons, not exclusively, but as a hallmark thing. Few men had the build to heft one. They were the crude, mechanical arms of a previous age, durable and reliable, with few sophisticated parts that could malfunction or jam. They were brute technology that, instead of being superseded and replaced by complex modern weapon systems, had simply been perfected and scaled up. An Astartes with a boltgun was a man with a carbine, nightmarishly exaggerated.

The sight of it reminded Hawser of how un-human the Wolves were. He had been amongst them for long enough to have become used to the look of them and the way they towered over him.

Still, they were positively reassuring compared to the forces of the Quietude.

Skull measurements and other biological data taken from captured Quietude specimens had confirmed their Terran ancestry. At some point long before the fall of Old Night, a branch of Terran expansion had brought the Quietude's gene pool into this out-flung, unremembered corner of the galaxy. The commander of the 40th Imperial Expedition Fleet, along with his technical advisors and savants, believed that this exodus had taken place during the First Great Age of Technology, perhaps as long as fifteen thousand years earlier. The Quietude possessed a level of technological aptitude that was extremely sophisticated, and so divergent from Terran or even Martian standards as to suggest a long incubation and, possibly, the influence of a xenobiological culture.

At some early stage in their post-Terran life, the humans of the Quietude had given up their humanity. They operated in social networks, cohered by communications webs neurally spliced into them at birth. They sacrificed most of their flesh anatomy to ritualised surgical procedures during childhood that prepared them to inhabit artificial bodies. Pretty much all that remained of a Quietude adult, organically speaking, were the brain, skull and spinal cord. These rested in the neck socket of an elegantly engineered humanoid chassis, which contained the machine-analogue organs that fed the brain and kept it alive.

That explained why the shot-up robusts were pooling almost purple fluids around their carcasses instead of blood.

The citizens of the Quietude wore hoods of silver circuitry over their skulls, and hologram masks instead of faces. As the boltguns killed them, the masks flickered out and failed, and revealed the self-inflicted inhumanity beneath.

Aeska had carried Hawser down with Tra, instructing Hawser to hold onto his neck. He'd clung on like a pelt, and Aeska had carried him as if his weight had no significance to the Astartes, and even when they'd been going hand-over-hand down through the dock's girder lattice, even when the only thing preventing Hawser from plunging to his death was the grip of his fingers around Aeska's neck, he'd kept his eyes open. He had not done this because he'd jumped down enough flues in the Aett to develop a head for heights. He'd done it because he'd known he had to. It was expected of him.

On the principal deck level, as the assault began, Aeska had set Hawser on the ground behind him and told him to walk in his shadow. The vast, polished deck yawned away on either side of them, curved like the surface of a world seen from orbit, and the lattice above was like the branches of a dense thorn thicket. The air was laced with bolter fire.

Hawser needed very little encouragement.

Five minutes into the fight, the Quietude finally began to claw back. The first Rout blood they spilled was from a warrior called Galeg, who was hit by a gravity pellet. The shot turned his left arm, from the elbow down, into a bloody twig, rattling with bracelets of shattered armour. Galeg shut the pain down and advanced on his attacker, swinging out a chain axe. Steam and blood-smoke sizzled from his injured limb.

The shot had not come from one of the robust warrior units. Three *graciles*, the lighter weight technical versions, had retrieved the weapon of a fallen robust and set it up on a lattice walkway. Galeg bounded up onto the walkway as they missed him with two more desperate shots, and dismembered them with his wailing axe. He did this with relish, and let out wet growls as their fracturing chassis shattered under his axe-blows and emitted strangulated electronic shrieks.

When Galeg had finished his kill, he signalled his ability to continue with a casual air-punch of his bloody, ruined fist, a gesture that Hawser found chilling.

Several robusts had defended the entrance to a major engineering underspace with what looked like a heavier, perhaps crew-served, version of the gravity rifle. The colossal bursts of fire, ripping up the underspace approach from an unseen source, vaporised Hjad, the first Wolf to come into view. Bear wheeled the rest of his pack aside. There was no point in providing further targets. Hawser saw Bear take out a small hand axe, a one-piece steel cast, and mark the bulkhead beside the underspace slope. He did it quickly and deftly. It was evidently a mark he'd made many times: four hard cuts to form a crude diamond shape, then a fifth notch bisecting the diamond. Hawser considered the mark gouged into the bulkhead metal, and realised what it was.

It was an incredibly simplified symbol for an eye. It was a mark of aversion.

❖

THE OLAMIC QUIETUDE had been hostile from the very point of contact. Suspicious and unwilling to formalise any kind of convergence, they had engaged the 40th Fleet in two separate ship actions in an attempt to drive the expedition out of Quietude space. During the second of these skirmishes, the Quietude managed to capture the crew of an Imperial warship.

The commander of the 40th Imperial Expedition Fleet sent a warning to the Quietude, explaining that peaceful contact and exchange was the primary goal of the Imperium of Terra, and the Quietude's aggressive stance would not be tolerated. The warship and its crew would be returned. Negotiations would begin. Dialogue with Imperial iterators would begin and understanding reached. The Quietude made its first direct response. It explained, as if to a child, or perhaps to a pet dog or bird that it was trying to train, that it was the true and sole heir of the Terran legacy. As its name suggested, it was resting in an everlasting state of readiness to resume contact with its birthworld. It had waited patiently through the apocalyptic ages of storm and tempest.

The Imperials who now approached its borders were pretenders. They were not what they claimed to be. Any fool could see that they were the crude artifice of some alien race trying to mock-up what it thought would pass for human.

The Quietude supported this verdict with copious annotated evidence from its interrogation of the Imperial prisoners. Each prisoner, the Quietude stated, displayed over fifteen thousand points of differential that revealed them to be non-human impostors, as the vivisections clearly demonstrated.

The commander of the 40th Expedition Fleet sent for the nearest Astartes.

THE LONGER HAWSER lived amongst the Rout, the more the Astartes had to do with him. Warriors he did not know, from companies he had not encountered, would come and seek him out, and regard him suspiciously with their abhuman gold eyes.

They hadn't learned to trust him. It wasn't trust. It was as though they had got used to his alien scent being in the Aett.

Either that, or someone, someone or something with the authority to call off a pack of the wildest killers on Fenris, had ordered them to accept him.

IT SEEMED, AS it had with Bitur Bercaw, that the telling of stories mattered to them.

'Why do the stories matter?' Hawser asked one night when he was permitted to eat with Skarssen and his game-circle. Board games like hneftafl were for sharpening strategy.

Skarssen shrugged. He was too busy scooping meat into his mouth in a manner that wasn't a human gesture. It wasn't even the gesture of a ravenous human being. It was the action of an animal fuelling itself, not knowing when it would feed again.

Hawser sat with a meagre bowl of fish broth and some dried fruit. The Astartes of Fyf had mjod, and haunches of raw meat so red and gamey it stank of cold copper and carbolic.

'Is it because you don't write things down?' Hawser pressed.

Lord Skarssen wiped blood from his lips.

'Remembering is all that counts. If you remember something, you can do it again. Or not do it again.'

'You learn?'

'It's learning,' Skarssen nodded. 'If you can tell something as an account, you know it.'

'And accounts are how we don't forget the dead,' put in Varangr.

'That too,' said Skarssen.

'The dead?' asked Hawser.

'They get lonely if we forget them. No man should be lonely and forgotten by his comrades, even if he's a wight and gone away to the dark and the Underverse.'

Hawser watched Varangr's face in the lamplight. There was no way to read it except as the dull-eyed mask of an apex predator.

'When I was sleeping,' Hawser said. It was the start of a sentence, but he hadn't thought it through to the end, and nothing else came out.

'What?' asked Skarssen, annoyed.

Hawser shook himself, coming out of a brief trance. 'When I was sleeping. In cold sleep, where you kept me. I heard a voice then. It said it didn't like it in the darkness. It missed the firelight and the sunlight. It said it had dreamed all of its dreams a hundred times over, a thousand times. It said it hadn't chosen the dark.'

He looked up and realised that Skarssen, Varangr and the other members of Fyf around him had stopped eating and were staring at him, listening intently. A couple had blood on their chins that they hadn't wiped away.

'It told me that the dark chooses us,' Hawser said. The Wolves murmured assent, though their throats made the murmur into a leopard-growl.

Hawser stared at them. The twitching firelight caught golden eyes and gleaming teeth in shadow shapes.

'Was it a wight?' he asked. 'Was I hearing a voice from the Underverse?'

'Did it have a name?' asked Varangr.

'Cormek Dod,' said Hawser.

'Not a wight, then,' said Skarssen. He sagged, as if disappointed. 'Almost but not.'

'Worse, probably,' grumbled Trunc.

'Don't say that!' Skarssen snapped.

Trunc bowed his head. 'I recognise my failing and will be sure to correct it,' he said.

Hawser asked what they meant, but they wouldn't be drawn. His story had briefly piqued their interest, but now they were deflated. The jarl turned back to the subject of death.

'We burn our dead,' said Skarssen. 'It's our practice. There's no soil on Fenris for burial. No ground that isn't iron hard in the long winter, and no ground with any permanence in summer. We don't leave markers or tombs, no graves for the worm-wed like other men. Why would a dead man want that? Why would he want his wight weighed down and anchored to one place? His thread's cut and he can finally roam as he pleases. Doesn't want a stone pinning him down.'

'A story is better than a stone,' said Varangr. 'Better for remembering the dead. Do you know how to remember the dead, skjald?'

✛

THE MEDICAE WHO tended him in the field station at Ost-Roznyka spent some time explaining that they'd nearly been able to save his leg.

'The shrapnel damage would have been repairable,' he said, as if discussing the re-liming of a wall. 'What cost you was the crush damage. The blast carried you into a building, and brought a lintel down on you.'

Hawser felt nothing. His senses had been entirely fogged by opiates, he presumed. The Lombardi Hort field station was grubby and painfully under-provided, and the medicae's scrub-smock, mask and cap were soiled so deeply it was clear he didn't change them between patients, but there were several freshly used opiate injectors in a chrome instrument tray by his cot. They'd used precious pharm supplies on him. He warranted special attention. He was high status, a visiting specialist.

It was likely several regular soldiers would die or at least suffer terrible and avoidable pain because of him.

He felt nothing.

'I think an augmetic will be viable,' the medicae said, encouragingly. He looked tired. His eyes looked tired. All Hawser could see of the medicae above his soiled mask were his tired eyes.

'I can't do a proper assessment here,' the medicae said. 'I really don't have the resources.'

Eyes, without a nose or mouth. Hawser felt nothing, but a current stirred deep down in his drugged torpor. Eyes without a nose or mouth, eyes above a soiled mask. That was wrong. He was used to seeing it the other way around. A mouth and no eyes. A mouth, smiling, and eyes hidden.

Really great eyes, hidden behind a tinted yellow slide-visor.

'Vasiliy,' Hawser said.

'Hmh?' replied the medicae. Someone was shouting outside. Cybernetica portage units were arriving with fresh casualties loaded onto their stretcher racks.

'Vasiliy. Captain Vasiliy.'

'Ahhh,' said the medicae. 'She didn't make it. We worked on her, but there was too much organ damage.'

Hawser felt nothing. It was a state of mind that was not destined to last.

'Murza,' he said. His lips felt like dough. His voice flowed like glue.

'Who?'

'The other inspector. The other specialist.'

'I'm sorry,' said the medicae. 'The blast killed him outright. There were barely any remains to recover.'

✣

HAWSER REMEMBERED THE names of the dead whose threads were cut taking the Quietude's graving dock. Five Astartes, five of Tra: Hjad, Adthung Greychin, Stormeye, Tjurl-On-The-Ice and Fultag Redknife.

He witnessed two of the deaths personally, and learned particulars of the others afterwards, so that he had at least one specific detail for each one, a piece that would make a proper end for each account.

For example, just before the robusts' crew-served weapon had turned him into bloodsmoke and a rattling drizzle of armour fragments, Hjad had carried over two of the Quietude's big fighting units by rushing them bodily. One had been too crippled to pick itself up again. The other had attempted to claw at Hjad, its face hologram blinking as it tried to reload into something more threatening. Hjad had punched his right fist through its torso and pulled out its spine. That was Hjad, the men of Tra agreed. Unflagging, unsentimental. A good account.

Hawser felt confident he had an idea of the desired form.

Adthung Greychin had cleared an entire deck level of the graving dock structure with his chainsword after a lucky shot damaged his bolter. He went through robusts and graciles alike, making them scatter. No one actually saw him take the two gravity penetrators that killed him, but Thel saw his body on the ground just after it dropped, and told Hawser that Adthung's famous grey beard had been dyed almost indigo by the spatter of the enemy's pseudo-blood. He had died well. He had left a litter of dead and a field of cut threads behind him. Hawser added a quip about sleeping on purple snow to

the finish of Adthung's tale, and that earned apprecia-
tive rumbles from Tra.

Stormeye went to the Underverse destroyed by beam
weapons. Blinded, his face all but scorched off by damage, his mouth fused shut, he had still managed to split
a robust from the shoulder to the waist with his axe
before falling. Hawser had seen this feat for himself. A
dead man pulling another down in death with him.
This account's ending was greeted by a grim but admir-
ing silence.

Erthung Redhand told Hawser about Tjurl. Tjurl was
known as Tjurl-On-The-Ice because he liked to hunt,
even in the alabaster silence of Helwinter on Fenris. He
would leave the mountain with his spear or his axe, and
go out into the high wastes of Asaheim. His blood never
froze, that's what they said about him. Because of all
that mjod he had drunk, Erthung liked to add.

Tjurl went hunting that day in the graving dock. He
took many trophies. That was how Hawser told it. Not
once did Tjurl's fury grow cold. Not once did he freeze.

Last to fall was Fultag Redknife. Last story to learn and
last to tell before the account of the taking of the graving dock could be finished. Fultag led the assault that
took the dock control centre and slashed the throat of
the Quietude's social network system so that all the data
drained out as useless noise.

The assault was not the act of vandalism that Hawser
had expected. Fultag's team did not smash the systems
indiscriminately with a heathen lust to defile the artefacts of a more sophisticated culture. They disabled
specific parts of the control centre using magnetic
mines, gunfire and blunt force, but spared enough of
the primary network architecture for the Mechanicum
to later examine and, if necessary, operate.

The higher beings of the Quietude were clearly concerned about accidental weapons discharge in the

control centre. None of the robusts there were armed.
Instead, the area – a geodesic dome structure in the central dock space directly beneath the caged Instrument –
was defended by squads of *super-robusts*. These were
titans, reinforced heavyweights armed with concussion
maces and accelerator hammers. Some of them had
double sets of upper limbs, like the blue-skinned gods
of the ancient Induz. Some even sported two heads,
twin side-by-side mountings for vestigial organic components, each with its own silver-circuit hood and
holomask.

Fultag's team gave them a lesson in axe work. Ullste,
moving in to support, witnessed the fight. Each blow
shook the deck, such was the strength in those limbs, he
said. Super-robusts and Wolves alike were knocked
down by bone-crushing blows. It was a clubbing, battering fight that churned through the split levels of the
centre, smashing the gleaming window ports, fracturing
console desks as bodies reeled into them. The matt fabric of the floor was quickly covered with chips of glass
and fragments of plastic and spots of purple pseudo-
blood.

Fultag knocked down his first super-robust on the
centre's entry ramp. He ducked the mace it swung at his
head. If it had connected, the blow would have pulverised even Fenrisian anatomy. The thwarted weapon
made a *woof* through the air instead, a *woof* like a
winded *fjorulalli*, the great seal-mother.

Fultag was wrong-footed by having to duck, and there
was no time to plant his feet better to swing the smile
of his axe in before the mace came back at him. He
managed a half-swing instead, and connected with the
poll of the axe-head. The blunt back of the head fractured the super-robust's shoulder armour and impaired
its limb function on one side. It compensated.

Fultag had already rotated his axe, reset his stance,

and brought the axe through in a downsweep that severed one of the super-robust's arms at the elbow and the other at the wrist. The detached pieces, still gripping the energy-sheathed mace, thumped onto the deck. Purple pseudo-blood jetted from the ruptured hydraulic tubes in the limb stumps.

The super-robust seemed to hesitate, as if it wasn't sure how it should proceed.

'Oh, fall down!' Fultag growled, and kicked it over the way he'd kick a door in.

Several members of his team were by then engaging enemy units in the mouth of the hatchway at the top of the ramp. The hatch was effectively blocked by the savage melee. Fultag vaulted the ramp's guardrail and edged along a parapet that ran around the dome's outer surface. When he got to the first window, he stove it in with his axe and jumped inside.

The graciles manning the consoles had begun to disconnect and flee the moment the window exploded in at them and showered the control area with glass shards. Fultag managed to kick one over and chop it in half. A super-robust came at him, and he used his axe-haft to deflect its hammer. Like a staff fighter, he brought the knob of the axe-haft up across his body, two-handed, and smacked the Quietude warrior in the sternum. Then the smile of his axe went into the super-robust's right shoulder.

It stuck fast, wedged. The thing wasn't dead. It lashed at him. Fultag pulled out his long knife, the knife he had cut so many threads with, the knife that had earned him his name, and propelled himself forwards into it. He crashed it backwards against a console. The combined weight of them partially dislodged the console from its floor socket and snapped underfloor cables. The super-robust got its hand to his throat, but Fultag stabbed his knife into the middle of its face.

It died under him and went limp, arms, head and legs slack over the console like a sacrificial victim on an altar slab.

Before he could slide back off his kill and regain his feet, Fultag was hit across the back by another super-robust. The blow was delivered with an accelerator hammer. It cracked Fultag's armour and broke his left hip.

He uttered a growl as he came around at his tormentor, his black-pinned golden eyes wide with rage. His transhuman Astartes biology had already shut the pain off, diverted ruptured blood vessels, and shunted adrenaline to keep Fultag moving on a half-shattered pelvis.

The super-robust was one of the quad-armed, two-headed monsters. Its upper torso and shoulder mount were wider than the driving cage of a Typhoon-pattern land speeder. It carried the concussion hammer with its upper limbs like a ceremonial sceptre-bearer. Fultag managed to evade its next blow, which folded and crushed the damaged console and the dead super-robust draped over it. The follow-up caught him across the right shoulder guard and hurled him sideways into another bank of consoles. Fultag growled, his teeth bared, and droplets of blood spraying from his lips, a wounded wolf now, hurt and deadly.

He went in at the super-robust and grappled to clamp its upper limbs and stop the hammer blows. The Quietude warrior actually found itself pushed back a few steps. It couldn't wrench its arms free. It dug in with its secondary upper limbs, ripping low at Fultag to break his grip. It clenched hard on the broken armour and mashed hip, and managed to get a yowl of pain out of him. He butted its left side head, making its holomask short out. The real face behind was a flayed human skull wired into a plastic cup of circuits. The lidless eyeballs stared back. The impact of the headbutt had caused one to fill almost instantly with pseudo-blood.

Fultag guttered out an ultrasonic purr and butted again. As the super-robust recoiled, he yanked the hammer from its upper set of limbs, but its haft was slick with purple sap and it flew out of his hands.

He tore the super-robust's left head implant out instead. He ripped it clean out of its shoulder socket – skull, neck mount and spinal cord. It came out in a spray like afterbirth. Fultag spat. He gripped the wrenched-out piece of anatomy in his right fist by the base of the spine and began to spin it like a slingshot. Then he swung it repeatedly at the super-robust in the manner of a ball and chain, and didn't stop until its other head was caved in.

The men of Tra approved of this.

More of the enemy came at Fultag after that, and the only weapon in reach was the accelerator hammer. This was his downfall. Stung by the use of its own weapons against it, the Quietude had adjusted its operational settings. When Fultag attempted to defend himself with the hammer, it fired a massive charge of power through the grip that cooked and killed him where he stood.

Around the circle, men nodded gravely. A trick, a trap, an enemy deception, these were all the hazards of war. They would all have made the same choice as Fultag. He'd gone with honour, and he'd held the super-robusts long enough for Tra to take the centre.

The wolf priests attended the dead. Hawser saw some of the dark figures he'd glimpsed in the kitchen-come-hospital-come-morgue on the day he woke up. The priest who served Tra was called Najot Threader.

The death of Fultag troubled Tra most of all. His

organics had broiled and burned. There was, Hawser learned, nothing for Najot Threader to recover.

Hawser didn't know what that meant.

✥

A WARSHIP CLOSED in as soon as Tra signalled that the graving dock was taken. They felt the megastructure shudder as it took disabling hits from the warship's massive batteries. The shots were annihilating secondary docks and support vessels, and crippling the graving dock's principal launch faculty.

The deck vibrated. There was a dull, dead sound like a giant gong striking arrhythmically in a distant palace of echoing marble. The air began to smell quite different: drier, as if there was ash or soot flowing into its intermix. Hawser felt afraid, more afraid than when he'd been in the thick of the close fighting with Tra. In his imagination, the warship's complement of monastically-hooded calculus bombardi, ranked in steeply-tiered golden stalls around the warship's gunnery station, were intoning their vast and complex targeting algorithms into the hard-wired sentiences of the gun batteries too rapidly. Mistakes were being made, or just one tiny mistake perhaps, a digit out of place, enough to place the delivery of a mega-watt laser or an accelerator beam a metre or two to the left or right over a range of sixty thousand kilometres. The graving dock would rupture and burst like a paper lantern lit and swollen from within by combusting gas.

Hawser realised it was because he trusted the men of Tra to keep him safe, safe from even the deadliest super-robust. He was only afraid of the things they couldn't control.

The next phase of the war unfolded. Word came that the Expedition Fleet's principal assaults on the Quietude's home world had begun. The men of Tra took themselves to the graving dock's polar bays to observe.

The polar bays had been opened to allow access for the shoals of Mechanicum and Army vessels ferrying personnel onto the dock structure. Hawser joined the Wolves looking down through networks of docking gibbets and anchored voidboats. Below, vast cantilevered hatches and payload doors were spread open like the wings of mythical rocs.

Beneath that, the planet filled the view like a giant orange. The sharp airless clarity of the view made the reflected sunlight almost neon in intensity.

The men of Tra took themselves out along the latticework of girders and struts to get the best view of the operations far below. They were oblivious to the precipitous drop. Hawser tried to seem as matter of fact, but he fought the urge to hold on to any and every guardrail or handgrip.

He edged onto a docking girder after Aeska Brokenlip, Godsmote and Oje. Other Wolves crowded onto the gantries around them.

A formation of bulk capacity deployment vessels was moving into line of sight about three kilometres below them, and the men were keen to watch. Some pointed, indicating certain technical aspects. What struck Hawser most was the way the three men of Tra with him comported themselves. They dropped down onto the gantry like eager animals watching prey from a clifftop, Oje crouching and the other two sprawled. Like dogs in the sun, Hawser thought, panting after exertion, alert, ready to bound up again at a moment's notice. The vast armour that cased them didn't appear to offer the slightest encumbrance.

A flurry of small but searing flashes across the neon-orange view below announced the start of the surface bombardment. Dark patterns immediately began to disfigure the atmosphere of the Quietude's world, as

vast quantities of smoke and particulate product began
to spill into it. The skin of the orange bruised. The slow-
moving deployment vessels began to sow their drop
vehicles: clouds of seed cases or chaff tumbling out
behind the monolithic carriers.

The Wolves made remarks. Oje dripped a little scorn
on the commander of the 40th Expedition Fleet and his
council of tacticians for not synchronising the surface
assault with the advancing nightside terminator, as he
would have done, and thus maximise the psychological
and tactical advantages of nightfall. Aeska agreed, but
added he'd have run the whole attack on the nightside,
except that the Army didn't like to fight at night.

'Poor eyes,' he said, as though talking of invalids or
unremarkable animals. 'Sorry,' he added. He cast the last
comment over his shoulder to Hawser, who was
perched behind them, holding on to a spar with white
knuckles.

'For what?' asked Hawser.

'He's apologising to your human eye,' said Godsmote.

'Maybe someone should do you a favour and poke
that out too,' said Oje.

The three Wolves laughed. Hawser laughed to show
he understood it was meant to be a joke.

The Wolves turned their attention back to the invasion below.

'Of course, if I'd been in charge,' said Aeska, 'I'd have
just dropped Ogvai into their main habitation, and
then come back a week later to collect him and hose
him down.'

The three Wolves laughed again, teeth bared. They
laughed so hard the gantry vibrated slightly under
Hawser.

A cry went up. They all turned to investigate.

Bear, and another of Tra named Orcir, had finally dislodged the crew of robusts who had earlier vaporised

Hjad on the underspace slope. They dragged them out into the open, where a gang of Tra members gathered and slaughtered them in a manner that seemed both ritualistic and unnecessarily gruesome. Despite the inhumanity of the Quietude creatures, Hawser found himself glancing away uncomfortably, unwilling to let his eyes record the scene. The two warriors saved the worst of their ministrations for the gracile commander of the weapon crew. The men of Tra watching yelled out encouragement. There was glee in the dismemberment.

'They are chasing out the maleficarum,' said Ogvai. Hawser looked up. He had not heard the massive, battle-black jarl come up to him.

'What?'

'They are casting it out,' said Ogvai. 'They are hurting it so badly it will know not to come back. They are punishing it, and explaining pain to it, so it will not be eager to return and bother us.'

'I see,' said Hawser.

'Make sure you do,' said Ogvai.

The gracile was dead. The Wolves left all the bodies where they had fallen.

Bear walked across to the top of the underspace slope and, as Hawser watched, used his axe to excise the mark of aversion he had made earlier.

SIX

Scintilla City

'I'VE SEEN SEVENTY-FIVE years come and go,' said Kasper Hawser, 'and I've worked fifty years on this project–'

'And the Prix Daumarl attests to the sterling–'

'Could I finish? Could I?'

Henrik Slussen nodded, and made a conciliatory gesture with his gloved hand.

Hawser swallowed. His mouth was dry.

'I have worked for fifty years,' he resumed, 'shepherding the concept of the Conservatory from nothing into this, this form. I was raised by a man who understood the value of information, of the preservation of learning.'

'That's something we all believe in, Doctor Hawser,' said one of the thirty-six rubricators sitting in a semicircle in the writing desks behind Slussen. Hawser had asked Vasiliy to arrange the meeting in the college's Innominandum Theatre, the lecture theatre panelled in brown wood, rather than the provost's office as Slussen had requested. A psychological ploy; he could get Slussen and his entourage to take the fold-down seats built for students, and diminish them in contrast to his authority.

'I believe the doctor was still a little way from finishing,' Vasiliy told the rubricator. His tone was smooth, but there was unmistakable chastisement in his voice. Vasiliy was standing at Hawser's left shoulder. Hawser could tell that his mediary had one hand inside his coat pocket, secretly holding on to the small vial of medication in case the tension of the situation became too much for Hawser.

The man worried too much. It was charming.

'The work the Conservatory has done,' said Hawser, 'the work *I* have done… It has all been about expanding mankind's understanding of the cosmos. It has not been about salvaging data and placing it in an inaccessible archive.'

'Explain to me how you think that is happening, doctor?' asked Slussen.

'Explain to me the process by which any average citizen can access information from the Administratum datastacks, undersecretary?' Hawser replied.

'There is a protocol. A request is made–'

'It requires approvals. Authorities. A positive request may take years to fill. A refusal may not be explained or appealed. Information assets, precious information assets, are being placed into the same vast pot as general global administrative data. Vasiliy?'

'Current assessments made by the Office of Efficiency predict that the centralised data-wealth of the Imperium is doubling every eight months. Simply navigating a catalogue of that data-wealth will soon be arduous. In a year or two…'

Slussen did not look at Hawser's mediary.

'So it's a problem of access, and of the architecture of our archives. These are issues that I am happy to explore–'

'I don't believe they are issues, undersecretary,' said Hawser. 'I believe they are symptoms and excuses. They are soft ways of censoring and forbidding. They are subtle ways of controlling data and deciding who gets to know what.'

'That's quite a claim,' said Slussen, entirely without tone.

'It's not the worst thing I'm going to claim today by any means, undersecretary,' said Hawser, 'so hold on tight. High level control of global information, that's bad enough. A conspiracy, if you will, that restricts and seeks to govern the free sharing of composited knowledge throughout mankind, that's bad enough. But what's worse is the implication of ignorance.'

'What?' asked Slussen.

Hawser looked up at the ceiling of the lecture hall, where egg tempera angels flew and cavorted through gesso clouds. He was feeling a little light-headed, truth be told.

'Ignorance,' he repeated. 'The Imperium is so anxious to retain proprietorial control of all data, it is simply stockpiling everything without evaluation or examination. We are owning data without learning it. We don't know what we know.'

'There are issues of security,' said one of the rubricators.

'I understand that!' Hawser snapped. 'I'm simply asking for some transparency. Perhaps an analytical forum to review data as it comes in. To assess it. It's six months since Emantine put you in charge, undersecretary. Six months since you began to steer the Conservatory into the dense fog of the Administratum. We are losing our rigour. We are no longer processing or questioning.'

'I think you're exaggerating,' said Slussen.

'Just this week alone,' said Hawser, taking the data-slate Vasiliy held out to him, 'one hundred and eighty-nine major archaeological or ethnological survey reports were filed directly to the Administratum through your office without going through the Conservatory. Ninety-six of those had been directly funded by us.'

Slussen said nothing.

'Many years ago,' said Hawser, 'so many years ago it alarms me to count them, I asked someone a question. In many respects, it was the question that led us to this place, the question that drives the whole ethos of the Conservatory. It comes in two parts, and I'd be very interested to know if you can answer either.'

'Go on,' said Slussen.

Hawser fixed him with an intent stare.

'Does anyone even know why the Age of Strife happened? How did we end up in the great darkness of Old Night to begin with?'

'WHAT ARE YOU going to do?' asked Vasiliy.

'Finish packing,' Hawser replied. 'Perhaps you'd like to help?'

'You can't leave.'

'I can.'

'You can't resign.'

'I did. You were there. I expressed a desire to Under-secretary Slussen to withdraw from the project for the time being. A sabbatical, I think it's called.'

'Where are you going to go?'

'Caliban, perhaps. An investigative mission has been sent to audit the Great and Fearsome Bestiaries in the bastion libraries. The idea appeals. Or Mars. I have a standing invitation to study at the Symposia Adeptus. Somewhere challenging, somewhere interesting.'

'This is just an overreaction,' said Vasiliy. The afternoon sunlight was piercing the mesh shutters of the high-hive dwelling, an academic's quarters, fully furnished, generous. The items in the room that were actually Hawser's belongings were few, and he was hurling them into his modular luggage. He packed some clothes, some favourite data-slates and paper books, his regicide board.

'The undersecretary's answer was just flippant,' said Vasiliy. 'Trite. He didn't mean anything by it. It was a politician's nonsense, and I'm sure he'll take it back on reflection.'

'He said it didn't matter,' said Hawser. He stopped what he was doing and looked at his mediary for a moment. He was holding a small toy horse made of wood, deciding whether to pack it or not. He'd owned it for a long time.

'He said it didn't matter, Vasiliy. The causes of the Age of Strife were of no consequence to this new golden age. I have never heard such folly!'

'It was certainly hubristic,' said Vasiliy.

Hawser let a thin smile cross his lips. His leg ached, as it always did in times of stress. He put the wooden horse back on a side shelf. He didn't need it.

'I'm going,' he said. 'It's been too long since I did any field work, far too long. I'm sick to the eye teeth of this bean-counting and political fancywork. I'm not made for it. There is no part of me that ever wanted to be a bureaucrat – you understand that, Vasiliy? No part. It disagrees with me. I need to work in a marked trench, or a library, with a trowel or a notebook or a picter. I'll only be gone a short while. A few years at most. Enough time to clear my head and refresh my perspective.'

Vasiliy shook his head.

'I know I'm not going to talk you out of this,' he said. 'I know that look, the one you've got in your eye. It says stay away from the crazy man.'

Hawser smiled.

'There, you see? You know the omens to look for. You've been warned.'

✣

THE QUIETUDE'S HOME world, that neon orange ball, was actually skinned with ice in the parts that mattered. The Quietude, it appeared, had artificially extended its ice caps like an armoured sheath.

A message was sent to Ogvai asking for further expertise.

'We're going to the surface,' Fith Godsmote said to Hawser. 'You'll come. Make an account.'

It almost sounded like a question, but it was really a statement of the imminent.

Stormbirds had been brought into the graving dock's extravagant facilities. As the men of Tra readied their weapons and kit, and lined up to board, Hawser saw that some of them were engaged in half-joking arguments.

'What's going on?' he asked Godsmote.

'They are debating which bird you should ride on,' said Godsmote. 'When you came to Fenris, you were a bad star and you fell out of the sky. No one wants to ride down the sky with a bad star.'

'I can imagine,' said Hawser.

He looked at the Astartes, and called out, 'Which craft is Bear travelling on?'

Some of the men pointed.

'That one, then,' said Hawser, walking towards the vehicle. 'Bear won't let me fall out of the sky twice.'

The men of Tra laughed, all except Bear. The laughter was edged with wet leopard-growls.

✥

HAWSER HAD TO wear a plastek rebreather over his nose and mouth, because there was something in the atmosphere that didn't agree with standard human biology. The Astartes had no need of support. Many went bareheaded.

The view was extraordinary. The sky, only faintly bruised by vapour, was an oceanic amber canopy that had such bright clarity it looked like blown glass. Everything had a slightly yellow cast to it, an orange tinge. It reminded Hawser of something, and it took him a little while to pull up the memory.

When he finally did, it was surprisingly sharp. Ossetia, a few days before his fortieth birthday; Captain Vasiliy sniggering as she allowed him to try on her heavyweight headgear, him blinking as he peered out through the giant slide-visor at a world tinted orange.

Then he heard, in his head, the *March of Unity* being played on an old clavier, and tried to think about something else.

They had set down on a great ice field. Under the orange sky, the landscape was flat but dimpled, like a textured flooring fabricated and rolled out from a machine. It was ice, though. The dimples were where small liquid ripples had flash-frozen, and punch samples had been taken by the engineer corps of the advancing Imperial Army brigades. The chemical composition matched those derived from orbital scanning. Stupendous towers the size of hive city spire caps, but of a design ethic that matched the graving dock far above, protruded from the ice field at regular intervals of approximately six hundred and seventy kilometres like cloves studding a pomander.

Almost the first thing the Wolf beside Hawser said was, 'There's no hunting here.'

He meant the ice was sterile. Hawser could sense it too. This was not the absolute white wilderness of Asaheim. This was an engineered landscape. The towers were generators, in his estimation. In the face of a massive extraplanetary invasion, the Olamic Quietude had used its appreciable technology to extend its natural ice caps to form shields. The thickness and composition were such that great parts of the orbital bombardment had been reflected or resisted.

There were cities under the ice where the Quietude
was preparing its counter-attack.

✧

THE IMPERIAL ARMY had targeted some of the towers, and
were attacking them in vast numbers. Hawser saw tides
of men and armoured fighting machines washing in
across the ice towards one, pouring in across pylon
bridges and support struts. Mass gunfire had stippled
the ice field, and the crust around the tower's structure
was beginning to melt, suggesting that damage had
been done to parts of its mechanism.

There were fires burning everywhere. Thousands of
threads of dirty smoke rose into the ochre sky across the
giant vista, each one spewing from a destroyed
machine, just dots on the ice in the general mass of
attackers. It was a scale that he could not really compre-
hend, like the scenic backdrop of some painting of a
general or warmaster with a raised sword and his boot
on a fallen helm. Hawser had always presumed the
apocalyptic battle scenes rendered behind them were
somewhat over-enthusiastic and largely intended to
fluff the sitter's importance.

But this was bigger than anything he had ever seen: a
battlefield the size of a continent, an armed host that
numbered millions, and that host only one of hundreds
of thousands that the Imperium had birthed upon the
awakening cosmos. In one repellant moment, he saw
the contradictory scales of mankind: the giant stature
that allowed the species pre-eminence in the galaxy, and
the individual stature of a great-coated trooper, one of
scores, falling and lost under the charging boots of his
comrades as they stormed the alien gates.

Quietude defences lashed the advancing lines with
withering disdain. Along the leading edge of the attack,
the air seemed to distort as the Quietude's weapon
effects impacted and mangled armour, ice and human

bodies. High on the ominous tower, massive lamp-like turrets rotated slowly and projected down beams of annihilating energy, washing them slowly as they turned like the beacons of fatal lighthouses. The beams left black, steaming, sticky scars gouged through the densely packed hosts of advancing Imperials.

Super-heavy tanks in deep formation braced for ice-firing and began to devastate the lower flanks of the tower. Parts of it blew out, ejecting huge sprays of debris. The explosions looked small from a distance, and the clouds of debris little more than exhalations of dust, but Hawser knew it was simply scale at work again. The tower was immense. The cloudbursts of debris were akin to those that might rain down after the destruction of a city block.

As he watched, a whole bridge section collapsed, spilling Imperial soldiers into the gulf between the tower and the ice shelf it was plugging. Hundreds of soldiers fell, tumbling, tiny, the sunlight catching braid and armour. Several armoured vehicles plunged with them, sliding off the bridge section as it caved, tracks snapping and lashing. They had been assaulting one of the main exterior gates, which had remained shut and unyielding throughout. Another bridge section collapsed about five minutes later when one of the tower's subturrets succumbed to bombardment from the super-heavy tanks and slumped like a landslip, its form unforming, its structure blurring, its weight ripping down off the face of the main tower and exploding the massive bridge into the gulf.

How many thousand Imperial lives went in that second, Hawser wondered? In that flash? In that senseless roar?

What am I doing here?

'Come on. You, skjald, come on.'

He turned from his ringside view of armageddon and

saw the flame-lit face of Bear. There was no smile or
expression of regard to be found there. Hawser had
learned this to be a character mark of the sullen Wolf.
He presumed that Bear was particularly sullen with him
because he, a human, had caused Bear, an Astartes,
embarrassing problems in the eyes of his company, and
the *Vlka Fenryka* as a whole.

'Where?' Hawser asked.

Bear bristled slightly.

'Where I tell you,' he said. He turned, and tilted his
head to indicate that Hawser should follow.

They left the powdery, yellow lip of an ice ridge where
most of Tra had settled to observe the assault. Behind
them, an expanding column of thick cream dust was
slowly filling the amber sky. It was emerging from the
tumult surrounding the tower assault, climbing into the
sky like a stained glacier, ponderous and threatening.
The upper parts, where it broadened, were already seventy kilometres across, and the formations of Army
gunships and ground-attack craft lining up on the tower
were having to fly instruments-only as they penetrated
the sulphurous pall.

Hawser followed Bear up the slope. The fine yellow
powder-ice was adhering to the Wolf's dark, almost
matt-grey armour. Sometimes Hawser stumbled or
slipped a little as the soft slope trickled or subsided
under him, but every single step Bear took was sure:
deep strides, planting his massive, armour-shod feet,
not once having to steady himself with a hand. He
began to leave Hawser behind.

Hawser fixated on the black leather braids and runic
totems tied to the Wolf's belt and carapace, imagined
himself grabbing hold of them and clinging on, and
tried to catch up.

They wound up the cliff slope, through groups of
lounging Wolves, past the brooding Terminator

monsters, their gross armour burnished and glinting in the sun, past teams of thralls making adjustments and spot repairs to seams and joints as their masters waited impatiently to go back and view the battle. The Terminators were as immobile and sinister as cast bronze sculptures, all arranged to face the nearby conflagration.

Away from the unmarked but defined perimeter of Tra's vantage point, the rear echelon and supply encampments of the Imperial Army group were spread out like a souk. There was a dead space, a fringe of about two kilometres, between Tra's position and the closest Army post, indicating the intense reluctance of any soldier, officer or even mediary of the Imperial Army to come within sight of a Fenrisian Wolf.

If only they knew, Hawser thought. There are no wolves on Fenris.

'Keep up!' Bear said, turning to glance back. Now at last there was an expression on his face. It was annoyance. His black hair made a ragged curtain that threw his eyes into shadow and made them shine with nocturnal malevolence.

Hawser was dripping with sweat under his body-suit and the pelt draped over his shoulders. He was out of breath, and the sun was burning his neck.

'I'm coming,' he said. He wiped perspiration off his face, and took a long suck from the water-straw that fed into his rebreather mask. He stopped deliberately to catch his breath. He was interested to see how far he could push Bear. He was interested to see what Bear would do.

He hoped it wouldn't be *hit him*.

Bear watched. He'd braided his jet-black hair around his brow and temples before the attack on the graving dock to afford and cushion the fit of his Mark-IV helm. One of the braids had worked loose, and was causing

the curtain across his eyes. Bear began to plait it back
into place, waiting for Hawser.

Hawser took another deep breath, flexed his neck in
the prickling heat, and caught up.

They entered the Army encampment. It had only been
there a few hours, but it was already the size of a large
colony town. Arvus- and Aves-pattern transatmospheric
lifters were still coming in and out to make drops in a
haze of ice vapour on the far edge. The vapour was
catching the sun and creating partial rainbows. The
encampment, a patchwork of prefab tents and enviro-
modules mixed with pods, containers, payload crates
and vehicles: some beige, some gold, some khaki, some
russet, some grey, looked to Hawser like a patch of
mould or lichen, spreading out across the clean surface
of the ice field. When he mentioned it later, this descrip-
tion also won him some approval from the Wolves.

No one challenged their entry into the encampment.
Around the edges of the mobile base were pickets of
Savarene Harriers with their shakos and gold-topped
staves, and G9K Division Kill eliters wearing long
dusters over semi-powered combat suits. Not a single
gun twitched in their direction. As the Wolf approached
with the human bumbling along behind him, the soldiers found other, far more important things to look at.
In the 'streets' of the tent town, the bustling military
personnel gave them a wide berth.

It was like a souk, a busy market, except all the traders
were provisioners of military service and all the produce
was munitions and materiel.

'Where are we going?' Hawser asked.

Bear didn't reply. He just kept striding on through the
camp.

'Hey!' Hawser shouted, and ran to catch up. He
reached out, and pulled at the thick, blunt edge of Bear's
left armour cuff. The ceramite was numbingly cold.

Bear stopped, and very slowly turned. He looked at Hawser. Then he looked down at the vulnerable human hand touching his arm.

'That was a bad idea, wasn't it?' said Hawser, removing his hand warily.

'Why don't you like me?' he asked.

Bear turned away and started walking again.

'I have no opinion either way,' said Bear. 'But I do not think you should be here.'

'Here?'

'With the Rout.'

Bear stopped again and looked back at him.

'Why did you come to Fenris?' he asked.

'That's a good question,' said Hawser.

'What's the answer?'

Hawser shrugged.

Bear turned and started walking again.

'The jarl wants you to see something,' he said.

Close to the centre of the vast encampment, which was feeling more and more like a carnival ground to Hawser, a large command shelter had been erected. There were tented shades overhead to screen off the harshest of the ice desert's hard sunlight, and walls of reinforced shock-boarding to baffle any stray or lucky munition strike. Nearby, a crew of polished silver servitors laboured to install and activate a portable void shield generator that would, by nightfall, be protecting the high-value section of the encampment under a fizzling blue parasol. The tent shades and shockboarding distorted the travelling roar of the conflict on the other side of the ridge, and somehow made it louder and more intrusive than it had been on the slope where the Wolves had gathered.

A crowd of perhaps two hundred had gathered under the central awning. They were surrounding a mobile strategium desk, the top of which was alight with active and moving hololithic displays.

The crowd, all Imperial Army officers, parted to let Hawser and his towering Astartes escort through. As he stepped up on to the self-levelling interlock staging, Hawser felt a pop in his ears and a chill on his face that announced he had just entered an artificial environment bubble. He unclasped his rebreather, and let the mask dangle around his neck. He smelled clean air, and the body sweat of hot, agitated, tired men.

Ogvai was at the centre of the crowd beside the strategium desk. He was not escorted by any of Tra, and he had removed his helm and some of the significant parts of his arm, shoulder and torso plating. Hugely armoured from the gut down, he stood with his long, white arms emerging from the rubberised black of his sleeveless underlayer with its feeder pipes and heat soaks like necrotised capillaries, and his long, black centre-parted hair, resembling a wager-bout pit fighter ringed by an audience at a country fair.

As a child at the commune, Hawser had seen men of that kind many times. Rector Uwe had sometimes taken the children to the festivals at the work camps of Ur where, in sight of the slowly forming, monolithic plan of the city-dream, the labour force would halt to celebrate the periodic feasts of Cathermas, Radmastide and the Divine Architect, as well as the observances of the builder-lodges. These holidays were basically excuses for spirited fairs and jubilees. Some of the larger labourers would strip to the waist and invite all-comers to bouts of sparring for beer, coins and the crowd's entertainment. They would tower head and shoulders above the onlookers too.

Except here, the onlookers were Army service personnel, many of them large and imposing men. Ogvai was a raw-boned monster in their midst. With his skin so white, he looked like he was carved out of ice and immune to the merciless heat, where they were all ruddy and sweating. The fat silver piercing in his lower lip made him look like he was taunting them all.

Why has he stripped back his armour, Hawser wondered? He looks... informal. Why does he want me here?

Bear stopped at the edge of the ring of onlookers with Hawser beside him. Ogvai saw them. He was in discussion with three senior Army officers around the desk. He leaned forwards, resting his palms on the edge of the desk and his weight straight-armed on his hands. It was casual and rather scornful. The officers looked uncomfortable. One was a field marshal of the Outremars, obediently holding up the holographic visage of his telepresent khedive master like a waiter holding a grox's head on a platter. Beside him was a thick-set, choleric G9K Division Kill combat master in a flak coat and a quilted tank driver's cap. The third was a freckled, pale-blond man in the austere uniform of the Jaggedpanzor Regiments. It was curious to hear Ogvai speaking in Low Gothic: curious to know that he could, curious to hear his jaw and dentition manage the brittle human noises.

'We are wasting time,' he was saying. 'This assault is not punching hard enough.'

The hololithic image of the Outremar khedive squealed in outrage, a sound distorted by the digital relay.

'That is a frank and open insult to the architects of this planetary attack,' the image declared. 'You exceed yourself, jarl.'

'I do not,' Ogvai corrected pleasantly.

'Your comment was certainly critical of the competency of this assault,' said the Jaggedpanzor officer, in a tone rather more conciliatory than the one the khedive had adopted, probably because he was actually standing in Ogvai's presence.

'It was,' Ogvai agreed.

'This is not "punching hard" enough for you?' asked the G9K commander, making a general gesture at the display in front of them.

'No,' said Ogvai. 'It's all very well as mass surface drops go. I guess one of you planned it?'

'I had the honour of rationalising the invasion scheme on behalf of the Expedition Commander,' said the khedive.

Ogvai nodded. He looked at the Jaggedpanzor officer.

'Can you kill a man with a rifle?' he asked.

'Of course,' said the man.

'Can you kill a man with a spade?' Ogvai asked.

The man frowned.

'Yes,' he replied.

Ogvai looked at the G9K man.

'You. Can you dig a hole with a spade?'

'Of course!' the man answered.

'Can you dig a hole with a rifle?'

The man didn't reply.

'You've got to use the right tool for the right job,' said Ogvai. 'You've got a big, well-supported army, and a world to take. It doesn't automatically follow that throwing the former at the latter will get you what you want.'

Ogvai looked over at Bear.

'Like you wouldn't try to hunt an *urdarkottur* with an axe, eh, Bear?'

Bear laughed a wet leopard-growl.

'Hjolda, no! You'd need a long-tooth spear to get through the fur.'

Ogvai looked at the Army commanders.

'The right tool for the job, see?'

'And are you the right tool?' the khedive asked.

Hawser heard the Jaggedpanzor officer gasp and recoil slightly.

'Don't push it,' Ogvai said to the hologram. 'I'm trying

to help you save a little face here. It's you the fleet
commander is going to drag over the coals if this
situation doesn't start to improve.'

'We are very grateful for any advice the Astartes can
offer,' the field marshal carrying the hololithic plate suddenly said, holding the platter to one side in case his
distant, holoform-represented master said anything else
provocative.

'That's why we sent the request to you,' said the G9K
man.

Ogvai nodded.

'Well, we all serve the great Emperor of Terra, don't
we?' he said, flashing a smile that showed teeth. 'We all
fight on the same side for the same goals. He made the
Wolves of Fenris to break the foes that couldn't otherwise be broken, so you don't have to ask twice, or even
that politely.'

Ogvai looked at the projected, slightly shimmering
face of the khedive.

'Though a little basic respect is always good,' he said.
'I want to be clear, mind. If you want us to do this, don't
get in the way. Go back to your superiors and make sure
they send official communiqués to the Commander of
the Expedition Fleet that my Astartes have been given
theatre control to end this war. I'm not moving until I
get that confirmed.'

Why did he want me to see that, Hawser wondered?
Does he want me to be impressed? Is that it? He wants
me to see him intimidate and bully senior and serious
Crusade commanders. And he wants them to see he can
do it stripped to the waist like he's relaxing.

The meeting began to disperse. Ogvai wandered
towards Bear and Hawser.

'You see?' he asked, in Juvjk.

'See what?' Hawser replied.

'What I brought you here to see,' snapped Bear.

'That everyone fears you?' asked Hawser.

Ogvai grinned.

'That, yes. But also that I abide by the codes of war. We abide by the codes of war. The *Vlka Fenryka* abide by the codes of rule.'

'Why is it important to you that I understand that?'

'The Sixth Legion Astartes has a reputation,' said Bear.

'All the Legions Astartes have reputations,' replied Hawser.

'Not like ours,' said Ogvai. 'We are known for our ferocity. We are thought to be feral and undisciplined. Even brother Legions consider us to be wild and bestial.'

'And you're not?' asked Hawser.

'If we need to be,' said Ogvai. 'But if that was our natural state, we'd all be dead by now.'

He leaned down towards Hawser like a parent addressing a child.

'It takes a vast amount of self control to be this dangerous,' he said.

⬥

HAWSER REQUESTED PERMISSION to stay in the Army encampment for an hour or two more, until it was time to depart. Ogvai had already wandered off. Bear gave Hawser a small homer wand and told him to return to the dropsite the moment it chimed.

It had been a long time since Hawser had been around regular humans, a lifetime in which he had been reborn as something that was not entirely human any more. After waking, he'd lived in the fastness of the Fang with the Rout for the best part of a great year, acclimatising, learning their customs, learning their stories, learning his way around the gloomy vaults of the Aett.

In all that time, three things had been kept from him. The first was the person of the Wolf King. Hawser didn't even know if the Sixth Primarch was actually on Fenris during that period. He doubted it. The Wolf King was more likely *upp*, leading companies in the service of the Emperor. Hawser reconciled himself to the fact that Skarssen and Ogvai would be the most senior Wolves he would have access to.

The second thing was a secret, something about Hawser himself. It was hard to say how Hawser knew this, but he did. It was a gut response, an instinct. Wolves often described to him particular moments in combat in such terms: visceral stimuli felt in their living bowels that made the split-second difference between living and dying. They always sounded proud of being sensitive to them. Hawser flattered himself that his immersion in their society was teaching him to recognise the same trick.

If it was, then it was telling him something. The Astartes and their thralls were withholding some details from him, one thing in particular. It was an intensely subtle thing. There were no crass signs like conversations abruptly halting when he entered rooms, or sentences suddenly trailing off when the speaker thought better of them.

The third thing was Imperial human company.

Towards the end of his first great year, Dekk Company returned to the Aett from a long tour of service in the Second Kobolt War, and Tra found itself rotated into the line, with instructions to shadow and support the 40th Expedition Fleet in the Gogmagog Cluster.

There never seemed any question that Hawser, as skjald, would go with them. He was part of their portage, part of company support, along with the thralls, the armourers, the pilots, the servitors, the musicians, the victuallers and the butchers.

They embarked onto *Nidhoggur*, one of the grim, comfortless warships that served the Sixth Legion, and made the translation to the immaterium with a flotilla of service tenders in support. Nine weeks later, at a mandeville point shy of Gogmagog Beta, they retranslated and made contact with the 40th Expedition Fleet, which was, by then, pressing fruitlessly into Olamic Quietude territory.

'What sort of thing are you?'

Hawser looked up from the strategium desk and found he was being addressed by the G9K Division Kill combat master who had been in conference with Ogvai.

'Do you have clearance to be here?' the man asked, clearly emboldened now that the brute Astartes had gone.

'You know I do,' Hawser replied with a confidence that surprised even him. The man was prepared to argue the toss, so Hawser brushed back his hair, which had grown long during the great year spent at the Aett, and properly revealed his gold and black-pinned eye.

'I am a watcher, chosen by the favour of the Sixth Legion Astartes,' said Hawser.

The combat master's expression registered distaste.

'But you're human?'

'Generally speaking.'

'How can you live with those beasts?'

'Well, I watch my tongue, for a start. What's your name?'

'Pawel Korine, combat master first class.'

'I get the distinct impression that no one here is comfortable having the Wolves as allies.'

Korine studied Hawser uncertainly.

'I'll watch *my* tongue, I think,' he said. 'I don't want them looking at me through your eyes and deciding I need to be taught a lesson in obedience.'

'It doesn't work like that,' Hawser smiled. 'I can be discreet and selective. I'd like to know what you think.'

'So you're some kind of... what? Chronicler? Remembrancer?'

'Something like that,' said Hawser. 'I make accounts.'

Korine sighed. He was a heavy-set man with Prussian ethnic traits, and he carried himself with the manner of a career soldier. G9K had a considerable reputation as a front-line force. It famously maintained an archaic performance-based pay and advancement model that was said to have its origins in the prediluvian traditions of mercantile-sponsored mercenaries. For Korine to have achieved the post of combat master first class, he had certainly seen some considerable active service.

'Tell me what you meant,' said Hawser.

Korine shrugged.

'I've witnessed plenty,' he said. 'I know, I know, that old soldier routine. But trust me. Thirty-seven years non-adjusted, that's what I've spent in this Crusade. Thirty-seven years, eight campaigns. I know what ugly looks like. I've seen Astartes fight four times. Every time, it's scared me.'

'They're designed to be scary. They wouldn't be effective if they weren't.'

Korine didn't look especially convinced.

'Well, that's a whole different issue,' he replied. 'I say if man's going to take back this great Imperium, he ought to do it by the sweat of his brow and the strength of his arm, and not build damned supermen to do the work for him.'

'I've heard that line of argument before. It has some merit. But we couldn't even unify Terra without the Astartes to–'

'Yes, yes. And what will we do when the work is done?' Korine asked. 'When the Crusade is over, what will we do with the almighty Space Marines? What do you do with something that can only ever be a weapon when the war is over?'

'Maybe there will always be war,' said Hawser.

Korine crinkled his thin lips distastefully.

'Then we really are all wasting our lives,' he replied.

His wrist-mounted communicator, thickly cushioned in black rubber, beeped, and he checked the display.

'Six hour evacuation has just been posted,' said Korine. 'I have to see what's going on. You can walk with me if you wish.'

They went out, back into the open and the roasting sunlight. Hawser felt the artificial atmosphere sleeve pop around him and replaced his rebreather. Activity levels in the camp had risen. Out in the rainbowed band of vapour beyond the camp edge, lifter craft were queuing out across the ice desert in a wavering, hovering line as they waited their turn to swing in and load up. The distant ones crinkled in an eerie heat-haze.

'You don't approve of Astartes then, combat master?' Hawser asked as they strode through the camp.

'Not at all. Extraordinary things. Like I said, I've seen them fight four times.'

They entered the combat master's command post, a large enviro-tent where dozens of G9K officers and technicians were already dismantling the site for withdrawal. Korine went to a small desk and began to sort through his personal equipment.

'The Death Guard, once,' he said, holding up a finger to begin a tally. 'Murderous efficiency with such small numbers. Blood Angels.' Another raised finger. 'A firefight gone bad in a casein works on one of the Fraemium moons. They arrived like... like angels. I don't mean to be glib. They saved us. It was like they were coming to save our souls.'

Korine looked at Hawser. He raised a third finger.

'White Scars, side by side, for six months on the plains of X173 Plural, hosing xeno-forms. Total focus and dedication, merciless. I cannot, hand on my heart, fault their duty, devotion to the Crusade cause, or their supreme effort as warriors.'

'You said four times,' Hawser pressed.

'I did,' said Korine. He raised a fourth finger in a gesture that reminded Hawser of surrender.

'The Space Wolves, two years ago non-adjusted. Dekk Company, they called themselves. They came in to support our actions during the Kobolt scrap. I'd heard stories. We'd all heard stories.'

'What kind of stories?'

'That there are Space Marines and there are Space Marines. That there are supermen and there are monsters. That in order to breed the Astartes perfection, the Emperor Who Guides Us All has gone too far once or twice, and made things he should not have made. Things that should have been stillborn or drowned in a sack.'

'Feral things?' asked Hawser.

'The worst of them all are the Space Wolves,' replied Korine. 'They were animals, Great Terra, they were *animals* those things that fought with us. When you have sympathy with the enemy, you know you have the wrong kind of allies. They killed everything, and destroyed everything and, worst of all, they took great relish in the apocalypse they had brought down upon their foe. There was nothing admirable about them, nothing rousing. They just left a sick taste in the mouth as if, by calling on their help, we had somehow demeaned ourselves in an effort to win.'

Korine paused and turned to hand out instructions to some of his men. They were obedient, well-drilled, attentive. Hawser could see that Korine was a soldier who expected an army to be supremely disciplined in order to function. One of his men, a burly second-classer with a chinstrap beard, brought a data-slate over for Korine's review. He glared belligerently at Hawser.

Korine handed the data-slate back to his officer.

'Full withdrawal from the surface,' he said. He sounded broken. 'All forces. We're to stand down and get clear so the Wolves can take it on alone. Shit. This assault has cost us thousands of men, and we're just scrapping it.'

'Better that than thousands more.'

Korine sat down, opened a haversack, and pulled out a slightly battered metal flask. He poured a generous measure into the cap and passed it to Hawser, and then took a swig from the flask.

'When the 40th discovered that the Wolves were the only Astartes in range who could help us tackle the Quietude, we almost cancelled the request. I heard that as a fact from one of the senior men close to the fleet commander. It was a genuine consideration that we didn't want to involve ourselves with the Wolves again.'

'You'd rather face defeat?'

'It's about ends, and the means that get you there,' Korine replied. 'It's about contemplating the question, what are the Wolves for? Why did the Emperor make them like that? What purpose could he possibly have for something so inhuman?'

'Do you have answers to any of those questions, Combat Master Korine?' asked Hawser.

'Either the Emperor is not as perfect an architect of this new age as we like to suppose, and he is capable of manufacturing nightmares, or he has anticipated threats we can't possibly imagine.'

'Which would you prefer?'

'Neither notion fills me with great confidence about the future,' replied Korine. 'Do you have an answer, as you keep their company?'

'I don't,' said Hawser. He'd finished his drink, and Korine refilled the cap. It was a strong spirit, an amasec or a schnapps, and there was a flush on Korine's cheeks, but Hawser felt nothing except the slightest burn in his throat. Life on Fenris had evidently bred a stronger constitution into him.

'The things we fought in Kobolt space,' said Korine quietly, 'they were lethal and proud. They had no interest in human ways or human business, and they were quite capable of fighting us to a standstill. They had mighty vessels, like cities. I saw one of them. I was part of an assault against it. Someone called it Scintilla City because it sparkled like it was all made of glass. We later found out it was called Thuyelsa in their language, and it was a structure they called a craftworld. Anyway, we never worked out why they were fighting us or what they were trying to defend, except perhaps that they were trying to keep us at bay, or keep for themselves whatever it was they had, but you knew, you just knew inside yourself they had something worth defending. A legacy, a history, a culture. And it was all lost.'

Korine looked down into his flask, as if some truth might lurk inside in the dark. Hawser suspected he might have been looking in that very same place for an answer for quite some time.

'At the end,' Korine said, 'they began to plead. The Wolves were upon them, and the city-vessel was shattering around them, and they realised that they were going to lose everything. They began to plead for terms, as if anything was better than losing everything. We never really understood what they were trying to tell us, or what kind of surrender they were trying to make. I personally believe that they would have given all of their lives if Scintilla City had been allowed to survive. But it was too late. The Wolves couldn't be called off. They sacked it. The Wolves destroyed it all. There wasn't even anything left for us to salvage, no treasure for us to plunder, nothing of value to claim as a prize. The Wolves destroyed it all.'

Korine fell silent.

The homer wand Bear had given to Hawser gave out a little beep.

Hawser set the cap down and nodded to the combat master.

'Thank you for the drink and the conversation.'

Korine shrugged.

'I think perhaps you malign the Wolves a little,' Hawser added. 'It may be that they are misunderstood.'

Korine made a sound, possibly a laugh.

'Isn't that what all monsters say?' he asked.

HAWSER LEFT THE G9K enviro-tent. All around him, personnel were busy dismantling the encampment for surface departure.

He stood for a moment, consulting the homer's direction indicator. Behind his back, someone cursed him.

He swung around.

Korine's second-classer, the man with the chinstrap, and several other G9Kers were loading impact-resistant crates onto a flatbed truck.

'Did you speak to me?' Hawser asked.

Chinstrap's glare was toxic. He set down the crate-end he had been lifting, and walked towards Hawser. His men looked on.

'Sack of shit animal,' Chinstrap hissed.

'What?'

'Go back to the filth you run with. You should be ashamed. They're not human. They're animals!'

Hawser turned aside. The man was big and aggressive, and he was evidently upset. It was the sort of confrontation Hawser had sought to avoid for most of his life.

Chinstrap grabbed Hawser's right arm. The grip was painful.

'You tell them that,' he said. 'Seventeen hundred men Division Kill's lost in one day of surface assault, and now those stupid animals tell us to piss off? Seventeen hundred lives wasted?'

PROSPERO BURNS   199

'You're clearly upset,' said Hawser. 'This has been a costly engagement, and I am sympathetic to–'

'Screw you.'

The other men, the members of Chinstrap's loading team, had closed in.

'Let go of my arm,' said Hawser.

'Or what?' Chinstrap asked.

'RUN!' MURZA TOLD him.

Murza was usually right about these things. It wasn't that Murza was a coward, Hawser supposed, it was simply because he was far more the rationalist. After all, neither of them were fighters. They were academics, field archaeologists, average men with above average minds. Neither of them had any military schooling and neither had been on any kind of self-defence training programme. They were armed only with their wits and their accreditation papers, which stated their names, the fact that they had both recently celebrated their thirtieth birthdays, and their status as conservators working in Lutetia for the Unification Council.

None of which was going to do them very much good.

'They can't be allowed to get away with this–' Hawser began.

'Oh, just run you idiot!' Murza shouted back.

The other members of the placement team were already running, no further encouragement needed. Their boots were clattering down the cobbled back alley as they scattered into the warren of unmapped streets criss-crossing the slum quarters of Lutetia around the dead cathedral.

The cathedral was just a giant corpse-building. It had died as a place of worship during the Nineteenth War of Uropan Succession three thousand years earlier, and since then its structure had been put to other uses: a parliament hall for three centuries, a mausoleum, an iceworks, an almshouse, and, latterly, a market when the last of the roof fell in. For the last eight hundred or so years, it had been an empty husk, a physicalised memory, lifting its rusting iron ribs at the overcast sky.

The rumours of its past had persisted as long as those ribs, if not longer. Murza had not been able to keep the excitement out of his voice when he'd briefed the team two days before. The site had been a place of worship for as long as records existed, and the cathedral stood upon the plot of previous structures called cathedrals, and was indeed only called a cathedral because of that masonic legacy.

There were cellars down there, deep under the foundations, the basements of previous incarnations, cisterns buried under the sub-fabric of later builds. Some said if you could trace your way down through the dark, you'd reach the centre of the Earth, and the catacombs of old Franc.

One of Murza's contacts (and he, as usual, had a network of well paid informers watching the traffic of artefacts and relics throughout the entire Lutetian city-node area) had reported that a gang of labourers had excavated the entrance to a drainage sump while reclaiming old stone. Some silver amulets and a ring scooped from the sump had been enough to convince the contact that the area was worth a look, and worth the fee that the conservators would have to pay the gang to reveal the precise location.

Hawser had been mistrustful from the start. The labourers, all local, were big men caked in black mud from street work. All of them showed signs of atomic mutation, a trait common in the slum. Hawser immediately felt threatened by them, physically intimidated, the way he had been by the bigger, older boys back at Rector Uwe's commune. He was no fighter.

Confrontation, especially physical confrontation, made him lock up and freeze.

The slum district was a maze. Nothing identifiable remained of the planned city that had once occupied the area. The streets had corroded into sub-streets and under-runs, alleys and cul-de-sacs, all of them dark and thick with filth, none of them charted or named. Children played in the piles of trash, and the sounds of wailing babies and arguing adults echoed down from the tenement levels rising above them. Washing lines were strung from building to building, like the canopy of a dingy, man-made jungle. It was shadowy and airless.

The labourers led them into the alley maze. It seemed an unnecessarily circuitous route to Hawser, and he said so to Murza, who told him to hush. After walking for about twenty minutes, the labourers turned and told Murza it was time to pay them the agreed fee.

The leader of the gang happened to add that what he meant by the agreed fee was significantly higher than anything Murza had discussed with the team.

Hawser realised they were in trouble. He realised it was all simply a trap designed to extort, and that its most likely consequences would be a beating or a kidnapping. It was going to cost the Conservatory programme: it was going to cost them in medical fees, or ransom or simply excess pay-offs. It might even cost them lives. He felt outrage. He felt stupid that he'd allowed Murza to walk them into another less than brilliant situation.

'This is no time to feel choleric!' Murza shouted. The gang was closing in on them, surly, barking threats. Some had shovels or picks.

'Run!' Murza yelled.

Hawser recognised that running was the only sensible course of action, but the physical threat had finally eclipsed his outrage, and intimidation had glued him to the spot. One of the labourers stepped towards him, spitting curses through buckled brown teeth, shaking a fist with kielbasa knuckles. Hawser tried to force his feet to work.

Murza grabbed his arm so hard it hurt and yanked him backwards.

'Come on! Come on, Kas!'

Hawser started to stumble, his legs beginning to move. The labourer was reaching for them. Hawser realised the labourer had drawn a gun, some kind of pistol.

Dragging Hawser after him, Murza looked over his shoulder and yelled something at the labourer, a single word or sound. There was an odd pulse, a pop like the equalisation of air at the skin of an environment bubble. The labourer yelled and fell backwards, writhing.

They ran, side by side, Murza still gripping his arm.

'What did you do?' Hawser yelled. 'What did you do? What did you say to him?'

Murza couldn't answer. There was blood drooling from his mouth.

⟡

CHINSTRAP'S FINGERS DUG into his arm like hooks. Scared, Hawser shoved. He just shoved to lurch the man away, so he could walk on, get past them, leave them behind.

Chinstrap hit the side of the pile of rubber-sleeved crates on the back of the track. He was airborne and travelling backwards. His spine and shoulders took the first impact, and his skull cracked back across the top of the uppermost crate. Then he plunged forwards and hit the ground flat on his face, loose as a sack of stones. His face just slapped into the gritty ice, shattering his plastek rebreather.

While Chinstrap was still in the air, one of his men

swung a punch at the back of Hawser's head. The punch seemed to Hawser to be ridiculously telegraphed, as if the man was trying to be sporting and give him a chance. He put his hand up to stop the fist from hitting his face and caught it in his palm. There was a little shock. He felt finger bones break and knuckles detonate, and none of them were his.

The third man decided to kill Hawser, and made an effort to insert a heavy, cast iron crate spanner into Hawser's skull. Once again, however, he appeared to be doing this in a delicate fashion, like an over-emphatic stage punch that goes wide of the mark but looks good from the audience. Hawser didn't want the spanner to come anywhere near him. He swung out his left hand in an impulsive, flinching gesture to brush the man's arm away.

The man screamed. He appeared to have developed a second elbow halfway down his forearm. The skin of his arm folded there like an empty sock. He fell over, the spanner bouncing solidly off the ice.

The other men fled.

⚜

BEAR WAS WAITING for him at the foot of a Stormbird ramp.

'You're late,' he said.

Hawser handed the homer back to him.

'I'm here now.'

'We would have left without you if you'd been much longer.'

'I'm sure you would.'

'You smell of blood,' said Bear.

'Yes, I do,' said Hawser. He looked at Bear.

'Why didn't you tell me how thoroughly you'd rebuilt me?' he asked.

SEVEN

Longfang

JARL OGVAI'S SOLUTION to the Quietude's resistance was as direct as it was effective. Having been granted an unequivocal mandate for theatre control by the commander of the Expedition Fleet, he gathered his iron priests, gave them instruction, and set them to work.

It took them about two days to complete the calculations and the preparation work. By then, the fleet's massive drop forces had been extracted from the planet's surface.

At a moment on the third day considered propitious by the jarl's closest advisors, the iron priests unleashed their handiwork.

A series of colossal controlled explosions tore the graving dock out of its stable orbit. Plumes of shredded, metallic debris streamed out behind it, glittering in the hard sunlight. The dock arced across the vast orange surface of the world, a tiny twin conjoined to it by the ligaments of gravity. They danced together, two encircling objects, like a child's brightly coloured spinning toy.

It took eighteen full rotations for the murdered orbit to decay to the inevitable, the terminal. The debris plumes had formed fine brown threads around the world by then, like the most delicate of rings around a gas giant. Friction and atmospheric retardation were beginning to burn the graving dock, to ablate its superstructure. It began to glow as it fell, like a metal ingot in a smithy, first dull red, then pink, then white with heat. Its curving descent, the steady unwinding of orbital passage, was tantalisingly slow.

It fell as all bad stars fall. Hawser knew about that. As bad stars went, it was the worst.

It struck the ice field between two of the stupendous towers, the towers that rose at intervals of approximately six hundred and seventy kilometres, and probably had been there for thousands of years. There was, at first, a wink of light, then a rapidly expanding brilliance like a sunburst squirting up through the ice. The brilliance became a dome of blinding radiance that travelled outwards in all directions, vaporising the ice crust and annihilating the towers like trees in a hurricane.

The impact event created a lethal pulse of infrared radiation. Ejecta clogged the air and scarred the atmosphere with a vast darkness of dust and aerosolised sulphuric acid. Incendiary fragments vomited up by the bolide-type impact pelted back down, adding to the firestorm outwash.

Tra had gathered on the embarkation deck of the ship to watch the mortal blow being delivered via pict-feed to several huge repeater screens designed for assault briefings. Thralls and deck crew gathered too. Some still had tools or polishing rags in their hands, or even weapons that they were in the process of repairing or cleaning.

There was general silence as they watched the languid descent, a little muttering, a few murmurs of impatience. When the impact came at last, the Wolves

exploded into life. They stamped their armour-shod feet
and smashed the hafts of their axes and hammers on
the deck; they beat their storm shields with their
swords; they threw their heads back and howled.

The noise was numbing. It sent a shockwave through
Hawser. All around him, the armoured giants bayed.
Exposed throats swelled, mouths opened to what
seemed like impossible widths, and spittle flew out
between exposed canines and carnassials. The pronounced, 'snouted' shape of the Fenrisian physiognomy
had never been more obvious to Hawser.

He only truly recognised that later. In the heat of the
moment, there on the embarkation deck, all that he was
able to register was the shock of the bestial noise. The
savagery of the Wolves' delight assaulted him like a
physical trauma. It reached into his chest and squeezed
with fingers that were prodigiously clawed. The hooded
Fenrisian thralls, and even some of the deck crew, had
begun to howl and shout too, shaking their fists. The
roaring was tribal and primal.

Just as he began to believe he couldn't tolerate it for a
second more, Hawser tipped his head back, closed his
eyes, and began to howl with them.

IN THE AFTERMATH, a deluge of acid rain began to fall,
and the stratosphere began to collapse. Tra's Stormbirds
led the way down into the toxin dust, into the discoloured smoke banks seething with crown-of-thorns
lightning.

The dark ships, wings broad, looked to Hawser like
their namesakes, circling ravens as black as thunder-
storm clouds, as they descended into the broken and
exposed heart of the ancient Quietude cities.

He said this to the Wolves, and they asked him what
'ravens' were.

✠

THE PACIFICATION TOOK three weeks, ship time. Time to learn things, Hawser decided. Some of the things would be about himself.

Accounts were already accumulating. Some were brought back from the sub-surface fighting by packs returning for replevin, others relayed by the members of packs waiting in reserve, stories that had filtered up from the planet through the links.

Some were worthy accounts of actions. Others seemed to Hawser to display, already, the hallmarks of the embroidered, the enhanced. *Mjod stories*, Aeska Bro-kenlip had called these, accounts exaggerated by the strength of the Fenrisians' lethal fuel.

Yet it didn't seem likely they were mjod stories, because Aeska had also made it clear that no self-respecting member of the Rout, and certainly no man of Tra, would ever be boastful. The braggart was one of the lowest forms of life, according to the traditions of the *Vlka Fenryka*. A warrior's stories were the measure of him, and the truth of them was the measure of his standing. A battlefield quickly exposed the braggart's lies: it tested his strength, his courage, his technical prowess.

And, Aeska had added, that was another reason why skjalds existed. They were brokers of truth, neutral mediators who would not let any fluctuations like pride or bias or mjod affect the agreed value of truth.

'So skjalds tell accounts to keep you entertained, to keep you honest, and to keep the history?' Hawser asked.

Aeska grinned.

'Yes, but mostly to keep us entertained.'

'What entertains the Wolves of Fenris?' Hawser pressed. 'What entertains them most?'

Aeska thought about it.

'We like stories about things that scare us,' he replied.

APART FROM THE stories that appeared to be exaggerations, there were others that puzzled Hawser.

According to the general picture, the battle far below was apocalyptic. With the ice-shield gone, the core cities of the Quietude were exposed, like the setts of some animal dug up by trappers. Conditions were hellish. There was acid rain and a pestilential sub-climate that included noxious gas clouds and hail. The irradiated cliffs of the impact crater were continuing to collapse into the continent-sized hole. The cities were mangled, pinned and crushed like passengers in a wrecked vehicle, leaking life and heat, bleeding power.

The forces of the Quietude had nowhere left to run, so they were fighting to the last.

Tra formed the strategic spearhead of the Imperial assault. Imperial Army hosts, now equipped for chemical war and hazard environs, followed their lead.

The accounts that puzzled Hawser were strange fragments reporting almost pernicious brutality. The Wolves seemed eager to record moments that did not portray them as heroic or daring or even lucky; they seemed almost gleeful about scraps that illuminated nothing but atrocity.

They were non-stories, with no point, no beginning, middle and end. They were not cause and effect. They were simply descriptions of murder and dismemberment committed on Quietude combatants.

Hawser wondered if he was supposed to weave some kind of narrative thread around these anecdotes, to sew them into a context that might make them more heroic and dramatic. He wondered if he had misunderstood something, something cultural that even the processes nanotically wired into his brain had not been able to translate.

Then he recalled the assault on the graving dock, and the episode when Bear and Orcir had finally dislodged

the crew of robusts who had earlier vaporised Hjad on
the underspace slope. He recalled the grisly ritual
slaughter that had followed.

They are chasing out the maleficarum, Ogvai had said.
*They are casting it out. They are hurting it so badly it will
know not to come back. They are punishing it, and explaining pain to it, so it will not be eager to return and bother us.*

These accounts, Hawser decided, were the same thing,
marks of aversion in word form. They were designed to
scare the maleficarum.

So what scares the Wolves, he wondered?

'You LOOK DISCOMFORTED,' remarked Ulvurul Heoroth.
Heoroth, called Longfang, was Tra's rune priest, a man
far older than Ohthere Wyrdmake. Like Ogvai and
many of Tra, he had a skin like ice, but it did not glow
with inner light like a glacier, the way that Ogvai's flesh
did. It was glassy and dark, like the half-translucent
plate of ice on a midwinter lake.

His skin was not the only evidence that he was old.
He was lean and bony, and his long hair was thin and
white. He appeared hunched and sclerotic in his runic
armour. Age had not afflicted him the way it had altered
other senior Wolves. It had bleached him and wizened
him, and grown out his canines into the teeth that had
given him his war-name. Some said there would be
other longfangs one day, if any of the Rout lived long
enough. Wyrd alone had kept Heoroth Longfang's
thread uncut. He was as old as it was possible for a Wolf
to be, the oldest of the last few Sixth Legion Astartes
who had been created on Terra and shipped to Fenris as
the foundation of the Wolf King's retinue.

The warship's massive embarkation deck, a long
gallery with Stormbirds racked laterally from overhead
rails ready for launch, was quieter than it had been at
the moment of impact. The priest was kneeling, like a

crusader knight of Old Terra at a Cruxian shrine, looking up at the repeater screens. The two packs he was
about to lead surfacewards in support of Ogvai were
preparing nearby. Hawser could hear the shrill buzz of
fitter drills screwing armour into place. He could hear
the hiss of hydraulics and the whirr of lifter gear. Fifty
metres away from him, along the main plain of the
deck, a circle of Wolves gathered to kneel around their
squad leader and take their pledge, the signifier known
to other Legions Astartes as the *oath of moment*.

'What are you doing?' Hawser asked the rune priest. It
was a blunt question, but he asked it anyway. Though
he had spent more time with Tra than with any other
portion of the Sixth Legion Astartes, he had exchanged
almost nothing with the saturnine priest. Longfang had
never given him a story to keep safe, nor offered comment on any account Hawser had delivered in his
capacity as skjald. Longfang was also far less approach-
able than Wyrdmake, though even Wyrdmake was a
chilling prospect.

Seeing Longfang alone for a moment, Hawser had
taken his chance. Longfang had not needed to look
around to know Hawser was behind him or, it seemed,
what expression was on Hawser's face.

The repeater screen showed the Quietude home world
from high above: the hard clarity of space, the brilliance
of direct sunlight. The world looked like an orange that
had had a red-hot poker rammed into its upper hemisphere.

No, it looked like a radapple, one of the late crop, fat
and russet pink, but marred with a huge, rusty blemish
of rot.

Longfang continued to stare at the screen.

'I'm listening,' he said.

'To?'

'The snapping of threads. The shaping of wyrd.'

'You're not watching, then?'

'Only the reflection of your face in the screen,' said Longfang.

Hawser snorted a small laugh at his own foolishness. The Wolves liked to wrap themselves in a cloak of mystery and solemn, supernatural power, but such nonsense was the superstitious talk of barbarians, inherited from the Fenrisians they drew their strength from. The truly abnormal thing about the Wolves was the sharpness of their perception. They had taught themselves to notice everything about their surroundings, and to use every scrap of information at their disposal. Their reputation helped. No one expected brutes who looked like ritual-obsessed, bestial clansmen to be underpinned by peerless combat intelligence.

It was what made them such efficient weapons.

'So why is there unhappiness in your visage?' Longfang asked.

'I am still uncertain of my place among you. Of my purpose.'

Longfang tutted.

'First, it is every man's lot to wonder at his own nature. That is life. To wonder at your own wyrd, that is the eternal state of contemplation for most men. You're not alone.'

'And second?' asked Hawser.

'It puzzles me, Kasper-Ansbach-Hawser-who-is-Ahmad-Ibn-Rustah-who-is-skjald-of-Tra, that you do not know yourself when, quite plainly, there are so many of you to know. It puzzles me that you chose to come to the Allwinter World, yet cannot account for that choice. Why did you come to Fenris?'

'I'd spent my whole life learning,' said Hawser. 'Gathering data, collecting it, preserving it. Always my motive had been the betterment of mankind. I reached a place where I felt that my life of effort was being... squandered. Passed over as insignificant.'

'Your pride was wounded?'

'No! No, nothing like that. It wasn't personal. The things I had cared enough about to conserve were just being forgotten. They weren't being put to use.'

Heoroth Longfang made a small movement deep inside his etched, bead-draped carapace that may or may not have been a shrug.

'Whatever the truth of that, it still does not explain Fenris.'

'When my life's work seemed to be stagnated,' said Hawser, 'I felt I should make one last voyage, broader and bolder than any I had made before, and close with some truth, some reality, greater than any I experienced in my career. Instead of probing mysteries of the distant past, I fancied to investigate curiosities of a more modern vintage. The Legions Astartes. Each one bound up in its own coat of mysteries, each one wrapped in its own trappings of ritual and lore. Mankind trusts his future to the diligent service of the Legions, yet does not know them. I thought I would choose a Legion, and go to them, and learn of them.'

'An ambitious thought.'

'Perhaps,' Hawser admitted.

'A dangerous one. No Legion makes its stronghold a welcoming place.'

'True.'

'So there was an element of bravado? Of risk taking? You would end your career with one last, bold flourish that would seal your reputation as an academic and repair your damaged pride?'

'That's not what I meant,' said Hawser sourly.

'No?'

'No.'

Longfang fixed his eyes on Hawser. The vox-feed built

into the helmet seal of his collar warbled and chittered. Longfang ignored it.

'I see anger in your face, though,' the priest said. 'I think I've come closer to the truth than you have so far. You still haven't really answered. Why Fenris? Why not another Legion-world? Why not a safer one?'

'I don't know.'

'Don't you?'

Hawser couldn't answer, but he had a nagging feeling he should have been able to.

He said, 'I was told it was good to face your fears. I have always been afraid of wolves. Always. Since childhood.'

'But there are no wolves on Fenris,' Longfang replied.

The priest moved to rise from his kneeling position. He seemed to struggle, like a weary, arthritic old man. Forgetting himself, Hawser stuck out his hand to offer support.

Longfang looked at the proffered hand as if it was a stick that had been used to scrape a midden hole. Hawser feared the priest might lunge forwards and snap it off with a single, furious bite, but he was too frozen to withdraw the offer.

Instead, grinning, Longfang closed his massive, plasteel gauntlet around Hawser's hand and accepted the support. He rose. Hawser meshed his teeth and let out a little squeak of effort as he fought not to collapse beneath the weight the huge rune priest leant on him.

Upright, Longfang towered over him. He let go of the skjald's hand and looked down at him.

'I'm grateful. My joints are old, and my bones are as cold as dead fish trapped in lake ice.'

He shuffled away towards the waiting packs, his wild, thin hair catching the light of the deck lamps like thistledown. Hawser rubbed his numb hand.

'You're leading a drop now?' Hawser called out after him. 'To the surface? A combat drop?'

'Yes. You should come.'

Hawser blinked.

'I'm allowed to come?'

'Go where you like,' said Longfang.

'Three weeks I've been on this ship, getting accounts of this war second-hand,' said Hawser, trying not to sound peevish. 'I thought I had to ask permission. I thought I had to wait until I was permitted or invited.'

'No, go where you like,' said Longfang. 'You're a skjald. That's the one great privilege and right of being what you are. No one in the Rout can bar you, or keep you at bay, or stop you from sticking your nose in.'

'I thought I had to be protected.'

'We'll protect you.'

'I thought I'd get in the way,' said Hawser.

'We'll worry about that.'

'So I can go anywhere? I can choose what I see?'

'Yes, yes.'

'Why did no one think to tell me that?' Hawser asked.

'Did you think to ask?' replied the priest.

'This is the logic of the *Vlka Fenryka*?' Hawser said.

'Yes. Catches in your flesh like a fish-hook, doesn't it?' replied the priest.

⚜

THE PACKS LONGFANG was leading down were not familiar to Hawser. He knew just a few of the warriors by name and reputation.

Their blood was up, but they seemed subdued. There had been a tone of this in the air for days. As the Stormbirds made their long, silent dive from the strike ship, Hawser strapped in beside Longfang.

'You said I looked discomforted, but there is a grim look in these eyes,' Hawser said.

'All of Tra wants to be away from here,' said Longfang. 'The glory's gone from this war.'

'Gone to Ullanor,' said a Wolf strapped into the row of arrestor cradles facing them. *Svessl*. Hawser attached a name.

'What's Ullanor?' Hawser asked.

'Where, you mean,' replied another Wolf, Emrah.

'Where is it?'

'A mighty victory,' said Svessl. 'Ten months ago, but word has just reached us. The Allfather made a mighty slaughter of the greenskins, laid them out on the red ground. Then he sank his sword tip into the soil and announced he was done.'

'Done?' asked Hawser. 'What do you mean? Are you talking about the Emperor?'

'He's done with the Crusade,' said Emrah. 'He's returning to Terra. He's left His anointed successor to continue the war in His absence.'

Longfang turned to look at Hawser. His eyes were hooded and dark, like lightless pools.

'Horus is chosen as Warmaster. We enter a new age. Perhaps the Crusade is nearing an end, and we will be put aside to let our teeth grow blunt.'

'I doubt that,' said Hawser.

'Ullanor was a great war,' said Longfang. 'The greatest of all, the culmination of decades of campaigning against the greenskins. The Rout had heard of it, and hoped that we would be able to stand with the Allfather when the culmination of the struggle came. But we were denied that honour. The Wolves of Fenris were too busy on other errands, fighting dirty fights no one else wanted to fight in other corners of the galaxy.'

'Fights like this one?' asked Hawser.

The Wolves nodded. There were several growls.

'No thanks we'll get for this,' said Longfang.

THE BITTER TRUTH had emerged later, after Ogvai had been granted theatre command, after the commander of the Expedition had agreed to let the iron priests blast the graving dock out of orbit, after it had impacted. The Instrument cradled within the graving dock's girder-work embrace was not the kill vehicle feared by the expedition's threat assessors.

After Tra had seized the facility, the Mechanicum had begun to examine it, especially the control centre area so scrupulously spared by Fultag's assault. The implications of that examination only became clear once the graving dock, at the Expedition commander's pleasure, had been used as a giant wrecking ball.

The Instrument was a data conveyor. The Olamic Quietude had been in the process of loading it with the sum total of its thinking, its artistry, its knowledge and its secrets. The intention was presumably to launch it, either as a bottle upon the ocean in the hope of some salvation, or towards some distant, unknown and unknowable outpost of the Quietude network.

Knowing what had been lost and, perhaps, understanding how that would reflect upon him in the eyes of men even more senior than himself, the commander of the Expedition Fleet flew into a recriminatory rage. He blamed poor intelligence. He blamed the slow function of the Mechanicum. He blamed factionalism in the Imperial Army. Most of all, he blamed the Astartes.

Ogvai was on the surface by that time, leading things, at the bloody end of the matter. When he heard of the commander's wrath, he transmitted a brief vox-statement, reminding the commander and the senior fleet officers that they had insisted he solve their problem and break the deadlock, and had approved his use of all resources. They had given him theatre command. As was ever the case, the Astartes had not made a mistake. They had simply done what was asked of them.

Once the message was transmitted, Ogvai vented the

spirit of his real responses on the warriors of the Quietude.

✧

THE STORMBIRD FELL as a bad star falls.

Hawser had dropped to the surface with Tra before,
but this time it was the suicidal plunge of a combat run.
Inertially locked straps and an arrestor cage kept him
stuck to the seating rig. The graduated compression pro-
vided by the tight bodyglove he was wearing as a base
for his lightweight environment armour kept the lym-
phatic and venous systems of his limbs functioning. His
heart banged like an x-ray star. His teeth chattered.

'What story will you tell about this?' Svessl asked, seeing his fear and enjoying it.

'Not many hearth stories to tell about soiling yourself,' said Emrah. Wolves laughed.

'What angered you the most?' Hawser asked, as loudly
as he could, to any who would listen.

'What?' asked Emrah. Others turned to look his way.
Full helms and knotwork leather masks glared at him.

'I said what pissed you off the most, Wolves of Tra?'
Hawser asked, raising his voice above the howl of the
engines and the judder of the airframe. 'Was it that you
missed the fight at Ullanor? The glory? Or was it that
our Allfather chose Horus as Warmaster, not the Wolf
King?'

They may kill me, thought Hawser, but at least the
process will take my mind off this hellish descent.
Besides, what better time to ask a pack of Wolves an
awkward question than when they are all lashed into
arrestor cages?

'Neither,' said Emrah.

'Neither,' agreed another Wolf, a red-haired monster
called Horune.

'We would have liked a taste of the glory,' said Svessl,
'to stand up in a great war and be counted.'

'Ullanor was no greater than a hundred campaigns of the last decade,' Longfang reminded the warrior.

'But it's the one where the Allfather laid down His sword and said His Crusade was done,' Svessl replied. 'It's the one that will be remembered.'

And that's what counts to you, thought Hawser.

'And the Wolf King would never have been named Warmaster,' said Emrah.

'Why?' asked Hawser.

'Because that was never his wyrd,' said Longfang. 'The Wolf King was not made to be Warmaster. It's not a slight. He hasn't been passed over. The Allfather has not played favourite with Horus Lupercal.'

'Explain,' said Hawser.

'When the Allfather sired His pups,' said the priest, 'He gave each one of them a different wyrd. Each one has a different life to make. One to be the heir to the Emperor's throne. One to fortify the defences of the Imperium. One to guard the hearth. One to watch the distant perimeter. One to command the armies. One to control intelligences. You see, skjald? You see how simple it is?'

Hawser tried to make his nodded reply obvious through the vibration shaking him.

'So what is the Wolf King's wyrd, Heoroth Longfang?' he asked. 'What life did the Allfather choose for him?'

'Executioner,' replied the old Wolf.

The Wolves were quiet for a moment. The Stormbird continued to shiver with intense violence. The engines had reached a strangled pitch that Hawser hadn't believed possible.

'What pisses us off,' said Emrah suddenly, 'is that we weren't present at the Great Triumph.'

'They say it was a fine sight,' said Horune, 'a whole world laid bare to salute Horus's ascendancy.'

'We would have liked to gather there,' said Longfang,

'shoulder to shoulder with brother Astartes, in numbers not seen since the start of the Crusade.'

'Shoulder to shoulder with Wolf companies we haven't seen for decades,' added Svessl.

'We would have liked to raise our voices and join the roar,' said Emrah. 'We would have liked to shake our fists at the sky, and show our proud allegiance to the new Warmaster.'

'*That's* what's pissing us off,' said Svessl.

'That, and you reminding us about it,' said Horune.

THE STORMBIRDS PUNCHED through the dense impact pall, poisonous vapour slipstreaming off their sleek wings and spiralling in the thunderclaps of their wakes like ink in fast water. Under the clouds, a nightmare rim of firestorms burned around the titanic entry wound. It was a kill-shot that had taken out a planet. The depth of the wound was astonishing. It did not look geological to Hawser. It looked as anatomical as the analogies filling his imagination. An exposed, surgical void of pulverised organs, muscles and bones, all tinted orange, all partially blackened as if blown out by a penetrating incendiary round.

Slower-moving Imperial Army dropships, vessels of much mightier draughts, were descending into the scalding pit. The Stormbirds streaked past them, and outpaced their Thunderhawk and gun-cutter escorts. The Astartes craft, in tight formation, passed below the level of the pit's burning lip and knifed into the sub-glacial void, down through smoke, through burning air, through the shattered ruins of the Quietude cities.

The cities ran deep. Hawser was astonished to glimpse the complex, interlocking layers of them, rising up like cyclopean towers from profound geological foundations. He was also stunned by the degree of destruction. Upper levels had all been vaporised, and below that, the

municipal stages and sections had been crushed down
into one another. Tower structures had collapsed and
pancaked into themselves, held in place only by the
remaining mantle of super-thick ice that acted like a setting resin around the delicate, shattered wreckage.
Hawser was reminded of the way Rector Uwe had
always folded almonds and pecan nuts in a white nap-
kin after supper, before striking the parcel with the back
of a spoon. The debris would have flown everywhere
but for that enveloping medium.

The ship's thrusters were suddenly making an entirely
different type of anguished scream.

'Ten more seconds!' Longfang yelled. The Wolves
began to beat their swords and axes against their storm
shields.

A savage change of momentum hammered Hawser's
innards. The bird had just used the bottom of its pow-
erdive and ferocious upturn to dump colossal amounts
of speed. Before he could adjust, the most violent
impact of all occurred. They just fell. They fell hard into
something with a noise like the steel gates of the Imperial Palace falling off their hinges.

They'd landed. They *had* landed, hadn't they? Hawser
couldn't be sure. They looked to be moving still, but
that could simply have been his head and his bewildered senses. There was a shrieking noise from outside,
metal-on-metal. The Wolves were slamming aside their
arrestor cages and leaping up.

'On! On!' Longfang yelled. Hawser realised they'd all
been speaking Wurgen for the last ten minutes.

The boarding ramp was opening. Light flooded into
the green twilight gloom of the drop cabin. Heat came
with it, roasting, fireball heat that Hawser could feel
sucking into his lungs down the chimney of his throat
like a backdraught, despite his armoured breather
mask.

'Great Terra!' he coughed.

The metal-on-metal squealing from outside was getting louder. They *were* moving. They were juddering and moving backwards.

The whole Stormbird was sliding.

Fleeting, jerking silhouettes loomed across the fire-bright gap of the open ramp in front of him. The Wolves, deploying. He could hear them howling.

No, it wasn't howling. It was the wet leopard-growl, amplified: the resonating, deep-chest purr of a megafauna predator. It was a paralysing, infrasonic panther-snarl throbbing and then surging up from the specially adapted larynxes of apex carnivores.

He followed them out into the light and the searing heat. Some of them brushed against him as they charged out down the ramp, knocking him aside, spinning him. He had no idea what he should be doing. A giant plasteel hand grabbed him by the scruff of his suit and his feet dangled off the ramp for a second.

'Stay with me!' Longfang growled in Wurgen.

Hawser followed the old priest as he lumbered forwards. He focussed in on the details of Longfang's armour, as he had done when instructed to follow Bear. Bear's armour had been simple compared to Longfang's, but then Bear was an ill-tempered youngster beside the veteran priest. His grey armour had been more modestly adorned and decorated.

Longfang's case of armour was old, a work of art that owed its richness to both the armourer and the etcher. It was covered in runic symbols, some of which had been picked out in brass, or gold leaf, or glossy red enamel. Apotropaic eyes had been scratched, emphatically, into the shoulder guards. Besides the huge, gossamer-white pelt, Longfang was draped with skeins of beads, strings of charms, small trophies, and clattering amulets.

They came out from under the Stormbird's shadow into the glare of a chemical firestorm. The Stormbirds had set down on a series of ornate platforms extending from monumental, fluted towers half encased in the surrounding ice-mantle. Great portions of the towers and their more massive neighbouring structures were ablaze. The wall of heat was oppressive. Light-rich flames boiled and tumbled up the ice chasm towards the top of the pit, drawn as if up a flue. Frequently oxygenated by sources Hawser couldn't identify, the firestorms swelled and flared, rushing white-hot and spitting out clouds of molten sparks and incendiary cinders that blizzarded into the depths below. Hawser realised some of the vertical firestorms were bigger than cities he had spent whole chunks of his life living in. His mind could barely cope with the scale. He found himself focussing on single sparks, drifting silently in the air in front of him, as large close up as the firestorms were far away. To hold focus on a single, drifting spark was to hold on to a precious moment of sane tranquillity.

The air was full of sparks. There was also a strange smell, more than decay and burning. It was the smell of some synthetic substance that should never have been exposed to heat.

Portions of the pit's upright city were collapsing into the yawning gulf below. Wars were happening on different levels. Hawser could see Imperial Army troops drop-landing on platforms above him, lit up by enemy fire as they swung in towards leaf-shaped platforms. To the west of his position, and slightly below, a tide of Expedition drop-troops assaulted across the spans of three or four intact inter-tower bridges, as gun-cutters and blitz ships swept in over them and raked the facades of the ancient citadels.

Longfang's packs were driving in across the ornate

platforms towards imposing, sullen mansions. The polished, orange material tiling the mansions and the platform surface was pitted and scorched. Everything was orange. The world was orange. It was partly the firestorm, and partly the ubiquitous material that the Quietude constructed everything from.

Again, for a split-second pang, Hawser was reminded of Vasiliy. To think she was a world and a life ago now was not even ironic.

Debris, including chunks of fallen masonry of considerable size, landscaped the platform. What had this place once been, Hawser wondered as he ran forwards through the murderous heat and the winnowing sparks. The landing stage of a parliament hall? The platform of a defence station? The private jetty of an aristocratic residence? Did the residents once look out over the platform and admire the view of the glowing ice caves beneath, or was it just a functional cavity to them? Had there been beauty here, before Ogvai's kill-shot? Deliberate beauty, or just the accidental marvel of the nature that only human eyes recognised? Did the beings of the Quietude have souls?

He fancied perhaps they did. The platforms had ornate decorations worked into them, especially on their undersides, where they fanned out like ribbed lilies or acanthus leaves. Similarly, around the high, wide door spaces and side columns of the mansions they were attacking, there were simple lines of relief that suggested an aesthetic.

Enemy fire licked at them, most of it gravity rifle shot that pulverised the platform surfaces into dust where it hit. He heard the unmistakable sound of bolters firing and saw Horune and the others ahead, bounding away across the tumbled slabs and crushed stonework. He made a mental note to improve his next story; he had no idea an Astartes could move so fast.

The metal-on-metal shriek came again. He turned.

The Stormbird that had brought them in was sliding backwards. Unlike the other Stormbirds in Longfang's flight, which had touched down securely on other landing levels and were already cycling back up for take-off, this craft had been forced to use the lip of its target platform by an overhead collapse. That it had landed at all was a testament to the devotion of the flight crew.

The weakened platform was shredding. The rear half of the Stormbird's bulk was tipping off. The metal-on-metal shriek was the sound of the Stormbird's landing claws as they tried to dig in and anchor on. The skids tore squealing gashes as they slipped backwards. The pilot was trying to fire mooring lines from under the nose. Each grapple rebounded from the polished orange tiles.

A Stormbird was a large transatmospheric craft with a broad, threatening profile designed to menace. It was considerably more substantial in both mass and sheer craftsmanship than the bulk-produced landers like the Thunderhawk and the dropfalcon models that had been churned out of constructor factories as short-term, utilitarian solutions to the Crusade's material demands. A Thunderhawk wasn't designed to last: it was just a cheap, functional, template-pressed disposable.

The Stormbirds were legacies of the Unification Wars on Terra, superb machines that were far more costly and time consuming to manufacture. Armadas of them were assembled for the Expansion, and only when the true scale of the Great Crusade became apparent was it realised that a cheap bulk supplement would be needed. They were not the sort of things that should look vulnerable or ungainly. They were lords of the air, soaring creatures that could dive from orbit straight down into the fires of hell, and survive.

Yet this one was stricken. It was doomed. Its

backwards slide was accelerating. Its nose was tipping
up, and the angle of that inclination was increasing.
Metal shrieked on metal until the landing claws began
to tear free, lifted too high by the dipping tail. Hawser
could clearly see the frantic, chalk-white faces of the
flight crew through the tinted cockpit canopy as they
fought to stabilise their situation. The engines suddenly
started racing, and hurricanes of loose debris and grit
swirled into the intakes as someone tried to throttle up
and... what? Push the ship back onto the platform?
Relaunch?

The Stormbird tipped. Hawser saw it pass the point of
no return. The boarding ramp was still down, and it
looked for all the world like an open beak, like the ship
was a fledgling bird, too damaged to fly, squawking in
terror as it pitched from a nest.

With a sudden, jarring lurch, it was gone, and the
shredded lip of the platform was gone too. Hawser felt
the deck quiver as the Stormbird let go.

He mumbled something, something obscene and
incoherent, unwilling to accept what he'd just seen. Part
of his mind told him that the Stormbird would surely
restart its engines as it fell and fly back up to them, magnificent and phoenix-like. Another part told him what a
fool that made him.

He realised Longfang was shouting at him. There was
a far more immediate issue.

The weight of the Stormbird, and the violent way it
had quit its perch, had entirely undermined the
integrity of the damaged platform.

Everything they were standing on was giving way.

He had once witnessed the explosive demolition of a
stratified favela in Sud Merica. The slum hive, cleared of
inhabitants and protesters by the Unification authority,
was a towering ziggurat, a landfill mountain that had
cast its shadow across a river basin for sixty generations.

Hydroelectric projects would replace it and, during that work, Hawser and Murza would be granted access to explore the impossibly ancient foundations for relics of the Proto-Cruxian faith that was said to have persisted there like an isotope in the water table.

The demolition had brought the vast structure down like an avalanche, folding level into level, collapsing storey into storey like riffle-shuffled playing cards. He had been astonished by the seismic violence of the destruction, and by the overwhelming noise. Most of all, he had been staggered by the quantity of dust exhaled by such annihilation.

The platform went the same way. It disintegrated, letting the rubble and massive fragments fallen from the city above slide off into the gulf. Noise was vibration and vibration noise, and there was no division between them, and both of them were a visual blur. Orange tiles and support beams exploded and shattered in clouds of dust like flour.

Hawser ran towards the mansions. His future fell away behind him in the pit in a raging landslip. The ground steepened in front of him, and he realised he was running uphill. An elephantine block of stone, part of some city structure demolished far above, slithered towards him. Its impact had undoubtedly contributed to the platform's fundamental weakness.

As it rushed down at him, he leapt up the face of it, hurling himself before it could turn him into a long red smear. He landed on the top of it, a hard, awkward landing that badly bruised his hip and ankle, but held on, his hands wrapped around the stub of a shattered finial.

The block kept sliding. Righting himself, he leapt again, clearing the slab and coming down on the other side, on the slope of the expiring platform. He scrabbled up, loose rocks pinging off his shoulders and his face mask. One hit so hard it crazed the left-hand eye-piece, and stunned him.

The noise of the tumult reached a peak. Blind, scrambling, he ran into something and found it was a wall.

'Sit down. Sit down!' a voice snarled in Wurgen. 'You're safe there, skjald.'

He could barely see. Most of the platform had gone, leaving a jagged strand of rockcrete stuck through with severed rib beams and shorting power lines. The destruction had exhaled so much dust into the air that there was a strange, farinaceous haze.

Hawser was hunkered right up against the foot of one of the mansion walls, spared from the fathomless drop by a ragged shelf of surviving platform no more than two metres broad at its most generous. Wolves were crouched with him, their pelts and armour dusted with yellow powder.

'Are you alive?' the Wolf beside him asked. Hawser didn't know his name. The Wolf had eschewed his full plate helm for a knotwork leather protector that had entwined furrows in the shape of Fenrisian sea-orms forming the nasal guard and the heavy brows.

'Yes,' said Hawser.

'You sure?' asked Serpent-mask. 'I see fear in that wrong eye of yours, and we don't want fear tripping us up.'

'I'm sure,' Hawser snapped. 'What's your name? I want to make certain my account of this day records your concern for me.'

Serpent-mask shrugged.

'Jormungndr,' he said. 'Called the Two-bladed Serpent. You insult me, skjald, that you haven't heard of the famous Two-blade.'

'I have,' Hawser lied quickly. 'But I have been shaken by that tangle with death, and I was slow to recognise the trait marks on your face guard.'

Jormungndr Two-blade nodded, as if this was accept-
able.

'Follow,' he said.

Svessl had blown a way into the nearest of the structures Hawser thought of as mansions.

They passed through a gatehouse into a courtyard
beyond. In amongst the debris of rubble, he saw the
first of the enemy dead: graciles and robusts, and also
other smaller forms new to him. The pale yellow dust,
sifting in the air, stuck to the spattered pools of purple
Quietude blood.

The Wolves were surging into the courtyard and splitting in all directions. Cloisters and inner entrances
beckoned. Hawser, uncertain which way to go, heard
enemy fire, and then answering blasts of bolter shot.
The gunning bolters, often one at first and then joined
by an emphatic chorus as multiple weapons were
brought to bear on an identified target, had a distinctive
metallic grinding note behind their deep shot-boom,
like a bitter aftertaste.

He could hear other sounds, deeper, bigger sounds.
They were the vast, echoing, booming noises of the
unstable cities, creaking and swaying, uttering their
slow and monumental death knell out across the
immense gulf of the impact pit.

Hawser found himself walking slowly through the
mansion zone, crossing from courtyard into cloister and
back again. He felt immune to the battle that rang
around him, incidental, close by, but not near enough
to trouble him. Sparks sailed like stars through the
dusty air. He stepped from the shadows of the covered
walkways into the bright orange glare of the open
courts, where the light of firestorms cast shadows of
him, long and lean across the tiled ground.

He looked at his shadow, so distorted and extended,
so longshanked and shifting in the flamelight. The pelt

Bitur Bercaw had given him on the night he awakened
in the Aett was still around his shoulders. He wore it at
all times. The grey wolf pelt lent his spectral shadow a
strangely hunched neck and shaggy back.

Much of the mansion complex's infrastructure had
been ripped out. He saw walls and ceilings where flush,
polished panels had been torn out, revealing curiously
organic layers of machinery. The purpose of the sub-
layer systems was not apparent. They seemed to be
complex arrangements, patterns that were both circuits
and organic valves, power cables and blood vessels
intertwined. Smouldering energy fumes wept out of
torn and dangling tubes. Unidentifiable fluids dribbled
from ruptured ducts.

He looked around. He looked up. The spavined city
rose above him as if it was trying to claw its way out of
its icy grave. Tracers of weapons fire, like bright lattices,
criss-crossed the smoke-streaked air. Heavy weapon
beams scored destructive lines several kilometres long
across the darkness of the pit, projected by assault craft
on attack runs. Where they touched, the city structures
dissolved in walls of light and threw out arches of burning gas like solar flares. Flurries of missiles, visible from
their exhaust flares alone, raced like schools of comets,
spat out by gunships too dark to be seen in the smoke.
At roof-level, to his left, two distant Warlord Titans were
leading the Army in towards a bastion gate across a
horizon formed by an inter-tower bridge. Clouds of tiny
munition impacts billowed around their inexorable figures like fireflies at dusk.

He heard the deep, booming, background instability
of the cities again. It sounded like a bell tolling in the
core of the planet.

A sharper sound made him start. Concussion slapped
him. Directly overhead, a formation of bulk landers was
attempting to deliver platoons of Outremars onto

upper platforms that jutted out like theatre balconies.
One had been hit by ground fire. It had exploded in a
staggering welter of flame and whizzing debris. The landers in formation with it attempted to steer out of the
blast wash. One clipped another and they both had to
pull off the drop target hard, engines protesting. A third
was struck soundly along its flank by projectile debris
from the lost unit. It shivered, mortally wounded. Black
smoke began to gout from its port-side engines. It tried
to get nose-up. It tried to get close enough to the platform to drop its ramp and let its cargo of soldiers
deploy.

It hit the platform instead. The planing impact tore
the underside away, peeling it off like the lid of a tin
can. As the main hull began to disintegrate and the four
engines exploded in a quick, fiery series, it began to rain
bodies.

The Outremar troopers spilled by the wreck fell on
the mansion complex, helpless, tumbling, flailing.
Some were already dead. Some were still screaming
when they made impact. They hit roofs, terraces, the
canopies of cloisters, the open tiles of the courtyards.
They glanced off sloping walls and made multiple further impacts before rolling to a halt. Burning debris
rained down with them. Some of the bodies were on
fire, or partially dismembered. Some struck with such
force, blood spatter went five or six metres up the face
of walls. Others landed whole and lay as if asleep.

Staring up, mesmerised by the human hail, it took
Hawser a moment to register that there was every possibility he might be struck by some of the falling bodies.
One came rushing down at him and he flinched to his
left. It hit the tiled courtyard ground with a noise like
smashing eggs and snapping celery. He looked down at
the anatomically impossible position it had chosen to
rest in for the remainder of eternity.

Another body impacted a few metres to his right like a bag of blood bursting. Hawser backed away. He looked up again in time to see a whirling piece of burning machine debris dropping towards him, end over end.

He ran. He made it to the cover of the nearest cloistered area as the wreckage struck. Then a human body smacked into the awning roof above him, splitting as it shattered orange tiles and produced a vile trickle of blood that pattered down onto the ground. He ran again, and sought greater sanctuary in the more substantial archway of the mansion proper.

He cowered briefly. The terrible downpour of bodies subsided. He looked up and took a step out of the shadowed archway.

A Quietude super-robust lunged at him. The towering beast had two heads and three surviving upper limbs. Something akin to a plasma beam had blown the other one off. The face-plates of its heads displayed hologram masks of psychopathic rage. It was wielding two large, hook-bladed weapons like tulwars with its upper limbs. It sliced at Hawser.

Hawser wasn't sure how he moved out of its path. He threw himself away from it and hit the tiled ground of the courtyard several metres back from the archway, landing in a clumsy and painful tumble. The superrobust came after him, slicing with one blade, then the next. The tip of one hooked blade struck sparks off the tiles. It reached out with its third limb to seize him so it could pin him and butcher him.

He evaded again, this time more aware of what he was doing, of how superhumanly fast his reactions were, how ridiculously instinctive. The wolf priests, geneweavers and fleshmakers of the *Vlka Fenryka*, had done so much more than repair his wounds and shave years off his life. They had given him so much more than the enhanced vision of a wolf.

They had accelerated him, his senses, his speed, his strength, his muscle power, his bone density. Even without any combat training, he had snapped the limbs of the G9K malcontents who had outnumbered him.

Nevertheless, a super-robust of the Olamic Quietude, spiking on battle-stimms, would kill him easily.

He ducked a lateral sweep, and then rolled to avoid a downward slash. The super-robust kept coming, kept swinging. Hawser slipped in a pool of Outremar blood, and lost his footing.

Longfang slammed into the super-robust from behind. The priest had appeared without warning, moving like a phantom. There was no hint of infirmity about him, no creak of age. His eyes were bright and wild, and his long white hair flew out like a mane. This was not a man who needed the hand of another to help him get up off his knees.

Longfang expertly hooked his arms around the super-robust from behind in a grip that resembled a wrestling hold. He lifted the enemy warrior away from Hawser while keeping its limbs locked so it could not strike with either tulwar. Longtooth grunted with the effort. Having turned it aside, he sent the super-robust staggering forwards with a serious kick to the arse to create some safety distance, and drew his sword, a huge broad blade that slept in a knotwork scabbard across his back. It had a two-handed grip, and a runic blade that glowed like frost. As soon as it was drawn, it began to keen, a weird song only wights or the soulless could sing. Power crackled and hissed through its fierce edge.

The super-robust turned around and strode back to face and kill the interloper who had interrupted its attack. It seemed undaunted by the searing glimmer of the glacial blade that was whispering a death-lament for it. It flung itself forwards with its powerful upper limbs raised, raining alternating downstrokes with its tulwars.

Longfang grunted, reacted, let his long blade and the
armour of his left forearm soak up the multiple
impacts. The super-robust was as strong as a template
construction press. Hawser saw that the old priest had
to plant one foot back to brace against the assault.

With a growl-bark, Longfang put a full body spin and
the weight of his shoulders into the answering stroke.
The blow sliced the third limb clean off the Quietude
warrior's torso. It staggered back, but it felt no pain. It
resumed its drive at Longfang, chopping down alternating blows again. This time it had effect. The hybrid alloy
of one of the tulwars smote through the forearm guard
of the rune priest's intricate armour. Leather bindings
split, and snake-stones, bezoars, sea-shells and beads
made of nacre scattered across the courtyard tiles. Blood
gushed out, down to the cuff, dripping off the ridges of
the huge gauntlet.

Longfang let out a wet leopard-growl that palpitated
Hawser's guts. He hacked at the super-robust with his
frostblade, driving it backwards across the blood-
stained, fire-lit yard. The last blow in the savage series
cracked the top fifteen centimetres off the left hand tulwar and stove a deep crack across the super-robust's
barrel chest.

At that point, two more super-robusts bounded into
the courtyard. The first, armed with an accelerator hammer, went immediately to reinforce the unit fighting
Longfang. The second, its hologrammatic face express-
ing first curiosity and then undisguised antipathy,
turned for Hawser.

Heoroth Longfang had no intention of breaking the
skjald-bond. He had told Hawser to go where he liked
because he would be protected by Tra, and that was a
compact he intended to honour, or forfeit with his life.
A long and, for the most part, secret heritage of genetic
engineering had culminated in the ability of Imperial

Terra to manufacture hyper-organisms like him. He leapt with all the agility and power that heritage had provided him with, not as a man leaps to jump an obstacle, but as an animal pounces to bring down its prey. He left his immediate adversaries standing, almost awkwardly, suddenly devoid of a combat opponent.

He landed behind the super-robust rushing Hawser, and saved the skjald's life for the second time in ninety seconds. The hissing frostblade went up over his white-haired head in a two-handed grip, and then came down in a single, splitting blow of extraordinary force that sheared the super-robust's torso medially. The sectioned halves parted in an explosive cloud of purple bio-fluid liberated by the rupture, and fell heavily in opposite directions.

There were beads of glittering purple blood in Long-fang's fine white hair. He looked at Hawser with his tired gold and black-pinned eyes. He knew what was coming.

'Find cover,' he said.

Shock took him away. There was a bang like a sonic boom. Heoroth Longfang was simply removed, side-ways, from Hawser's field of vision.

Hawser reeled from the concussive blow, stunned, dazed, his breather mask cracking, his nose filling with blood from vessels burst by the over-pressure. The super-robust's accelerator hammer had buried itself in Longfang's left side and hurled him clean across the courtyard. The priest hit a wall, cracking the tiles, and landed on the ground.

Both super-robusts hastened to finish him as he tried to rise. Blood was leaking out of Longfang, from his lips, from the waist-joint and hip seals of his runic armour.

As the Quietude brutes closed in, Longfang raised his hand, as if he could fend them off with force of will

alone, as if he could unleash magic, or even maleficarum, under such a miserable duress. For a moment,
Hawser almost believed he could. He almost believed
the wights of the Underverse might come howling
down like an ice storm in response to Longfang's furious will.

Nothing happened. No magic, no ice storm, no
maleficarum. No wights from the Underverse wailing
with rapturous glee.

Hawser snatched up a blood-flecked Outremar lasri-
fle, yanking the weapon's strap free of its previous
owner's broken arm. The rifle had fallen out of the sky,
but its mechanism was intact. He opened fire, raking
the two super-robusts. His shots struck their backs and
shoulders, denting the plasticated finish of their
armour, scoring little holes and blemishes. The super-
robust with the accelerator hammer even took a shot in
the back of the head, causing its neck to whiplash
slightly.

Both stopped, and turned slowly, smoke wisping
from the superficial damage.

'Tra! Tra! Help here! Help here!' Hawser yelled, in
Wurgen. He started firing again, unloading the entire
energy clip at the super-robusts. They paced towards
him, and the paces became faster and turned into running strides. The hammer and the tulwars were lifted up
to strike. Hawser backed away, blasting, yelling.

Jormungndr Two-blade entered the courtyard. He
came in over one of the cloister roofs where Outremar
bodies had collected like autumn leaves. True to his
name, he had a blade in each hand, a matched pair of
power swords, shorter and broader than Longfang's
hissing frostblade.

He uttered the loudest roar of all, and landed hard on
the tiles in front of the charging super-robusts. The
impact made a sound like a dropped anvil, and pavers

cracked under him. He met their united attack aggressively, hammering aside the super-robust with the tulwars with his right blade, and then blocking the hammer with his left.

The super-robust with the tulwars re-joined without hesitation, hacking at him. Two-blade blocked and parried with matching speed, allowing neither of the tulwars to slip past his guard. Simultaneously, his left-hand weapon fended away the follow-up swing from the super-robust with the hammer.

Now that one of the tulwars had lost a section in the clash with Longfang, the mis-matched lengths played to the super-robust's advantage. As his left-hand sword was occupied with the other opponent, Two-blade found it supremely difficult to counter the rain of blows from the twin swords unless he managed to catch both down near the hilt. Twice, the broken tulwar flew past a parry that had blocked the long hook of its partner and gouged Two-blade. Within a few seconds of the struggle beginning, Two-blade was bleeding from a deep injury in his right arm.

He resolved the problem directly. Ducking a vicious but telegraphed swing from the accelerator hammer, he kicked out at the super-robust with the tulwars, catching it in the left kneecap. The huge plasteel boot delivered a torsion injury that twisted the super-robust off balance, and Two-blade put his right-hand sword through one of its faces.

The super-robust tottered backwards with sparks shorting and spitting from its splintered face mask. Purple gore splashed down its chest from under the mask's rim.

Jormungndr Two-blade did not pause to enjoy the satisfaction of this advantage. He had to jerk his head back hard to avoid the hammer again. The evasion was whisker-close. The hammer-wielder had thrown such bodily force behind the latest blow that the swing had described an almost complete circle. The hammer-head, missing Two-blade on the downward half of the orbit, ended up striking the ground of the yard and creating, with a painful, plosive bang, a radiating crater in the tilework that looked like a bullet hole in a mirror, or the ripple of a stone hitting the surface of still water.

Two-blade struck the super-robust with his left-hand sword. The super-robust deflected the slash with the long haft of its hammer, bringing it up level in front of its face like a stave, before swinging it up higher for another downward, post-setting blow. Two-blade managed to get his swords up and crossed against each other, and caught the neck of the hammer in the V formed by their blades. Even so, the impact drove him down onto one knee.

Straining, Two-blade kept the swords locked. The super-robust with the tulwars was recovering its wits as its secondary head took over its biological operations. It moved in from the side to attack Two-blade while his weapons were occupied.

Two-blade sliced his swords together, uttering a bellow of effort. The swords scissored the neck of the accelerator hammer. The hammer head was not entirely cut off, but the haft just below the head exploded and buckled as the Astartes' blades sliced through grip, trunking, liner and core.

Two-blade came up off his knees and drove in against the super-robust, head-down, stabbing it repeatedly through the torso with murderous, under-arm punches, first with the right sword, then the left, and then alternating, jabbing blow after vicious blow. He drove it backwards, killing it three or four times over to make sure it was dead. By the end, it was only held upright by his blades.

He let it fall. The other one had reached him. He spun to greet its tulwars, and delivered a rotating lateral slash that knocked it flying. It landed on its face, and tried to rise. Two-blade pounced onto its back, held it face-down with his knee, and drove a sword down through it, pinning it to the ground.

Purple liquid began to creep out from under it.

Hawser crossed the yard to where Longfang lay. Two-blade wrenched his sword out of the super-robust's corpse and followed. Two-blade's escalated Astartes metabolism had already kicked in, and his wounds had stopped bleeding.

Heoroth Longfang's wounds had not stopped bleeding. The priest had propped himself against a wall, his legs out straight in front of him. He was breathing hard. Blood was seeping out of far too many of the seams in his armour.

'A fine day for sitting on your arse,' remarked Jormungndr Two-blade.

'I like the weather here,' replied Longfang.

'We'll do all the work, then,' said Two-blade. He was silent for a while, staring down at the old rune priest.

'I'll send Najot Threader back to you, when I find him.'

'Not necessary,' replied Longfang.

'I won't let you go without honour,' said Two-blade. There was a tiny hitch in his voice that surprised Hawser. 'When I find Najot Threader–'

'No,' Longfang replied more emphatically. 'Eager though you are to see me off, I'm not going anywhere. I just need to rest. Enjoy this nice weather for a while.'

Hawser looked at Two-blade, and saw he was smiling a broad smile under his mask that showed his teeth.

'I recognise my failing and will be sure to correct it,' he said.

'There's a good boy,' said Longfang. 'Now go and kill

something. The skjald here can stay and keep me company.'

Two-blade looked at Hawser.

'Amuse him,' he said.

'What?' asked Hawser.

'I said amuse him,' replied Two-blade. 'You're Tra's skjald. Amuse him. Take his mind off what's coming.'

'Why?' asked Hawser. 'What's coming?'

Two-blade snorted.

'What do you think?' he asked.

The big Wolf knelt down quickly, and bowed his head to Longfang.

'Until next winter,' he said.

Longfang nodded back. They clasped fists, and then Two-blade stood and walked away without looking back. His massive plasteel boots crunched on the grit coating the courtyard ground. By the time he was on the far side and vanishing from view, he had accelerated into a run.

Hawser glanced back at Longfang.

'I know it's an indelicate question, but what is coming?' he asked.

Longfang laughed and shook his head.

'You're dying, aren't you?' asked Hawser.

'Maybe. You don't know much about Astartes anatomy. We can shrug off a hell of a lot of damage. But sometimes there's a hell of a lot of pain in that process, and you're never sure if you're going to get there.'

'What should I do?' Hawser asked.

'Your job,' said the priest.

HE SAT DOWN beside the priest.

Longfang's skin looked even more translucent than before. He was speckled with blood, both purple and red, both human and foe. Some of it was drying and streaking.

His respiration was laboured. Something was critically wrong with his lungs. Every breath produced a blood mist.

'So I... I am to amuse you, then?' asked Hawser. 'You want me to recite an account?'

'Why not?'

'You might want to tell me some of yours,' said Hawser. 'You might want to tell me anything that matters to you. In case.'

'You'd be my confessor, would you?' said Longfang.

'That's not what I meant. Aeska Brokenlip told me that the accounts that entertain the Rout most are the ones that scare them.'

'True enough.'

'So what scares you?'

'You want to know?'

'I want to know.'

'What scares us most,' said Heoroth Longfang, 'are the things that even we can't kill.'

EIGHT

Longfang's Dream of Winter

'WE ARE THE Allfather's killers,' said the rune priest.

'You're soldiers,' said Hawser. 'You're Astartes born.
Astartes are the finest warriors Terra has ever manufac-
tured. You're *all* killers.'

Longfang coughed. Blood from the mist he was exhal-
ing was beginning to collect around his mouth and
soak his beard. It dripped onto the gossamer-white pelt
he wore.

'That's too simple a view,' he said. 'I told you this. A
role for each primarch-son. A role for each primarch's
Legion. Defenders and champions, storm troops and
praetorians… we all have our duties. Sixth Legion are
the executioners. We are the last line. When all else fails,
we are the ones expected to do whatever is necessary.'

'Isn't that true of all Legions?' Hawser asked.

'You still don't understand, skjald. I'm talking about
degree. There are lines that other Legions will not cross.
There are divides of honour and fealty and devotion.
There are some acts so ruthless, some deeds so

unpalatable, that only the *Vlka Fenryka* are capable of undertaking them. It's what we were bred for. It's the way we were designed. Without qualm or sentiment, without hesitation or whimsy. We take pride in being the only Astartes who will never, under any circumstances, refuse to strike on the Allfather's behalf, no matter what the target, no matter what the cause.'

'It's why the Sixth Legion Astartes is considered so bestial,' said Hawser.

'That's secondary,' Longfang replied. 'It's a by-product of our ruthlessness. We are not feral savages. It's just that two centuries of doing things that other Legions find distasteful have earned us that reputation. The other Legions think we are untamed, untrained dogs, but the truth is that we are the most harshly trained of all.'

Longfang was about to say something else, but a tremor ran through him. He closed his eyes for a moment.

'Pain?' asked Hawser.

'Nothing,' Longfang replied with a dismissive wave of his right hand. 'It'll pass.'

He wiped the blood from his mouth.

'We are the Allfather's killers,' he repeated. 'It is a matter of honour that we will face anything down. This also may explain why others may regard us as deranged. We deny fear. It plays no part in our lives. Once we deploy, fear is gone from us. It doesn't ride with us. It doesn't stay our hands. We exclude it from our hearts and from our heads.'

'So the stories?' asked Hawser.

'Think of the extremity of our lives,' said Longfang. 'The unremitting punishment of Fenris, the unstinting combat against mankind's foes. Where do we find release from that? Not in the dainty pleasures of mortal men. Not in wine or song, or womenfolk, or banquet feasting.'

'What then?'

'The one thing denied to us.'

'Fear.'

Longfang chuckled, though the chuckle was half-drowned in blood.

'Now you understand. In the Aett, at the hearth-side, when the skjald speaks, then and only then do we allow the fear back. And only if the account is good enough.'

'Letting yourself feel fear? That's your release?'

Longfang nodded.

'So what sort of account? A tale of war, or of hunting an ocean orm and–'

'No, no,' said Longfang. 'Those are things we *can* kill, even if it's hard and we don't succeed every time. There is no fear there. A skjald has to find a story about something we *can't* kill. I told you that. Something that is proof against our blades and our bolts. Something that will not fall down when you strike it with a back-breaker. Something with a thread that cannot be cut.'

'Maleficarum,' said Hawser.

'Maleficarum,' the priest agreed.

He looked at Hawser, and coughed again, aspirating more particles of blood.

'Make it a good one, then,' he said.

'I was born on Terra,' said Hawser.

'Like me,' put in Longfang proudly.

'Like you,' Hawser agreed. He began again. 'I was born on Terra. Old Earth, as it was called in the First Age. Most of my life, I worked as a conservator for the Unification Council. When I was about thirty years old, I was working in Old Franc, in the centre of the great city-node Lutetia. It was ruins, most of it, ruins and sub-hive slums. I had a friend. A colleague, actually. His name was Navid Murza. He's dead now. He died in Ossetia about a decade later. He wasn't a friend at all, really. We were rivals. He was an extremely accomplished academic and very capable, but he was ruthless too. He'd use people. He didn't care who he had to go through to get what he wanted. We worked together because that's how things had turned out. I was always wary of him. He frequently took things too far.'

'Go on,' said Longfang. 'Describe this Murza so I can see him.'

A CLAVIER WAS playing. It was a recording, one of the high quality audio files that Seelia insisted on listening to in the *pension*. Hawser was sure that Murza had put it on. Hawser was sure that Murza was sleeping with Seelia. The woman was gorgeous and dark-skinned, with a cloud of tawny hair. During the first few days of the Lutetian placement, she'd seemed quite interested in Hawser. Then Murza had turned up the charm and that had been that.

If Murza had put the music on, then Murza had got back to the pension ahead of him. They'd become separated during the headlong flight. Hawser let himself in through the side entrance, using the gene-code keypad, and made sure the shutters were secure. The work gang who had tried to trap them at the old cathedral site knew where they were based. Some of them had come to the pension to discuss details with members of the Conservatory team.

Hawser took off his coat. His hands were unsteady. They'd nearly been beaten. They'd been threatened and nearly been assaulted, and they'd been forced to run for their lives, and adrenaline was thumping around his body, and that still wasn't the reason he felt so badly shaken.

It was getting dark. He turned on some glow-globes. The whole team had scattered into the backstreets. They'd make their way back to the pension, one by one, given luck and time.

Hawser poured himself an amasec to steady his nerves. The bottle of ten year-old, his preference, was missing from the tray. He made do with the cheaper stuff. The decanter clink-clinked against the glass in his fidgety hands.

'Navid?' he called out. 'Navid?'

There was no answer except the melody of the clavier, an old pastoral piece.

'Murza!' he shouted. 'Answer me!'

He poured himself another amasec and went up the stairs into the dorm level.

The pension was a fortified manse in a gated block called Boborg, just off a thoroughfare called Sanantwun. It was one of a number of safe-homes that a big Uropan mercantile house used as accommodation for visiting trade delegates, and the Conservatory had leased it for a three-month period. It came furnished, with servitor staff, and was as safe as anywhere in Lutetia. The city was a sprawling, blackened, uncouth place, venerably old, but deteriorating into slums. Though Hawser appreciated it for its history, he couldn't understand why anyone would choose to live there any more if they didn't have to. For the wealthy and aristocratic who still dwelt in the city-node, and there were many enclaves, surely the Atlantic platforms offered a much higher standard of living, and the superorbital plates vastly more security.

Halfway up the stairs, at the turn, there was a tall slit of a window that allowed a view of the city over the block wall. It was getting dark, and the roofs were a lumpy black slope like the scaly ridge of a reptile's back. The largest ragged lump, sticking up like a broken thorn, was the dead cathedral. It looked like a fang-shaped mountain, dwarfing other mountains around it. The sun, gone from the sky, had left pink smears on the western horizon behind it. Most of the evening light

was the artificially bright and oddly unreal radiance cast
by the plate that was presently gliding over the city in a
north-western direction. Hawser wasn't exactly sure
which one it was, but from the time of day and the
geography of its leading coast, he believed it to be
Lemurya.

Hawser sipped his drink. He looked up the rest of the
flight of stairs.

'Murza?'

He went up. The music got louder. He realised how
warm it was in the pension. It wasn't just the amasec in
his belly. Someone had cranked the heating system
right up.

'Murza? Where are you?'

Most of the bedrooms were dark. Lamplight and
clavier music were coming out of the room Murza had
picked when the team first moved in.

'Navid?'

He went in. The rooms were only small, and Murza's
was almost stifling with heat. It was cluttered too, piled
high with kit bags, discarded clothes, books, data-slates.
The music was playing from a small device beside the
bed. Hawser saw female garments jumbled amongst the
others on the floor and a kitbag that wasn't Murza's.
Seelia had moved her lovely, trusting self in with him.

Murza had left Seelia to run home on her own
through the slum-streets of Lutetia after curfew, which
was fairly standard behaviour for Navid Murza.

Hawser took another sip, and tried to quell his anger.
Murza had got them all into danger, and not for the first
time. That wasn't the worst of it. The worst of it was
something he didn't really want to consider but knew
he was going to have to face up to.

The bedroom wasn't just hot. It was fuggy. Humid.

Hawser pulled open the folding door into the wash
closet.

Murza was sitting in the bottom of the little shower stall with his knees tucked up under his chin and his arms wrapped around his shins. He was naked. Water, hot water from the stream coming out under the stall's worn plastek bubble, was hosing down on him. He looked forlorn and blank-eyed, his dark hair plastered to his scalp and neck. He was holding the decanter of ten year-old amasec by its neck.

'Navid? What are you doing?'

Murza didn't answer.

'Navid!' Hawser called, and rapped his knuckles on the clear plastek bubble. Murza looked up at him, slowly focussing. It seemed to take him a long time to recognise Hawser.

'What are you doing?' Hawser repeated.

'I was cold,' Murza replied. His words came out slurred, and his voice was so quiet, it was hard to hear over the rush of the water.

'You were cold?'

'I came back here and I needed to be warm. Have you ever been that cold, Kas?'

'What happened, Navid? That was a disaster!'

'I know. I know it was.'

'Navid, get out of the shower and talk to me.'

'I'm cold.'

'Get out of the damn shower, Navid. Come out here and tell me what you think you were playing at setting up a deal like that?'

Murza looked at him and blinked. Water dripped off his eyelashes.

'Are the others back?'

'Not yet,' said Hawser.

'Seelia?'

'None of them.'

'They'll be all right, won't they?' Murza asked. His voice slurred again.

'No thanks to you,' Hawser snapped. He softened slightly as he saw the anguished look in Murza's eyes.

'They'll be fine, I'm sure. She'll be fine. We've planned for this. We know the contingency plan, the back-up. None of them are stupid.'

Murza nodded.

'I'm not so sure about you,' Hawser added.

Murza grimaced and lifted the decanter he was holding to his mouth. A lot of the amasec was already gone. He took a big swig, swallowed some and then swooshed the rest around inside his cheeks as if it was mouthwash.

When he spat into the shower floor, Hawser saw blood swirling away down the chrome drain.

'What did you do, Navid?' he asked. 'What the hell did you do to that man? How did you know how to do it?'

'Please don't ask me,' Murza replied.

'What did you do?'

'I saved your life! I saved your life, didn't I?'

'I'm not sure, Navid.'

Murza glared at him.

'I didn't have to do that. I saved your life.'

He spat again, and more blood swirled in the water.

'Get out of there,' said Hawser. 'You're going to have to explain everything to me.'

'I don't want to,' replied Murza.

'That's bad luck. Get out of that cubicle. I'll come back in ten minutes. You'll need to be ready to explain things. Then I'll decide what we tell the others.'

'Kas, no one else has to know about–'

'Get out of there and we'll discuss it.'

HAWSER WENT DOWN to the common room, refilled his glass and sat in an armchair trying to steady his wits. He'd been at it five minutes when the others came back, first Polk and Lesher, then the twins from Odessa, then Zirian and his pale, tearful assistant Maris. Finally, just as Hawser was really beginning to worry, Seelia appeared, escorted by Thamer.

'Are we all here?' she asked, trying to sound confident, but clearly exhausted and rattled. Several of the returning team had already disappeared to wash and change.

'Yes,' said Hawser.

'Even Navid?' she asked.

'Yes.'

'Bastard,' Thamer muttered.

'I'm going to talk to him,' Hawser said. 'Just leave it, please.'

'All right,' said Thamer, sounding unconvinced.

Hawser told Polk and the twins to prepare some supper for the team, and got Lesher and Zirian to begin planning some other ideas so that their placement wouldn't be an entire waste of time. He knew it would be, but at least the semblance of activity kept their minds off the day's unpleasantness. He couldn't get the image of the pistol out of his mind. He kept seeing the black hole of the end of its muzzle aiming at him.

He went back upstairs. Murza's shower was off, and Murza was sitting on the end of his bed wearing an undershirt and combat trousers. He had not bothered to dry himself off. Water dripped from his hair. He'd poured some amasec into a small porcelain cup and was drinking from that, nursing it morosely with both hands. The decanter was on the floor beside him.

'We shouldn't have gone into that,' said Hawser, jumping straight in without preamble.

'No,' Murza agreed without looking up.

'Your call, and it was a bad one.'

'Agreed.'

'You assured us the intelligence was good and we'd be safe. I shouldn't have listened to you. I should have had security checked, and I should have set up a proper route for abort extraction, a vehicle, probably.'

Murza looked up at him.

'Yes,' he said. 'But you didn't, and you didn't because you're supposed to be able to trust me.'

'Why do you do it, Navid?'

Murza shrugged. He reached one hand up to his mouth, and probed under his lip with a finger as if one of his teeth was loose. He winced.

'Do you get greedy?' Hawser asked.

'Greedy?'

'I know what that feels like, Navid. We're two of a kind. We're driven by a real hunger to discover and pre-serve these things, to find the lost treasures of our species. It's a worthy, worthy cause, but it's an obsession too. I know it. You know we're more alike than either of us care to admit.'

Murza raised his eyebrows in a slightly amused agree-ment.

'Sometimes you go too far,' said Hawser. 'I know I've done that. Pushed too hard, paid too much of a bribe, gone somewhere I shouldn't have gone, faked up some paperwork.'

Murza sniffed. It was a sort-of laugh.

Hawser sat down on the end of the bed beside him.

'You just take it further than I do, Navid,' he said.

'Sorry.'

'It feels like you don't care who gets hurt. It feels like you'd sacrifice everyone just to get what you want.'

'Sorry, Kas.'

'That's greedy on a whole new level.'

'I know.'

'It makes me think that it's greedy in a very different way. Not a worthy way, a selfish one.'

Murza stared at the floor.

'Any truth in that?' asked Hawser. 'Is it a *selfish* flaw, do you think?'

'Yes. Yes, I think so.'

'All right.'

Hawser picked up the decanter at Murza's feet and refilled his own glass. Then he leaned over and poured some amasec into the porcelain cup Murza was clutching.

'Listen to me, Navid,' he said. 'Today you could have got us all hurt or worse. It was a total screw-up. Things like it have happened before. I'm not going to let them happen again. We play by the rulebook. We don't mess around with safety and take chances from now on, all right?'

'Yes. Yes, Kas.'

'All right, let's draw a line under that. It's done. Conversation over. Clean slate tomorrow. It's not what really troubles me, and you know that.'

Murza nodded.

'You did something this evening in the shadow of the dead cathedral. I don't know what it was. I've never seen or heard anything like it. I think you said a word or something like a word to that thug with the gun and knocked him right over.'

'I think...' said Murza very quietly. 'I think I quite probably killed him, Kas.'

'Fug me,' Hawser murmured. 'I need to know how that's even possible, Navid.'

'No, you don't,' Murza replied. 'Can we not just leave it? If I hadn't done it, he would have shot you.'

'I accept that,' said Hawser. 'I accept you did it for good reasons. I accept you saved my life, probably, and reacted in a bad situation. But I need to know what you did.'

'Why?' asked Murza. 'It'd be so much better for you if you didn't.'

'Two reasons,' Hawser replied. 'If we're going to work together at all from this point on, I'm going to need to be able to trust you. I'm going to need to know what you're capable of.'

'Fair enough,' Murza replied. 'And the other reason?'

'I'm greedy too,' said Hawser.

✧

HAWSER STOPPED SPEAKING. For a moment, he thought Longfang was asleep, or worse, but the rune priest opened his eyes.

'You stopped,' Longfang said in Juvjk. 'Keep going. This man Murza you talk of, he has maleficarum in him, and yet you toast with him like a brother.'

Blood was still misting out of Longfang's mouth with every halting breath. The fold of gossamer-white pelt below his chin had become quite dark and wet.

Hawser took a deep breath. His throat was dry. The rumble and flare of the doom come to the Quietude's cities continued to roll around the vast, firelit darkness of the space around them. In the distance, beyond the high, tiled walls of the mansion complex, apocalyptic firestorms coiled up the far side of the pit, consuming citadel structures in showers of sparks like heartwood caught in a bonfire. Closer at hand, bolters and plasma weapons traumatised the air with their discharge.

'This man,' said Longfang, 'this Murza. Did you kill him? Because of his maleficarum, I mean. Did you cut his thread?'

'I saved his life,' said Hawser.

✧

'YOU'VE NEVER TOLD me much about your childhood, or your education,' Hawser remarked.

'I don't intend to start now,' Murza replied.

He hesitated.

'Sorry. Sorry, I didn't mean to be sharp. It's just that

it's all so complicated, and it will take time we haven't got. Here's the simple version. I was privately educated. The schooling was a tradition that mixed classical training with an emphasis on the esoteric.'

'Esoterica is a very important branch of classical study,' said Hawser. 'For millennia, occulted knowledge has been passionately, jealously guarded.'

Murza smiled.

'Why is that, Kas, do you suppose?'

'Because men have always believed in supernatural forces that would grant them great powers, and give them mastery over the cosmos. We've been thinking that way since we watched the shadows play on the cave walls.'

'There is another possible reason, though, isn't there?' Murza asked. 'I mean, there has to be, logically?'

Hawser sipped his glass and looked at Murza beside him.

'Is that a serious question?' he asked.

'Do I look like I'm serious, Kas?'

'You're smiling like an idiot,' said Hawser.

'All right… Did what I did tonight look serious?'

'Are you suggesting that was something? Some kind of… *what*? It was a trick.'

'Was it?' asked Murza.

'Some kind of trick.'

'And if it wasn't, Kas, if it *wasn't*, then there's another, logical reason why certain knowledge has always been very jealously guarded. Wouldn't you say?'

Hawser stood up. He did it rather suddenly, and swayed, surprised by how considerably the amasec had gone to his head.

'This is ridiculous, Navid. Are you saying you… you can perform magic? You honestly expect me to believe you're some kind of sorcerer?'

'Of course not.'

'Good.'

'I haven't studied for anything like long enough.'

'What?' said Hawser.

'Sorcerer's the wrong word. Better terms would be adept or magus. At my very junior level, acolyte or apprentice.'

'No. No, no, no. You had a weapon of some kind. Something small, concealed. Under your cuff or in a ring. Digitally based.'

Murza looked up at him. He ran his left hand through his dripping hair, trying to comb it back. There was a glitter in his eyes, an appealing, predatory thing. Navid Murza had always benefited from excess charisma. It was what carried him so far.

'You wanted to know, Kas. You asked to know. I'm telling you. Do you want to hear it?'

'Yes.'

MURZA GOT DRESSED. Hawser went down to the others and made up some excuse about stepping out with Murza to 'have a serious talk about his shortcomings'.

Murza was waiting for him on the small, rusty landing platform at the rear of the pension. It was dark and surprisingly cold. The petrochemical whiff of traffic exhaust mixed with the vent-off of cooking smells from the eating houses along Sanantwun. Beyond the secure walls of Boborg, the lights of Lutetia glimmered like a draped constellation.

Murza was wearing a long coat, and he had a small rucksack over his shoulder. He'd called a skike for them, and it was sitting on the platform with its potent little lifter motors revving. They checked with the Boborg watchman, signed their gene-codes out of the gated perimeter, and took the little transponder that would admit them back into the pension's airspace later.

'Where are we going?' Hawser asked as they ducked in

under the rain hood and took their seats behind the skike's centrally-mounted servitor pilot.

'It's a secret,' Murza smiled back, locking his seat-belt in place. 'It's all about secrets, Kas.'

He pressed the 'go' switch, and the skike rose off the platform with a whine, carried by its three engines, the two under the passenger cage and the other one under the nose forks. At rooftop height, it rotated to face north, and then took off at a high rate of knots. From the high vantage, with the cold wind in his face, Hawser could see what seemed like the whole spread of night-shadowed Lutetia. They shared the darkness with the zipping running lights of other skikes and speeders.

'You look nervous?' Hawser said to Murza.

'Do I?'

'Are you nervous?'

Murza laughed.

'A little,' he admitted. 'This is a big night, Kas. It's been a while coming. I've wanted to tell you about this stuff for years, since we first met, really. I thought you'd understand. I knew you'd understand.'

'But?'

'You're so serious! There was always a danger you'd go all disapproving and *older brother* on me, and spoil everything.'

'Am I really like that?'

'You know you are,' chuckled Murza.

'So this interest of yours has been going on for a long time?'

'When I was still quite young, at the end of my schooling, I was inducted into a private society dedicated to the rediscovery and restoration of the powers man used to command.'

'So, some foolish schoolboy club?'

'No, the society is old. Hundreds of years old, at least.'

'And does it have a name?'

'Of course,' smiled Murza. 'But it's too soon to tell you that.'

'But its remit is essentially similar to the Conservatory's?'

'Yes, but more specific.'

'It only concerns itself with what I might regard as occult material?'

'Yes,' said Murza.

'Is this why you joined the Conservatory, Navid?'

'Conservatory work gave me great access to the sorts of material the society was seeking, yes.'

Hawser glowered. He looked out of the skike to give himself time to check his annoyance. The superorbital plate Lemurya had long since slid out of the sky, but the immense moonshadow of Gondavana was passing silently over the world, east to west like a giant cyclonic pattern, and the slightly smaller ghost of Vaalbara was crossing beneath it, south-west to north-east.

'So what do I conclude from that, Murza?' Hawser asked at length. 'That for years you've been passing stuff to this mysterious society? That the Conservatory work is just a cover for you? That you've been exploiting the Council's investments and–'

'You see? You see this? Just like an older brother! Listen to me, Kas. I have never betrayed the Conservatory. I have never withheld anything, not a single find, not a book, not a page, not a button or a bead. I have dedicated myself to my work. I have never given the society anything that I haven't given to the Conservatory.'

'But you've shared?'

'Yes. At certain times, I've shared certain discoveries with the society. Isn't sharing the point? Isn't that the guiding principle of the Conservatory?'

'Not in such a clandestine way, Navid. There's a nuance here, and you know it. You're observing letter, not spirit.'

'Maybe this was a mistake,' said Murza, sullenly. 'We can get the skike to turn back.'

'No, we've come too far,' Hawser replied.

'Yes, I think we have,' said Murza.

LONGFANG LURCHED FORWARDS violently as another spasm of pain shook him. Hawser recoiled. He wasn't sure what to do. There was little help he could offer. He couldn't do anything to make the rune priest more comfortable, and he felt in some physical danger from the convulsions. An armoured Astartes, even a dying one, was not something a human being could cradle in his arms.

'I'm not dying,' said Longfang.

'I didn't say you were,' said Hawser.

'I can see it in your eyes, skjald. I can see your thoughts.'

'No.'

'Don't tell me "no". You're afraid of me dying. You're afraid of what to do if that happens. You're afraid of being left here on your own with a corpse.'

'I'm not.'

'And I'm not dying. This is just healing. Sometimes healing hurts.'

Hawser heard a sharp noise from somewhere close by. He glanced at Longfang. The priest had heard it too. Before the priest could do or signal anything, Hawser had put a finger to his lips and signed for quiet. He got up off the ground, and picked up the nearest weapon.

Slowly, with the weapon raised, he edged around the courtyard, checking each archway and cloister. There was no sign of anything. The noise had probably been debris falling from above, a false alarm.

Hawser went back to Longfang, sat down with him again, and handed the weapon over.

'Sorry,' he said. 'I needed something.'

Longfang looked down at the frostblade in his hands and then back up at Hawser.

'You realise I'd have killed any other man for taking this without asking, don't you?' he said.

'You'd have had to get up first, wouldn't you?' Hawser replied.

Longfang laughed. The laugh turned into a bloody cough.

'I don't remember Terra,' he said.

'What?'

'I don't remember it. I'm oldest of all, and I don't remember it. I was made there, one of the last few that was, and I remind all the brothers of our proud link to the birth-sphere. But the truth is, I remember very little. Dark barrack fortresses, exercise camps, fight-zones, off-world expeditions. That's all. I don't remember Terra.'

'Maybe one day you'll go back,' suggested Hawser.

'Maybe one day you'll finish this account and tell me something about it,' replied Longfang.

✣

THE SKIKE DROPPED them in a puddle of floodlights outside a sulking monster of a building in the western quarter of the city-node.

'The Bibliotech,' said Hawser.

'Indeed.' Murza was smiling, but his nerves were getting worse.

'I called ahead. I'm hoping they'll meet you.'

'They?'

Murza led him up the steps into the vast portico. The ancient stone columns soared away into the darkness above them. The floor was tiled black and white. Hawser could smell the dry air of climate control. He'd been to the Bibliotech many times before, for study and research. Never in the middle of the night. The sodium lamps cast a frosty, yellow glare on everything.

'The society has had its eye on you,' Murza said. 'For

quite a while now, in fact. I told them about you, and they think you might be very useful to them. A useful ally, like me.'

'Do they pay you for what you deliver to them, Navid?'

'No,' Murza said quickly. 'No money. I'm not rewarded financially.'

'But you are rewarded. How?'

'With… secrets.'

'Like how to kill a man with a word?'

'I shouldn't have done that.'

'No, you shouldn't.'

Murza shook his head.

'No, I mean that was beyond my skill-set. Way beyond my skill-set. It was an abuse of my power. I don't have anything like that level of control, which is why I damaged my mouth trying to do it. Besides, *Enuncia* shouldn't be used for harm.'

'What's "Enuncia", Navid?'

Murza didn't answer. They had already taken stimm shots to lessen the effects of the alcohol in their systems, and used enzyme sprays to neutralise the stink of amasec in their mouths. The Bibliotech's book priests were waiting for them, robed and silent in their ceremonial vestments. Murza and Hawser removed their boots and outer clothes, and the book priests dressed them in the visitor gowns: the soft, cream-felt, one-piece robes with integral gloves and slippers. The book priests fastened the robes around the men's throats, then gathered their hair and added tight skull caps. Murza took two data-slates out of his rucksack and led the way into the Bibliotech. Book priests opened the towering screen doors.

The grand hall was empty. None of the long reading desks was occupied. Three hundred pendant lights hung from the high ceiling on long brass chains, and lit

the great length of the room in pairs that marched away
from them. It was like stepping into the stomach of a
great whale. The light from the pendant lamps reflected
in soft, brushed spots off the warm wood of the reading
desks, and glittered wetly off the polished black ironwork of the shelf cages lining the walls.

'Where are they then?' Hawser asked.

'They're all over the world,' Murza replied cockily. 'But
I'm hoping a few of the members who operate in Lutetia will be able to meet us here.'

'This is about recruiting me, then?'

'This could be the most exceptional night of your life,
Kas.'

'Answer the damn question!'

'All right, all right,' Murza hissed. 'Keep your voice
down, the book priests are looking at us.'

Hawser glanced and saw the disapproving faces of the
priest officers peering in through decorative holes in the
screen door. He lowered his voice.

'This is about recruiting me?'

'Yes. I don't know what it is, Kas. I just can't seem to
keep them happy. They keep wanting more. I thought if
I brought you in–'

'I don't like any of this, Navid. I don't like where this
is going.'

'Just wait here, all right? Wait here and then hear them
out.'

'You probably can't keep them happy because you're
such a liability, Navid! I don't want to get drawn into
your games!'

'Please, Kas! Please! I need this! I need to show them
I can deliver! And you'll see! You'll see what it can do
for you!'

'I'm not meeting anybody without knowing their
names.'

Murza handed him one of the data-slates.

'Sit down here. Read this. I've marked the file. I'll be back in a minute.'

He hurried away.

Hawser sighed, and then pulled out a chair at one of the reading tables. He switched on the data-slate, lit it, saw the item Murza had called 'For Kasper', and selected it. It had a little marker image in the shape of a toy horse beside it. Preferring to read things on a large view, he plugged the slate into the reading table's terminal jack, and opened the full screen. A seamless slot in the edge of the wooden desk top opened, and a hololithic screen a metre square projected up in front of Hawser, tilting to the optimum angle.

Images began to form and move.

It was random notes at first, digital facsimile pages copied from Murza's tattered work journal. Hawser had seen the kind of thing before, because he had peer reviewed and worked up a lot of Murza's material over the years. They counted on each other for that. Quite often, after a Conservatory expedition, one of them would supervise the physical archiving of any artefacts recovered, while the other collated and audited their working notes for the Imperial Catalogue and for scholastic publication. He was used to Murza's short-hands, his annoying tics, his habit of skipping, and sometimes annotating laterally.

It was definitely Murza's rough journal. Hawser found himself smiling at the old copperplate typeface that Murza always chose to work in, and the occasional doodles and sketches that he'd copied into the memory.

The pages seemed to have come from a number of different sources, though. They were extracts, bits that Murza had snipped and sampled from his journal from different times. Hawser recognised notes recorded during more than a dozen different expeditions they had made together over the previous few years. If this was all linked to Murza's underlying obsession, then his madness did indeed run back a long way. Hawser saw reference to an expedition to Tartus that he knew Murza had made the year before their first meeting.

He looked up from the light screen. A sound.

One of the book priests, perhaps? There was no sign of anyone.

He went on reading, trying to make sense of what Murza had loaded into the file. There seemed to be no particular connection between the facts and locations Murza had put together. What was he missing? What had Murza found?

Just his own madness?

He looked up again.

He could have sworn that he'd heard footsteps, soft felt steps approaching across the stone tiles of the Bibliotech floor. Murza returning, perhaps.

There was no one there.

Hawser got to his feet. He walked down the table to the far end and back again. He stopped. He swung around sharply.

He thought he caught a glimpse of someone flitting past the backlit holes of the main screen doors. Just a glimpse. A robed figure.

'Navid?' he called out.

There was no reply.

He went and sat down again, and turned the display to the next sequence of pages. These were annotated pictures of excavation finds, artefacts removed from dig sites around the world. The annotations were all in Murza's style. Two of the artefact specimens were from lunar excavations.

Had Murza been to the moon? He'd never said so. That was special permit work. You needed direct Council authority.

Hawser sat back for a moment. Maybe this was Murza

simply studying artefacts retrieved by other field workers. He tried to find dig dates and source codes.

There weren't any.

The artefacts were all figurines or amulets, worked in
stone, in clay, in metal. They were, in no particular
order, a sampler of the uncounted ethnic cultures that
had formed the long and half-known patchwork of
mankind's history. Some were a thousand years old,
some were tens of thousands. Some were so old or
obscure in origin that it was impossible to cite their
provenance. There was no commonality of age, or geo-
graphical location, no shared thread of ritual
significance or religious practice, no unity of script or
language. A five hundred year-old Panpacific Dumaic
battle standard had been placed in the file between a
four thousand year-old ceremonial synapse shunt from
the Nanothaerid Domination and a thirty thousand
year-old votive bowl from Byzantine Konstantinopal.
There was absolutely no–

There was one linking element.

Hawser began to see it. He was trained to notice these
things, and he'd been doing his job well for a long time.
He had a memory that leaned towards the eidetic, and
as he switched between the holo-images, rotating some
in three dimensions with quick gestures of his felt-
gloved hands, he saw what Murza had seen.

Eyes. Stylised eyes. A whole varied symbology of eyes,
of eye-like dots, of circumpuncts, of monads, of ompha-
los, of aversion marks.

'The all-seeing singularity,' Hawser whispered to
himself. *You idiot, Navid. This is so simplistic. Every culture
in human history has noted and reflected the significance of
the eye in its ritual and art. You are making connections
where there are no connections. These tiny similarities are
only due to the fact that all of these things were made by
human beings. For fug's sake, Navid. You're seeing some kind*

*of conspiracy in history, some kind of illuminating tradition,
an occult continuity, and it's all nonsense! Your mind is
simply making sense of shadows on the cave wall! There is no
sense! They're only shadows, Navid, they're only–*

Hawser blinked. His skin was prickling. It was the dry
heat of the Bibliotech and the over-warmth of the felt
robes. He had stopped at the annotated image of an
uraeus or *wedjat*. It was an amulet, partially damaged,
formed in the traditional *eye-and-teardrop* shape. Navid's
careful note indicated it was between thirty and thirty-
five millennia old, and was composed of carnelian,
gold, lapis lazuli and faience.

> 'The wedjat/uraeus ~~perfectly~~ typifies ABSOLUTELY
> ambiguity of eye as symbol/motif,' Navid's rambling
> note went on, 'espc. in the <u>Faeronik Era</u>, it seems it was
> both a <u>talisman of protection, of guarding</u>, AND of
> wrath & malice. It is good & evil AT ONCE, it is ~~good~~
> & light and dark, it is positive & negative. The wedjat,
> later known as the *Eye of Horus*, may perhaps be said to
> represent DUPLICITY: a thing or person that can
> present one face to the world & then turn to present a
> contrary aspect. But this <u>'traitorous'or 'treacherous'</u>
> interpretation may be offset/modified/qualified by
> notion that wedjat is COSMOLOGICALLY NEUTRAL.
> Eye is both aggressive AND passive, protective AND
> proactive. Alignment depends upon WHO or WHAT is
> employing device.'

It was a simplistic conclusion, one that Hawser felt
was beneath Murza's range as a scholar. Why had Navid
made these jottings with such haste and imprecision.
Hawser wondered–

Hawser wondered why he couldn't stop looking at the
eye on the hololithic projection. It was gazing at him, as
if challenging him to look away and defying his dis-
missal of Navid Murza's scribblings. It was staring at
him. It was unblinking. The pupil was static, black iris

set in blue, hard as the sky. It made his eyes water. He couldn't blink. He couldn't break its stare. He tried to turn his head or fight off the force that was pinning his eyelids open and making his eyeballs itch and well up. His hands tightened on the edge of the reading table. He tried to push himself away, push himself back, break contact, as if the image was a live electrical wire he had brushed against and couldn't break away from. It was like trying to haul out of the undertow of a bad dream that didn't want to let him go.

The eye was no longer blue.

It was gold and black-pinned.

The back of his head hit the floor with a crack. Pain arrowed into his skull. He'd managed to tip his chair over and had ended up on his back. With his felt-slippered feet sticking up in the air, it would have been comical, except for the pain. He'd struck himself a serious blow hitting the floor.

Maybe he was concussed. He felt sick.

He felt weird.

What had just happened? Had Murza built some kind of hypnotic feedback pattern into his file? Was there some subliminal imaging?

He got up, and leaned hard on the edge of the table to steady himself. Then he pulled the data-slate link out of the table-jack without looking directly at the hololithic display. The light screen went out. He took a few deep breaths, and then leaned down and righted the chair. Bending over made his head pound and his stomach slosh. He stood up straight again to get some stability.

There was someone at the far end of the room.

The figure was about twenty metres away, at the end of the reading tables, standing by the inner stacks furthest from the screen door entranceway. It was looking at him.

He couldn't see its face. It was wearing the same soft, beige felt robes of the Bibliotech he was, but it had raised the suit's hood, like a monk's cowl. Its arms were by its side. Everything about its outline was soft, almost plump. In the cream library robes, it looked like the naked form of a person who had lost great amounts of weight very dramatically, and whose flesh had become baggy and empty. In the Bibliotech's half-light, it looked like a ghost.

Hawser called out, 'Hello?'

His voice rolled around the twilight cavern of the Bibliotech like a marble in a foot locker. The figure did not move. It was staring right at him. He couldn't see its eyes, but he knew it was. He wanted to see its eyes. He felt as if he needed to.

'Hello?' he called out again.

He took a step forwards.

'Navid? Is that you? What are you doing?'

He walked towards the figure. It remained where it was, staring at him, its creamy form so soft in the gloom, it seemed phantasmal.

'Navid?'

The hooded figure turned suddenly and began to walk away towards the carved black ironwork screen into the inner stacks.

'Wait!' Hawser called out. 'Navid, come back! Navid!'

The hooded figure kept walking. It passed under the ironwork frame and disappeared into the shadows.

Hawser started to run.

'Navid?'

He entered the inner stacks. Rows of shelving fanned out before him in the low light. The beautifully made wooden stacks were each twelve metres high, and each row ran off as far as he could see. Sets of brass library steps with complex gears were attached to each stack at intervals and could be run along the shelves on inertia-less rails to allow readers access to the higher levels. As Hawser moved, his body heat triggered catalogue tags on adjacent shelves. Hololithic tags lit up, and a pleasant voice spoke.

Eastern Literature, Hol to Hom.
Eastern Literature, sub-section, Homezel, Tomas, works of.
Eastern Literature, Hom to Hom continued.

'Mute,' Hawser instructed. The pleasant voice faded. The hololithic tags continued to flare up and then gradually fade as he hurried past.

'Hello?' he called. He ducked back and tried another row. How could a walking figure have vanished so quickly?

He caught movement out of the corner of his eye, and turned in time to see the hooded figure, just for a second, as it crossed a division between stacks. He broke into an urgent sprint to catch up with it, but when he got to the division, there was no sign.

Except a couple of hololithic shelf tags slowly fading away again, as if passing body heat had only recently brought them to life.

'Navid! I've had enough of this!' Hawser yelled out. 'Stop playing games!'

Something made him turn. The hooded figure was behind him, right behind him, silent and ghostly. It slowly raised its hands up from its sides, raising them out straight like wings, or like a celebrant priest invoking a deity.

The softly gloved right hand held a knife.

It was a ceremonial blade. An *athame*. Hawser recognised its form at once. It was a sacrificial blade.

'You're not Navid,' he whispered.

'Choices have to be made, Kasper Hawser,' said a voice. It wasn't Murza, and it wasn't the hooded figure either. Fear crushed Hawser's heart.

'What choices?' he managed to ask.

'You have much to offer, and we would be pleased to have a relationship with you. It would be of mutual benefit. But you have to make a choice, Kasper Hawser.'

'I still don't understand,' Hawser replied. 'Where's Murza? He said he was bringing me to meet with the people he works with.'

'He did. He has. Navid Murza is a disappointment. He is rash. He is unreliable. An unreliable servant. An unreliable witness.'

'So?'

'We are looking for someone more suited to our needs. Someone who knows what he's looking for. Someone who can recognise the truth. Someone who can see with better eyes. You.'

'I think you've mistaken me for some kind of idiot who wants to join a pathetic secret club,' Hawser answered fiercely. 'Take off that stupid hood. Let me see your face. Is that you, Murza? Is this another of your stupid games?'

The hooded figure took a step forwards. It almost seemed to glide.

'You have to make a choice, Kasper Hawser,' said the voice.

Hawser realised the voice was coming from all around him. It definitely wasn't coming from the figure. It was the soft and pleasant system voice of the stack shelves. How could anything or anyone speak to him through the Bibliotech's artificial system?

'You have to make a choice, Kasper Hawser.'

Hawser heard Navid cry out. It wasn't a vocalisation. It was a tremor of pain. He turned his back on the hooded figure, and started to stride down the aisle, not quite running, but moving more urgently than a walk.

'You have to make a choice,' the shelves whispered to him as he walked by. 'You have to make a choice. See for us, and we will show you such things.'

'Navid?' Hawser called out, ignoring the voice,

A four-way junction in the stacks lay ahead. A set of library steps had been rolled to the end of one of the adjacent stacks, and Murza had been bound to its brass rail by his wrists. He was lying on the floor, half twisted, with his legs stretched out into the centre of the junction area and his arms pulled up painfully by the restraint. He looked half-drugged, or woozy as if he'd been felled by violence.

There were six more hooded figures standing in a vague semi-circle around him.

'You have to make a choice,' said the voice.

'What are you doing to him?' Hawser demanded.

'You have to make a choice. See for us, and we will show you such things. Things you cannot imagine.'

Murza let out a low moan.

Hawser ignored the hooded figures and crouched down by Murza. He tilted the man's face up. Murza was flushed and sweaty. Fear pricked his eyes.

'Kas,' he stammered. 'Kas, help me. I'm so sorry. They like you. You interest them.'

'Why?'

'I don't know! They won't tell me! I just wanted to make an introduction, that's all. Show that I was useful to them too, that I could bring them the people they needed.'

'Oh, Navid, you're such a fool...'

'Please, Kas.'

Hawser looked up at the robed figures behind him.

'We're going to walk out of here now,' he said, with more conviction than he actually felt. 'Navid and I, we're going to get up and walk out of here.'

'You have to make a choice, Kasper Hawser,' said the pleasant, artificial voice.

'No, I don't.'

'Yes. We have extended an invitation to you. We do

not extend invitations like this to just anybody. You are a rare creature, and this is a rare offer. Do not underestimate the potency of the things we are inviting you to share. They are the things you have spent your life seeking.'

'This is a mistake,' said Hawser.

'The only mistake would be if you said no, Kasper Hawser,' said the voice. 'A yes is far simpler. The signifier of yes should be easy for a man of your education to recognise. It is around you.'

Hawser blinked. He looked at Murza, the figures, the looming shapes of the stacks, the extending perspective of the aisles.

'Of course,' he said. 'A ritual conducted on a crossed point, representing the unity of approaching directions. Eight adepts offering admission to one novitiate. Identities are masked, representing the mysteries awaiting beyond initiation. This is a variation on the initiation rites of the witch-cults of the Age of Strife. Which one? The Knower Sect? The Illuminated? The Cognitae?'

'It doesn't matter,' said the voice.

'No, because that's the whole sell, isn't it?' said Hawser. '*Caveat emptor*. The initiate gets to know nothing: no truths, no names, no identities, until after initiation, when it's too late. Revelation breaks the compact of secrecy. I know what you want from me.'

'You have a choice to make.'

'Eight adepts, but there can be only eight. The sacred number. One must step aside to let a replacement in. And one has made a mistake and broken the compact of secrecy.'

Murza moaned again. He pulled weakly at his bonds, making the set of brass library steps rattle.

The hooded figure with the athame held the blade out to Hawser.

'Oh, please, Kas,' Murza whimpered. 'Please.'

Hawser took the blade.

'You really have got yourself in a mess, Navid,' he said.

Hawser made a quick, simple, strike with the dagger. Murza yelped. The cord binding his wrists parted.

Hawser turned to the hooded figures, brandishing the athame.

'Now fug off!' he said.

The semi-circle of figures hesitated for a moment. Then they began to tremble. Each soft, cream suit began to shudder, as if pressurised air hoses had been attached to them to inflate them. They swelled slightly, in ugly, lumpen ways that evoked malformation and defect, and they began to writhe, stirred by ethereal things moving inside them. The felt suits grew plump, distending like balloons. A whine began, a high-pitched note growing louder and louder. It was a shrill wail coming from the stack voice system. Murza and Hawser clamped their hands to their ears. When the noise reached its peak, it cut off abruptly. The hoods of the shuddering figures slipped back and released vapour into the gloomy air. The vapour was golden and it vanished almost as soon as it emerged, like smoke, from the neck holes of the suits. Empty and slack, the seven felt body-robes fell softly onto the floor.

Hawser stared down at the empty suits, at the impossibility of them. There had been men inside them. Even the most subtle and fine-scale teleportation work could not have removed them from inside their robes. He realised he was breathing hard, and tried to contain his panic. He had a peculiar fear inside him, a kind he only rarely experienced, a kind that had followed him from childhood at the commune, from the nightmares he'd had of something scratching at the door.

Murza was clinging to the base of the library steps he'd been tied to. He was sobbing.

'Get up, Murza,' Hawser said. He felt something on his cheek, something too cold for a tear.

It had begun to snow in the library.

The snow was gentle and silent. It drifted down out of the fusty darkness above the stack tops, and glittered like starshine as it passed through the glow of the aisle lamps.

'Snow?' Hawser whispered.

'What?' Murza murmured.

'Snow? How can it be snow?' Hawser said.

'What are you talking about?' Murza said, not really interested.

Hawser stepped away from him, looking up into the darkness, his hands out, upturned, to feel the cold sting of snowflakes landing on his palms.

'Great Terra,' he whispered. 'This isn't right. Snow, that's not right.'

'Why do you keep talking about snow?' Murza moaned.

'This isn't how it happened,' said Hawser.

'It's enough like how it happened for the story to stay true,' said Longfang.

Tra's rune priest was lying at the mouth of the aisle to Hawser's left, propped up against the stack as if it was the orange-tiled wall of a mansion in a city near another star. The blood down his front had caked dry like rust, and he was no longer breathing out a bloody steam, but his lips were wet and red, in sharp contrast to his almost colourless skin.

'How can you be here with me?' Hawser asked.

'I'm not,' said Longfang, his voice a sigh. 'You're here with me. Remember that? This is only your account.'

'Kas?' Murza called. 'Kas, who are you talking to?'

'No one,' said Hawser.

The snow was falling a little more heavily. Hawser knelt down beside Longfang.

'So, did you like my story?'

'I did. I felt your fear. I felt his more.'

Longfang nodded his head towards Murza.

'Who are you talking to, Kas?' Murza called out. 'Kas, what's happening?'

'He got in over his head,' Hawser said to Longfang.

'He was never trustworthy,' the priest replied. 'You should have smelled that on him from the start. In your tale, he was nicer, a better friend to you, than he is now I see him myself. You're too trusting, skjald. People use you because of that.'

'I don't think that's true,' said Hawser.

'What isn't true?' Murza whined.

'You look old,' said Longfang looking up at Hawser.

'I'm a lot younger here than I am as you know me.'

'We made a better you,' replied Longfang.

'Why is it snowing in here?' asked Hawser.

'Because the snow comforts me,' said Longfang. 'It's the snow of Fenris. Of winter approaching. Get me up.'

Hawser reached out his hand. The priest took it and got to his feet. There seemed to be no weight to him this time. He left a pool of blood on the library floor.

The snowfall grew a little heavier.

'Come on,' he said. He started to shuffle down the aisle. Hawser walked with him.

'Kas? Kas, where are you going?' Murza called out behind them.

'What happens?' Longfang asked.

'I'll take him back to the pension, clean him up. We do some soul-searching. I try to weigh up the huge asset he represents to the Conservation programme in terms of his scholarship, ability and sheer tenacity against the huge liability of him consorting with dilettante occultists.'

'What do you decide?'

'That he was a valuable commodity. That I should

keep any inquiry internal. That I believed him when he swore to me he was renouncing all his old connections and associations so he could dedicate himself to th–'

'You should have smelled his treachery.'

'Maybe. But for ten years after that night we worked together. There was never any more trouble. He was a superb field researcher. We kept working together until… until he was killed in Ossetia.'

'There was never any more trouble?' asked Longfang.

'No.'

'Never?'

'Never,' said Hawser.

'Kas?' Murza's voice echoed out. It was a long way behind them, muffled by the distance and the snow. 'Kas? Kas?'

'So you liked the account?' Hawser asked. 'It amused you? It distracted you?'

'It was amusing enough,' said Longfang. 'It wasn't your best.'

'I can assure you it was,' said Hawser.

Longfang shook his head. Droplets of blood flecked from his beard.

'No, you'll learn better ones,' he said. 'Far better ones. And even now, it's not the best you know.'

'It's the most unnerving thing that happened to me in my old life,' said Hawser with some defiance. 'It has the most… maleficarum.'

'You know that's not true,' said Longfang. 'In your heart, you know better. You're denying yourself.'

'What do you mean?'

The snow had become quite heavy. It was lying on the ground, and their feet were crunching over it. Hawser saw his breath in the air in front of him. It was getting lighter. The stacks were just black slabs in the blizzard, like stone monoliths or impossibly giant tree trunks.

'Where are we going?' Hawser asked.

'Winter,' said Longfang.

'So this is a dream too?'

'No more than your tale was, skjald. Look.'

THE SNOW WAS a kind of neon white, scorching the eye as it reflected a sun high up on a noon apex, the brief, bright bite of a winter day.

The air was as clear as glass. To the west of them, beyond a vast, rolling field of snow and a mighty evergreen forest, mountains rose. They were white, as clean and sharp as carnassials. Hawser realised the murderous gun-metal skies behind them weren't storm clouds. They were more mountains, *greater* mountains, mountains so immense the sheer scale of them broke a man's spirit. Where their crags ended, buried like thorns in the skin of the sky, the black-hearted wrath of the winter season Fenrisian storms were gathering and clotting, angry as patriarch gods and malign as trickster daemons. In no more than an hour, two at the most pleading limits of a man's prayers, the sun would be gone and the light too, and the storms would have come in over the peaks on their murder-make. The fury would be suicidal, like men rushing a firm shield wall, and the snow-clouds would disembowel themselves on the mountain tops and spill their contents on the valley.

'Asaheim,' said Hawser, so cold he could barely speak. It felt as if all of his blood had gone solid.

'Yes,' said Longfang.

'A whole great year I lived in the Aett, I never went outside of it. I never saw the top of the world.'

'Now you're seeing it,' said Longfang.

'What are we doing?'

'We're being quiet,' said Longfang. 'This is my tale.'

The rune priest began to advance down the long white shoulder of the vast snow field. His head was low, his stance wide-spaced. The gossamer-white pelt across his back caused him to almost vanish into the lying snow. He had a long steel spear in his right hand.

Hawser followed him, head down, putting his feet in Longfang's footprints. The prints were shallow: the snow was as hard as rock. Their breath came out of their mouths in long sideways streams like silk banners.

Snow stopped its slow, gentle fall and began coming in from the direction of the mountains, loose flakes driven by the wind in circling, dizzy patterns. Hawser felt it sting his face. The nature of light in the world around them changed. A shadow against the sky tilted. The horizon was filling up with a grey vapour. The sun seemed to look away. It was as though a veil had been drawn, or a screen pulled across a door. There was still sunlight, bright yellow sunlight, at the top of the sky, and it was reflecting its neon-burn off the ridge of the snow line, but down where they were, the snow was suddenly a dark, cold pearl colour.

Longfang pointed. Down at the tree line, huge, slow shapes processed in a loose, plodding group. They were vast quadruped herbivores, part bison, part elk, darkly pelted in black, woolly coats. Their bone antler branches were the size of tree canopies. Hawser could hear the snort and huff of them.

'Saeneyti,' whispered Longfang. 'Stay low and quiet. Their antlers work as acoustic reflectors. They'll hear us long before they're in spear-throwing range.'

Hawser realised he had a spear of his own.

'Are we hunting?'

'We're always hunting,' said Longfang.

'So if they heard us, they'd run?'

'No, they'd turn on us to defend the calves. Those antlers are longer and sharper than our spears, skjald. Remember to put that in your account.'

'I thought this was *your* account, priest?'

Longfang grinned.

'I just want you to get the details right.'

'All right.'

'And watch the treeline,' Longfang added.

Hawser turned to look at the edge of the forest. He could see its shadowed, evergreen blackness through the snow. The towering tree trunks looked like the ends of Bibliotech book stacks. He knew that even in full sunshine, light didn't dare penetrate the mossy darkness of the fir glades.

'Why?' he asked.

'Because we may not be the only ones hunting,' Longfang replied.

Hawser swallowed.

'Priest?'

'Yes?'

'What is the point of this tale? What is the purpose of telling it to me?'

'Its point is its point.'

'Very gnomic. I mean what am I supposed to learn from it?'

'It's about time we trusted you with one of our secrets,' Longfang replied. 'A good one. A blood one.'

As if to emphasise the word, Hawser realised he could suddenly smell blood. He could smell Longfang's blood. Immediately afterwards, he smelled something else too: the dung-stink and ferment-odour of cattle. He could smell the *saeneyti*.

The wind had changed. It was bringing the stink of the herd up towards them. The clouds moved, shoved by the wind, racing and scudding. The sun came back out and turned its glare on them like a lamp. They were black dots in a broad neon snow field.

They were painfully visible.

The big bull leading the herd turned its bearded head and made a booming, trumpeting sound through nostrils the size of sewer pipes. It shook its crown of antlers.

The herd took off in agitation, hooting and braying, waddling their huge bodies away double-time, kicking up powder snow.

The bull peeled away from the fleeing herd and came back up the slope.

'Shit!' said Hawser. He hadn't fully appreciated the size of the creature. Four, perhaps five metres tall? How many tonnes? And the width of those antlers, like the spread wings of a drop-ship.

'Move yourself!' Longfang shouted. He had his arm crooked back, the spear locked to throw, standing his ground. The bull was coming on. It was too big, too tall, too cumbersome to develop any real speed, but it was inexorable and it was angry.

'I said move!' Longfang cried.

Hawser started to stumble across the snow away from Longfang.

'No. To the side. The side!' Longfang ordered.

Hawser was running away from Longfang and the approaching bull. If it ran Longfang down, it would simply run him down too. Longfang intended him to turn wide, out of its line of charge.

Given the breadth of its antler crown, that was going to be some distance.

The snow was hard to run on. He was already out of breath. It felt like he was struggling with his old, human body, the one he had worn before Fenris, the weak, aging Kasper Hawser. Every step was an effort to lift his feet high enough to clear the snow. He had to bound. The light, fluorescent-bright, burned his eyes.

He looked back in time to see Longfang cast. The spear flashed in the bright sunlight. It seemed to strike the huge beast, but it vanished against shaggy black hair. The bull saeneyti kept coming. Longfang vanished in a welter of pulverised snow.

Hawser yelled the priest's name involuntarily.

The bull swung towards him.

Hawser turned and fled. He knew it was futile. He could hear its muffled thunder, its snorting and grunting, the oceanic surge of its gastric caverns. He could smell its rank breath, its spittle, its giant mauve tongue. It boomed again like a carnyx.

Hawser knew he wasn't going to outrun it. Expecting an antler spike to split through his torso from the back at any moment, he turned and threw his spear.

It weighed too much. It didn't even reach the saeneyti, even though the bull was closing the distance and was scarcely five metres away.

Hawser fell on his backside. Wide-eyed and helpless, he watched death ploughing towards him, head down.

A black wolf hit the saeneyti from the side. It looked like a normal wolf, until Hawser tried to reconcile the size of it compared to the saeneyti bull, which he knew to be the size of the very largest prehistoric Terran saurians. The wolf had gone for the nape of the neck. It had closed its jaws just in front of the humped shoulder mass where the saeneyti carried its winter fat.

The bull lifted its head and let out an excruciating, throttled noise. It tried to twist its head to hook the predator with its crown of antlers and toss it away, but the wolf was tenacious and held on. Jaws clamped, it made a wet leopard-growl that was half muffled by the bull's pelt.

Blood as black as ink was running down the bull's wattle, spattering the snow between its front feet. It was streaming down through the black wool. The saeneyti snorted again, pink froth foaming at its mouth and nose. Its eyes were wild and mad, red-rimmed, staring insanely out from under the thick fringe of winter fur.

It went down hard, front legs collapsing first. It fell onto its front knees, and then the back end followed. Finally, its body went over in a catastrophic roll onto its side like the hull of a capsizing yacht. Hawser could see the saeneyti's huge, protruding tongue shuddering between its yellow teeth, lips peeled back. Its breath pumped out in clouds like a malfunctioning steam engine. Blood vomited out of its mouth across the snow and lay there smoking.

The wolf maintained its grip until the bull gave up its last, trembling rumble, then it let go. Blood dripped from its snout. It padded around the massive corpse twice, moving quickly, head low, sniffing.

It stopped beside the head of its kill, and raised its own head, ears upright, to stare at Hawser. Its eyes were golden and black-pinned. Hawser stared back. He knew if he tried to get back on his feet, the wolf would still be taller than him.

'There are no wolves on Fenris.'

Hawser looked up. Longfang was standing beside him, staring at the wolf.

'That's evidently not true at all,' Hawser replied in a tiny voice.

Longfang grinned down at him.

'Try to keep up, skjald. There were no wolves on Fenris until we got here.'

Longfang looked back at the wolf.

'Twice he's helped protect you,' he said.

'What?' asked Hawser.

'He had a different name last time you were in his company,' said Longfang. 'Then, he was called Brom.'

The black wolf turned and ran for the forest, accelerating as only a mammalian apex predator can. It vanished into the enormous darkness under the evergreens.

After a few seconds, Hawser saw its eyes staring out of the blackness at them: luminous, gold and black-pinned.

It took him another few moments to realise that there

were another ten thousand pairs of eyes watching them
from the shadows of the forest.

'I THINK YOU should explain,' said Hawser. He felt angry,
and curiously cold given the heat washing across the
courtyard. 'What do you mean he was called Brom?
What do you mean by that?'

Longfang didn't answer. He stared back at Hawser
with a sneering look that defied argument.

'This is ridiculous!' Hawser exclaimed. 'This is just
some of your myth-making! This is a mjod story! A
mjod story!'

He hoped this would provoke a reaction, stir something in the old rune priest that would make him reveal
some actual truth.

Longfang remained silent.

'Well, I don't think much of your account then,' said
Hawser.

He heard footsteps behind him and turned. Bear was
walking towards him, with Aeska Brokenlip close
behind him. They were both spattered with Quietude
gore. Hawser became aware again of the constant noise
around him, the swirling din of end-war circling the pit.

'Tell him to speak plainly to me!' Hawser said to Bear,
rising. 'Tell him not to insult me with riddles!'

Bear crouched down beside the priest. He leaned his
axe against the orange-tiled wall and reached out to the
priest's throat. Aeska looked on, wiping spats of blood
off his nose.

Bear stood again and looked at Aeska.

'What?' asked Hawser.

'Heoroth Longfang has gone,' said Aeska.

'What? No. He's hurt but he's mending.'

'Bio-track on his armour says his thread parted twelve
minutes ago,' said Bear flatly.

'But I was just talking to him,' said Hawser. 'I was just

talking to him. I was watching over him while he healed himself.'

'No, skjald, you were seeing him through the last of the pain,' said Aeska. 'I hope your account was a good one.'

'I was watching over him while he healed!' Hawser insisted.

Bear shook his head.

'He was holding on long enough to watch over you,' he said.

Hawser gazed down at the body of the rune priest propped up in a sitting position against the alien wall. He had words in his mouth, but they were all broken and none of them worked.

Others were approaching. Hawser saw it was Najot Threader, Tra's wolf priest. He approached with a retinue of thralls clad in cloaks of patchwork skin.

'Look away,' said Aeska Brokenlip.

NINE

Twelve Minutes

FOR ALL OF the forty-week voyage, he considered those twelve minutes.

Their work done, Tra left the 40th Expedition to stamp out the ashes of the Olamic Quietude, a miserable effort of funereal cleansing that would eventually take three years, and effectively end the 40th Expedition's exploration. Tra had been summoned to its next operation. Hawser was not told what it was. He did not ask. He did not expect to be told.

What he did expect was censure for the death of Heoroth Longfang. He felt the loss was essentially down to him and, adding the fact of Longfang's high status as a veteran, he didn't hold out much hope for a continuing relationship with the *Vlka Fenryka*.

Or, indeed, with breathing.

No censure was made. As the ship got under way, the company just gathered quietly to make its respects. Hawser was given simple instructions.

'They'll each come to you,' Bear told him. 'Learn their accounts.'

'Who will?' Hawser asked.

'All of them,' Bear replied, as if it was a stupid question.

'Was that a stupid question?' asked Hawser.

'You have no other kind,' replied Bear. 'Learn their accounts.'

THEY CAME TO him, all right. Every single member of Tra, one at a time, or in small groups. They came to Hawser and they told him the stories they had of Heoroth Longfang.

There were a lot of them. Some were multiple versions of the same event, retold by different witnesses. Some were contradictory. Some were short. Some were long and ungainly. Some were funny. Some were scary. Most were fearsome and bloody. Many recounted incidents when Longfang had saved the storyteller's life, or taught the storyteller a valuable wisdom. There were expressions of gratitude, and respect and appreciation.

Hawser listened to them all and he learned them all, relying on all his eidetic tricks and Conservatory training. By the end of the process, he had committed four hundred and thirty-two discrete accounts of the rune priest to memory.

Some of the stories had been given to him flat and expressionless, matter-of-fact. Others had been related grimly by men moved over the loss. Some had been told to him by men who were plainly poor storytellers, and he'd had to go back several times and quiz the teller to make sense of what he was being told. Some had crucial elements missed out accidentally due to enthusiasm. Some were just tangled messes he'd had to unpick. Some were stories related with mirth, remembering Longfang with considerable affection. In such cases, the process of conveying the stories to Hawser was often

interrupted as the tellers struggled to stop laughing so
they could finish their accounts.

All the while, listening to the stories with a serious or
smiling aspect as was appropriate, Hawser thought of
the twelve minutes. Heoroth Longfang had stayed with
him for twelve minutes, talking, finishing his story,
sharing his truth. Twelve minutes from his bio-track
flatlining. Twelve minutes of postmortem survival.

Heoroth Longfang had stolen twelve minutes from
the Underverse's tally-stick for a reason. To keep him
safe? To show Hawser something? To prove something?

ONCE THE STORIES were his, the sending away began.
Longfang's body, held in a stasis casket, would be
shipped back to Fenris to be burned out on the ice fields
of Asaheim, at some high point overlooking the forest
migration trails of the saeneyti where the old priest had
liked to hunt, but this was another kind of letting go.
The company gathered in one of the ship's main chambers to feast in memory of Longfang for as many days
and nights as Hawser's account lasted.

Godsmote had shown Hawser some pity. He had
warned him to rehearse well, to practise dramatic recita-
tion, to space the stories out so that smaller reflections
were worked in between longer epics. He told the skjald
that, under no circumstance, should he hurry along.
Long rests should be built in, long rests of ten hours or
more. These periods of reflection also prolonged the
event. The recitations would be done in Juvjk, the
hearth-cant, because that was one of the solemn and
sacred uses of the hearth-cant. Wurgen terminology
could only be used for technical embellishment.

Tra was using a warship called *Nidhoggur*. Hawser did
not imagine that the warships of the *Vlka Fenryka* resembled the ships of other Legions Astartes except, perhaps,
in their basic construction. Hawser had not seen other

Astartes warships, but he'd travelled on several Imperial
Fleet vessels, and *Nidhoggur* was a strange craft by com-
parison. He got the impression that the *Vlka Fenryka*
regarded both their starships and their transatmospher-
ics as boats, and the void simply an extension of the
gale-wracked oceans of their home world. Interior
spaces had been finished with bone, polished ivory and
wood, like the inside of the Aett. It was a Unification Era
cruiser that had been progressively altered and adorned
until most of its old identity had been lost, and a great
deal of new identity imposed.

Environmental controls were set several points down
from Imperial standard, so *Nidhoggur* was darker and
colder than any vessel he'd travelled on before. Too
much warmth, Hawser was reminded as he shivered in
a corner of the living spaces, made a man sluggish. Too
much light, and a man's vision grew blunt. A lamplit
dusk prevailed in most of the deck spaces.

The chamber employed for the sending off was a hold
space that was left unused except for such events. Only
a member of the *Vlka Fenryka* as venerable as Longfang
deserved such a ceremonial farewell.

The hold reminded Hawser of a slice of urban under-
hive, a piece of favela wasteland from the slums of an
old-Terra city. It was dirty and littered, and twilight-
dark. Most of the surfaces of the place were blackened
with soot. Piles of loose cables, insulation, broken
metal spars, ceiling liners and tangled wire suggested
that the space had been either vandalised or customised
over the years, perhaps both.

Combustible material was dragged in, heaped up,
and lit under the scorched vents of the hold's extractor
ducts. Eye-watering smoke filled the chamber. On this
deck level, Hawser presumed, the ship's emergency
detection and containment systems had been disabled,
or had long since fried out.

He sat by a wall, watching the ceremony take shape. Over time, sitting exactly where he now sat, others had worried away at the wall by the jumping firelight. The ivory panelling lining most of the hold was covered in intricate, hand-done knotwork, the same ancient weave pattern that marked the Rout's weapons and armour, especially their leatherware. He felt the surface with his fingertips in the shadows, touching where one pattern ended and another took up, blade marks as distinctive as handwriting or voices. He realised how old *Nidhoggur* was. Two hundred, maybe even two hundred and fifty years old. He thought of the *Vlka Fenryka* as a well established order, with old and honoured traditions, but this vessel had come out of the fitters' yards before the Sixth Legion Astartes had even left Terra and been rehoused on bleak Fenris. Hawser had committed most of his life to the search for history, and here it was right under his fingertips. He knew the scale of history, but he'd never really thought about its varying intensities. The long, slow tracts of stability, the abiding Ages of Technology, like endless hot summers, were bland and uneventful compared to the furious two centuries *Niddhoggur* had witnessed. The remaking of mankind's fortunes. The rebuilding of mankind's estate. Would any ship ever last so long or see so much of that which mattered?

Tra assembled. The men came dressed in their pelts and their leatherwork. They were shadows with beast faces, shades with knotwork masks. Hawser could smell the petroleum reek of mjod, mjod in copious quantities. Thralls in horned head-dresses and long, ragged cloaks of patchwork hide moved through the assembling company with drink to fill and refill each lanx. They brought red meat too; panniers of it to stoke the accelerated metabolisms of the Astartes.

Drums were sounding. There was no unifying rhythm. It seemed to be more a matter of pride for a man to be

belligerently out of tempo with the neighbouring beats.
Playing along with crude pipes and trumpets, made
from bone and animal horn, the drums were designed
to make noise, a kind of assaulting anti-music. Some of
the drums were hoops of wood or bone, or even heated
and bent tusk that had been covered in tight skins. Others were giant fish scales, or plates of hammered metal
that Hawser eventually realised were pieces of armour
taken as trophies from enemies. These hardskin drums
made battering rows like cymbals or sistra.

In no order of seniority, and apparently casually, the
men came up to the main fires and placed offerings in
the ash spill. Hawser saw them leave beads or small trophies, claws and fish teeth, small graven figures shaped
from bones and wax, and shell cases etched with knotwork scratches and plumed with seabird feathers. When
they left a gift, they took a handful of ash and, removing
their leather masks or their entire headgear in some cases,
marked their faces with smudges of grey. Najot Threader,
his head covered in a tight leather mask that crowned in
two vast, winter-black antlers, stood by the fires and
watched the men make their marks. He spoke to some,
stopping them, a hand on their shoulders, making marks
of his own sometimes with ash or red paste on their
brows or on their cheekbones under their eyes.

'What do I give?' Hawser asked.

Fith Godsmote was sitting beside him, gnawing at a
handful of raw meat. Hawser could smell the blood, a
pervasive metal stink that was turning his stomach.

'You've got your account to give, so that's enough,'
Godsmote said. 'But you should go and get marked by
the priest.'

'I've got this feeling,' said Hawser.

'What?' asked Oje from the other side of him.

'This whole thing is going to end up with me cere-
monially offered up in Longfang's memory.'

'Hjolda!' Oje laughed. 'That's an idea that would please some!'

'It's not how it works,' said Godsmote, wiping his mouth, 'but I could have a word with the jarl if you like.'

Hawser scowled at him.

'You think we blame you for Longfang?' Godsmote asked.

Hawser nodded.

'That's not how it works,' Godsmote repeated. 'Wyrd sometimes takes and sometimes gives. Some things seem more important than others when they're not. Other things, they seem less important than others, when in fact they're the most important things of all. You didn't take Longfang from us. It was his time to go. And you've brought things to the Rout that they're grateful for.'

'Such as?'

Godsmote shrugged.

'Me,' he said.

'You've got a pretty high opinion of yourself, Fith of the Ascommani,' said Hawser.

'I don't mean it like that,' said Godsmote. 'But I'm useful, a useful arm. I've done good work for the jarl and the Rout. I wouldn't be here unless I was meant to be here. But I wouldn't be here if you hadn't fallen out of Uppland that spring.'

'So I wasn't such a bad star for you, then?'

'Neither of us would be here unless we were supposed to be here,' said Godsmote. 'You see what I'm saying?'

'I still feel I'm here on sufferance,' said Hawser.

'What does that mean?' asked Godsmote.

'I feel I'm tolerated because there's not a lot else you can do with me.'

'Oh, there were plenty of things we could have done with you,' said Oje matter-of-factly as he bit into some meat.

'Ignore him,' said Godsmote. 'Look, they're closing the bounds so we can begin. Go up now and show us the value of a skjald, and you'll know you're not with us under sufferance.'

At the exits and entrances of the hold space, members of Tra were using plasteel hand-axes to strike marks of aversion into the hatch sills and door frames, duplicating the device Hawser had seen Bear make on the graving dock. The area was now contained and access from the outside forbidden until the ceremony was played out. The anti-music noise rose to a peak, and then stopped.

Hawser approached the flames.

NAJOT THREADER, WOLF priest, loomed over him like a bull saeneyti, his antlered head backlit by the fire. Despite the crackling blaze and the throat-closing smoke, Hawser felt cold. He pulled the fur that Bitur Bercaw gave him close around his throat and shivered inside his clammy bodyglove. Someone, the priest perhaps, had thrown seedcases and dried leaves on the fire, and they were burning with an unpleasantly sweet aroma.

'Name yourself,' said Najot Threader.

'Ahmad Ibn Rustah, skjald of Tra,' Hawser replied.

'And what do you bring to the fireside?'

'The account of Ulvurul Heoroth, called *Longfang*, as is my calling,' said Hawser.

The priest nodded, and marked Hawser's cheeks with grey paste. Then he leaned forwards with a small straw made from a hollow fish bone. Hawser closed his eyes just in time as Najot Threader used the straw to blow a spray of black paint across his eyes.

His tear ducts stinging, Hawser turned to face the company, circling the main fire as boldly as he felt able. He was trying to control his breathing, trying to remember to pace himself and project his voice. His throat was dry.

With a gesture of confidence and command, he held out a hand. One of the thralls obediently handed him a lanx, and Hawser drank without even checking to see if it was mjod. It wasn't. The thralls were aware of his biological limits and careful not to cripple him by accident.

Hawser took another sip of watered-down wine, rinsed it around his gums, and handed back the drinking bowl.

'The first account,' he said, 'is the story of Olafer.'

Olafer rose from his place amongst one group and nodded, raising his lanx. There was a ragged cheer.

'On Prokofief,' Hawser began, 'forty great years ago, Olafer and Longfang fought against the greenskins. Bitter winter, dark sea, black islands where the greenskins massed in numbers like the shingle on a beach. A hard fight. Anyone who was there will remember it. On the first day...'

✧

SOME PARTS OF the account were greeted with roaring enthusiasm, others with grim silence. Some provoked laughter and others barks of sorrow or regret. Hawser warmed to his task, and began to recognise which of his techniques worked well and which seemed to impress the least.

His only real mis-step came when he described some fallen enemies in one account as 'finally succumbing to the worms in the soil'.

Someone stopped him. It was Ogvai.

The jarl held up a ring-heavy hand. His look of confusion was accentuated by the heavy piercing in his lower lip.

'What is that word?' he asked.

Hawser established that the word 'worms' wasn't known to any of the Wolves. Somehow, he'd slipped out of Juvjk and fallen back on his Low Gothic vocabulary.

It was strange, because he knew the Juvjk word for worms perfectly well.

'Ah,' said Ogvai, nodding and sitting back. 'I understand now. Why didn't you say so?'

'I'm sorry,' said Hawser. 'I have travelled a long way, and picked up as many words as I have stories.'

'Continue,' Ogvai instructed.

HE CONTINUED. HE built in the rests he'd been advised to incorporate, and slept for a few hours at a time as the men drank mjod, and talked. Sometimes, the drumming and the anti-music would start up again, and some of the men would dance a sort of furious anti-dance, a wild, heedless, ecstatic frenzy that looked as if they had been possessed or suffered a mass psychogenic chorea. It grew so warm in the chamber that Hawser began to go to the fireside without his pelt when he was called.

It was a test of endurance. He ate what the thralls brought him, and drank copiously to maintain his fluid levels. The stories, even the shortest and most incomplete tales, seemed to crawl by, etching out Longfang's lifespan slowly, like careful knotwork. Four hundred and thirty-two stories took time to tell properly.

The last of all would be the account of Longfang's death, a tale that combined Hawser's memories with those of Jormungndr Two-blade. Hawser knew he would be tired by the time he reached it.

He also knew he had to make it the best of all.

It was still a long way off, with over sixty stories left to tell, when Ogvai rose to his feet. They had stopped to rest. Aeska shook Hawser awake. The drumming was quietening down from another frenzied bout, and dancers were slumping to the deck, laughing and reaching out for mjod.

'What's happening?' Hawser asked.

'Part of the sending off is the choosing of the next,' said Aeska.

There were several men in Tra who were alleged to have the sight like Longfang. They also served in priest-like capacities, and one would be selected to fulfil Longfang's senior role.

They came forwards and knelt in a circle around Ogvai. The jarl's centre-parted hair fell straight on either side of his face like black-water cataracts. He was stripped to the waist. He tilted his head back and reached out his hands, flexing the huge muscles of his arms, his shoulders and his neck. Grey ash had been smeared on his snow-white flesh. Like Hawser, Ogvai had black paint across his eyes.

In his right hand, he held a ceremonial blade. An *athame*.

The jarl started to speak, intoning in turn the virtues of each candidate.

Hawser wasn't listening. The athame, the pose with the arms outstretched, it violently reminded him of the figure in the Lutetian Bibliotech, a story that had been locked in his head for decades, a story he had only brought out again for Heoroth Longfang.

He stared at the athame.

It wasn't just similar. Kasper Hawser was an expert in these things. He knew about types and styles. This wasn't a misidentification based on similarity.

It was precisely the same blade.

He rose to his feet.

'What are you doing?' asked Godsmote.

'Sit down, skjald,' said Oje. 'It's not your turn.'

'How is that the same?' asked Hawser, staring at the ceremony.

'How is what the same?' asked Aeska, annoyed.

'Sit down and shut up,' growled another Wolf.

'How is that blade the same?' Hawser asked, pointing.

'Sit down,' said Godsmote. 'Hjolda! I'll smite you myself if you don't sit down!'

Ogvai had made his choice. The other candidates bowed their faces down to the deck to acknowledge the authority of the decision. The chosen man rose to his feet to face the jarl.

Tra's new rune priest was young, one of the younger candidates. Aun Helwintr had earned his name because his long hair was as white as deep season snow, despite his age. The leatherwork of his mask was so dark it was almost black, and he wore the pelt of a tawny animal. He was known for his strange, distant manner, his odd bearing, and his habit of getting into impetuous fights that he miraculously survived. Wyrd gathered inside Aun Helwintr in a way that Ogvai wanted to harness.

Some rite was about to take place. Hawser felt the silence close in. He believed himself to be the cause of it.

That was not the case. The Wolves had turned to look towards one of the chamber hatches, golden eyes baleful in the firelight.

A group of thralls stood there, escorting a terrified-looking member of *Niddhoggur's* bridge crew. They had entered despite the marks of aversion at the doorways.

Ogvai Ogvai Helmschrot swapped the athame into his left hand and picked up his war axe. He strode across the hold space to dismember them for their violation.

Halfway across the deck, he stopped and checked himself. Only an idiot would ignore a mark and break in on such a private ceremony.

Only an idiot, or a man with a message so important that it couldn't wait.

'So you liked the account?' Hawser asked. 'It amused you? It distracted you?'

'It was amusing enough,' said Longfang. 'It wasn't your best.'

'I can assure you it was,' said Hawser.

Longfang shook his head. Droplets of blood flecked from his beard.

'No, you'll learn better ones,' he said. 'Far better ones. And even now, it's not the best you know.'

'It's the most unnerving thing that happened to me in my old life,' said Hawser with some defiance. 'It has the most… maleficarum.'

'You know that's not true,' said Longfang. 'In your heart, you know better. You're denying yourself.'

Hawser woke with a start. For a terrible, rushing moment, he thought he was back in the Bibliotech, or out on the ice fields with Longfang, or even in the burning courtyard of the Quietude's sundered city.

But it was all a dream. He lay back, calming down, trying to slow his panicked breathing, his bolting heart. Just a dream. Just a dream.

Hawser settled back onto his bed. He felt tired and unrefreshed, as if his sleep had been sour, or sedative assisted. His limbs ached. Sustained artificial gravity always did that to him.

Golden light was knifing into his chamber around the window shutter, gilding everything, giving the room a soft, burnished feel.

There was an electronic chime.

'Yes?' he said.

'Ser Hawser? It is your hour five alarm,' said a softly modulated servitor voice.

'Thank you,' said Hawser. He sat up. He was so stiff, so worn out. He hadn't felt this bad for a long time. His leg was sore. Maybe there were painkillers in the drawer.

He limped to the window, and pressed the stud to open the shutter. It rose into its frame recess with a low hum, allowing golden light to flood in. He looked out. It was a hell of a view.

The sun, source of the ethereal radiance, was just coming up over the hemisphere below him. He was looking straight down on Terra in all its magnificence. He could see the night side and the constellation pattern of hive lights in the darkness behind the chasing terminator, he could see the sunlit blue of oceans and the whipped-cream swirl of clouds, and, below, he could see the glittering light points of the superorbital plate Rodinia gliding majestically under the one he was aboard, which was...

Lemurya. Yes, that was it. Lemurya. A luxury suite on the underside of the Lemuryan plate.

His eyes refocussed. He saw his own sunlit reflection in the thick glass of the window port. Old! So old! *So old!* How old was he? Eighty? Eighty years standard? He recoiled. This was wrong. On Fenris, they'd remade him, they'd–

Except he hadn't been to Fenris yet. He hadn't even left Terra.

Bathed in golden sunlight, he stared at his aghast reflection. He saw the face of the other figure reflected in the glass, the figure standing just behind him.

Terror constricted him.

'How can you be here?' he asked.

And woke.

The chamber was cold and dark, and he was on the deck under his pelt. He could feel the distant grumble of *Nidhoggur's* drive. Nightmare sweat was cold on his gooseflesh.

No one had seen Ogvai since the interruption to the ceremony. Fith said that Tra had received an urgent notification and been retasked, but there was nothing concrete. As usual, Hawser didn't expect to be told much. He waited a while to see if the ceremony would be resumed, but it was clear the moment had passed. The fires were allowed to go out, and the men of Tra dispersed. Hawser found most of them in the arming chambers, readying their weapons and their battlegear, or in the practice cages. Blades were being whetted so they held the best edge, armour was being polished and adjusted. Small refinements were being added, small trinkets or decorations. Beads and loops of teeth were being wired in place. Marks of aversion were being notched onto the tips of bolter rounds. In the harder gantry lighting of the arming chambers, Hawser reflected how much like flayed humans the Wolves looked in their leatherwork gear. The knotwork and straked pieces resembled sinews, tendons and sheets of muscle.

No one paid him any heed. His head bubbling with unhappy dreams and a sense that he had slept too long for his own good, he wandered back to the hold space.

The air smelled of cold smoke. He touched the marks of aversion on the door sills, felt the rough metal edges where they, like the others marked in place before them, had been defaced and robbed of potency.

Hawser wandered into the hold space, and stood for a while beside the smouldering heap of the main fire. He saw the glitter of the offerings the men had left in the grey ashes, and the stains of mjod splashed on the decking. He saw the discarded drums and sistra. Thralls had collected up all the lanx dishes and flasks. There were no signs of the ritual items used by either Najot Threader, the wolf priest, or Ogvai.

Go where you like.

That's what Longfang had told him.

'You're a skjald. That's the one great privilege and right of being what you are. No one in the Rout can bar you, or keep you at bay, or stop you from sticking your nose in.'

Hawser headed for the jarl's chamber.

Ogvai occupied a stateroom near the core of the starship. If *Nidhoggur* was Tra's lair, then the chamber was
the darkness at the very back of the cave reserved for the
alpha male. It was sparsely furnished, and screened with
veils of metal link, like curtains of chainmail. Hawser's
Fenrisian eye found no trace of body heat in the chilly
shadows, and his nose detected barely any pheromones
in the pelts scattered around the deck.

Adjoining Ogvai's sleeping chamber was a weaponarium. Most of the items and devices on display were
trophies that the jarl had taken from vanquished foes.
There were xenosform weapons whose form and function Hawser could barely imagine: staves, wands, fans,
sceptres, small delicate machines. On other shelves and
racks were arranged biological weapons: teeth, claws,
spines, toe-hooks, mandibles, stingers. Some were preserved in jars of fluid suspension. Others were dried. A
few were burnished, as if for use. Hawser paused for a
moment to marvel at the grotesque size of some of the
specimens. One sickle talon was as long as his arm.
There was a quill as big as a harpoon. He tried to imagine the proportions of the creatures that had once been
attached to them.

On other stands, firearms and blades were displayed.
Hawser hunted along the lines of them until he found
the collection of daggers and shorter blades.

There were several athames. Some were Fenrisian. The
conservator in Hawser wished to hell he knew where
Ogvai had come by the others. They were priceless relics
from before the Age of Strife.

'You could ask him.'

Hawser snapped around. Without hesitating, he had
slipped one of the displayed athames off its hooks and
aimed it at the shadow that had spoken.

'It's one of a number of questions you have for him,
isn't it?'

'Show yourself,' said Hawser.

Something took the athame out of his hand. Hawser felt a painful bump, and then he was being strangled, his feet kicking free in loose air.

He had been picked up and hung from the tip of the sickle talon by his pelt. The athame he had been brandishing was embedded in the wall, quivering. He tried to pull away the knot holding the pelt in place. It was hanging him. He couldn't get his head free. His legs pinwheeled frantically.

He was lifted down and thrown onto the deck, choking and gasping.

Aun Helwintr crouched down beside him, his elbows on his knees.

'I don't care who you are,' said the new rune priest. 'You don't pull a blade on me.'

'I recognise my failing and will be sure to correct it,' Hawser coughed out, snidely.

'You were looking for something, weren't you?' remarked Aun Helwintr. 'You were looking for something and it's not here.'

'How do you know?'

'Your mind is loud, skjald.'

'My what?'

Aun Helwintr gestured to the racks containing the daggers and athames.

'It's not here. The particular blade you were looking for.'

Helwintr's skin was almost gelid blue under his mane of straight, white hair. His features were long and sharp, like a blade, and his eyes were edged in kohl. He looked amused, like some kind of cunning, dangerous boreal trickster-god.

Hawser stared up at the rune priest in quiet alarm. He could hear Aun Helwintr's voice, but the priest's lips were not moving.

'The measure of your surprise, Ahmad Ibn Rustah,' the rune priest murmured without using his mouth, 'reflects the unconscious contempt you have for the Sixth Legion Astartes.'

'Contempt? No–'

'You cannot hide it. We are barbarians, arctic savages, gene-fixed and dressed up with war-tech, and sent off to do unseemly labour for our more cultured masters. It is a common belief.'

'I never said that–' Hawser protested.

'Or even consciously thought it. But deep down inside you, there is a patronising sense of superiority. You are a civilised man, and you've come to study us, like a magos biologis observing some primitive tribe of throwbacks. We live like animals, and we follow shamans. And yet… Great Terra! Could it be that our shamans have real gifts? *Genuine* powers? Could it be that they are *more* than just bone-rattling, bead-jangling gothi, out of their heads on mushrooms, howling at the sky?'

'Psionics,' whispered Hawser.

'Psionics,' Aun Helwintr echoed, smiling. He used his real voice.

'I had heard that some of the Legions actually had psyker contingents,' said Hawser.

'Most of them have,' replied Helwintr.

'But the occurrence is so very rare,' Hawser said. 'The mutation is a–'

'The psyker mutation is a priceless asset to our species,' said Helwintr. 'Without it, we would be condemned to captivity on Terra. The Great Houses of the Navigators allow us to expand our reach. The astrotelepaths allow us to communicate over the gulfs. But caution must always be exercised. Control.'

'Why?'

'Because when you gaze out with your mind, you never know what will stare back.'

Hawser got up and faced the rune priest.

'Was there a purpose to this demonstration, apart from scaring me?' he asked.

'The purpose was the fear,' Helwintr replied. 'Just for a second, you thought some kind of fell magic had swept you away. Some kind of maleficarum. You felt the same way that night, years ago, beside that cathedral corpse.'

Hawser looked at him sharply.

'I can read the pin-sharp memory you shared with Longfang,' Helwintr told him.

'Are you saying,' Hawser began, 'are you saying that my colleague Navid Murza was a psyker, and I never knew it?'

'You come from a society that accepts and uses psykers, skjald. On Old Terra, they walked amongst you on a daily basis. Did you recognise them all? On Fenris, could you tell a ranting shaman from a man who truly has the sight?'

Hawser tightened his lips. He had no answer. Helwintr leaned closer, and stared down into Hawser's eyes.

'The truth of it all is that your colleague probably wasn't a psyker. He had found a crude shortcut to something else. And that is the point. That is the lesson. Psyker ability is not a thing of itself. It allows us to draw on a greater power. It is just another path to that same something else. The best path. The safest path. Even then, it's not without its pitfalls. If you'd care to, you may define maleficarum as any sorcery that is not performed under the most stringent application of psyker control.'

'Just like that, you tell me I live in a universe of magic,' said Hawser.

'Just like that,' agreed Helwintr. 'Is it so hard to reconcile with all the other wonders and horrors?'

'What about the knife?' asked Hawser. 'It was the knife.'

'It was not the same,' Helwintr replied. 'But something

wanted you to think it was. Something wanted you to
think that the Sixth Legion Astartes had manipulated
you and intervened in your life at some point in the
past. Something wanted you to mistrust us and make us
enemies.'

He took an athame off the stand and showed it to
Hawser.

'This is the blade Ogvai used,' he said. 'You recognise
it well enough now, don't you?'

'Yes,' said Hawser.

'It was made to look like the one you remembered,'
said Helwintr. 'Something got into your memories and
altered them to turn you against us.'

Hawser swallowed.

'What could do that?' he asked. 'Who could do that?'

Helwintr shrugged, as though he didn't care.

'Perhaps it was whoever made sure you could speak
Juvjk and Wurgen from the moment you arrived on
Fenris,' he said.

⚜

AUN HELWINTR RAISED his left hand and beckoned,
though Hawser was sure the gesture was unnecessary.
Fith Godsmote disengaged his practice cage and
jumped down to approach them.

It was extremely noisy in the training hall of *Niddhoggur's* company deck. Godsmote's cage was whining to a
halt, but most of the others were still occupied, and
their mechanised armatures of blades of target drones
were emitting high pitched screams as they whirled
around. On the open deck mats, Wolves in leatherwork
armour sparred with each other using staves of bone.

Godsmote, like all of them, looked like a flayed
human in his leatherware. His black-pinned gold eyes
blazed inside the slits of his gleaming brown mask. He
had been training with two axes, and he held on to
them as he came over rather than racking them.

'Priest?' he said.

'A duty for you,' said Helwintr.

'I serve,' Godsmote nodded.

Helwintr glanced at Hawser.

'Say to him what you said to me,' the priest prompted.

'I've never been a fighter,' said Hawser.

Godsmote snorted.

'This is known about you,' he remarked, amused.

'Can I finish?' Hawser asked.

Godsmote shrugged.

'I've never been a fighter, but the *Vlka Fenryka* have seen fit to rebuild me with great strength and speed. I have the physical capacity, but none of the skills.'

'He wants to learn how to handle a weapon,' said Helwintr.

'Why?' asked Godsmote. 'He's our skjald. We'll protect him.'

'If he wants to, it's his choice,' said Helwintr. 'Tell yourself that part of our duty to protect him is teaching him to protect himself.'

Godsmote looked down at Hawser dubiously.

'There's no sense trying to teach you everything,' he said. 'We'll pick one thing and focus on that.'

'What do you suggest?' asked Hawser.

THE AXE WAS a single-bladed weapon with an almost silvered finish to the plasteel head. Its haft was a touch under a metre long, and hand shaped from a piece of bone from Asaheim. The polished ivory possessed a yellow glow. Hawser wasn't sure what kind of animal the bone had been taken from, but he had been told it was supple and pretty much unbreakable.

Unbreakable for his purposes, anyway.

The axe lived on his hip in a loop of plasteel that was held to his belt by a piece of leatherwork.

'Don't loiter,' Bear warned him.

Hawser didn't intend to, but he was sweating like a pig in the heat, and it was a considerable effort to keep up with the striding Astartes.

He was the only regular human amongst them; a slight figure dwarfed by the two dozen fully armoured Wolves thundering down the tunnel around him. The thralls and the regular human-sized servants were following them at a distance.

Ogvai Ogvai Helmschrot led the party, his helm clamped under his arm. There was no orderly ranking to the group, but Aun Helwintr and Jormungndr Twoblade flanked the jarl, and Najot Threader and the other wolf priests seemed to glide along in the rear part of the group.

The Wolves were marching purposefully, as if Ogvai was in a hurry to be somewhere. After forty weeks of transit, Hawser wondered what could be so important it couldn't have been undertaken with more circumspection. They had deployed from *Nidhoggur* the moment it achieved high anchor, which made it feel like an urgent combat drop, but it was clearly not that at all. They had come in blind, through terrifying atmospherics that had required instrumentation-only guidance, and eventually slid under a volcanic shelf and set down in deep, sheltered landing pits.

The local heat was immense. The rock around them was black and volcanic, and there was a bad-egg whiff of sulphur in the air. The air itself shimmered with a haze of heat. As he walked down the Stormbird's ramp behind Godsmote, Hawser had felt an ear-pop sensation that suggested that vast, hidden atmosphere processors were waging a monumental war to maintain a viable environment.

This wasn't a world designed to support life.

The landing pits, and the tunnels that led away from them into the core of the planet, had been clean cut on a massive scale, as if with industrial meltas. The tunnels sliced through the volcanic rock, leaving an unnaturally smooth surface like glass. There was a constant rumble of the storms outside, and the seismic growing pains of the young planet under their feet. Fiery light, undulating and seething, oozed through the glassy walls and floor of the tunnels, and lit their way. It was like being stoppered inside a glass bottle that had been cast into a bonfire. Hawser was disconcerted by an odd sense of the very old and the very new. The subterranean spaces were like ancient habitation cave sites he had investigated on many Conservatory expeditions during his life, yet these had been cut recently, by hand. There was an odd disconnection between the temporary and the permanent too: someone had commanded enough power and resources to bore holes and chambers out of the solid rock of a supervolcano, and to install a zone of safe environment on an inimical world, both of them monumental feats of physical engineering.

Yet Hawser had the distinct feeling that once the intended business here, whatever it was, was done, the whole site would be abandoned. It was purpose built. It was not beyond reason to presume that the lifelessness of the world was part of that purpose. Whatever that business, there was a chance it might turn ugly. Of course there was. An entire company of the *Vlka Fenryka* had been summoned to achieve it.

Whoever had ordered the construction of this environment, had wanted it done in a remote place where there was no danger anyone could get caught in the crossfire.

'What is this place?' Hawser asked, scrambling to keep up.

'Quiet,' Bear hissed.

'Forty weeks! How much longer before you tell me anything?'

'Quiet,' Bear hissed, with greater emphasis.

'I can't tell the account if I don't know the details,' said Hawser, a little more loudly. 'It'd be a poor story then, not at all fitting for Tra's fireside.'

Ogvai came to a sudden halt, so sudden it almost took the fast moving group by surprise. Everyone stopped obediently. Ogvai turned, and glowered back through the figures at Hawser. Sweat was running down Hawser's face in the heat. All the Wolves had mouths half-open, teeth bared, and were slightly panting, like dogs on a warm day.

'What's he saying?' he growled.

'I'm asking how I'm supposed to be a skjald if you don't tell me anything, jarl,' Hawser called back.

Ogvai looked at Aun Helwintr. The rune priest closed his eyes for a second, took a calming breath, and nodded.

Ogvai acknowledged the nod and turned back to Hawser.

'This place is called Nikaea,' he said.

✧

THEY ENTERED A great circular chamber, melta-cut from the bedrock. The surfaces of the room were like black glass shot with glittering mica, but still it reminded Hawser of the ivory-cased chambers of the Aett.

People were waiting for them. Warriors of the Sixth Legion Astartes had been posted around the perimeter, but they were not from Tra. Another company was present.

Amlodhi Skarssen Skarssensson, Jarl of Fyf, rose to his feet from a stone bench.

'Og!' he growled, and the two mighty jarls bear-hugged, banging their armoured chests against each other. Ogvai exchanged some rough sparring remarks with Skarssen and then turned to the other alpha wolf who had been sitting with the Jarl of Fyf.

'Lord Gunn,' Ogvai acknowledged with a tip of his head. The other warrior was older and bigger than either Skarssen and Ogvai. His beard was waxed into two, sharp, up-and-forward-curving tusks, and the left side of his face was inked with dark lines that resembled knotwork.

'Who's that?' Hawser asked Godsmote.

'Gunnar Gunnhilt, called Lord Gunn, Jarl of Onn,' Godsmote replied.

'He's jarl of the First Company?' Hawser asked.

Godsmote nodded.

Three companies. *Three* companies? What could be happening on this place Nikaea that demanded the presence of three companies of Wolves?

Lord Gunn pushed past Ogvai and confronted Hawser.

'Is this the skjald?' he asked. He took Hawser's head between his huge hands and wrestled it back, stretching Hawser's eyes wide to peer into them, and then pulled open Hawser's jaw and leaned down to sniff Hawser's breath, as though he was livestock.

He let go of Hawser and turned away.

'Has it begun?' asked Ogvai.

'Yes,' Skarssen replied, 'but only in a preliminary way. They don't know we're here yet.'

'I don't want them to know,' said Ohthere Wyrdmake. Wyrdmake was one of a number of rune priests who had been standing, silent, spectral and attentive, behind the seated jarls. They were all panting slightly, open-mouthed. The volcanic heat of the chamber didn't seem to touch Skarssen's priest. Even the diffuse, pulsating light of it on his face took a greenish cast, like cold fire. Wyrdmake looked at Aun Helwintr. Something passed between them.

'I don't want them to know,' Wyrdmake repeated.

'We're here purely as a safety measure,' said Lord

Gunn. 'Make that understood. We only reveal our strength if wyrd turns against us. If that happens, this becomes a no-quarter operation, where our only purpose is to secure the primary. Anything and everything that moves contrary to us under those circumstances gets a kill-stroke. Are we clear? I don't care who it is. This is why we exist. Make sure that all in Tra know that–'

Wyrdmake cleared his throat.

'Something to say, priest?' Lord Gunn asked.

Wyrdmake nodded his head towards Hawser.

'You said it was safe enough to talk,' said Lord Gunn.

'We're as safe as we can be down here,' Wyrdmake replied. 'However, I don't see the need to discuss Rout strategy in front of a skjald. He can wait somewhere.'

'Varangr!' Skarssen called. His herald appeared from the ranks around the chamber walls.

'Yes, Skarsi?'

'Var, take Ibn Rustah and put him somewhere.'

'Where, Skarsi?'

'I think it was suggested earlier today that he should be put in the quiet room as soon as he made planetfall.'

'Really, Skarsi? Really? The quiet room?'

'Yes, Var!' Skarssen snapped. He looked at Lord Gunn. 'You have a problem with that?' he asked.

Lord Gunn shrugged and chuckled a little wet leopard-chuckle.

'Valdor made a special point of asking us not to do anything provocative, but we don't take our orders from him. What do you think, priest?'

Wyrdmake gently bowed his head.

'Whatever pleases my Lord Gunn,' he said.

'Very little ever pleases me, gothi,' replied Lord Gunn. 'Being here doesn't please me. The nature of this council, the gravity of what's at stake here, the infernal politicking and pussy-footing, none of it pleases me.

However, sticking this little runt in the quiet room might amuse me for a short while.'

All of the Wolves in the group laughed. Hawser shivered.

'This way,' said Varangr.

Wyrdmake stopped Hawser as the herald of Fyf began to lead him away.

'I am told you were with Longfang when his thread was cut.'

'I was,' said Hawser.

'Don't forget where he led you,' said Wyrdmake. 'He would have led you further, except he couldn't follow.'

✣

VARANGR LED HAWSER out of the chamber, and down a melta-cut tunnel towards the enigmatic 'quiet room'. They had barely entered the tunnel when Hawser started to feel queasy.

'Gets into your guts, doesn't it?' asked Varangr with relish. 'Like a knife. No, a branding iron.'

'What is that?'

'It's them,' the herald replied, as if that explained everything. Tectonic booming echoed up through the tunnel floor, and luminous orange blossoms of lava lit up and flowed past the vitreous walls. Hawser felt unsteady, his head swimmy. He leant against the tunnel wall for support, not caring how painfully warm the glassy surface felt.

'You'll get used to it,' said Varangr. 'Don't know what's worse, the feeling of them, or the feeling of what they keep out.'

At the end of the tunnel, there was a rough-notched mark of aversion staring out of the rock lintel.

They passed by it, and Varangr led him out into a large, square chamber, smaller than the space that had housed the Fenrisian jarls. The floor was made of a rough, grey pyroclastic rock, though displays of volcanic firelight still shimmered through the glassy walls and ceiling to provide light. Six tall figures were sitting on bench blocks cut from the flaky grey rock. They rose to their feet as one the moment Varangr and Hawser entered and faced them.

'Refreshments,' Varangr said, gesturing at a tray that had been placed on a smaller grey block. On the tray were some dried field kit rations, a jug of tepid water, a flask of mjod and a lidded bowl. From the smell, Hawser could tell that the bowl contained fresh meat that had begun to turn in the sweltering heat.

'Help yourself,' Varangr said, and left.

Hawser looked at the six figures facing him. They were tall, taller than him, and female, all dressed in ornate, high-collared war armour. The armour looked gold or hammered bronze in the firelight. Despite the heat, the females wore floor length cloaks of a rich, crimson fabric. Exquisite parchments, manuscripts and prayer strips hung from their belts and armour plates, attached by red wax seals and ribbons. Kasper Hawser could recite copious amounts of evidentiary research on the historical use and significance of prayer strips. He knew a great deal about the importance, the actual psychophysical potency, that primitive cultures had once invested in the written word. To many human civilisations in the past, prayers or wards or imprecations written down in some ritual fashion and pinned or otherwise attached to a person in a ceremonial manner were things of supernatural force. They protected the wearer. They were marks of aversion, or the means to vouchsafe good fortune. They were ways of making hoped-for futures become reality. They were charms for fending off bad things.

The fact that the women wore such adornments, like old Cruxian pilgrims, felt like the most spectacularly pagan thing Hawser had seen in a long time, and that was saying something given how long he'd lived with the *Vlka Fenryka*. The Fenrisians were tempered by the primitive climate of their planet. These females were coldly beguiling, their arms and armour the product of High Terran technology. Each one had a silver longsword, a powerblade of horrible beauty. The swords rested upright, tips to the floor between the women's feet. Each female had her armoured wrists crossed on the pommel of her sword.

None of the females wore a helmet, but the grilled throat guards of their golden armour rose up high, obscuring their mouths and the lower halves of their faces. Eyes without a nose or mouth, eyes above golden grilles. They reminded him of an old memory, faded and creased. A mouth, smiling, and eyes hidden.

The eyes of each of the females were intense and unblinking. Their heads were shaved except for bound top knots of long hair.

'Who are you?' he asked, wiping sweat off his brow. His skin had gone clammy.

They didn't reply. He didn't want to look at them. It was the strangest thing. The swimmy, bilious feeling returned, far more unpleasantly than before. The females were fascinating, beautiful figures, but he did not want to regard them. He wanted to do anything but. The sight of them repelled him. The very fact of them made him recoil.

'Who are you?' he demanded, turning away. 'What are you?'

No reply came. He heard the faintest metal scratch as a sword tip lifted away from pyroclastic rock floor. Still looking aside, Hawser drew his axe. It was a firm, fluid draw, just the way Godsmote had taught him: left hand under the head, thumb behind the shoulder, pulling to almost throw it clear of the plasteel belt-loop before letting it go, so he caught the haft around the belly with his right hand and clamped the throat with his left hand again, and there it was across his chest, ready to knock into someone.

A voice rumbled something. A command. The voice was so deep, it sounded like an extension of the seismic turmoil beneath them.

Hawser dared to raise his eye line. He maintained his grip on his axe, fully prepared to strike.

The beautifully hideous, hideously beautiful females had encircled him. Their longswords were all aimed at him in double-handed grips. Any one of them could extinguish his life with a turn of her wrists.

The voice rumbled again. It was louder this time: the throat-noise of an animal mixed with a volcanic detonation, the furious blast of the top coming off a mountain.

As one, the females took a step back, all switching to a formal 'rest' position, with their swords raised at their right shoulders and no longer directly threatening. The voice muttered a third noise, a softer growl, and the females stepped back, breaking the circle around Hawser.

Hawser moved clear of them, further into the chamber. He could see a dark shape ahead of him, a mass of shadows in the ruddy firelight. It was the source of the voice.

Hawser could hear the soft, deep, quick panting of a big animal bothered by heat.

The figure spoke. Hawser felt its voice vibrate his diaphragm. He felt terror through to his core, but, curiously, it was a clean, simple feeling, preferable to the revulsion the females had inspired.

'I don't understand,' Hawser said. 'I don't understand what you're saying to me.'

The voice trembled him again.

'Ser, I can hear your words, but I don't know the language,' Hawser insisted.

The figure stirred and looked directly at him. Hawser saw its face.

'I was told you spoke the cants of the *Vlka Fenryka*,' said Leman Russ.

TEN

Witness

THE WOLF KING straightened up, like some elemental giant rousing from its telluric slumber.

'Juvjk. Wurgen,' he said. 'I was informed you spoke both fluently.'

The distinctive wet leopard-growl of the Fenrisian Astartes haunted every syllable of his words. Hawser was mesmerised by the primarch's size. Every physical dimension exceeded that of an Astartes. It was like meeting a god. It was as though one of the great and perfectly proportioned statues of classical antiquity, one scaled fifty or seventy-five per cent bigger than human standard, had come to life.

'Well?' asked Russ. 'Or have you lost your command of Low Gothic too?'

'Ser, I…' Hawser began. 'Ser… you're speaking Low Gothic?'

'I am now.'

'Then I don't know,' said Hawser. He wished, desperately, his voice didn't sound so pathetic and paper-thin.

'I could speak both Juvjk and Wurgen before I was brought to this quiet room. Then again, I could speak neither of them until I came to Fenris, so make of that what you will.'

The Wolf King pouted thoughtfully.

'I think it confirms what Wyrdmake and the others have believed all along. You've been tampered with, Ahmad Ibn Rustah. At some point prior to your arrival on Fenris, some agency, probably a psyker, altered your mind.'

'Aun Helwintr suggested as much to me, ser. It's quite a thing to take in. If it's true, then I can't trust myself.'

'Imagine how we feel.'

Hawser stared at the Wolf King.

'Why do you even tolerate me, then? I'm untrustworthy. I'm maleficarum.'

'Oh, sit down,' said the Wolf King. He held out a huge open hand and gestured to a stone bench beside him. 'Sit down and we'll talk about it.'

The Wolf King was also seated on a stone bench. He had a deep silver lanx near to hand, brimming with mjod. His armour appeared almost black, as if it had been scorched and tarnished in a smithy, but Hawser felt that was just the way the gloom of the firelight played upon it. Under an open sky, he thought, it would be tempest grey.

The armour was by far the heaviest and most marked power plate Hawser had ever seen. It dwarfed the formidable suits of the Terminators. It was notched and gouged, and the damage was as much decoration as the knotwork and tooled etching on the main plates. Around his shoulders, Russ wore a black wolf-skin. The pelt seemed to surround him and clothe him, like a forest beards a hillslope or a stormcloud smokes a peak. His face was shaved clean, and his skin was white like marble. Close to, Hawser could see light freckles on it.

The Wolf King's hair was long. Thick plaits of it hung down across his chest plate, weighted at the tips by polished stones. The rest of it was lacquered into a spiked mane. Hawser had heard many stories about the Wolf King from the men of Tra. They had all described his hair as red, or the colour of rust, or of molten copper. Hawser wasn't so sure. To him, the Wolf King's mane looked like bright blond hair stained in blood.

Russ watched Hawser take his seat. He sipped from his lanx. He was panting still, through parted lips, like a large mammal made uncomfortable by the heat but unable to shed its fur.

'This chamber has proved the tampering.'

'They called it the quiet room,' said Hawser. 'Who are those females, ser?'

He gestured towards the armoured figures waiting near the mouth of the chamber, but he could not bring himself to look at them.

'Members of the Silent Sisterhood,' Russ replied. 'An ancient Terran order. Null Maidens, some call them.'

'Why do I find them so… distressing?'

Russ smiled. It was an odd expression. He had a long philtrum and a heavy lower lip. These, combined with the high, freckled cheekbones, made his mouth into something of a muzzle, and his smile into a threat display of teeth.

'That's their function… aside from the fact they fight like bastards. They're blanks. Untouchables. Psyker-inert. Got the pariah gene in them. Nothing on Nikaea can see us or hear our minds while we're in here with them. There are more of them stationed throughout these chambers, and their effect is general enough to cloak the presence of the *Vlka Fenryka*. But Gunn thought it a good idea if I stayed in here, in the heart of it.'

'Why?'

'I don't want to upset my brother,' replied Russ.

'Why? What might he do?' asked Hawser, swallowing hard. The question he'd really wanted to ask was, *who is your brother?*

'Something stupid that we'd all regret for a damned long time,' said Russ. 'We're just here to make sure he arrives at the right decision. And if he doesn't, we're here to make sure the repercussions of the wrong decision are restricted to a bare minimum.'

'You're talking about another primarch,' said Hawser.

'Yes, I am.'

'You're talking about taking arms against another primarch?'

'Yes. If needs be. Funny, I always seem to get the dirty jobs.'

The Wolf King rose to his feet and stretched.

'The moment you came in here, *ser*,' Russ said, mocking Hawser's use of the honorific, 'the scramble-your-guts sisters blocked whatever was playing with your head. I'd be very interested to know who was handling you.'

'Handling?'

'My dear Ahmad Ibn Rustah, wake up and see where you are. You're a spy. A pawn in a very long game.'

'A spy? I assure you, not willingly, ser! I–'

'Oh, be quiet, little man!' the Wolf King growled. The vibratory force alone sat Hawser back on his stone bench. 'I know you're not. We've spent a long time and a lot of effort testing you. We want to know what kind of spy you are: a basic intelligence gatherer, or something with a more insidious mission. We want to know who's running you, and who sent you to infiltrate the *Vlka Fenryka* twenty years ago.'

'That was my choice. I chose Fenris, out of academic interest and–'

'No,' said Leman Russ. 'No, you didn't. You think you did. You feel like you did, but it's not true.'

'But–'

'It's not true, and you'll see that yourself in time.'

The Wolf King sat down again, facing Hawser. He leaned in and stared into Hawser's eyes. Hawser trembled. He wasn't able not to.

'People think the Sixth are just savages. But you've spent enough time among us to know that's not true. We fight smart. We don't just charge in howling, even if it looks like we do. We gather impeccable intelligence and we use it. We exploit any crack, any weakness. We are ruthless. We're not stupid.'

'I've been told this,' said Hawser. 'I've witnessed it with my own eyes. I've heard Jarl Ogvai repeat the lesson to the men of Tra.'

'Jarl Ogvai knows how I like my Legion run. He would not have been named jarl otherwise. There are certain philosophies of war that I adhere to. Does that surprise you?'

'No, ser.'

'You may have been placed among us by an enemy, or a potential enemy,' said the Wolf King. 'Rather than just disposing of you as a threat, I'd like to use you. Are you willing to help me?'

'I serve,' said Hawser, blinking fast.

'It might get your thread cut,' rumbled Leman Russ through a smile, 'but I want you to test the ice and see if you can't get whoever sent you to show themselves.'

RUSS ROSE AGAIN.

'Women!' he shouted, and made a great beckoning gesture for the Sisters of Silence to follow them. All six moved in perfect coordination, and swung their longswords up to a shoulder guard position from the tip-down stance. Hawser heard six, quick simultaneous scratches of metal on rock.

Russ took another swig of mjod, set his lanx aside,

and lumbered out of the cavern through a melta-cut gap opposite the corridor Hawser had entered by. Following close behind him, Hawser had time to appreciate the size of the broadsword the Wolf King wore in a leather-work and nacre scabbard across his back. He was struck by its beauty. It had the same hypnotic perfection as an approaching storm, or the gape of an apex predator a millisecond away from biting. The sword was bigger than him, taller. It would not have fitted into a coffin built for Kasper Hawser.

The gold-plated female warriors fell in step around them as an honour guard, three on each side. Hawser felt his skin crawl at their proximity. He had not put his axe away since drawing it at the chamber mouth, and his hands white-knuckled around the warm bone grip. Sweat beaded on his face.

The gap was short, and led down a series of crude, torch-cut steps into a soaring, lofty chamber. After the confines of the tunnels and the quiet room, its size took Hawser's breath away. An immense bubble had once been trapped in the lava stream that had solidified to compose this part of the mountain. The floor had been levelled off with melta work, but the upper reaches of the cavern were naturally arched, mimicking a cathedral's nave. Though the air was warm, there was a murmur in it, the echo of many voices dwarfed by a great space.

The chamber had been set up as a command post. On top of the metal decking plates set up on the heat-levelled floor, portable power units were running cogitator sets and deep-gain vox-casters. There were lighting rigs and, Hawser noted, automated sentry guns and field generators at the outer exits. This was a strongpoint. The area had been made defensible. Solemn rows of Imperial banners and flags had been suspended down the length of the chamber from the ceiling, hanging limp and heavy in the heat. They were martial symbols and honour rolls, vast sheets of cloth and gold thread evidencing the dignity and import of the Imperium of Man. Here, even here in a rock-cut facility built for temporary purposes, it had been considered necessary to make such a display, as though the chamber was one of the great halls of the Royal Palace of Terra.

A curious mix of personnel manned the command post. There were hundreds of humans and servitors at work. More of the silent sisters lurked around the corners of the vast space, lending their distressing absence to the location. At the bustling console positions, most of the personnel were uniformed officers of the Imperial Fleet and the Hegemonic Corps, though Hawser saw some Sixth Legion thralls along with liveried human servants from other institutions.

The most striking figures were the giants dressed in gold. There were at least a dozen of them in the chamber, supervising different tasks. Their armour was ornate, like that worn by the Astartes, but it was more lightly and finely built, as if forged by more subtle craftsmen. Some of the giants were bareheaded. Others wore conical golden helmets with green-glowing eye slits and red horse-hair plumes.

They were Custodes, the praetorian bodyguards of High Terra. Their accelerated post-human nature had been derived by yet another different principle to those which had produced the Astartes and the primarchs, and they fitted in magnitude between the two: far fewer in number yet greater in faculty than the Astartes.

'I can think,' Hawser began.

'What?' asked Russ gruffly, swinging round to look at the skjald behind him. 'What did you say?'

'I said I can think of only one reason why the warriors of the Legio Custodes would be here,' said Hawser.

'Then you're thinking well,' Russ snapped.

'He's here,' said Hawser.

'Yes, he's here.'

Kasper Hawser slowly tilted his head back and looked up at the roof of the glass-rock cave. Magmatic light pulsed inside the volcanic walls, but all he really saw was the light in his imagination. He had never thought, never ever thought, he would stand in such proximity–

'He's here?' he whispered.

'Yes! That's why we're on our best behaviour.'

The Wolf King gestured insistently at one of the noble golden figures who was standing at a codifier not far away, observing the crew of operators at work. The figure had already noticed the entry of the glowering Wolf King. So had other people in the room. They were approaching with some haste, as if they didn't want to keep him waiting.

Or they didn't want to leave him alone long enough to cause a problem.

The Custodes reached them first. Close up, it became clear how ornamented the surface of his gilded armour was. Serpents curled around the seals of the gorget, and writhed around the shoulders and breastplate. Suns, stars and moons of all phases ran around the vambraces and the arm-guards. There were trees, flames, petals, diamonds, daggers, figures of tarot and open palms. Eyes and circumpuncts gazed out. The symbological historian in Hawser saw a lifetime's work in every part of the Custodes's plate, in the heraldic and cultural significance of every mark and engraving, every inscription and device. The man was a walking artefact. An incomplete but tantalising primer to mankind's esoteric tradition presented itself in the form of power armour.

Over his armour, the Custodes wore a long red cloak and a red kilt covered by a war skirt of studded leather. His all-enclosing conical helm with its flowing plume of red hair made him a towering prospect. He regarded the Wolf King with his softly glowing green eye slits, and curtly nodded his head in deference.

'My lord, is there something the matter?' he asked, his voice sounding slightly boxy due to the helmet vox.

'I was just saying, we're on our best behaviour, Constantin.'

'Indeed, my lord. Now, is there something? I thought you were resting in the quiet room. We are rather occupied at the moment.'

'Yes. Constantin, this is the skjald of Tra Company. I've said he can look around. Skjald, I present to you Constantin Valdor, Praetor of the Custodes. Look suitably impressed. He's a very important fellow. It's his job to keep my father safe.'

'My lord, might I speak to you privately for a moment?' Valdor asked.

'I'm making introductions here, Constantin,' snapped Russ.

'I insist,' said Valdor, his vox-clipped tones sounding threatening. A second Custodes had arrived behind Valdor, along with two fully armoured Astartes, one in crimson armour, the other in heavy Terminator plate that was ash grey trimmed with green. A single horn protruded from his helmet like a tusk. A lot of other personnel in the immediate area were stopping to watch the exchange. Two cherub servitors, the size of real human babies, flew in low on damselfly wings. Their faces were silver masks and their wings made drowsy, thrumming beats like outboard motors.

'You know what?' said the Wolf King. 'The last time anyone insisted anything to me, I twisted their arms off and stuck them up their arse.'

The cherubs squealed and swooped into Valdor's shadow to hide.

'My lord,' replied Valdor levelly. 'This constant need of

yours to playfully maintain the role of barbarian king is most amusing, but we are busily occupied with–'

'Oh, Constantin!' Russ chuckled. 'I honestly hoped you'd go for it!' He gave the Praetor an open-handed slap on the arm that Hawser was quite sure left a dent in the golden plate.

'Lord Russ, I must support Lord Valdor's statement,' said the Astartes in red. 'This is no place for a…'

His voice trailed off to the crackle-stop of a vox speaker turning off. He nodded his head at Hawser.

'A person brandishing an axe,' he finished.

Hawser realised the axe was still in his hands. He quickly slipped it back into the loop at his hip.

'Look now, skjald,' said the Wolf King, sweeping his hand out to encompass all four imposing figures confronting them. 'They're ganging up on you. You see the one in red? That's Raldoron, Chapter Master of my brother Sanguinius's Blood Angels. And the handsome brute in grey, that's Typhon, First Captain of the Death Guard. Remember their names so you can tell the account of this day in all detail and particulars at Tra's hearth-side.'

'Enough, my lord,' said Typhon. 'There are matters of security–'

'Oh-ho! Over-stepping your mark, First Captain!' said Russ, taking a step forwards and aiming an accusing finger at the Astartes in ash grey. 'You do not… You do *not* tell a primarch "enough".'

'Maybe I'm allowed to, then,' said another voice. They turned. The towering newcomer had the presence of Leman Russ and the charisma of a main sequence star. He was light and aesthetic perfection where Russ was visceral dynamism and blood-gold hair. Between them, they outshone even the magnificent Custodes.

'You,' said Russ grudgingly. 'Yes, you're allowed to, I suppose.'

He glanced at Hawser.

'You know who this is?'

'No, ser,' mumbled Hawser.

'Well, ser, this, ser, is my brother Fulgrim.'

The Primarch of the Emperor's Children was dressed in finely wrought wargear of purple and gold. His white hair framed a face of almost painfully perfect grace. He smiled down at Hawser politely, briefly.

'Were you getting fretful in your quiet room again, brother?' Fulgrim asked.

'Yes,' Russ admitted, looking away.

'You realise you need to stay there for now? Your presence might be seen as inflammatory, especially when he finds out you pushed for this censure.'

'Yes, yes,' said Russ impatiently.

Fulgrim smiled again. 'Console yourself. Concealing you means that the revelation of the evidence we have at our disposal will carry more effect. Your man Wyrdmake is about to step up to make account.'

'Good. Then the secrecy will be done with and I can stop hiding behind the sisters,' said Russ.

'Still,' he added, with a plaintive tone, 'how I would love to see the look on his face when Wyrdmake is revealed. Or, at least, how I would love to hear that look described at the fireside in years to come by my skjald here.'

The Wolf King got hold of Hawser's upper arm and dragged him forwards, shaking him a little for emphasis.

'We're trying to be patient with you, brother,' said Fulgrim.

'Please, my lord,' added Valdor. 'It's inappropriate for–'

'You never let me introduce him properly,' said Russ, blithely cutting them off. 'Not very polite of you. He is skjald of Tra, also called Ahmad Ibn Rustah, also called Kasper Ansbach Hawser.'

There was a pause, a hesitation.

'You dog, Russ,' murmured Fulgrim.

Valdor reached his hands up to the sides of his steeple helmet, disengaged the neck seals with a pneumatic hiss, and removed it. He handed the helm to his fellow Custodes.

'Playing games with us a little, my lord?' he asked. It sounded from his tone as though he was trying to appear amused. Valdor's head was shaved back to a stubble of white, and he was deep-browed and aquiline. It looked like he seldom found cause to smile at anything.

'Yes, Constantin,' Russ purred. 'I got bored in my quiet room. I had to find something to do.'

'You might have told us this man's identity a little sooner,' said Valdor. He took a hand scanner from his companion and swept Hawser.

'Because my identity matters somehow?' asked Hawser.

'Of course, Kasper,' said Fulgrim.

'You know who I am?' Hawser stammered.

'We've been briefed,' said Raldoron in a crackle of helmet vox.

'Kasper Hawser, distinguished and fêted scholar and academician,' said Typhon, 'founder and director of the Conservatory project that enjoys the Emperor's personal approval.'

Typhon removed his brutally horned helm. The choleric face beneath was bearded and framed by long dark hair. 'Resigned suddenly about seventy years ago adjusted, and subsequently disappeared, apparently while making an inexplicable and ill-advised voyage to Fenris.'

'You know who I am,' Hawser breathed.

'Let's get him debriefed,' said Constantin Valdor.

✠

'You TALK AS if my whole life has been played out to someone else's rules,' said Hawser. The servitors hummed around him.

'Perhaps it has,' said Valdor.

'I refuse to accept that,' said Hawser.

'How many people have got to tell you before you start listening?' asked Russ, his voice a rumble.

'Please, my lord,' chided the other Custodes attending them.

'Constantin, keep your puppy in check,' warned Russ.

Valdor nodded in the direction of the other Custodes, who had removed his engraved helm to reveal the face of a younger man.

'Amon Tauromachian is a bit more than a puppy, Wolf King. Don't goad him.'

Russ laughed. He was sitting on the raised edge of the command post's staging area, watching the bio-checks. Standing at his side, arms folded, Fulgrim smirked and shook his head.

They had taken Hawser to a small medical monitoring area set up in a corner of the main hall. He had been required to lie down on a padded couch. Specialist personnel were running biometric scans using both paddles and skin-patch contacts. Servitors were swabbing spots on Hawser's skin so that small terminals could be attached.

'I went to Fenris because I was driven by the same urge to learn and discover that has inspired me since childhood,' said Hawser, aware that his tone was defensive. 'The decision was prompted by dissatisfaction that after long and devoted service to the cause of Unification, my work was being sidelined and shelved. I was frustrated. I was disappointed. I decided to turn my back on the ridiculous politicking of Terra that was foundering my efforts, and undertake an expedition of pure research, as a cultural historian, to one of the wildest and most mysterious worlds in the Imperium.'

'Even though you've suffered from a crippling fear of wolves since your earliest years?' asked Valdor.

'There are no wolves on Fenris,' replied Hawser.

'Oh, you know there are,' growled Russ, his voice a wet leopard-purr, 'and you know what they are.'

Hawser realised his hands were trembling slightly.

'Then… then if you're searching for some deep-seated psychological reason, perhaps I was seeking to face and overcome my childhood phobia.'

Aun Helwintr had joined them from the outer halls. He sat nearby on one of the other padded couches, rolling polished sea shells out of one gloved palm into the other. The weight of him put huge strain on the adjustable rod frame of the couch.

'Doubtful,' he said. 'I think it's the key. The fear. That specific fear. It has potency. I think it's how they found a way into you in the first place. Still, we've never been able to discern the trigger, despite what we milked from your thoughts during the cold dreaming, and despite how close Longfang came to seeing it. The trigger remains too well clouded.'

'What trigger?' asked Hawser. 'What cold dreaming?'

Constantin Valdor was consulting a data-slate.

'You won the Prix Daumarl among many other citations. Your work was acclaimed by academicians throughout the inner systems. Some of your papers became springboards for lines of research and development that have had profound and positive implications for society. The Conservatory wielded formidable political influence.'

'That's not true,' said Hawser. 'We had to fight for every centimetre of ground.'

'And other political bodies did not?' asked Raldoron, who stood nearby.

'No,' said Hawser, moving so sharply that one of the

terminals detached from his skin. 'The Conservatory was an academic foundation with a simple mandate. We had no influence. By the time I left, we were going to be absorbed into the Hegemonic administration. I couldn't stomach it. Don't tell me we had influence. We were thrown to the wolves.'

He looked over at the Wolf King.

'No offence, ser.'

Russ boomed another laugh that showed his teeth in a distressing way.

'Try not to do that, dear brother,' said Fulgrim. 'You're scaring him.'

'I believe you may have had a great deal of influence,' said Valdor. 'If I may say, ser, your greatest crime was naivety. At the very highest level, your work was admired, and received tacit protection. Other institutions of the Imperium's political machine were aware of that. They were afraid of you. They were jealous of you. You didn't see it and you didn't know it. It's a common mistake. You were a superb academic trying to run an academic foundation. You should have got on with your study and left the job of management to someone more suited to the task. Someone sharp and savvy who could have kept the wolves at bay.'

Valdor turned to Russ.

'I speak metaphorically, my lord,' he said.

Russ nodded, still amused.

'That's all right, Constantin. Sometimes I dismember metaphorically.'

'Navid always filled that role,' Hawser said quietly, to himself. 'He loved the machinations of the Hegemony and the academies. He was never happier than when competing for a stipend or negotiating for a procurement fund.'

'This is Navid Murza?' asked Valdor, consulting the slate. 'Died young, I see. Yes, you were quite a team.

Your brilliance at field work supported by his boundless enthusiasm in the bureaucratic arena. He was killed in Ossetia.'

'The death may have been significant,' said the other Custodes.

'Oh, please!' Hawser snorted. 'Navid was killed by an insurgent's bomb.'

'Nevertheless,' said Valdor, 'it removed him from the Conservatory and took him from your side.'

'I did not decide to go to Fenris because Navid Murza was killed in Ossetia,' said Hawser angrily. 'A number of decades separate those two events. I refuse to believe–'

'The scale of your thinking is too small, ser,' said the other Custodes, the one called Amon. 'Murza was eliminated, and the benefits he brought to you and the Conservatory were eliminated with him. Did you ever replace him? No. He had been your friend for a long time, you were used to him. You took on the responsibilities yourself, even though you knew you weren't suited to them like he was. You forced yourself to be a political animal because to find a replacement would have felt like a betrayal. You didn't want to dishonour his memory.'

'So you were much more worn down when the time came, Kasper,' said Fulgrim. 'You were tired from years of bureaucracy, years of doing the job Murza always should have done, years of not getting on with the work you really enjoyed. You were absolutely primed and ready to throw it all away and go to Fenris.'

'There's still the matter of a trigger,' said Aun Helwintr.

'Yes, that remains a mystery,' Valdor agreed.

'Not the timing,' said Typhon. The ash-grey Terminator stood on the far side of the medical couch. Like Valdor, he was consulting a data-slate.

'He was ripe,' said Fulgrim.

'With respect, yes, my lord,' said Typhon. 'The subject

was ready. I meant the timing in terms of who was directing the subject.'

He looked at his data-slate again.

'Spool eight-six-nine-alpha,' he said. Valdor consulted his slate, and Fulgrim produced one of his own.

'I refer you to the report filed by Henrik Slussen, the undersecretary brought in to facilitate the Conservatory's incorporation into the Administration.'

'That was the straw that broke my spirit,' said Hawser. 'Slussen was an odious man. He didn't begin to appreciate what I was–'

'He may have been a more sympathetic ally than you thought, Kasper,' said Fulgrim. The primarch's smile was calm and reassuring, and his tone supportive. 'At the time of your resignation and disappearance, Slussen filed a report to his superiors. There's a copy in the file spool here. He was recommending that the Conservatory's independence be preserved. He suggested that absorption into the Administratum would seriously hamstring the Conservatory's work, and the benefits it could offer.'

'The proposal was approved by Lord Malcador,' said Valdor. 'The Sigillite placed his personal seal upon the ratification of the Conservatory's autonomy.'

'The Sigillite?' asked Hawser.

'He always took a great interest in your work,' Valdor replied. 'I think he was your champion behind the scenes. If you had not vanished, ser, you would have been granted the authority you craved. Your staff would have increased, along with the scope of your operation. I believe that within three to five years, you would have found yourself with a secretarial position on the advisory council of the Inner Hegemony. You would have been a man of great influence.'

'First Captain Typhon is quite probably correct,' said Fulgrim. 'You would have been less malleable. Your frustrations would have receded. Whoever was running

you had to pull the trigger, in that small window, or run
the risk of losing all control over an agent they had
spent upwards of five decades developing.'

Hawser stood up. The sensors that had been attached
to him pinged off under tension, one by one.

'Ser, we haven't quite finished–' a medical orderly
began to protest.

Fulgrim held up a hand to hush the man gently.

'No one spends that long grooming and deploying an
agent,' Hawser said quietly.

'Yes, they do, Kasper,' said Fulgrim. 'The main institutions of the Imperium wouldn't think twice about
procuring agents at birth and arranging deployments
that saw out their lifetimes. Most of these things are
done without the agents in question even knowing.'

'You'd do it, ser?' Hawser asked, looking up at him.

'We'd all do it,' said Valdor bluntly. 'The business of
intelligence is vital.'

'We kept you on ice for nineteen great years just to
find out who had sent you,' said Russ.

'Predictions may be made,' said Aun Helwintr. 'Wyrd
may be parsed. A man's character may be analysed, and
that analysis extrapolated to foresee what career he
might take, and where he might find himself at certain
points in his life. An experienced diviner can chart a
man's life, and train him like a plant, tend him, make
him grow in a specific direction for a specific purpose.'

'Who did that to me?' asked Hawser.

'Someone who exploited your innate characteristics,
Kasper,' said Fulgrim. 'Someone who saw that your
innocent hunger for lost knowledge could be harnessed
for their benefit.'

'He means our benighted brother,' said the Wolf King.

THE CUSTODES CALLED Amon took Hawser out of the vast
cathedral of the command post, and up through melta-

cut tunnel levels guarded by Astartes of the Ninth and
Fourteenth Legions Astartes. The Custodes carried his
ceremonial weapon, the guardian spear, an ornate
golden halberd that incorporated a master-crafted
bolter. The tunnels were smoky and hazed with heat.
Hawser could feel the steady and monumental pump of
the atmosphere processors preserving the engineered
enclave of Nikaea from instant incineration. His heart
thumped and he felt sick. The beautiful Primarch Fulgrim had suggested he be allowed to walk and settle his
thoughts, though Hawser suspected that, yet again,
other hands were directing his life.

He was glad to be away from the group of worthies,
however. To be the focus of attention for two primarchs,
two Custodes and three senior Astartes was overwhelming. They had all loomed over him literally and in terms
of potency. He had felt like a child in a room with
adults, or an insect in a specimen jar.

Or a livestock animal tethered out as an offering for
predators.

'Are we not moving out of the range of the untouchables?' Hawser asked his escort.

'Yes,' replied the Custodes. 'Only the lower levels are
thought-proofed.'

'So my mind is about to become visible?' Hawser
asked. 'Visible, perhaps to my manipulator? Isn't there a
risk that I'm about to give a great deal away?'

Amon nodded.

'There's also a good chance of securing some leverage,'
he said. 'The Wolf King knew you were a spy, but he
kept you around for a long time. He kept you on Fenris
and took you out into the Crusade. He wanted whoever
was spying on him to see what you saw, and to
understand that he was aware of them. The Wolf King
believes that he doesn't win battles by hiding secrets
from his enemies. He believes he wins them by showing

his enemies exactly what they're up against and how miserably they're going to lose.'

'That's arrogant.'

'That's his way.'

'This enemy, it's not really an enemy, is it? Another primarch? We're talking about rivalry, aren't we?'

'All of the Legions run networks of intelligencers,' replied the Custodes. 'But they do it for different reasons. The Space Wolves do it to strategically evaluate any opponent they might ever, even theoretically, face. The Thousand Sons do it primarily to feed their hunger for learning.'

'Learning?' Hawser echoed. 'What do they want to know?'

'As I understand it,' replied the Custodes, 'everything.'

He ushered Hawser ahead of him with a subservient gesture. There was a light ahead of them, as if the sun was rising, shafting its rays down the throat of a specially aligned barrow-grave. The tunnel was broadening out and opening.

Hawser stepped out onto a platform of black rock like an immense gallery that curved around the upper level of the vast volcanic interior. The ragged lip of the cone above him was backlit by a sky lit pink with Nikaea's vulcanism. It reminded Hawser, for a swift, unmanning moment, of the view up out of the entry-wound pit on the Quietude's home world, the view he had turned to look up at so he did not have to behold Longfang's doom.

Above the pink horizon, the open sky above the cone was still. There was an eerie calm inside the colossal space that the supervolcano enclosed.

Hawser glanced at the Custodes, who nodded reassuringly. Around the curved range of the huge gallery, other figures had gathered, looking down into the volcanic bowl. Hawser stepped forwards to the lip, a waist-high wall of glittering black basalt. He felt its gritty surface as he leaned against it. He felt the tug of soft wind stirring far below, the tremor of an atmosphere subjugated but defiant.

The gallery and its lip had been melta-cut. Below, similar industry had carved out more galleries in concentric rings, stepping down the inner slopes of the cone flue until they became, in turn, stacked tiers of black benches, hewn from the rock, forming a monumental amphitheatre.

Figures crowded the watching galleries, and packed the benched tiers. Hawser peered to make them out. Most were so far away, they were specks: robed adepts, nobles in finery with attendants, groups of Astartes.

Hawser glanced back at Amon, his escort.

'What is happening here?' he asked.

'Philosophies are being tested,' replied the Custodes. 'The uses and abuses of power are being considered and weighed.'

'By whom?' asked Hawser.

Amon Tauromachian made a sound that was probably laughter.

'My dear ser,' he said, 'look again.'

Hawser looked down. The wind stirred up at him. Vertigo tugged his belly at the soaring plunge past the galleries beneath, down the sculpted slopes, over the banked tiers of seating, staged like an ancient Romanii arena, where freemen would bay and jeer as slaves were thrown to wolves.

Down, down, over the heads of some of the Imperium's most potent and significant beings, to the polished floor of the amphitheatre, where a spread eagle the size of a Stormbird had been inlaid in gold in the black marble.

Adjacent to the inlaid eagle's head was a stepped dais.

The dais held light.

The light had been there all the time, too bright to be reconciled, so sublime that his mind had denied it rather than recognise it. It was the source of the rays he had mistaken as sunrise. It was a supernova of blue-white radiance that shafted light into the sky like a spear.

It was a light and it was a figure, and the thought and reality of both made him sob out loud. He had been looking right at it, but his brain had been too afraid to consciously acknowledge what it was seeing.

The Master of Mankind was holding audience, and the light of his magnitude was humbling to behold.

It was the second most extraordinary thing Kasper Hawser would ever witness.

⚜

'You HAVE TO look,' said Amon.

'I can't bear to,' mumbled Hawser, wiping the tears from his eyes.

'You can't look away either,' replied the Custodes.

Shaking, Hawser gazed down. He perceived the shape of a throne in the radiance, a seat of flaring wings. Black banners hung above the seated figure, suspended by choirs of cherubs that were barely visible in the glare.

Flanking the throne on the dais were Custodes warriors, their lance weapons held at attention. The outflung light seemed to infuse them too, transforming their lustrous golden armour into living, writhing magma.

'Who are those other men?' asked Hawser. 'They can't even be men, to stand on the dais so close to the light and not be burned away.'

Amon stepped in beside him, and identified the figures one by one, pointing his index finger.

'The Choirmaster of the Astropaths, the Lord Militant of the Imperial Army, my lord Kelbor-Hal, Fabricator

General of Mars, the Master of Navigators, and my lord
Malcador, the Sigillite.'

'Ser, I have lost the ability to feel,' said Hawser. 'This
day has numbed me. Awe has given way to some kind
of trauma, I think. My mind is broken. My sanity has
fled. I can no longer register shock, or be impressed.
You have just named the five principals of the
Emperor's court, and they are just words to me. Words.
You might as well tell me I have sunk with Atlantys or
been buried in the caves of Agarttha. A man should not
be forced to face the myths that underpin his universe.'

'Unfortunately, some men must,' said Amon. 'And
isn't that what you've been doing your entire life? So
your bio-briefing ran, anyway. You've searched your
whole career for the myths that have been hidden by the
dust of ages, and now they confront you, you shy away?
It suggests a lack of backbone.'

Hawser jerked his gaze away from the spectacle and
stared at the towering Custodes by his side.

'I think I might be permitted a little recoil! I'm not
used to this rarefied society like you!'

'I apologise, ser,' said Amon, 'if I offended you, but it
is your inquisitive quality that caused you to be selected
as a player in the game. It's what made you appealing to
the Fifteenth Legion Astartes. You were already an eager
seeker of knowledge. They merely had to harness it.'

'How could they do that? I've never even encountered
one of their kind.'

'Never?' asked Amon.

'Never! I–'

Hawser's voice dried up. Another memory swam close
out of the lightless abyss at the back of his mind.

Boeotia. So long ago, so very, very long ago.

*He had asked, 'Ser, which Legion do I have the honour of
being protected by?'*

'The Fifteenth.'

The Fifteenth. So. The Thousand Sons.

'What is your name?'

Hawser had turned. The Tupelov Lancers had led most of the team out of the shrine, leaving only him behind. Two more Astartes, each as immense as the first, had manifested behind him. How could something that big have moved so stealthily?

'What is your name?' the new arrival had repeated.

'Hawser, ser. Kasper Hawser, conservator, assigned to–'

'Is that a joke?'

'What?' Hawser had asked. The other Astartes had spoken. 'Is that supposed to be a joke?'

'I don't understand, ser.'

'You told us your name. Was it supposed to be a joke? Is it some nickname?'

'I don't understand. That's my name. Why would you think it's a joke?'

'Kasper Hawser? You don't get the reference?'

'It was years ago,' Hawser said to Amon. 'Just once, and so briefly. I had barely remembered it. It couldn't have been then. It was so… insignificant. They asked about my name.'

'Your name?'

'There's nothing wrong with my name, is there?' Hawser asked.

'Names are important,' said Amon. 'They invest power on those who own them, and grant power over those who own them to those who learn them.'

'I… what?'

'When you know someone's name, you have power over them. Why do you suppose no one knows the Emperor by anything other than his rank?'

'You speak of this as if it were sorcery!' exclaimed Hawser.

'Sorcery? Now *there's* an accusation. You know the power of words. You saw what Murza did with words in Lutetia.'

'Has the damn rune priest shared that story with everybody?' Hawser snapped.

'Who gave you your name?'

'Rector Uwe, when I was a foundling. No one knew my name when I was brought to the commune. He chose it for me.'

'It is a name from a folktale. Kaspar Hawser, Casper Hauser, there are variant forms. In ancient times, in the city of Nuremborg, before even the Age of Technology, he was a boy from nowhere, without parents or a past, who had been raised in nothing but a darkened cell, with nothing but a toy horse carved of wood to play with, who emerged into the world only to die in equal mystery, a riddle, in the gardens of Ansbach. This rector, he chose your name well. It is suffused with a sublime power derived from significance. The foundling child. The past of utter darkness. The quest for truth. Even the wooden horse, an attendant symbolism, representing the deceit by which one party may penetrate the defences of a rival.'

'The Strategy of Ilios?' asked Hawser. 'Is that what I am?'

'Of course,' said Amon. 'Though the Wolves, with their senses sharper than any of the Astartes, saw through it in a second.'

'It is simply preposterous to suggest my life has been controlled through my name,' spat Hawser. 'Where would you come by such a notion?'

The Custodes tapped the throat of his armour.

'Names are crucial signifiers for my kind. A Custodes's name is engraved inside the chest plate of his gold armour. The name begins at the collar, on the right side, with just the first element exposed, and then runs around the inside of the plate. For some of the oldest veterans, the accumulated names filled up the linings of their torso plates, and were engraved outside like belts across the abdomen. Constantin Valdor's name is nineteen hundred and thirty-two elements long.'

'I know this tradition amongst the Custodes,' said Hawser.

'Then you will understand that "Amon" is just the start of his name, the earliest part of it. The second part is "Tauromachian", then "Xigaze", the site of his organic birth, then "Lepron", the house of his formative study, then "Cairn Hedrossa", the place where he was first tutored in weapon use–'

'Stop. Stop! You mean to say *your* name, not *his*,' protested Hawser.

'When one shares a name,' said the voice that belonged to Amon, Custodes of the first circle, 'it becomes especially easy to achieve mastery and control. My name is *also* Amon. For the moment, I have used that coincidence to eclipse your noble escort. Turn and know me, Kasper Ansbach Hawser.'

Hawser was abruptly aware that the Custodes was oddly still, as if paralysis had seized him, or his burnished armour had been used to clothe a statue. Amon Tauromachian, Custodes, stood with one hand resting on the gallery parapet, gazing out into the amphitheatre, utterly still.

Hawser began to turn, looking to his right. His skin began to crawl. An emotion finally pierced the traumatic numbness that had overwhelmed his mind.

It was fear.

Something else stood behind him, something that had approached behind his back without betraying its presence. It was an Astartes warrior in red and gold, his bulk half blurred by the distortion field of a falsehood device. He leaned his massive elbows on the parapet, like a casual spectator, the gaze of his green-lensed visor on the theatre below rather than on Hawser.

'I am Amon of the Fifteenth Astartes, Captain of the

Ninth Fellowship, Equerry to the Primarch.' The Astartes was using his own voice now.

'How long have I been conversing with you rather than the Custodes?'

'Since we came into the open air,' the Equerry replied.

'Did you create me?' asked Hawser. 'Did you twist me to your will?'

'We guided you to our pathway,' the warrior replied. 'Hidden Ones are more obliging if they are not bent against their will, even unconsciously.'

'So you freely admit I'm an asset?'

'Curious, is it not? We know you're our spy, and so do the Wolves. One might be tempted to presume you were useless.'

'Why am I not?'

'Because things are not yet played out.'

The Equerry of the Thousand Sons gestured down at the bowl of the amphitheatre. Far below, a shock-haired giant was ascending a small plinth to stand at a wooden lectern facing the radiant dais.

'This is not a council,' said the Equerry. 'This is a trial without legitimacy or statute. My beloved primarch, behold him there, is about to plead for mercy on behalf of knowledge to a court driven by superstition and credulity. The Emperor has been steered into this. He has been manipulated into serving judgement on the Crimson King.'

'By who? How is that even possible?' asked Hawser.

'By the Crimson King's brothers. Other primarchs are jealous of the Thousand Sons, and the arts we have mastered for the benefit of the Imperium. They call our talents sorcery, and rail against them, but it is simply jealousy. Some hide their envy well. Sanguinius, for example, and the Khan, they pretend it is a minor concern that should simply be settled for the good of everyone, but inside they burn with a jealous rage. Others cannot even begin to hide it. Mortarion. The Wolf King. Their hatred is perhaps more honest because it is open.'

The Equerry looked at Hawser for the first time. The red and gold visage of his crested helm was threatening. The lens slits shone with green light, but the light died as the Equerry lifted the helmet clear of his head. The Equerry was a veteran soldier, with a close-cropped grizzle of hair, and skin like aged paper.

'The Council of Nikaea is intended to resolve the issues surrounding the use of Librarian adepts in the Legions,' he said. His voice, no longer disguised by the helmet-mic, was deep and rich. 'We believe that what some call magic is a tool vital to the continued survival of the Imperium. Our opponents call us heretics and decry the lore we have accumulated. If the Emperor rules against us, a divisive wedge will be driven so deeply into the brotherhood of primarchs it will never recover.'

'Especially if you defy the Emperor's ruling,' said Hawser.

'He would have no choice but to sanction us,' the Equerry of the Thousand Sons agreed.

'And that sanction would be the Sixth.'

'Sanction is the only reason he permits the feral and monstrous Sixth to endure. The only way he can justify their creation and continued existence is as his ultimate deterrent.'

'And I am your early warning. Through me, you will see them coming.'

'Yes, Kasper Hawser. Just so.'

'He will rule against you,' said Hawser. 'No matter how you dress it up, the art you speak of is maleficarum, and that, I have come to believe, is what led mankind into Old Night.'

The Equerry turned to look back at the scene below. Hawser studied his profile. He wondered what a warlock was supposed to look like. He wondered if sorcery had a smell.

He tried to remember if it had been this warrior's face that had been waiting behind him that morning when he had woken on the orbital plate and looked down at Terra. Had it been this face? Was it familiar?

'Let me tell you of Old Night,' said the Equerry, 'since you've spent your career trying to uncover its traces. It was the catastrophe of universal proportions the myths say it was. A cosmological apocalypse. And yes, the abuse of certain arcane and transformatory talents were specific causal events. But I stress the word *abuse*. I'm talking about whole cultures and societies misusing and misapplying esoteric practices, often because they had no understanding of what they were doing. But do you know the most frightening thing about Old Night, Kasper?'

'No,' Kasper replied.

'I'll tell you. The term is imprecise. There was no Old Night. When we look back across time, across the train of history, it is possible to discern hundreds of disasters. Whole eras lost to the outer darkness, from which man rebuilt, only to be swept down again. Civilisation has come and gone more times than can be remembered. Atlantys *and* Agarttha, ser. There have been versions of the rule of man before that have left no lasting trace. This is a natural process.'

'Natural? Surely it's testament to man's meddling with destructive powers!'

'No,' said the Equerry, adopting a patient tone as though he was a tutor coaching a faltering student. 'Think of a forest, afflicted by raging fires from time to time. The fires denude and raze, but they are part of the cycle because they allow for vigorous new growth. Mankind is regrowing from the ashes of the last conflagration, Kasper. What we learned from that is that knowledge is the only continuity. Knowledge is the only strength. Without it, we will burn again, so the primary devotion of the Fifteenth Astartes is the accumulation of knowledge. Just like you, Kasper. That was why you were such a suitable candidate for recruitment. That's why your mind didn't even murmur in protest when we yoked your ambitions to ours. Knowledge is life and power, and protection against the dark. Forgetfulness is the true abomination, and the wound that darkness tries to inflict upon us.'

He touched his fingertips to his brow.

'Here, more than anywhere, is where it matters. Commitment to knowledge. Not in books or in slates or data-stores, but in the memory. Tell me, don't the Wolves themselves, for all their protestations against *maleficarum*, proudly pursue a tradition of oral histories? Isn't memory and retelling the only form they respect, *skjald*?'

'Yes,' Hawser admitted, quietly and grudgingly.

'There is an old myth,' said the Equerry. He paused, and looked up at the frozen violence of the Nikaean sky. 'It is a story of Thoth, a god of the Faeronik Era. He invented writing, and he showed it to the King of Aegypt. The king was horrified, because he thought it would promote forgetfulness.'

The Equerry turned and looked directly at him again.

'We did not come to you with words, or instructions on a page. We did not try to influence you with things that could be erased or tampered with. We spoke in your dreams, and wrote on your memories, where it would matter.'

'You gave me no choice, you mean,' replied Hawser. 'You altered my life and shaped my wyrd, and I had no say in the course of it.'

'Kasper–'

'You say forgetfulness is the true abomination? Then

why do you employ it? Why can I remember some things so clearly, while others are invisible to me? If forgetfulness is the greatest evil of all, why did you use it to shape me? Why is my memory selective? What is it that you don't want me to see?'

The Equerry's eyes became cold.

'What are you saying?' he asked.

'He's saying step back,' said Bear.

ELEVEN

Blood and Names

'STEP BACK,' BEAR repeated, with greater emphasis.

Amon of the Thousand Sons turned and looked at the Space Wolf over Hawser's shoulder. He reignited his smile.

'You're aiming a weapon at a fellow Astartes, wolf-brother?' he asked. He looked slightly amused. 'Is that wise? Is it even… decent?'

Bear's bolter did not waver.

'I'm protecting the skjald, as is my bond. Step back.'

Amon of the Thousand Sons laughed. He took a step or two away from Hawser and the parapet. The Custodes was still frozen in place, but he was trembling ever so slightly, like a sleeper trying to swim clear of a dream and awake.

'Are we to bicker and brawl while history is made below us?' the Equerry asked.

'It's a possibility,' said Aun Helwintr. The rune priest had approached silently from the other side, flanking the Thousand Sons Equerry.

'Two of you?' Amon declared, with mock delight.

'The skjald is under our protection,' replied the priest.

'But I make no threat towards him,' Amon answered lightly. 'We were just talking.'

'Of what?' asked Helwintr.

'Idle things,' Amon replied. 'Innocent things. A toy horse made of wood, the inlay of a regicide board, the taste of radapples, the playing of a clavier. The things that string a life together. Nostalgia. Memories.'

'Step back,' Bear repeated.

'Oh, so terse and humourless that one,' said Amon.

'Step back and take your magic with you,' said Aun Helwintr. The rune priest moved forwards, left foot ahead of right, assuming a ritual-specific stance. His hands locked, the left arm up like a lindorm about to strike, the right low at the waist and palm-up with the fingers curled like fish hooks. Hawser suddenly felt an increase in air pressure.

'What I especially admire,' said the Thousand Sons Equerry, 'is your hypocrisy. You hound us and harass us over our so-called sorcery, yet you do not shrink from using it, *shaman*.'

'There is a vast gulf between what I employ for the good of the Rout and what you practise, *warlock*,' Helwintr replied, 'and the chief part of that gulf is control. Only the naive would think that mankind could survive in the cosmos without some measure of craft and cunning to protect him, but there is a limit. A limit. We must know what we can master and what we cannot, and we must never allow ourselves to step beyond that line. Tell me, how many steps have you taken? One? Three? A dozen? A thousand?'

'And thanks to our innate superiority to your gothi fumblings, we have mastered every one,' Amon returned. 'You have barely dipped your toe in the Great Ocean. There is always something more to know.'

'There is such a thing as too much,' said Hawser.

Amon smiled.

'Words said to you by that treacherous priest Wyrd-make on the day you awoke on Fenris.'

Hawser looked at Helwintr.

'From his own mouth,' Hawser said. 'I don't know what further proof we'd need that the Fifteenth have been using me as a spyglass since I entered the Aett.'

The smile left Amon's lips. He glanced at the poised rune priest.

'Aun Helwintr!' he cried. 'Plainly named in the bright thoughts of the skjald! You have no sway over me now I have your name in my mouth!'

The air seemed to buckle explosively between the Equerry and the rune priest. The force of it knocked Hawser to the ground. Light blistered. Helwintr was hurled back against the rear wall of the gallery space, his hands smoking. His impact grazed a dent in the wall's basalt face.

Bear fired three precise shots with his bolter. It was ridiculously close range, and Bear was taking no chances. Each one was a kill-shot. Each one was a man-stopper. He did not even consider laming the Thousand Sons Equerry when a hostile act had been made against his priest-brother, and a threat remained to his skjald. His response was automatic, and no Astartes could miss under such circumstances with his signature weapon.

On the ground, rolling over, Hawser felt time bulge and contort. He could see the mass-reactive shells in flight as they went over him, smudging out lines of grease-on-glass slipstream behind them, like comet tails, like bad stars streaking towards impact.

The shots burst before they could hit Amon. They ruptured into little flattened disks of shockwave fire and filled the air with white, papery dust that rained down like ash or deep winter snow. Amon came through the

swirling blizzard at Bear, arms outstretched, roaring
Bear's name aloud. Hawser knew the name had been
stolen from his mind, just as Helwintr's had been. The
Equerry had Bear's name, and so had power over him.

Bear threw aside his bolter, its dependability found
wanting, and put his right fist into Amon's face.

The Equerry crashed backwards into the parapet wall,
his lips and nose mashed and bloody. His recoil from
the blow was so sudden, Hawser had to squirm away to
avoid being trampled underfoot. Indignant fury blazed
from the Equerry, along with a measure of shock. The
name should have stopped Bear in his tracks.

Bear hit him again, twice more, both body blows. The
Wolf was snarling. Amon went back against the parapet,
and the force of his impacts knapped flakes of basalt off
the lip of the wall. He threw a blow at Bear that Bear
seemed not to feel.

The impacts and the shock had broken Amon's concentration. The noble Custodes, pinned like a specimen
by the power of his name since the Equerry's first
appearance, let out a strangled cry as he tore himself
back into mobility. It was an awful sound, the sound of
a man who had been drowning and had never thought
to breathe air again, the sound of a man waking from
an immobilising nightmare. He shuddered backwards
out of his stance, and then tried to lunge at the Thousand Sons warrior.

'Amon Tauromachian!' the Equerry proclaimed, and
the Custodes slammed over onto his back. It was as
though he had been knocked down by typhoon winds.
He slid backwards along the gallery floor for a dozen
metres, his armour scraping up flurries of sparks off the
rock, driven by a hurricane-force blast no one else could
feel.

The Equerry held out his right hand, and Amon Tauromachian's guardian spear flew to him from where it

had fallen. It landed in his palm with a solid *smack*. Wielding it expertly, and transferring it into a two-handed grip, he swept it laterally at Bear. The toe of the blade caught Bear's left shoulder-plate and rotated him brutally. Slivers of ceramite plating spun away from the impact.

Bear drew out his axe, and used the haft to stop the next swing. He tried to hook the attacking weapon away, but the guardian spear had a much greater reach. Amon's use of it was so precise, Hawser had no doubt that the Equerry had simply lifted decades of practice drill and technique from the mind of the Custodes. The halberd's blade ripped the Fenrisian war axe from Bear's grip, and then came back again to cripple him.

All the men of Tra, indeed every man of the Rout, had been taught that the only thing of consequence was victory. Outsiders considered the Sixth Astartes notorious for their wild belligerence, but that was simply an inevitable by-product of their defining mindset. The *Vlka Fenryka* were stoically resolved to take any action necessary in order to win.

The truth is that we are the most harshly trained of all.

Bear tilted slightly and took the blade in his side. It cut through the torso plating under his left arm. An Astartes from another Legion might, if faced with the same dire threat, perhaps have tried to hunch and shield himself with his shoulder plate. The result would have cost him an arm. Bear threw his guard wide, arm raised, and absorbed the hit in his physical core. The impact made him roar to vent the pain. Hawser, watching wide-eyed in horror, saw the daggers of Bear's fangs. He saw the blood gout from the trench wound puncturing Bear's flank.

Bear clamped his left arm down like a vice and trapped the halberd buried in his ribs. He gripped the golden haft, slippery with blood, and yanked Amon close. The Equerry couldn't pull it out. With his free right fist, Bear punched Amon in the face repeatedly, each blow delivered with a roar of pain and triumph, each blow causing blood to spray. The fifth or sixth blow caught the Thousand Sons warrior in the throat. Gore from his pulverised face covered the front of his glorious armour.

Amon slipped backwards, swaying, releasing his grip on the guardian spear. Bear wrenched it out of him and hurled it away. Hawser ducked as the blood-splattered weapon clattered past him.

Bear grasped Amon by the chest plating with one hand and the scalp by the other. He twisted the Equerry's head back, exposing his throat, and lunged in, teeth bared.

'No!' Hawser yelled.

Poised to bite and finish his prey, Bear snarled a wet leopard-growl at Hawser. His black-pinned golden eyes had gone dark with pain, pain and some other feral property.

'Don't!' Hawser cried, holding out a staying hand. 'We need him alive! Alive, he's testimony for us! Dead, he's proof simply of our aggression!'

Bear relaxed his grip slightly, and pulled back from the threatened bite, though his mouth still gaped hungrily and his teeth gleamed. He punched Amon again, punishingly hard, and laid him out on the basalt floor.

'Blade!' he demanded.

Hawser unlooped his axe, and tossed it to Bear. The Wolf caught it neatly in his right hand, knelt down over the Equerry, and hacked the mark of aversion into his chest plating.

The Equerry of the Thousand Sons screamed. He thrashed and convulsed with demented fury and threw Bear backwards. His fists and feet hammered the floor in an insane blur, and his screams turned to choking

gulps as blood and plasmic matter sprayed from his
mouth. As his convulsions reached a pitch, a torus of
sizzling, foul-smelling energy blasted out of him, soiling the air with streaks of sooty smoke.

Shuddering and wailing, he clambered to his feet. He
was aspirating blood and other fluids through the
pulped ruin Bear had made of his face. His shaking was
like a palsy, a nervous judder. Clouds of vapour were
pouring off him, rank and oily. Almost at once he was
moving, fleeing, thumping quickly but unsteadily away
along the gallery, his arms clenched around his torso.

Bear struggled to rise and give chase. He was inter-
cepted by the Custodes, who was finally back on his feet
and free of the sorcerous yoke. Deep gouges marked the
Custodes's golden armour.

'Wait,' he said to Bear. 'I've signalled the Custodian
force. The upper galleries will be sealed. He cannot
escape. The Sisterhood will silence him, and my
brothers of the Legio Custodes will bring him down.'

'I will hunt him myself!' Bear insisted.

'No,' said the Custodes, more firmly. He looked over
at Hawser.

'Ser,' he said. 'I apologise. I failed you badly.'

Hawser shook his head. He walked to the parapet and
looked down. Far below, the proceedings of the great
council were continuing without interruption. The cone
of the supervolcano was so vast, no one on the chamber
floor had been aware of the violent altercation in the
upper parts of the auditorium.

Aun Helwintr appeared at Hawser's side. His face was
paler than usual, as if he had been starved of light and
food for a year. He had removed the gauntlets of his
power armour. His hands were miserably scorched, raw-
red and blistered. He gazed down into the bowl of the
amphitheatre.

'A report must be passed to the Emperor without

delay,' he said, speaking not to Hawser but to Amon Tau-romachian and Bear. He was staring straight down at the bright form on the dais, and the shock-haired giant pleading his case from the wooden lectern before him.

'No matter what argument the Crimson King presents,' said Helwintr, 'this will surely influence whatever decision the Master of Mankind makes.'

'It's the most unnerving thing that happened to me in my old life,' said Hawser. 'It has the most… maleficarum.'

'You know that's not true,' said Longfang. 'In your heart, you know better. You're denying yourself.'

Hawser woke with a start. For a terrible, rushing moment, he thought he was somewhere else, but it was a dream. He lay back, trying to slow his bolting heart. Just a dream.

Hawser settled back onto his bed. He felt tired and unrefreshed. Sustained artificial gravity always did that to him.

There was an electronic chime.

'Yes?' he said.

'Ser Hawser? It is your hour five alarm,' said a softly modulated servitor voice.

'Thank you,' said Hawser. He sat up. He was so stiff, so worn out. He hadn't felt this bad for a long time. His leg was sore. Maybe there were painkillers in the drawer.

He limped to the window. The shutter rose into its frame recess with a low hum, allowing golden light to flood in.

The sun was just coming up over the hemisphere below him. He was looking straight down on Terra in all its magnificence. He could see the night side and the sunlit blue of oceans and the whipped-cream swirl of clouds and the glittering light points of a superorbital plate gliding majestically past beneath him.

He saw his own sunlit reflection in the thick glass of

the window port. Old! So old! *So old!* How old was he? Eighty? Eighty years standard? He recoiled. This was wrong. On Fenris, they'd remade him, they'd–

Except he hadn't been to Fenris yet. He hadn't even left Terra.

Bathed in golden sunlight, he stared at his aghast reflection. He saw the face of the other figure reflected in the glass, the figure standing just behind him.

Terror constricted him.

'How can you be here?' he asked.

And woke.

'Who were you talking to?' asked Ogvai.

'His dreams,' said Aun Helwintr. 'They're getting louder.'

Hawser sat up. They were in the chamber beyond the quiet room. The moving light of magmatic turmoil dappled the walls. It was uncomfortably hot. The warmth of the smoky air had caused him to doze. He imagined that sleep was an attempt by his mind and body at self-preservation after the unsettling clash with the Thousand Sons warlock.

Considerable numbers of Tra were gathered in the chamber, along with Wolves from Onn and Fyf.

'Did they catch him?' Hawser asked.

Helwintr glanced at him, and then shook his head. He was applying salve to the weeping burns on his hands. Given the damage Hawser had seen earlier, the flesh was healing with astonishing speed.

'He slipped into the shadows,' said Helwintr.

'Spineless Custodes lost him,' said Skarssen.

'It doesn't matter anyway,' rumbled a voice. 'It doesn't matter a damn now.'

The Wolf King loomed into the chamber, a hulking mass of shadow backlit by the fire-glow. He was flanked by the painfully beautiful maidens bearing their raised longswords.

He came closer, and the men bowed their heads, even Ogvai and Lord Gunn. The flickering flame light revealed his face, half shadowed, and the broad smile that exposed his inhuman teeth.

When he spoke, it was with a wet leopard-growl.

'The Emperor has made His ruling,' he said.

TWELVE

Thardia

'So you LIKED the account?' Hawser asked. 'It amused you? It distracted you?'

'It was amusing enough,' said Longfang. 'It wasn't your best.'

No…

'I can assure you it was,' said Hawser.

Longfang shook his head. Droplets of blood flecked from his beard.

'No, you'll learn better ones,' he said. 'Far better ones. And even now, it's not the best you know.'

No, again… not this memory… You keep sticking on this memory… We have to get past it…

'It's the most unnerving thing that happened to me in my old life,' said Hawser with some defiance. 'It has the most… maleficarum.'

'You know that's not true,' said Longfang. 'In your heart, you know better. You're denying yourself.'

Hawser woke with a start. It was all a dream. He lay back, calming down, trying to slow his panicked breathing, his bolting heart. Just a dream. Just a dream.

Better. We're closer now. Past the memory of Longfang, closer to the one that matters.

Hawser felt tired and unrefreshed, as if his sleep had been sour, or sedative assisted. His limbs ached. Sustained artificial gravity always did that to him.

Golden light was knifing into his chamber around the window shutter, gilding everything, giving the room a soft, burnished feel.

There was an electronic chime.

Keep with it. Focus.

'Yes?' he said.

'Ser Hawser? It is your hour five alarm,' said a softly modulated servitor voice.

'Thank you,' said Hawser. He sat up. He was so stiff, so worn out. He hadn't felt this bad for a long time. His leg was sore. Maybe there were painkillers in the drawer.

He limped to the window, and pressed the stud to open the shutter. It rose into its frame recess with a low hum, allowing golden light to flood in. He looked out. It was a hell of a view.

Ignore the view. Who cares about the view? You've seen it before, over and over, in life and in your dreams. It's what's behind you that matters. Focus!

The sun, source of the ethereal radiance, was just coming up over the hemisphere below him. He was looking straight down on Terra in all its magnificence. He could see the night side and the constellation pattern of hive lights in the darkness behind the chasing terminator, he could see the sunlit blue of oceans and the whipped-cream swirl of clouds and, below, he could see the glittering light points of the superorbital plate Rodinia gliding majestically under the one he was aboard, which was...

It doesn't matter. It. Doesn't. Matter. Stay in that

moment. Focus your mind on that memory, on the one part of the memory that's really important!

Lemurya. Yes, that was it. Lemurya. A luxury suite on the underside of the Lemuryan plate.

His eyes refocussed. He saw his own sunlit reflection in the thick glass of the window port.

You're distracted! Don't be distracted! Ignore what you look like! This is a dream! A memory! Behind you, that's all that counts! Turn around! Look behind you! Focus! Who's behind you?

Old! So old! *So old!* How old was he? Eighty? Eighty years standard? He recoiled. This was wrong. On Fenris, they'd remade him, they'd–

Except he hadn't been to Fenris yet. He hadn't even left Terra.

Focus! Who's behind you?

Bathed in golden sunlight, he stared at his aghast reflection. He saw the face of the other figure reflected in the glass, the figure standing just behind him.

Yes! Yes!

Terror constricted him.

'How can you be here?' he asked.

And woke.

Hawser groaned. He was covered in sweat and his heart was palpitating. The astringent smells of herbal ointments and body paint assaulted his nose.

'Did you see?' asked Aun Helwintr.

'No,' said Hawser.

'Ah,' said the priest.

'I'm sorry,' said Hawser.

The priest shrugged.

'We'll try again,' he said. 'Tomorrow, or later tonight if there's strength in you.'

'It was very close this time,' said Hawser. 'I mean this time, I actually turned around earlier. I changed my memory, I behaved differently in it. I turned around, but it still wasn't fast enough.'

'Next time,' said Helwintr. He seemed distracted.

They had come up through the silent stands of forest into the crags above the high station, a two-hour trek they had made every day for a week. It was cold, and if they made an early start, frost could be found lingering on the trail. The rocks of the crags, grey and cream, were sheathed in beards of winter lichen: purple, mauve, blue, red, some as rough as sandpaper or as soft as moleskin.

Aun Helwintr claimed that the loneliness of the crags aided contemplation and inner sight. It was away from the traffic of voices and everyday life, and on Thardia, where humans had only inhabited the high station and the research facility, there was no legacy of wights or ghost memories to tangle a man's threads.

Helwintr liked the cold too. Even at its polar extremes, Thardia barely approached the lethal majesty of a Fenrisian winter, but the priest liked the bracing climate and the marks a man's breath left in the air.

Helwintr collected up the pots of salve, the talismans, and the other paraphernalia he had arranged around the table rock they had chosen for the day's effort. The rock, low, flat-topped and large enough for Hawser to lie on it, full length, like a man stretched out on a bed, had a bluish coat of lichen on it. It reminded Hawser of the worn velvet lining of an Ossetian prayer box or an old gaming board.

The priest was fully caparisoned with winter pelts and his leatherware garb. His mask, head-binding, chest and shoulder wear and arm guards were all of glossy black leather with involuted knotwork. His long white hair, lacquered into an S-tail, was protruding from the back of his scalp-case. His black face-guard was a prophylactic fear-mask with a daemon-snarl to the mouth and snout intended to scare wights away.

Hawser wore leather gear of his own, dark brown and of simpler design, with a half-mask and no full-head casing. It had been a twenty-six week translation from Nikaea to Thardia, and he'd used his time to learn and practise some basic hideworking skills. Men from Tra, at different times, had shown him various techniques, and had reviewed his work and suggested refinements. Hawser had begun some rudimentary knotwork decoration down the left arm guard, but it was slow, and he was disgruntled at his lack of ability. The rest of the leatherware was plain and undecorated.

His accoutrements gathered, Helwintr crouched on a slab of rock, his legs bent wide, his back hunched. The pose reminded Hawser, just for a moment, of an amphibian on a lily-pad. Then it reminded him of something else: a lupine predator, vigilant on a rock, calm but alert in the sunlight, resting but surveying the forest below.

Helwintr took an athame from his belt and began to make marks in the lichen covering the rock he was squatting on.

Hawser was cold. He left the priest to whatever abstruse gothi business had engaged him. The open air of any planet's biosphere was more conducive to such activities than the chambers of a void-borne starship. Helwintr was making the best use of the taskforce's brief stay-over at Thardia.

To the east, in the glassy sky, a constellation unfamiliar to the heavenscape of Thardia glimmered and shone. It was a star-pattern that this world's sky had never seen before, and never would again, a star-pattern that even a spiritually bankrupt gothi could read as an astral house of doom and destruction.

It was the lights of the taskforce ships at high anchor. Taskforce Geata, six companies of the Sixth, along with their support vessels and enthralled servers. A notable concentration of strength by the standards of any Legion, especially in this age when the demands of the Great Crusade diluted the Astartes across the vast celestial stage. By the standards of the Sixth, almost unheard of. The official line was that the companies were assembling at Thardia for a moot and resupply, but Hawser knew something else was going on.

There was a chill in his bones. Hawser drew his axe and moved down the slope away from the priest, beginning his long, repetitive regimen of practice strokes and turns that Godsmote had taught him. He was beginning to handle the weapon well enough to have earned Godsmote's approval once or twice. Hawser could turn the axe, rotate and check the angles of stroke and attack, block, and switch hands, either from one to another or from a single to a double-handed grip. He had even mastered a showy little spin, a rapid, one-handed rotation that mimicked some of the dazzling blade skills he'd seen displayed by warriors like Bear and Erthung, but Godsmote had warned him against it. Too flashy, he'd said. Too much risk of losing control or grip, just for the sake of showing off.

Axe-fighting was a complex and demanding dance. It looked much more brutal and simplistic than swordwork, but in some respects it was vastly more subtle than the ballet of the swordsman. The killing edge of an axe was in a position to harm an opponent for a much smaller percentage of engagement time than the killing surfaces of a sword. Axe fighting was about swinging and circling, moving and evading, choosing the moment to land the blow. It was about seeing that opening coming three or four steps ahead, like a good regicide player, and then taking advantage of it without telegraphing the stroke. It was about predicting the interface between swing and moving target. Misjudge that, and you'd lose the fight.

Axes were cold-climate weapons, because they were as much working tools for ice and firewood and butchery as they were weapons. But the art of using an axe in a fight was about predictive judgement, so it was no wonder that cultures like the Fenrisians had become preoccupied by prophecy. Reading the future was a survival skill at the micro level, and thus had become bred into their culture at the macro. Games of predictive strategy were compulsory activities in the Rout.

For his part, Hawser had spent many of his childhood hours playing regicide with Rector Uwe.

Hawser put his shoulders and back into the loops and turns, making his weapon hum as it cut the air. The exercise began to warm him up too.

He turned hard, swinging around, chopping the axe in a figure of eight, and as he did so, he realised that he was clearly beginning to inherit the *Vlka Fenryka*'s gift for prophecy. He knew before he'd even turned that he was going to have to stop the axe swing short.

Ohthere Wyrdmake was standing right behind him. The keen bite of Hawser's redirected axe still barely missed him.

'Move,' said Wyrdmake. 'With me, now.'

'What?'

'Now!'

Wyrdmake's manner was hard to read at the best of times. His inscrutability, the sheer imposing threat of him, made him an uncomfortable presence to be around, and the rune priests were the most remote and inhuman of all the *Vlka Fenryka*.

He was blinking rather rapidly, though, and there was a touch of perspiration on his brow. To Hawser, Wyrdmake seemed agitated and uncomfortable.

'There's danger here,' he said.

'We must warn Helwintr,' Hawser replied. He looked back up the slope to the rock where Aun Helwintr had been crouching. There was no sign of Tra's rune priest.

Hawser looked back at Wyrdmake. The priest put an index finger against his lips, seized Hawser by the wrist, and started to drag him towards the forest line.

The forest vegetation was dark, tuberous growths with glossy black trunks and lacy foliage like the ragged wings of dead insects. Only at a distance, in general, structural terms, did it resemble actual trees.

Some of the growths were of fantastic size, bloated and wizened with age. Hawser had paid them little attention each day as he'd trekked through the glades. Now he was among them, furtive and confused, he became aware of how alien they were. There was a smell of dust and cinnamon. A black humus of decaying leaves covered the soil, and insects, tiny as pepper dust, billowed in the sunlit spaces between the plant shadows.

Hawser tried to make as little noise as possible, desperately trying to apply the techniques of stalking and foot-placement Godsmote had taught him, but he was like a noisy sack that Wyrdmake was dragging behind him. The priest moved in utter silence.

They got into cover in the shadow of a vast tubergrowth. The veined filigree of its canopy hung overhead like a widow's veil. Hawser had leaf dust in his throat and tried not to cough.

Wyrdmake pushed Hawser back against the plant bole. The bark of the tuber was as glossy and black as the skin of an aubergine. The priest held up a hand indicating that Hawser should keep himself there, and then raised his head.

Hawser could half-see Wyrdmake in the shadows in front of him. Like Hawser and Helwintr, the priest of Fyf was clad in leatherwork gear, pelts and mask. Totemic strings of beads and animal teeth were looped around his neck. Hawser wondered how they didn't make a sound when he moved. He became locked on the question. It was so silly. It almost made him laugh out loud. How did they not make a noise? Was there a trick to it?

Wyrdmake kept himself raised up for a moment, panning his head around, watching the glade, listening. Then he crouched down beside Hawser and started to fiddle with one of the bead strings around his neck.

'I know what Helwintr's been doing this past week,' Wyrdmake whispered to him. 'He's had my blessing and advice on the matter. Getting past your sculpted memories is a very worthwhile goal for you and the *Vlka Fenryka*.'

Hawser swallowed and nodded. Wyrdmake had taken two black feathers off his necklace, and he was using a small length of thin silver wire to bind them to a garnet bead and a human finger bone he'd produced from a belt pouch.

'The memory architecture is very strong,' Wyrdmake continued as he worked, his voice barely a whisper. 'There is cunning in it. Maleficarum. Helwintr reports to me every day. He is frustrated. Today, he tried a new technique. A new way, perhaps to unlock your thoughts. You know Eada Haelfwulf?'

Hawser nodded. Haelfwulf was another rune priest attached to Tra Company, serving their needs as one of Helwintr's senior gothi. He was a tall, raw-boned warrior who dyed his leather gear red to match his flame-hair and beard.

'Haelfwulf came with you today.'

'I didn't see him,' Hawser whispered.

'That was the idea,' Wyrdmake whispered back. 'He stayed back, out of sight, to secretly push at your memories from another angle while Helwintr kept you occupied.'

'So? What's happened?'

Wyrdmake shook his head.

'I don't know. But about an hour ago, I felt a terrible presentiment. A beforehand sense that something ill was about to take place up here in the crags. I came at once.'

'You're scaring me,' Hawser whispered.

'Good. That means you're taking me seriously.'

'Where's Helwintr?'

'When I arrived, all I saw was you, busy at your axe-work.'

'Helwintr was right there!' Hawser hissed. 'He was on the rock not twenty metres back from me.'

'Not when I arrived.'

'He wouldn't just disappear. He was busy with something. Some cunning work. He was listening.'

'He'd sensed it too,' Wyrdmake said. He had finished what he'd been doing with the feathers and the trinkets from his pouch. He cupped them in his hands, blew on them, and then threw his hands up.

Something black fluttered away into the canopy. Hawser heard its noisy wings. He got the brief impression of a raven, even though he knew no raven could have been hidden about Wyrdmake's person.

'What–' he began.

Wyrdmake silenced him.

'Wait now.'

The priest closed his eyes, as if concentrating hard. Hawser became acutely conscious of the sound of his own breathing. The forest was eerily quiet. There was an occasional sound: the fidget of the wind, or of some small creature, the tick of burrowing insects, the soft brush of leaf litter drifting down from the tuber-trees.

He heard a flutter from not far away. The sound of a large bird moving through the upper levels of the canopy.

'Did you… did you make a crow?' Hawser asked.

Wyrdmake peered at him.

'A what?' he whispered.

'A crow.'

'What word is that, skjald?'

'Crow.'

'You mean *crow*?' the priest asked.

'That's what I said,' Hawser whispered.

'Not in Juvjk or Wurgen you didn't. You spoke the Terran-tongue name for it.'

'No, I didn't, I–'

'Be. *Quiet*.'

Wyrdmake closed his eyes again. Hawser shut up. He heard the wings beating once more, but further off. He heard another noise too, the faintest suggestion of something moving somewhere through the trees. Whatever it was, it was bigger than a burrowing insect or a forest floor creature.

Wyrdmake's eyes snapped open.

'I see it,' he whispered, almost to himself. 'Hjolda, it's big.'

He looked at Hawser.

'Head up towards the crags as fast and as quietly as you can. Don't look back.'

Wyrdmake reached under his pelts and produced a compact plasma pistol. He armed it. It looked utterly incongruous and yet utterly appropriate in his leather-clad hands.

'Go!' he said.

The priest turned and sprang out of the shadows of the vast tuber-tree. His pelts flowed out behind him like a cloak as he headed deeper into the forest with great, bounding strides, towards the source of the noise. Within seconds, he had vanished from view.

Hawser waited a moment, willing the priest to reappear. Then he got up, axe in hand, and started to move as he had been instructed. He cursed every noisy step he took, every crunch of leaf-mould, every crack of dry twig. He felt like a blundering fool.

He hadn't gone far when he heard a sound. He stopped and looked around. The forest space was black shadows and bars of white light. Tiny flies danced in the beams. Withered leaf shapes made shadows like calcified wing membranes. He heard the sound again.

A flutter. A flutter of wings, not far away. A slight disturbance in the forest cover. Branches rustled. Another flutter.

Without warning there was a frenzy of noise, a violent thrashing that was over as fast and as abruptly as it began. Not ten metres from him, undergrowth shook and tore. He dropped down low, weapon ready. Something that wasn't human let out a brief, raucous shriek.

There was a wet leopard-snarl.

Then, from behind him, deep in the forest, came a cry of agony.

Hawser knew it was Wyrdmake.

He rose and turned. The priest was hurt. In trouble. He couldn't just...

He heard a throb of sound, the throat-rumble of a carnivore. It was close by. He couldn't tell which direction it had come from. Fear-sweat was trickling down his back. He raised the axe ready to strike. He moved forwards. He edged around a massive tuber bole that came up out of the dusty forest brush like an inverted mushroom. He kept his back to it. Slowly, ever so slowly, he leaned forwards to peer around the trunk.

He saw the wolf.

Half-saw it. It was just a shadow. A wolf-shaped shadow. A shadow-shaped wolf. Vast and ominous, like a blood-dark midnight sky; spectral and malevolent like the final whispered curses of a dying lunatic. It existed in the shadows but not in the patches of sunlight. Hawser could feel the grumble of its throat-noise. Terror was upon him, like all the cold of Fenris concentrated in a hyperdense lump inside his heart.

The almost-wolf had something in its jaws, a gleaming black tangle of something. It dropped it onto the forest floor. It let out a growl that sounded like the lowest bass thump of a tribal bodhran. Hawser waited for it to turn. He waited for it to turn and see him. He stopped breathing. He pressed himself into the sticky black skin of the tuber bole.

He waited. He waited. He waited for the jaws to close on him. He waited for eternity to pass so he could breathe again.

The almost-wolf uttered another wet leopard-growl.

Hawser heard the dry ground cover stirring, leaf-mulch sifting.

He risked a second look.

There was no sign of the almost-wolf. It had moved away. It had slipped into the darkness, into the forest.

Hawser waited a moment more. Hands tight around the haft of his axe, he slid from the tree shadow and stepped into the gloom of the glade where the almost-wolf had been standing.

In the mid-point of the clearing, the something that the almost-wolf had dropped was lying on the leaf-loam. It was a muddle of torn black feathers. The feathers were sheened like jet silk. It was Wyrdmake's crow. It was dead, mangled, one wing almost bitten off. Droplets of blood spattered the feathers and the ground around it, glinting in the dim light like amber beads. Under the feathers, the cunningly wrought thing was just the bones it had always been.

Hawser had been with the *Vlka Fenryka* long enough to understand Wyrdmake's distant cry of pain. Sympathetic magic. What had been done to his cunning spy had also been done to him.

Hawser straightened up. He tried to remember which direction the priest's cry of pain had come from. He tried to orientate himself. It was hard. The clotted fear inside him was very great and very cold. It was sliding up his gullet like a glacier. He tried to think like a Wolf, like a man of Tra. He tried to think strategically, as if all he was contemplating was the next move or two on Skarssensson's hneftafl board, or Rector Uwe's regicide set.

He let the axe slip down through both palms, until he had it clenched around the very throat and knob of the haft. This was a battle-ready grip called 'the open bite' in Wurgen. It was the maximum extension of arms and haft, so it afforded the longest reach and the greatest leverage. It was not a subtle position from which to start a fight. If he encountered the almost-wolf again, Hawser didn't expect the fight to be subtle.

He moved forwards, through the light and shadow, under the canopy of insect-wing leaves. He kept the axe at full extension in the double-handed brace. He became aware of a new sound. It was breathing. Laboured, human breathing. The struggling respiration of someone injured.

Hawser ducked under a low band of ghost leaves, and saw a large body crumpled in the shade of a misshapen tuber trunk. The man was Astartes. His leatherwork wargear was red.

'Eada?' Hawser whispered, crouching down beside him.

Eada Haelfwulf blinked and looked up at him.

'Skjald,' he smiled. His face was drawn with pain. His torso was wet with gore. Something had delivered several crippling bites to his flank and hip.

'Shhhhh!' Hawser hissed.

'The wolf had me,' Eada whispered. 'Came out of nowhere. Something brought it forth. Someone here today is working against us.'

'I saw it. Stay still.'

'Give me another minute. My wounds are knitting

and the blood vessels are closing off. I'll be on my feet again in a moment.'

'Wyrdmake's hurt,' said Hawser.

'I heard him. We have to find him,' Eada replied.

'I don't know what happened to Helwintr,' said Hawser.

Eada Haelfwulf looked at him in a grave way that suggested he really ought to know. Haelfwulf had pulled off his leather mask. There were specks of blood all over the white skin of his cheek and brow.

'What did you mean, Eada? What did you mean when you said that someone here today was working against us?'

Eada Haelfwulf coughed, and the action of it made him wince slightly.

'Helwintr and I were working into your memories, skjald.'

'I know,' said Hawser.

'Imagine your mind like a fortress. Well defended, high ramparts. Helwintr was trying to get in through the front gate. He was out where you could see him, an open approach. I was behind the fort, trying to scale the ramparts while Helwintr's attack engaged your attention. My aim was to get into an inner chamber next door to the one you keep locked.'

'What happened?' asked Hawser.

'He broke into someone else's memories,' said a voice from behind him.

Hawser turned.

Aun Helwintr was standing at the edge of the glade, staring at them. He had a short, thick-bladed fighting sword drawn.

'Come here, skjald,' he said.

'Hjolda!' Eada exclaimed. 'In the name of all the wights of the Underverse, skjald, stay here by me!'

'What?' Hawser stammered.

DAN ABNETT

Helwintr took a step closer. Hawser kept staring at him, his grip on his axe tight. He could hear Haelfwulf making a huge effort to rise behind him. He heard Haelfwulf drawing his blade.

'Stay close by me,' Eada Haelfwulf hissed. 'I broke through into someone else's memories, all right. Some *thing* else's. It was whatever had reshaped your thoughts, skjald. It had left a doorway open, a doorway back to its own mind, so it could slip back and revisit you whenever it wanted. I looked through the doorway. So did Helwintr. It saw us looking, and it didn't like it.'

'Come here, skjald,' said Helwintr, taking another step forwards. He beckoned with his free hand, the warrior's cocky invitation to an enemy. 'Come on. Don't listen to him.'

'Stay where you are,' Haelfwulf grunted, straightening up behind Hawser. 'Get ready to move behind me. I'll defend you.'

'But Helwintr–' Hawser began.

'Hjolda, listen to me!' Haelfwulf rasped, his voice cut by a throb of pain. 'Understand me! The thing that saw us, it didn't like us prying. It lashed out at us. We fell back, but not fast enough. It touched us with its malefi-carum. It touched Helwintr.'

Hawser gazed in horrid disbelief at Aun Helwintr. The priest took another step forwards. A deep rumble came out of him, a wolf-growl. Through the slits of his mask, his eyes were black-pinned gold.

'You're the wolf,' Hawser said, his voice tiny.

'Everything Eada Haelfwulf said is pretty much true,' said Helwintr. 'Except one part.'

Helwintr took another step closer.

'It was Eada that was touched by the maleficarum.'

Hawser froze up. He heard the sounds coming from the wounded rune priest behind him. The ragged, pained breathing slowly became a deeper, panting, huffing noise. He heard skin and sinew stretching, he heard the phlegmy click and gurgle of cartilage and joint fluid. He heard bones protesting as they deformed, and organs bubble and slosh as they realigned. He heard the stifled agony of something enduring extreme physical transmutation.

'Don't look around,' said Aun Helwintr. The priest stood his ground and brought his sword up to a ready stance.

Hawser felt the hot breath on the nape of his neck, the wet, frothing leopard-purr.

He turned. The open bite grip delivered the axe in a full, chest-height rotation swing, a half-circle blow that buried the axe-head in the right shoulder of the thing behind him.

The almost-wolf that had been Eada Haelfwulf roared in frustrated pain. The weight of it struck Hawser and smashed him over onto his back. He couldn't even see it. It was just a shadow blur and a predator sound. He glimpsed teeth. He rolled hard on the leaf-loam, seeing the teeth raking for him.

Helwintr charged the almost-wolf head-on. The pair clashed, grappled and went over in a thrashing, struggling tangle. Even as an insubstantial shadow, a smoke-wisp that only existed where the sunlight didn't fall, the almost-wolf was twice the size of the Astartes. Locked together, they became a furious blur. Hawser tried to get up. He couldn't find his axe. He cried out as blood jetted out of the fight and spattered his face and chest. He couldn't tell if the blood had been spilled by teeth or sword. He couldn't tell if it belonged to Helwintr or the almost-wolf.

He circled the tumult of the fight. Helwintr had almost disappeared into the spreading shadow the almost-wolf cast around it. Both combatants were moving too fast for him to track.

There was a crack of bone, a sound of flesh shredding. Helwintr flew backwards in a shower of blood. He hit a tuber bole and somersaulted onto the forest floor. His leather gear was ripped and his sword was missing. He was wounded badly in the face, neck and left leg. He tried to rise, yelling at his limbs to move, to obey.

The almost-wolf uttered its loudest throat-noise yet. It swung its massive snout around to face Hawser, ignoring the Astartes it had maimed. All Hawser could see was the shadow of it, like a piece of night cut out and pasted onto daylight. At the heart of the darkness, the huge teeth glimmered like icicles.

A thin, searing beam of light squealed across the glade and exploded the ground underneath the almost-wolf. As it tried to recover, a second beam hit it squarely in the chest and threw it backwards. It demolished two large tuber trees as it went tumbling over. The dry boles burst like ripe seed cases and filled the air with a choking blizzard of string vegetable pulp. Broken, parts of the canopy foliage came crashing down.

Ohthere Wyrdmake lowered his plasma pistol. His left arm hung slack and limp. Blood around the shoulder, not yet dried, made it look as though his arm had almost been bitten clean off.

On the far side of the demolished tuber trees, sunlight fell on Eada Haelfwulf lying tangled in a sticky mass of broken bark and vegetable matter. Dense clouds of disturbed spores and plant dust billowed in the sunlit air.

Smoke rose from the terrible plasma weapon wound that scorched Eada's chest. Hawser's axe was still buried in his right shoulder.

THE THRALLS AND wolf priests backed off, and slipped out of the deep armoured chamber in the heart of *Nidhoggur*. Powerful banks of lights had been secured to the ceiling to bathe the chamber in a constant, simulated daylight. Marks of aversion had been notched into the chamber floor.

Eada Haelfwulf, stripped of his pelt, his wargear and his armour, was chained to an upright cruciform of plasteel in the centre of the chamber. He was near death. The apparatus that secured him was the work of the wolf priests, part restraint, part interrogation device, part life support mechanism. Tube lines and feeds ran from beating vital units on the floor behind the cross, and burrowed like worms into the sutured flesh graft that patched the wound cavity in his chest.

He looked out at Hawser and the Wolves, imploring, ashamed, knowing what he had done, what he had been. Clear fluid, viscous, wept from his nose, mouth and tear ducts, matting his beard and drying like glue on his bare flesh. There was a musky animal stink in the chamber that overwhelmed the astringent smell of counterseptic and the odour of blood.

'Forgive me,' he gurgled. 'I could not fight it.'

'What did you see?' asked Ohthere Wyrdmake.

Eada whined, as if the memory was too painful to recall. He closed his eyes and turned his head from side to side reluctantly. Mucus ran from his mouth and nose.

'Even if he answers, we can't trust anything he says now,' said Helwintr. 'It's been inside him. It's used him. Its touch is on him and he won't ever cast it out in this life.'

'I'd still like to hear his answer,' replied Wyrdmake. The senior priest of Fyf flexed his left arm. The injury done by sympathetic magic was healing with the usual, startling speed of Astartes self-repair, but it was still sore.

'And I'd like it if he wasn't on my damn ship,' grumbled Ogvai from behind them. 'He's poison. He's spoiled. He's turned.'

Wyrdmake raised a hand to crave the jarl's indulgence.

'A little of Eada Haelfwulf yet remains,' he said.

Eada moaned. Spittle and flecks of mucus flew from his lips and face as he shook his head.

'I recognise my failing and will be sure to correct it,' he moaned.

'Too late,' said Ogvai.

'The maleficarum could have taken any of us,' said Wyrdmake.

'It could just as easily have swallowed me,' added Helwintr. Helwintr's wounds were bound up too. He looked up at Haelfwulf.

'Do what you can, Eada,' he said. 'You can't make this right, but you can carve some honour out of this yet. What did you see?'

'I saw through the doorway in the skjald's memories,' Eada said. He shuddered, and a thick curd of mucus welled up over his lower lip and rolled down his chin into his beard.

'And what did you see there?' asked Hawser.

'Whatever redesigned the architecture of your mind,' Eada said, struggling to speak, 'it left a link into you, a trap door so it could creep back in and make further adjustments as necessary. When I probed you from the blindside, I went through the trap door by mistake. The thing in there, it was focussed on keeping Helwintr out. Like you, it was looking at him. I stepped into one of its memories for a moment.'

'I'm waiting,' said Ogvai.

'I saw a blade, lord,' said Eada Haelfwulf. 'A sacred dagger like the ritual knives we use, but an old and wretched thing, crafted by alien hands, shaped by alien thoughts. Its proportions are wrong. It is a nemesis weapon. It is sentient. It lies within the rusting hulk of a ship cast down from the stars, a ship that wallows in the depths of a miasmal fen. The blade is called the Anathame.'

Eada broke off as more coughing wracked him, and foul, syrupy matter splattered down his chest.

'So?' asked Ogvai.

'It didn't want me to see it, lord,' said Eada Haelfwulf. 'It didn't want me to be able to tell you about it. It seized me, and skinwrought me, and turned me against the skjald and my brothers. The only good that comes of this is that I can tell you about this thing. This Anathame.'

'And what is it for?' asked Wyrdmake.

'It will split the race of men,' said Eada. 'It will warp the future. It will murder the Wolf King's brother, great Horus, honoured Warmaster.'

'Murder him?' Ogvai echoed.

'The Warmaster we admire and follow will cease to be,' said Eada.

'Lies,' said Ogvai. He turned away from the chained figure. 'These are just the false things the maleficarum wants us to hear. His mouth lies. That is how he wants to split the race of men, by dividing us with mistrust and infamy.'

'Please, lord!' Eada cried.

'Perhaps we should listen to this,' said Hawser. 'Perhaps there is some kernel of truth here that Eada Haelfwulf is trying to impart. He–'

'No,' said Ogvai.

'He may yet–'

'No!' Ogvai snapped. He looked down at Hawser. 'Don't listen to his lies, skjald. Look for yourself.'

Hawser looked at the figure chained to the plasteel cruciform. The chamber's harsh overhead lights were casting a sharp, black shadow on the deck below the structure's base. The shadow silhouette of the spread-eagled figure did not belong to a man.

It belonged to a monstrous wolf.

Hawser recoiled from the sight.

Ogvai looked over at Helwintr. Wyrdmake had turned his gaze towards the aversion marks on the deck.

The Jarl of Tra walked up to the foot of the heavy shacklepost, and looked up at the miserable body suspended on it. Mucus dripped out of Haelfwulf's mouth.

He gazed down at his lord and whispered, 'I recognise my failing and will be sure to correct it.'

'I know,' said Ogvai. 'Until next winter.'

Ogvai drew his bolt pistol, pressed the muzzle up under Eada's chin, and vaporised his head with a single mass-reactive round.

⭧

'So you LIKED the account?' Hawser asked. 'It amused you? It distracted you?'

'It was amusing enough,' said Longfang. 'It wasn't your best.'

'I can assure you it was,' said Hawser.

Longfang shook his head. Droplets of blood flecked from his beard.

'No, you'll learn better ones,' he said. 'Far better ones. And even now, it's not the best you know.'

'It's the most unnerving thing that happened to me in my old life,' said Hawser with some defiance. 'It has the most… maleficarum.'

'You know that's not true,' said Longfang. 'In your heart, you know better. You're denying yourself.'

Hawser woke with a start.

Godsmote was shaking him.

'Wake up,' the warrior said.

'What?' Hawser murmured, his head still murky with sleep. He was in his quarters aboard *Nidhoggur*. Godsmote had interrupted his repeating dream pattern and, somehow, that was more distressing and confusing than following it to its usual frustrating conclusion.

'Get up,' said Godsmote.

'What's happening?' Hawser asked.

'Someone's calling for you,' said Godsmote.

A pinnace carried Hawser and his escort from Tra's cruiser to the Wolf King's massive warship. The anchored fleet components looked like monolithic blocks of dark grey stone suspended over the disk of Thardia. Everything had the hard-edged shadow of light in a vacuum.

Hawser peered out. The scale of the vessel was incredible. Even the smaller escorts and fleet tenders were blunt-nosed slabs like slices of mountain cliff. The principal warships were shockingly vast. The surface detail of their flanks took forever to flash past the ports as the pinnace flitted between them.

The most massive ship of all was a slate-grey monster with a ploughshare prow. This was the apex predator, the alpha male of the fleet.

'The *Hrafnkel*,' said Godsmote. 'Flagship of the Wolf King.'

The deck spaces of the flagship, vast as cityscapes, were heaving with activity. Hundreds of thousands of ratings, thralls and servitors worked to status-sweep the colossal ship from its last translation and prep it for the next immaterial transfer. Deck plates and interior struts were being examined and reinforced. Powerlines were being tested. In some stretches of companionway, inspection plates had been lifted in forty- or fifty- metre long trenches. In the lofty arming chambers, cathedrals of war, automated hoists raised payloads of void munitions from the armoured magazines to delivery points where gunnery trains coiled like sea-orms, waiting to thread the service arteries of the ship and deliver the titanic warheads to the *Hrafnkel*'s batteries. Regiments

of men, dwarfed by the arched vaults, unpacked
weapons and laid them out in rows along the deck to be
stripped and hand-checked before distribution to the
troop contingents.

The moaning shiver of the ship's vast engines rose
and fell, swelling and dying away, making the intensity
of the deck lights rise and fall. The drive was being
tested. It was like a warrior limbering his shoulders and
flexing his sword arm.

'War,' said Hawser as they strode along.

'Always,' said Bear.

'This isn't normal readiness,' said Hawser. 'This is
something particular. It's–'

'It's only war,' said Helwintr. 'Whatever else it is, it's
only ever war.'

✠

LEMAN RUSS DOMINATED the command bridge, even
though the command bridge was a multi-levelled vault
that reminded Hawser of a palace throne room. Officers
and servitors attended control positions wrought from
brass and gold which encircled the great dome of the
bridge and plugged into the bulkhead walls with fat
braids of gilded cables, circuits and tubes. These extending fans of tubework made the consoles resemble giant
pipe organs. To reinforce the mental image, most control positions had triple or quadruple sets of keyboards.
The keys were made of bone, inlaid with instructional
marks. Use and age had yellowed some. They looked
like the grin of old teeth.

They looked like the keys of a battered clavier.

Hololithic screens, many projected from overhead or
under-deck emitters, turned the central part of the command area into a flickering picture gallery. The crew
moved among the images, surrounding some for study,
adjusting the data flow of others with finger touches of
their reactive gloves. Some images were large, others

small, or arranged in stacked series that could be flipped through with a deft gesture. As Helwintr, Bear and Godsmote brought him in, Hawser saw one ensign slide a luminous rectangular map of fleet dispersal through the air for his superior's attention. Some of the slightly incandescent images showed topographical maps, contour overlays, positional guides or course computations. Others scrolled with constant feeds of written data, or showed, in small frames, real-time pict-links to the talking heads of other ship commanders as they reported in.

The air was filled by the mechanical chatter of machinery, the brittle stenographic clack of keys, the crackle of voxed voice messages or Mechanicum vocalisers, the drone of background chatter. Command officers with cuffs and high collars stiff with gold braid rasped orders into vox-mics that were attached to the consoles by flex leads. They held the mics up to their mouths, and the small acoustic side-baffles of the microphone heads obscured the lower parts of their faces like half-masks. Just eyes, without noses or mouths, which reminded Hawser of something.

Cherubs, giggling at private jokes, buzzed through the bridge hustle, carrying messages and communiqué pouches. Insectoid remotes, as perfect and intricate as dragonflies, kept obedient station in the air at the shoulders of their Mechanicum masters, their wings droning in hover-mode at a disturbingly low vibrational threshold.

In the centre of the command bridge was a massive brass and silver armature, an instrument designed for complex celestial display and calculation. It resembled an orrery with its skeletal metal hemispheres and its surrounding discs and measuring orbits, but it was ten metres in diameter and grew out of the desk grille on a stand as thick as a tree trunk. Attendants manned small

lectern consoles around it, tapping out small
adjustments that caused the main frame of it to turn,
realign and spin in subtle measures.

The hemispheric theatre of the planetarium was cur-
rently used to display a large-scale hololithic image of a
planet. The glowing topographical light map, three
dimensional and rotating in an authentic orbital spin
showed day and night side and was contained inside
the moving, spherical cage of the brass instrument.
Smaller side projections hung in the air, enlarging particular surface details, and various declinations,
aspectarians, and astronomical ephemerides.

The planet under scrutiny was as beautiful as a star
sapphire. The hololithic resolution imaged its greens
and blues, its ribbons of cloud and mountain range, its
traceries of river basins, its sheened oceans, its turquoise
aura of atmosphere. As he got closer, Hawser saw that
the vast image was actually a mosaic compiled from
thousands of separate detailed pict scans, a work composition that suggested a vast effort of careful and
systematic intelligence gathering.

Despite the size and majesty of the planetarium display, Russ was still the most compelling thing in the
chamber. As soon as he saw Hawser and his escort
arrive, he pushed aside the huddle of Navigators clutching their dossiers of sidereal times and zodiacal
interlocks.

'Bring him!' he growled, and pointed to the shipmaster's reclusiam.

Helwintr, Bear and Godsmote led Hawser into the
reclusiam space behind the Wolf King. The shipmaster,
a stern giant with a long, wirewool beard of grey and an
extravagantly peaked cap, saluted and withdrew to give
the primarch privacy. Command officers scurried after
their immaculately uniformed master, clutching arm-
fuls of data-slates and dockets.

Russ waved a jewelled sceptre and raised falsehood screens around the reclusiam space. The ambient noise of the bridge chatter dropped away. It was suddenly as quiet as a monastic chapel.

The Wolf King idly tossed the sceptre away. It bounced into the seat of the shipmaster's red-leather throne. He turned to face Hawser. His presence was almost intolerable. A dynamic, lethal energy pulsed within him. He was hunched, his arms clamped around his body, as though he was trying to prevent himself from exploding. If the explosion happened, Hawser had no doubt it would take the entire flagship with it.

'Do you hear me, brother?' he asked Hawser.

'What?' Hawser replied, trembling. 'Lord, what are you asking me?'

'I know you can hear me, brother,' Russ said. 'I know you can.'

'Lord, please,' said Hawser. 'Explain to me what you're saying.'

The Wolf King ignored his words. He continued to stare into Hawser's eyes, as though they were murky pools out of which something might suddenly surface.

'Magnus, Magnus, Crimson King, brother of mine,' he said. 'I know you can hear me. You planted this instrument, this poor unwilling fellow, Ibn Rustah, you planted him among us so you could learn our secrets. Guess what? We're as smart as you. Smarter, perhaps. We saw your spy for what he was, and we made no effort to remove him. We kept him with us so we could look back at you, Magnus. So we could learn *your* secrets. An eye can look out and it can look in. You should know that, you who look deeper than most.'

The Wolf King turned and walked a few paces away. He picked up the sceptre again, and sat down in the throne. He rested the sceptre in his lap, leaned his head on one fist and gazed back at Hawser.

'I've got nothing to hide from you, Magnus. Nothing. You know how I work. My enemies should know what's coming to greet them. It fixes them in the right mental place to be annihilated. I don't like to hide my strengths or my approach. I'd rather my foe knows the full, unimaginable fury that is about to descend upon him.'

The Wolf King paused. He swallowed. He seemed to be considering his next words.

'That's not why I'm talking to you now. I'm talking to you because I hope you'll listen. I'm talking to you as the personal courtesy extended from one brother to another. What is about to happen should not be happening. You know I do not want this. You know it tears my heart to commit against you, and it breaks the very soul of our father to place his sons in opposition. But you have done this. You have brought this. You have brought this action.'

Russ swallowed again. He looked down at the deck, though he was still directing his words at Hawser.

Hawser stood numb, shaking, rooted to the spot.

'We gave you every chance, Magnus. We indulged your learning, we gave you room to explore. When we became fearful of where those explorations were leading you, and how they might endanger everything we value, we told you of our concerns. The Council at Nikaea, that was supposed to be a moment of reconciliation. You swore you would renounce the cunning arts. You swore! You swore you would abide by our father's ruling!'

His voice dropped to a whisper.

'You did not. You have proved your intent to ignore the Ruling of Nikaea beyond all doubt. So this is on you. You must have known our father's hands would be tied. He would have no other option than to turn to me to issue sanction.'

Russ looked up into Hawser's eyes.

'This is a courtesy, then. From brother to brother. A grace period I would extend to no other enemy. Settle your affairs. Evacuate the civilians from your cities. Deactivate your defence systems. Bring yourself and your Thousand Sons out into the open, and prepare to surrender to me upon my arrival. Please, Magnus. The Wolves of Fenris have been unleashed upon you. Only you have the power to make the consequences bloodless.'

He rose to his feet.

'Please, Magnus. Please.'

The Wolf King looked away. He turned his back on Hawser.

'Does he answer?' he asked, distractedly.

'I cannot feel an answer,' Hawser replied, his voice wobbling. 'But then, I've never really known how I work as a conduit.'

Russ grunted.

'Or if I do,' Hawser added. He was painfully aware that the other Wolves, especially Helwintr, were glaring at him.

'I've never been totally convinced of that either,' he said.

The Wolf King made no comment.

'My lord,' said Hawser. 'What… what did your brother do?'

'He performed an act of maleficarum that drove his sorcery right to the heart of Terra and into the presence of the Emperor,' said Helwintr.

'But… why?' asked Hawser.

'It was an alleged attempt to communicate a warning,' said Russ without turning. His voice was a soft grumble, like thunder grinding in the far distance.

'A warning, my lord?'

'One of such terrible importance, Magnus felt it was worth exposing his own treachery to reveal it,' Russ murmured.

'Forgive me,' said Hawser, 'but does that not speak to some loyalty in your brother? Has the warning been examined? Has it been taken seriously?'

Russ turned back to face him.

'Why would it? My brother is a madman. A dabbling warlock.'

'Lord,' said Hawser, 'he was prepared to admit he was ignoring the edicts of Nikaea, and risk the censure that he knew must result from that admission, to relay a warning. Why would he do that unless the warning was valid?'

'You're not a warrior, skjald,' said the Wolf King in an almost kindly tone. 'Strategy is not your strong suit. Consider the reverse of your proposition. Magnus wants the ruling of Nikaea overturned. He wants permission and approval to continue with his arcane tinkerings and his foul magics. So he manufactures a threat, something he can warn us about that is so astonishing we would have to forgive him, and set aside our objections. Something so unthinkable, we would have to thank him and tell him he had been right all along. All along. This is his ploy.'

'Do you know what was so unthinkable? asked Hawser.

'Magnus claimed that great Horus was about to turn against the Imperium,' said Russ. 'From the look on your face, Ahmad Ibn Rustah, I see you recognise how ridiculous that sounds.'

Hawser switched his gaze to Helwintr. The priest's masked face was unreadable.

'Wolf King, great lord,' Hawser began, 'that's not the first time that warnings concerning the Warmaster have been voiced. Please, lord–'

'Our skjald refers to the incident involving Eada Haelfwulf, lord,' said Helwintr.

'I know of it,' said Russ. 'It seems corroborative, I grant you. But once again, consider the strategy. It involved maleficarum turning and twisting one of our own gothi, in the immediate vicinity of you, an identified conduit for the enemy's power. Of course poor Haelfwulf would gabble out the same damned lie with his dying breath. It's supposed to make Magnus's story sound more credible by coming from a secondary source.'

Russ looked down into Hawser's eyes.

'Truth is, it's the proof I need that Magnus is desperately trying to coordinate a campaign of disinformation to support his ruse. He doesn't need to answer through you, skjald. He's answered already.'

The Wolf King turned to Helwintr and the escort.

'Take him away, but keep him with us, right to the advance. I want that channel to my brother left open. My poor brother. I want him to see us coming. I want him to know it'll never be too late for him to beg for mercy.'

'My lord,' said Hawser. 'What happens now?'

'Now?' Leman Russ replied. 'Now, Prospero falls.'

PART THREE

ACCOUNT

THIRTEEN

The Sanction of the Sixth

I NAME MYSELF Ahmad Ibn Rustah, skjald of Tra, and I bring to this hearth the account of the *Vlka Fenryka*'s raid upon Prospero, as is my calling.

Many voices can be heard in mine, many memories, for as skjald of Tra I have done my duty, the duty given to me by Ogvai Ogvai Helmschrot, Jarl of Tra and, before him, Gedrath Gedrathsa, Jarl of Tra, to gather all the stories the men of Tra have, and make memories out of them so that they can be retold, over and again, until wyrd decides when my thread must be cut.

You who gather here at the hearthside, you who listen to me by the firelight, and sip your mjod, and wait for your part of the account to be recited, you will need to forgive me. This is my story too, and I am inside it, my voice and my memories, and I cannot be taken out. For I name myself also, Kasper Hawser, visitor to Fenris, comrade of the Sixth, pawn of the Fifteenth, witness, outsider.

The account of Prospero is several things. We all know

that. Foremost, it is a testament to the courage and loyalty of the Sixth Astartes. It is the story of a duty performed without hesitation or equivocation. The Allfather told the Rout what task he needed them to do, and it was done. No one will ever hear this account and question the devotion of the *Vlka Fenryka*.

It is also a lament. This was a sad necessity regretted by all. It gave no pleasure to perform it, not even the reward of glory. The prosecution of a fellow Legion, even when it is done so successfully, is no easy thing to square in a man's mind. This has ever been the burden of the Wolves of the Sixth Astartes that their calling as the Allfather's chosen hunters places a solemn burden of responsibility on their shoulders greater than any endured by other Legions. There is no shame in admitting this is an account of sorrow, a mournful thing. It is an account we could happily wash away from our memories and wish undone.

Prospero burned. The Wolves of Fenris fell upon it, and it blazed up brightly, and died into the darkness. Though strong in many arts of war and lorefare, the brotherhood of Tizca could not withstand the murdermake. Bloody was the fighting, savage and unholy. Only one result was ever likely. No one survives the coming of the Wolves, not even the Crimson King and his Thousand Sons.

We know the conclusion. We know how it ends. We know that Magnus fled, broken, with the last surviving scraps of his once noble force, and, in fleeing, proved beyond any doubt the extent of his necromantic talents. Only the darkest magics allowed him to escape the field of war alive.

There is one part of the account you do not know, however, and it is my part, and I will tell it once.

Here and now.

✠

THERE WAS DRUMMING; the anti-music of a sending off. I had been given armour, thrall-armour, to wear under my pelt and reinforce the knotwork leather that had become my everyday garment. I had my axe, and a displacer field unit, and I had been given a short-form laspistol of excellent manufacture. I believe it had come from Jarl Ogvai's weaponarium. The weapon was old, but in pristine condition. It had been disassembled and reassembled many times to keep its component parts clean and serviceable. During its life, which had been longer than mine, the hand grip had been removed, perhaps due to wear, and replaced with a simple shaped piece of radapple wood that fitted around the frame's handle-spur. On the faces of the wooden grip, the symbol of Ur was inlaid in gold wire. The weapon had once been the property of an officer in the Defence Corps of the great, doomed Catheric city-project of Ur. Aun Helwintr, proud rune priest, had selected it for me, knowing the account I had made of my own past, and my connection, as a child, to the Ur labour communes.

'Ur was one of many grand and admirable schemes to achieve a finer future for mankind,' Helwintr told me when he presented me with the weapon. 'It failed, just as many of them failed, but its spirit was great, and its intention beyond fault. I give this to you to remind you of that spirit. What we do today, however bloody, is done with the same intent. Unification. Salvation. The betterment of man.'

I could not argue with his words. Toil and blood, effort and hardship, these were payments worth making in return for a greater future. Ideals were never won cheaply, whether the cost was the raising of one dream city or the razing of another.

My only doubt, and I confess doubt lurked in my heart, was that Ur had any significance for me at all. I had lived my life assuming it did. I had lived my life trusting the solidity of my identity and my memories. Now I trusted nothing. I heard a clavier playing. I saw a toy horse made of wood. I watched the dawn rising over Terra, and turned from a window port to see a face I could not recall. Eyes without features. Features without eyes. Pieces on an old game board. An athame, softly glowing in the darkness like a blade of ice.

I took the weapon anyway.

Nidhoggur's carrier decks were swarming. Hoists conveyed drop-ships overhead to the catapult ramps. Munition trains clattered across the deck grilles. Smoke as white and fine as summer cloud filled the embarkation space to thigh level, because so many transatmospheric drive units were test firing and venting. Under the brilliant light-banks of the ceiling rigs, it felt as though we were gods of Uppland, walking abroad in the heavenscape, masters of creation and destruction. We could hear the rapid hammer and air-gun stutter of the armourers making their last minute adjustments. Wyrd was being forged here.

I was placed with Jormungndr Two-blade's pack. Bear was amongst them, and Godsmote and Aeska and Helwintr. Every member of the pack kept their eyes on me, watching to see if I would fall down and roll back my eyes, and froth at the lips and plead for mercy in the voice of the Crimson King.

I never did. He never chose to speak through me.

THE WOLF KING had brought the entire Sixth to sanction Prospero. A full Legion to punish a full Legion. The fleet components that had assembled at Thardia translated to three further assembly points, gathering strength as they went. Amongst them were forces of the Silent Sisterhood and the Custodes, bequeathed by the Allfather himself to strengthen our cause.

The full force of the Sixth was something I did not

believe needed strengthening. There is not an Astartes
in the Imperium who can out-match a warrior of the
Rout, one to one, and we held a significant numerical
superiority. Much is said of Prospero's noble Spireguard, and other auxiliary contingents, but the only true
consideration was Astartes numbers, and Magnus the
Red's Legion was small compared to the *Vlka Fenryka*.

However, there was an ugly mood of caution amongst
the Sixth. The Crimson King's edge derived from maleficarum, the very root of the entire dispute. Now it came
down to a bare fight, he would show his sharpest claws.
No matter that we had ten or a hundred or even a thousand times his Thousand Sons, magic could level any
fight. All the pack leaders agreed, loath as they were to
admit it out loud, that the Silent Sisterhood might
make the difference between triumph or destruction.
Only they, Allfather willing, might cancel out or dilute
the sorcery of Magnus and his disciple-sons.

There was fear. You could feel it in the thralls at least,
and in the support forces. I do not think an Astartes can
feel fear, not fear as a man knows it. Trepidation, perhaps. But I knew that the Rout always craved stories of
maleficarum, because it was the only thing they
couldn't kill, and thus the only thing that lent their lives
even a thrill of apprehension.

We were slamming out of the immaterium into the
face of maleficarum.

I felt fear. Fear was in my heart. I put on my mask to
scare it away.

※

I HAD FINISHED my Rout-mask and leatherware during
the passage from Thardia to the target system. Aeska
Brokenlip had lent me some general advice, and both
Orcir and Erthung Redhand had shown me knotwork
designs that I chose to copy. I chose to make the mask
with the stylised antlers of a bull saeneyti spreading out

from the bridge of the nose to form the brow ridges. I
did this in honour of the memory of Ulvurul Heoroth,
called Longfang, who sleeps upon the red snow. I
stained my mask and all my leather gear black, and
added the circumpunct, the mark of aversion, to the
centre of the mask's forehead. With its warding eye, and
flaring bull antlers and snarling lips, the mask's threat
would drive off all but the darkest maleficarum.

The men of Tra armed for the onslaught. This was a
murder-make, and they had come to cut threads, and
they wore all the faces that Death needed to wear to get
the task done. Blades and boltguns predominated, of
course: the true, trusted weapons of the *Vlka Fenryka*
were their primary resource. But all the jarls had opened
their weaponariums, and Ogvai had shared out devices
amongst men in his company who were willing and
skilled to operate them. I was not the only soul that day
to have received a weapon from the hoard as a gift.

Some Wolves had enhancements that turned their
armoured gauntlets into huge wrecking fists, or even
industrial talons. Others prepared enormous melta-
weapons with armoured feeder cables, ornately
engraved lascannons, or colossal assault cannons with
rotating barrels that seemed barely man-portable.

On the repeater screens up in the rafters of the
embarkation deck between the Stormbirds hung like
game in a larder, the forward-scan images of ghostly,
utopian Prospero grew steadily larger.

ON THE FINAL night, a dream came to me. It was the
dream I had been having since I left Terra, the dream I
no longer trust. It purports to be a memory, but it is
laced with deceit. I know that I stayed aboard the superorbital plate Lemurya during the last months before my
departure. I leased a luxury suite on the underside of the
plate. That much is real. I know that the prolonged

exposure to artificial gravity made me feel tired and unrefreshed.

I remember that golden light sliced into my chamber around the window shutter every morning, gilding everything, giving the room a soft, burnished feel.

I remember there was always an electronic chime before the hour five alarm.

I had gone to Lemurya to void-acclimate before transferring to the ship on which I had arranged passage. I had also gone there to avoid people. I was hell-bent on taking my sabbatical, on freeing myself from the chains of Terra, and I did not need well meaning souls like Vasiliy trying to convince me otherwise.

Of course, now I realise that the circumstances were not quite as I understood them. My situation with the Conservatory was not as untenable and unappreciated as I had thought. These facts I have had from exemplary sources.

I do not think I was in my right mind. I was being influenced even then. Indeed, perhaps the manipulation long pre-dated that moment. The urge to leave Terra had been put into me. So had the urge to experience Fenris. Honestly, brothers, tell me, what man who is afraid of wolves goes to face his fear by voyaging to a *planet* of wolves? It is nonsense. I was not, forgive me, even especially interested in Fenrisian culture.

The fascination was put into me too.

The other reason I spent time on the superorbital was to visit the biomech clinics. Some instinct, or implanted instinct, had warned me that Fenris was not a place where a man could make notes or keep written records. I had therefore undertaken an elective procedure to replace my right eye with an augmetic copy that was also an optical recording device. My real eye, surgically removed, is being held in stasis in the clinic's organ banks, ready to be replanted on my return.

Sometimes I wonder what dreams it is seeing.

My recurring dream finds me waking in my room as the hour five alarm rings. It is the day of the scheduled implant surgery. I am old, older than I am now in every respect except years. My body is weary. I rise and limp to the window, and press the stud to open the shutter. It rises into its frame recess with a low hum, allowing golden light to flood in. I look out and drink in the view. I have done this every morning of my stay, because I know these may be the last chances I get to see such a magnificent view with my own eyes. My real eyes.

On that last night before Prospero, the dream had been embellished. I do not believe any new elements had been added, I just think that I had stepped through the dream so many times, I was noticing things in finer and finer detail.

Through the half-open doors of the closet, I glimpsed a toy horse made of wood standing on top of the foot locker. I could hear clavier music playing from a neighbouring room. I could smell fresh-pressed radapple juice. On a shelf in the corner, my Prix Daumarl sat in its pretty little casket beside an old Ossetian prayer box. By the window, a regicide set lay open on a small table. From the look of the pieces, the game was just two or three moves away from its end.

I stepped to the window, waiting to see the reflection of the face of the figure standing just behind me. I waited for the terror to constrict me.

I waited to ask, 'How can you be here?'

I turned, hoping the face would be another detail I could resolve in greater clarity than before.

All I glimpsed before I woke were eyes. They were eyes without features, and they blazed like marks of aversion.

We had anticipated resistance. Of course we had. For all our confidence and innate superiority, for all our show of terrible force, we did not expect to be unopposed. Never let it be said that the Thousand Sons of Prospero were not great warriors. They were Astartes! That fact alone puts them on a different order of being. During the Great Crusade, we had respected them as brothers and comrades in arms, and now we respected them as mortal foes. Even without their warlock sorcery, they were to be taken seriously.

Moreover, Prospero was their home world. A Legion is always strongest at its base. The fortress homes of the Allfather's eighteen Legions Astartes are the most formidable and impregnable sites in the new Imperium.

As the sanction fleet burned in towards Prospero like a massed, migrating pod of hrossvalur, it became evident that the planet had not lit its defences. The grids were down from outer orbital to close surface. Individual cities were screened, but that was standard operation and not a response to the approaching threat. There were signs that civilian ships had fled or were fleeing the planet and the system in considerable numbers.

Some of the escaping vessels were overtaken and boarded. Their crews and passengers were taken captive and interrogated by the rune priests, so that every useful scrap of information could be gathered. Later, I heard that one such ship, the *Cypria Selene*, was carrying Imperial remembrancers who had been posted to Prospero to observe the Fifteenth Astartes. One of them, I was told, was an old man described as 'the Scribe of Magnus'.

I would like to have met them, and spoken with them. I would dearly like to have listened to their accounts, and heard the voice of the other side. I did not get the opportunity. I only learned of their presence long after the day was done, and their ultimate fates are unknown to me.

Two-blade conjectured that the Crimson King had capitulated. Magnus the Red had not signalled surrender, but he had seen the error of his actions and the disgrace he had brought upon the Fifteenth Astartes, so he had sent the innocents away and thrown his defences wide open in order to accept his fate with humility, as a guilty man places his exposed neck upon the headsman's block. If true, this spoke to great remorse and contrition on Magnus's part. Two-blade ventured that the action would be over in hours.

But Ogvai gainsayed him. With wise counsel, the jarl reminded us all that witchcraft had brought this sentence of doom upon Prospero and the Crimson King. It was likely that he had defences, raised and ready, lethal and primed, that were maleficarum and invisible to our sensors.

We waited. The high-resolution image of Prospero was so large that it filled the repeater screens. We began to feel the slight artificial gravity tugs of orbital corrections.

An hour later, the main lights on the embarkation deck began to dim for periods of several seconds at a time.

'What's doing that?' I asked Aeska Brokenlip.

'The main batteries are drawing power,' he replied. 'We have begun the orbital bombardment.'

WHEN THE TIME came for the drop, I think I was dozing, or daydreaming. I had been thinking about the commune where I had grown up, the tent fields on the desert highlands, the long room, the teaching desks in the library annex, the bedtime stories of wolves to keep us in our place.

Godsmote nudged me.

'We're ready,' he said.

The drums were thundering. We boarded our

Stormbird. As skjald, I had the right to go where I wanted, and choose any accelerator seat I liked, but I took one of the spares at the back of the cabin and not one of the numerical ranks. I would not insult my brothers by breaking their cohort.

Each seat's arrestor cage locked down with a pneumatic hiss. We checked our restraints. Thralls and servitors secured bulkier weapons to the overhead racks or the magnetic stowage plates, and then scurried clear as the ramp began to rise. The entire airframe was already rattling with pent-up main-engine fury, and the burner roar almost drowned out the screaming vox-chatter of pilots, ground crew and deck supervisors.

Then the lights went as red as blood, and the sirens howled like carnyx horns, and the hydraulic bolts fired like lightning stones, and acceleration hit us like a warhammer blow.

One after another, our Stormbirds spat out of *Nidhoggur's* belly like tracer rounds from a basket magazine. In the sky around us, a score of other ships discharged their cargoes in similar fashion.

I looked at Godsmote.

'We are all bad stars now,' I said.

THE HEARTH-FIRE STILL burns brightly. There is still meat on your plate and mjod in your lanx, and I still have more of this account to tell.

So then, on Prospero, many great years ago, we fought against the Traitor Fifteenth. A hard fight. The hardest. The most bitter in the history of the *Vlka Fenryka*. Firestorms, burning air, crystal cities where the Thousand Sons waited for us with flame-light reflecting off their casement glass. Anyone who was there will remember it. No one who was there could forget it.

We descended through flames. We speared down past orbital defence platforms ablaze from end to end, great rigs that had been crippled before they could take a shot. They burned as they tumbled and rolled away in slow, decaying orbits, spilling out trails of debris or shorting out great blossoms of reactor energy.

Below, the world burned too. The fleet's bombardment had torched Prospero, and ignited the atmosphere. Spiral patterns of soot and particulated debris thousands of leagues across cycled like hurricanes. Giant columns of plasma energy had roasted all vegetation and wildlife, and turned the seas into scalding banks of steam and toxic gas. Vast las bombardments from the heavy batteries had evaporated river deltas and flash-thawed ice-caps. Kinetic munitions and gravity bombs had fallen like Helwinter hail, and planted new forests of bright liquid flame that sprouted and grew, spread and died back, all in a few minutes. Shoals of targeted missiles, silver-swift as midsummer fish running from a catcher's net, delivered warheads that blasted the soil into the sky and thickened the air into poisonous soup. Magma bombs and atomics, the godhammers, had altered the geography itself. Mountains had been levelled, plains split, valleys thrown up into new hills of rubble and spoil. Prospero's crust had fractured. We saw the throbbing, glowing tracks of its mortal wounds, brand new canyons of fire that split entire continents. This was the grand alchemy of war. Heat and light, and energy and fission had transformed water into steam, rock into dust, sand into glass, bone into gas. Swirling mushroom clouds, as tall as our Aett on Fenris, punctuated the horizon we rushed towards.

The ride was not smooth. No power dive from a low anchored carrier ever is. We dropped straight, like stooping hawks, and only levelled out when the surface was right under us. As our nose came up, fighting like a great ocean orm on a hook, the gravity force was huge.

The Stormbird shook as if it was intent on shredding to pieces. Then we were level and hugging the topography. Our pilots did not stint on speed. The craft continued to quake. We bellied and bounced as the terrain shifted, and banked hard at every squeal of the collision alarms.

Some of our drop-boats did not survive the experience. Some failed to recover from their dive approaches. Two that I know of were destroyed when they collided and tore the wings off one another. By then, of course, the warriors of Prospero had finally begun to respond. Battery fire was coming up from the main city. Inbound boats were blown out of the air, exploding outright or veering wildly away like burning moths. Wyrd's hand was on us. Threads were being cut. We–

BROTHER, WHAT? I said we were like stooping hawks. Hawks. You know the word, surely? Ah. Ah, I see what has happened. Sometimes, in my excitement, in my enthusiasm for the drama of the account, I lapse back into my old ways, and use a word of Low Gothic instead of Juvjk. It is a habit of mine that I have never left behind, the last traces of the language I spoke in my previous life. I ask your pardon. I did not mean to interrupt the tale.

THE FIRST THING I did when I set foot on Prospero was kill a man.

This is an important part of my personal account, for until that day, I had never cut a thread. No, not ever. I am a skjald, not a warrior, but that day, that dark day, I was determined I would be more than a helpless observer. On the home world of the Olamic Quietude, men had given of themselves to protect me during the fighting. I did not want to be a burden of that sort again. I had asked for weapons and armour so I could protect myself, and on Prospero I intended to do more than that, and fight with my brothers as the need arose. The wolf priests built my arms and back strong for just such a purpose, after all.

The Stormbird carrying us, its lifters howling, settled us down with a hard slam on a space of flat rockcrete below some derrick or manufacturing facility in the industrial quarters of Tizca, Prospero's glorious city of cities. Even now, brothers, even now it is gone, the idea of Tizca will persist down the ages like Roma and Aleksandrya and Memphys as one of the great cities of mankind. It was and is a Carthage, a L'Undone, an Atlantys even, its thread burned and cut, its towers fallen, its rubble long since ploughed under, yet persisting in the memory of our race. It had been planned and raised as a magnificent open city, with beautiful acres of parkland and urban gardens spacing out the vast towers of glass and the crystal ziggurats. Their sheer glass faces reflected either the sun, so they radiated light like mirrors, or the bruise-blue sky, so they became part of heaven. At night, they were reflecting bowls for the stars, perfect scrying surfaces in which the constellations could be watched as they performed their ritual choreography. There were busy quarters of bustling streets and squares, of fine markets and elegant public spaces, especially leading down towards the harbour.

We set down in one of the vast city's less glamorous wards, one of the necessary, functional sectors, and even here there was splendour. Buildings of the most mundane and unremarkable function were clad in glass, or raised to be crowned with majestic finials or spires. Tizca's basic functions of trade and produce-handling, cargo transfer, manufacturing, provision and distribution were all contained by a mask of aesthetic perfection where most cities wear such crude organs around their skirts away from the sites of civic refinement.

When we arrived, the mask was already knocked

away. The hammering shock of the bombardment, as well as several munition strikes, had shattered most of the glass off the buildings around us, exposing their superstructures and girderwork. Some burned furiously. The air wobbled with heat distortion. The open spaces and loading yards were littered with mirror shards, like beaches of polished glass shingle, and every last fragment reflected back a version of the flames so they twinkled and flashed like trillions of fireflies. Each step we took as we bounded from the Stormbird's ramp crunched. Penetrating warheads had blown titanic holes in the rockcrete ground, revealing some of the service tunnels below, the hidden network of arteries that invisibly maintained the city's needs.

Other Stormbirds shrieked overhead, so low it felt we could reach up and touch them. Some set down on nearby sites. The daylight had turned an odd, murky colour, a violet hue that suggested the blue sky had contracted some kind of disease. Smoke moved in the wind, swirling and spinning, reducing our visibility. All I could smell was burning. All I could hear was howling: transatmospheric engines howling, infernos howling, voices howling.

Then I began to hear, behind the howling, the distant thump of bombs and the nearby bang of bolter fire.

We entered the derrick tower, a multi-levelled manufacturing plant that had been skinned of its glass cladding. Fire squirmed in its upper levels, silhouetting the black ribs of the girders against bright orange. Low down, where we were, the fire cast hectic, jumping shadows. The Wolves did not hesitate. They ploughed in, hunting targets, dividing to quarter the area. Godsmote and Aeska were the first two to mount the metal-mesh stairs up to the second level, where a railed hoist platform connected to a larger gantry over some kind of machine bay. I ran with them. I jumped as I heard the

sudden, shocking retort of bolters discharging underneath us as our comrades met the first resistance. Aeska
yelled something and began firing at a walkway on the
level above us. His mass-reactive rounds bit chunks out
of the decking and the rail. I saw human bodies fall into
the flames far below. I realised we were being shot at.

I saw men on the same platform level as us, men in
crimson coats and silver helmets. They had golden
braid frogging on their coats, as though they had
dressed for a parade in the sun. Some had sabres in
their hands, drawn and ready. All of them were blasting
with lasweapons.

Godsmote roared and ran at some, his axe raised. I
saw one of the red-coated figures burst as a bolt from
Aeska's gun struck him. Smoke from the fires above us
suddenly gusted down as the wind direction changed,
and fogged my location, blinding me for a moment.

As the smoke sucked back out, I felt a dull concussion
from the front, then another. Two las-rounds had struck
my displacer field, and been dissipated in crackling
balls of energy. The shooter was directly ahead of me,
six spans away, beside the gantry rail. He was a young
man, handsome, regal in his gold-frogged red coat and
his silver helm. He was aiming his lasweapon and
yelling at me. He fired again, and the shot crackled off
my body-shield.

The pistol from Ur was in my right hand. I didn't even
think about it. My reaction was instinctive, but made
swift and effective by the training I received from
Godsmote. I fired back and killed him.

The only thing that betrayed my novice status, the
only thing that gave me away as a combat virgin, was
the fact that I employed overkill. Godsmote had taught
me to aim and shoot. I could pull a gun and hit a target
at twenty spans. My first shot went into his chest and
would have been entirely sufficient. But he was

shooting at me, and he'd have killed me already had it not been for the displacer field, so I kept the trigger squeezed.

The pistol from Ur put three more rounds into his belly, and the sheer force of impact doubled him up so the next two shots punched into the side of his neck and the top of his head. He fell against the rail, and then collapsed in a sort of sitting position, all very suddenly and untidily. I kept waiting for him to fall down completely and stretch out dead on the deck, but he did not. He remained tangled and contorted, half-raised by the rail behind him.

I stepped towards him. My shots had killed him three or four times over. Blood from the rupturing torso wounds was streaming out of his corpse and spattering down through the deck grille into the darkness below. There was a huge, scorched puncture mark in the crown of his polished silver helmet as though a blacksmith had hammered a sooty augur through it. A steam of blood vapour wafted out of it from his cooked brain-case.

I expected his expression to register something. Anger, perhaps, defiance, or full on hatred for me. I expected at least a rictus of agony, or even a look of sadness or dismay.

There was nothing. His face was slack. Not one hint of a vital emotion could be read. I have come to learn since that is the case with the faces of the dead. We find no messages or legacies there, no final communication. Life departs, and the face sinks. As the thread is cut, the tension goes, and only the untended ruin of absence remains.

⚓

THE SOLDIERS IN red coats were the Prosperine Spire-guard. Their noble and well-appointed regiments were the domestic defence forces. They were as finely drilled and effective as any elite division of the Imperial Army.

They looked too civilised and decorative to bear the brunt of the Wolves' assault. They looked like men confounded by disruption to some formal colours ceremony. They looked as if they ought to be running away.

They did not run away. Let us agree on their courage and make it part of this account. They met the Sixth Astartes, the most efficient and ruthless killing machine in the entire arsenal of the Imperium, and did not give ground. They faced demented, barbarian giants that looked like feral caricatures of Astartes, and did not break. They had been ordered to defend Tizca, and they did not falter from that order.

And so they died. This is what happens when loyalty meets loyalty. Neither side was going to leave its grim and onerous duty undone, and so destruction of at least one was assured.

The Spireguard had ballistic armour woven into their distinctive red coats, but this could not withstand the mass-reactive devastation of bolter rounds. Some carried displacer fields or riot shields, but neither could cope with the withering ferocity of autocannons. Their silvered helms, some plumed, all alloyed from plasteel, were unable to block the slicing edge of axes or frostblades. Their gun-carriages and fighting vehicles were well plated and, in some cases, shielded, but all crumpled into mangled wreckage when struck by shoulder-launched missiles or conversion beamers, or burned like corpseboxes on funeral pyres when caught by heavy flamers or melta effects. Jarl Ogvai, so several brothers attest, faced one gun-carriage down as if it was a saeneyti calf that he intended to wrestle to the ground and hog-tie. He gutted it with his power claws, shredding metal like scraps of foil. He split its casing wide open and then filled its interior with bolter fire that pulped the crew.

The devastation was heartbreaking. The ground, as we advanced, was littered with the tattered and disfigured dead. Blade weapons had sectioned some, heat weapons had blackened and fused others. The marks of bolter impacts had left huge wounds that looked like deep bitemark craters in radapples. For their part, the Spireguards' lasguns and autoweapons barely scratched the marauding Rout. Minor injuries were taken. Only crew-served weapons and fighting vehicles offered any genuine hazard. Once the Sixth's armoured support began their advance, clanking and clattering up from the steam-haze of the seafront zones where their heavy landers had come in, even that small hope was extinguished. Predators and Land Raiders, grey as granite and just as monolithic, crushed through buildings in the lower town, levelled structures and demolished towers. Their tracks cut new roads into the city's streetplan, death roads of pulverised rubble. Their weapons selected and annihilated anything that crossed their range.

Dark shapes ran with them and around them, bounding along the new-made death roads into the fire of combat. They looked like wolves, or the shadows of wolves at least. I am not sure if they were real, or just the product of my imagination. The smoke was treacherous, and played many tricks.

I HAVE NEVER known my Rout brothers as savage as they were that day, nor have I ever known them so grim. There is a strange lightness to them in most times of war, an execution yard humour that allows them to bond and endure, and to laugh wyrd in the face. It is almost a glee, a relish, the eagerness of a duty well done. Even during the war with the Olamic Quietude I saw it: the caustic jokes, the barracking, the acid comments, the bleak, phlegmatic mindset.

But not on Prospero. The task was too dark, too thankless. Nothing could lighten the burden of what they were about, so they lost themselves in the fury of their actions. In some ways, this made Prospero's punishment all the more extreme and unholy. Not only was no quarter offered, no quarter was even considered. Teeth were only bared in wet leopard-snarls of rage and hatred, not in menacing grins. The only words uttered were curses and condemnations. Golden, black-pinned eyes darkened with resolve and hardened with duress. Blood begat blood. Slaughter begat slaughter. Fire fed fire, and in that fuelled frenzy, a planet perished, a society bled out, and a wound was torn in the flank of the Imperium that would never heal.

The Rout of the *Vlka Fenryka* did everything that was asked of them, without question or dubiety. They were not in the wrong. They were the perfect warriors, the perfect executioners, precisely as they were engineered and bred to be. They were the Emperor's sanction. This account, my account, absolves them of all blame and celebrates their trueheartedness.

It must also reflect one other thing. This account must reflect one other, secret thing. Hear it, and decide what must be done, even if what must be done is slit my throat and cut my thread so I can never recite this account again.

✣

THE DAY BLURS in my memory. An experience of such extreme intensity, of such violence and unending cacophony, will always do that. Moments conflate, events knock into one another and overlap.

I remember I was in a park, or what was left of some public garden. All the vegetation was burning. There was a small shrine structure, which had taken an indirect hit and was bleeding smoke into the violet air. We had entered from the east, with crossfire coming at us. I had temporarily turned off my displacer field because it was beginning to lose its charge.

Then we met the Thousand Sons for the first time.

Something had made them hold back. It was not fear. Perhaps they could not stomach the heresy of a fight against their Astartes kin. Perhaps it was some kind of tactical ploy intended to achieve an advantage.

Perhaps it was restraint. As though accepting their punishment, they had not opposed our initial advance, but, like the Spireguard, they ultimately found they could not stand by and watch their city burn.

They were resplendent in gold-edged red, their helmets marked with the distinctive nasal crest of their Legion. Though in form and armour and stature they were equivalent to the warriors of the Sixth, they could not have been more different. They moved differently. The Wolves bounded and sprang; they seemed to glide and stride. The Wolves were head-down and fast moving; they were upright and measured. The Wolves were howling; they were silent.

I was standing in the middle of the burning lawns as the lines of rival Astartes first engaged, wild grey shapes hurling themselves at gold and red centurions. The noise was like a thunderclap. It was the slap of great masses crashing together, like the clashing rocks of myth, but there was a ringing peal to it as well. It sounded like the voice of the monstrous storms that sheer altitude sometimes detonated outside the high places of the Aett on Fenris.

This was how battles must have looked when only gods and their demigod offspring walked upon Terra. Humanoid giants in regal armour, some dark and pelt-clad like sky deities of boreal Aesir, some golden and haughty like scholar gods of Faeronik Aegypt. Immense blows were landed by warriors of either side: men were smashed off their feet, or cut apart, bodies were rotated hard, heads snapped around. Fenrisian blades hammered into Prosperine armour, Prosperine force burned back into Fenrisian plate. The line faltered in both directions as it compensated for the force of collision. Then it seemed as though the carnivorous lust of the *Vlka Fenryka* would entirely overwhelm the warriors of the Fifteenth.

That was the moment we started to die, my brothers. That is the moment we started to die in any significant numbers. The Thousand Sons unleashed their maleficarum, the poison in their veins.

Electrical discharge leapt from staffs and fingertips. Radiant filth, like the *unlight* of the warp, spilled out of eye slits and speared from warding palms. Wolves were torn apart by the touch of their battle magic, or thrown back, mangled and scorched. Some were petrified into smouldering attitudes of excruciation. Their weapons charged with sorcerous power, fuming with *helsmoke* and sick light, the accursed traitors launched into our assaulting ranks.

Threads were cut in swathes, like scythed corn. Threads were more than cut. Some were torched back along their lengths, so that men did not merely die; the lives they had led before their deaths burned away into forgetfulness. Some were left as smears of blood, or haphazardly butchered carcasses. Some were pulled limb from limb by invisible wights and the sprites of the air. Some were left as nothing but heaped white bones and scads of blackened armour.

Oje died there, turned inside out by a warlock's gesture. I saw Svessl too, split in two by an invisible blade. His blood came out of him with great, explosive force, like liquid from a pressurised cask. Hekken: cooked inside his armour. Orm Ormssen: exsanguinated. Vossul: blinded and pulped. Lycas Snowpelt: gutted and decapitated. Bane Fel: engulfed in a cold blue fire that consumed him but would not go out. Sfen Saarl: withered to a vile powder. Aerdor: transmogrified into a twisted, steaming, inhuman stump.

Too many. *Too many!* The accounts needed for all their sendings off would last for months. The kindling needed for all their funeral pyres would exhaust an entire great year's supply.

I felt vindication, for the maleficarum of the Thousand Sons was everything it had been accused of being. Our prosecution was legitimised. But I felt fear, for I did not believe we would win or even live. For all our fury, for all our might as warriors, we would be exterminated, proving that the Thousand Sons of Prospero were monsters and warlocks.

I did the one thing a skjald should not do. I looked away. I averted my gaze so that I did not have to witness the fall of the Rout.

I missed, therefore, the beginning of salvation. I missed the first glimpse of the Null Maidens pouring down the black heaps of burning rubble into the fight. Their blades were bright. Pulsing beads and beams of energy spat from their weapons. They uttered no war cry or challenge.

The *blankness* of them washed across the line. The rank clouds of maleficarum burned away, or blew aside like fog in a night wind. The warlocks of the Fifteenth choked on the abominable words of their conjurations. They gagged on the pestilential utterance of their spells. I saw them stagger back, clutching at their throats, pawing at the neck seals of their helms. I saw blood spurting and leaking through visor slits in stringy ropes. I saw arcane gestures and motions seize up and cripple hands into palsied, arthritic claws.

Seconds after they had stunned and disempowered the traitors of the Fifteenth with their insidious silence, the sister-warriors struck. They surged through the

recoiled mass of Wolves and began to hack and slice
with their longswords. Their assault was an odd mixture
of frenzy and elegance. Every stroke, every cut, every
turn was the skilled action of an elite swordfighter, yet
it was driven along by a berserk mania, a hysterical orgy
of wounding and killing.

The Wolves did not hold back either. Released from
the hammerblow onslaught of magic, they set in beside
the Sisters, matching them blow for blow and kill for
kill. The war was physical again. It was kinetic, concussive, visceral and explosive. Blood lay like dew upon
what was left of the grass, and hung in the air like a mist.

Custodes had appeared with the Null Maidens. Their
golden forms gleamed amid the swirling scrum of fighting bodies. Released into battle from their normal,
solemn duties, they were as unrestrained as any Wolf.
The blades of their halberds were thirsty for blood–

PUT DRINK IN my lanx. I am thirsty too. My throat is dry
from the urgency of this account. I want you to hear all
of this. I want you to see it in your minds.

See? Do you see? Prospero burns.

WE WERE DRIVING them back towards the great glass
pyramids of Tizca. Drop-pods rained down through the
stained sky like meteor showers. The light was bad: not
insufficient, I mean. The daylight had gone bad, like
meat goes bad.

Tizca had been violated and deformed. Most of its
street plan had been erased, and its buildings and monuments demolished. The landscape was a tangle of
black rubble and debris, some of it heaped into steep
mountains and ridges, some of it cratered by vast munition strikes. There were corpses everywhere, and in the
craters and the gullies, blood had pooled. In places, it

ran in gurgling brooks between broken pipes and shattered masonry. Pulped organic matter spattered amongst the debris was the only residue of some fallen souls.

Each phase of assault was another climb up another hill that had not been there an hour earlier. The rubble slopes were sooty and treacherous. The air was full of beams and pulsed lasers, of hard rounds and rockets and squealing missiles. There was an almost constant downpour of micro debris, and, with that, oily rain as the boiled oceans began to condense and fall back onto the persecuted land. War machines, soiled by smoke-wash, streaked by rainfall, rolled and clanked and strode through the rubble-wastes, their weapons banks flashing and spitting. Pneumatic cannons recoiled pugnaciously into their mounts as they discharged. Main turret weapons boomed like the voice of the All-father. Flocks of whooping rockets flew together in search of roosts.

I was with Godsmote and Orcir. We scrambled up another ridge of jumbled wreckage. I was trying to keep up with their fierce rate of advance.

To the west of us, as we arrived at the summit, one of the great glass pyramids began to collapse, devoured by a languorously slow bloom of fiery light that swelled and expanded, and allowed the monumental structure to fall into its incandescent embrace.

There was howling in the air once more, the growing chorus of Wolves. Over the din of war and even the tumult of material collapse, the sacking of Prospero was dominated by that sound: part wail, part wet leopard-growl. We know ourselves, my brothers, as Astartes warriors, but I tell you this as an outsider. It is the most chilling sound in the cosmos. It is the primal noise that accompanies death. Nobody who hears it ever forgets it, and few who hear it ever survive. It heralds the approaching destruction, and gives notice that the time for any parlay or mercy is long gone. It is the sound of the sanction of the Sixth, the hunting call of the Space Wolves. It is the dread-sound of wyrdmakers. It turns the blood to ice and the gut to water. I do not believe, and I speak in all honesty, that the Thousand Sons, even though they were Astartes and therefore engineered to be free of fear, were not inspired to terror when they heard it.

You scare me, wolf-brothers. You scare *everything*.

As a prelude to my recurring dream, I often remember a conversation I had with Longfang. I had shared with him, at his request, an account of maleficarum, an event that had befallen me in my previous life, in the ancient city of Lutetia. Longfang told me it was a good tale, but it wasn't my best. He told me I would learn better ones. He told me I already knew a better one, but I was simply denying it.

I'm not sure how he was certain of these things. Right then and there, with his thread breaking, I believe he could perceive time in ways that we cannot. I believe he was not bound by the thread of life and could, in those twelve minutes surrounding his death, look up and down its length, and know the elusive past and the inescapable future.

For the latter point, the account I was denying, I believe he meant the event-memory that forms the kernel of my recurring dream. The face I could never turn in time to see, the face at my shoulder, that was the truth he wanted me to admit. By the time I came to Prospero, I was desperate to free myself of the burden too.

I did, though in doing so, I merely replaced it with a greater one.

I RAN WITH Tra, with the wolf-shadows in the smoke, across the ravished landscape. It was late in the day. The flame-light of the tortured world was keeping the encroaching gloom of evening at bay, but when night finally fell, as it must, I knew it would be eternal and no sunrise would ever dispel it.

I had killed six men – two with my axe, four with my pistol. These are the ones I know of, clean kills in the dizzy incoherence of war. I had also helped to slay one of the Thousand Sons. He would have killed me, one to one. He had felled Two-blade in a bruising clash, and pinned him to the ground with the tongue of a fighting spear, which had gone through-and-through Two-blade's hip and into the soil. Leaning on the spear to keep the brave Wolf down, he was drawing his bolt pistol to cut Two-blade's thread.

I suppose he considered me of no consequence: a thrall, a less-than-Astartes thing blundering in the smoke. He reckoned without the Fenrisian strength the wolf priests had woven into my limbs when they re-engineered me. I cried out a battle curse in Wurgen, and sprang at him, putting the momentum of my running leap into a two-handed downstroke that buried the smile of my axe in the top of his skull. The attack left me rolling on the blood-mire of the earth. The Thousand Sons warrior lurched backwards off Two-blade, uttering some foul, gurgling sound. He let go of the fighting spear's shaft and clawed at his scalp with his left hand, trying to grasp the blood-slick axe and wrench it out. I had not killed him. His helm had cushioned most of the blow. He swung around and aimed his bolt pistol at me, to punish me for the affront I had caused.

Two-blade pulled himself up, the spear still through him. He unpinned himself from the ground and came for the traitor foe from behind. He used his famous paired swords like shears and snipped off the warrior's head. Blood jetted into the air. I had to brace my foot against the detached head to twist my axe free.

Jormungndr Two-blade dragged the spear out of himself, glanced at me, and continued on his way.

Some enemy resistance had collected in the glass precincts and annexes of one of the great pyramids. I wanted to see one of these places for myself. I wanted to see its fine decoration and soaring majesty before it was lost to the eyes of man.

Fine alabaster steps detailed with gold led up to a portico of glass and silver. The only thing that marred the entranceway was the stream of blood running down the fine steps from the sprawled body near the top. Orcir and Godsmote were ahead of me. The doors and walls and ceiling were vitreous mirrors. Shots had struck the mirroring in places, punching holes that were encircled by crazed lines and the talcum scurf of powdered glass. Inside, it was still, the horror without muffled and kept at bay. We could hear the distant rumble of the war, the patter of debris and rain on the high roof panes. Wisps of smoke drifted in the air like holy incense. The mirrored structure of the precinct hall trapped light and bathed us in an ethereal radiance. We slowed our surging advance down to a walking pace and cast our eyes around the glory of the interior. This was but an annex, a side chapel. What wonders must the pyramids contain? The conservator part of me, relic of my old lifetime, stirred within my breast, and urged me to examine the complex symbology of the designs wrought in the gold and silver frames of the looking-glass walls, and to record the delicate tracery of glyphs chased into the crystal.

We saw ourselves too, reflected in the gleaming surfaces: startled and uneasy, dark and hunched, barbaric intruders besmirched with gore, framed in the honeyed light. We were uninvited, invaders, like wild animals that had worried a fence post loose or leapt a boundary ditch and found their way into some civilised commune to desecrate and befoul the place, and scavenge for food, and kill.

Predators. We were predators. We were why walls were raised and watchfires lit at night.

Shots came at us down the length of the hall and broke our contemplation. They whipped past us, small bad stars. Some struck the floor and excavated sprays of pulverised stone. Some struck the mirror-walls and punched holes through them. The impacts made the glass walls shiver. The reflections of us hastening to cover wobbled and shuddered. We returned fire, positioned behind turned glass pillars and rows of silver statues. Some of the gunshots screaming at us were bolter rounds. Terrible bites were torn from the gleaming pillars. Silver figures lost their heads or limbs, or toppled from their plinths. I saw one of the Thousand Sons at the end of the hall, unloading his bolter at us. An aura surrounded him, as if he was wearing his own personal storm. Orcir swung from cover and let rip with his heavy bolter. The shots annihilated the traitor, and threw his torn corpse back into the mirrored wall behind him, which promptly shattered and came down in a deafening cascade of glass.

Orcir and Godsmote moved up. Enemy fire was still coming our way. From the gauge of it, we suspected Spireguard. I could hardly bear to see the incrementally increasing damage that was being done to the grand hall: the spreading cracks, the falling glass, the shot holes, the collapsing statuary, the destroyed detailing. Orcir fired his huge, underslung weapon again, clearing the way. I slipped to the left behind him, into the mouth of a side hallway, hoping to find better cover. My displacer field had still not recharged. The rate of gunfire suddenly increased again, and drove me back along the side hall. I lost sight of Godsmote and Orcir. Mirrors were around me. Looking glass, reflecting me. I pressed on, gun drawn, axe slung but ready, to the end of the side hall, and opened a glass door. There was a room beyond. I stepped through.

Golden light was knifing into the chamber, gilding everything, giving the room a soft, burnished feel.

I stepped forwards, wary. There was an electronic chime.

'Yes?' I whispered.

'Ser Hawser? It is your hour five alarm,' said a softly modulated servitor voice.

'Thank you,' I replied. I was so stiff, so worn out. I hadn't felt so bad for a long time. My leg was sore. I thought, maybe there are painkillers in the drawer.

I limped to the window, and pressed the stud to open the shutter. It rose into its frame recess with a low hum, allowing more of the golden light to flood in. I looked out. It was a hell of a view.

The sun, source of the ethereal radiance, was just coming up over the hemisphere below me. Solar disc, circumpunct, it stared at me, an eye. I was looking straight down on Terra in all its magnificence. I could see the night side and the constellation pattern of hive lights in the darkness behind the chasing terminator, I could see the sunlit blue of oceans and the whipped-cream swirl of clouds and, below, I could see the glittering light points of the superorbital plate Rodinia gliding majestically under the one I was aboard.

I knew where I was. I had reached the end of my dream.

My eyes refocussed. I saw my own sunlit reflection in the mirror of the window port. I saw the face of the other figure reflected in the glass, the figure standing just behind me.

Terror constricted me.

'How can you be here?' I asked.

I did not wake.

'I have always been here,' answered Horus Lupercal.

FOURTEEN

Looking Glass

HE DID NOT need to name himself. I had seen his proud likeness many times on posters and pict-casts, on souvenir medals and holo-portraits: Primarch, Warmaster, the beautiful one, the foremost of the first sons. He was a giant, like all of his brothers. The little sleepchamber of the superorbital suite barely contained the scale of him. He was wearing the striking, Imperial white-gold armour of his Legion. A single, staring eye was fashioned across the breastplate. It was surrounded by an eight-pointed star.

He smiled down at me, a reassuring smile, the smile bestowed by a wise father on a miscreant child.

'I don't understand,' I said.

'You were never supposed to, Kasper,' he said. 'You were only ever a playing piece on a board. But I have grown fond of you down the years, and I wanted to see you one last time before the game was over.'

'We've never met before, my lord,' I said. 'I would have remembered.'

'Would you? I doubt it,' he replied.

'Ser,' I said. 'I have been privy to warnings. Grave warnings. A threat upon your life. I was shown a weapon–'

'This?' he asked. He drew the Anathame from his belt. It shone with malign light, just as it had done in my *un-memories*. 'It's too late. A year or so from now, this blade will have done its work upon me. I will be finished, and I will be renewed.'

'A year or so from now? How can you speak of time in such a topsy-turvy sense?'

He smiled again.

'When this blade cuts my thread, Kasper, occulted gods will take me in their arms. They will warp me. My life will change from mortal order to immortal Chaos. I will defy the laws of the cosmos and the rules of creation. Look at the two of us here, standing in your past. Prospero burns in your present, Kasper, but neither of us is there.'

'Why?' I cried. 'Why? What have you done? What madness have you wrought?'

'I am clearing the board for the game to come,' he said. 'I am setting it out the way I want it. Two key obstacles to my ambitions are the Sons of Prospero and the Wolves of Fenris. The former is the only Legion that has lorecraft enough to hinder me magically; the latter is the only Legion dangerous enough to represent a genuine military threat. The Emperor's sorcerers and the Emperor's executioners. I have no wish to store up a fight with either for my future, so I have invested time and energy arranging events to turn them upon each other.'

I gazed at him in disbelief. He shrugged, ruefully.

'I had hoped for more, if I am honest,' he said. 'Magnus is terribly misguided. His dabblings have brought him perilously close to damnation, and my father was right to restrain him. But he would never have toppled over the brink without this violent provocation. I had so wanted the Wolves and the Sons to annihilate each other here on Prospero, and remove themselves as threats at a stroke. But Magnus and Russ have remained true to character. Magnus, high-minded and pious, has accepted his punishment and been destroyed. Russ, relentless and brute-loyal, has not wavered in his appalling task. The Thousand Sons have been destroyed. The Wolves remain in play.'

He looked at me, and there was a glitter in his eye.

'But in the fate of Magnus and his sons, there is compensation for me. Broken by defeat, they nevertheless come across to my side. As a consequence, I earn some redress against the fact that the *Vlka Fenryka* remain a stark and extant danger to me.'

'No man can do this,' I cried, shaking my head. 'No man can orchestrate events on such a scale!'

'No? Not with years of gamesmanship and manipulation? Not with the dissemination of secrets and lies? Ugly rumours of Magnus's necromantic practices? Blunt questions about Russ's psychopathic tactics? Plus, of course, the deliberate manufacture of a network of spies like you, Kasper, real spies and pawns to make both sides paranoid, to make both sides suspect the worst and prepare for reaction? I turned the very traits and habits of each Legion's character into weapons of self-destruction.'

'No!' I insisted. 'No man can do such a thing.'

'Whoever said I was a man?' he replied.

I backed away. I felt the cold glass of a window or a mirror against my back.

'What are you really?' I asked.

'You know my name,' he laughed.

'That's just a mask, isn't it?' I said, pointing at his face. 'What are you really?'

'Which mask would you prefer?' he asked. He raised his hand to his face, and tore away the flesh. It split like the husk of a pea-pod, like fibrous vegetable matter, spilling sap like languid honey. The features of Horus Lupercal parted, and underneath them was the laughing face of Amon, Equerry to the Crimson King.

'This one? The one you spoke to on Nikaea? The real Amon was far below at his primarch's side.'

He dropped the shredded *Horus* face onto the deck. It landed with the *splat* of rotten fruit. Then he peeled the *Amon* face away too. Milky sap spurted out and spattered down his breastplate, drooling across the great staring eye. Now the sadly knowing features of my old colleague Navid Murza gazed at me.

'Or this one?'

'The real one,' I said. 'The real one. No mask, just your real face.'

'You could not bear to look upon it,' Navid said. 'No one can behold the baleful light of the Primordial Annihilator and survive. Your sanity would be the last thing to burn up, Kasper. Oh, Kasper. I was not lying when I said I had grown fond of you. You were good to me. I am sorry for the life I have given you.'

'What is the Primordial Annihilator, Navid?' I asked. 'What is it?'

'The warp, Kasper,' he said. 'The warp. The warp is everything, and everything is the warp. Your Allfather thinks He can win a war against it where other, greater races have lost. He can't. Mankind will be the warp's finest victory.'

He took a step towards me. At his throat, I could see the glint of the Catheric crux he always wore. It was melting.

'We got rid of our gods, Kas. Something was always going to take their place.'

His face was pleading. It was the face I had known for

years, un-aged since the day he perished in Ossetia. He
was no longer wearing the Warmaster's armour. He was
human-sized, and dressed in the soft, cream-felt robes
of the Lutetian Bibliotech.

I knew, with painful certainty, that Navid Murza's face
had been the one I had turned around and seen that
day, long ago, in my suite aboard the Lemuryan superorbital. His was the face that my dreams had blocked,
the face my memories had refused to recover. This had
been the trigger event: a man, dead for so long, come
back to find me in a locked room to warp my mind with
fear, reboot my memories, adjust my will and drive me
to Fenris.

This was the 'best piece' of maleficarum, the one that
Longfang knew I had.

'So all this is for nothing?' I whispered. 'Prospero has
burned, for nothing? Astartes has murdered Astartes, for
nothing?'

Navid grinned.

'It's *exquisite*, isn't it?'

'The Crimson King was loyal. Misguided, but loyal. So
this tragedy need never have happened?'

'I know!' he said, exalted, his eyes bright. 'But now
this has happened, oh Kas, now this has happened, a
door has been opened. A precedent has been set. If you
think Prospero is a tragedy, an abomination, a terrible
mistake, you should see what happens next. Two
Legions Astartes, locked in mortal combat? Kas, that's
just the *overture*.'

He was close to me. His hands were reaching out. He
had folded back the integral gloves of the soft robes to
free his hands. I did not want him to touch me.

'How long did I know you before you weren't Navid
Murza any more?' I asked.

'I was always me, Kas,' he cooed. He touched the side
of my face with one hand. I felt his fingers against the

knotwork of my mask. My headgear's marks of aversion were not keeping him at bay.

Him. *It*, I think. I could smell its breath, the charnel stink of a predator's bacteria-swilling mouth, the venomous air of Prospero outside my private dream, burning up at the end of all its days.

'Always you?' I asked. 'No, I think there was a Navid Murza once, and you took his place.'

'It's naive of you to think so, Kas,' it said, stroking my cheek.

'It's naive of you to get this close,' I replied, and spoke the word Navid had spoken, all those years before, in the back alley behind the cathedral corpse. *Enuncia*, he had called it, part of the primeval vocabulary of magic. He had been so cocky, so arrogant; he had never expected me to retain its form, not after so many years and so brief an exposure, but I had spent a long time with the rune priests of Fenris recovering and replaying my memories. I had heard it over and over again, enough times to commit its jagged, razor-edged shape to memory.

I had it, word perfect.

I spat it into the thing's face. It was the single most important word I have ever uttered as a skjald.

Its face exploded in a blizzard of flesh and blood. Its head snapped back as though it had been struck in the face with an axe. It tumbled away from me, screaming and howling, the sounds horribly muted by its mangled mouth.

I was hurt too. I could feel how raw my throat was from retching up the word. I could taste the blood in my mouth. My lip was split. Several of my teeth were loose.

Caring little for any of that, I moved forwards, raising my pistol.

'Tra! Tra! Help here!' I shouted, and then had to spit blood through the slit of my mask.

I fired at the writhing, robed form. Its cream-felt shape crashed over the chamber's bed and fell on the floor on the other side, squealing like a butchered pig. Furniture toppled over. Books spilled from broken shelves. Damaged, the bedside dataplate began to repeat, 'Ser Hawser? It is your hour five alarm. Ser Hawser? It is your hour five alarm...'

I fired at the thrashing shape again.

'Skjald? Skjald?'

Voices were calling me in Wurgen. The chamber door opened, and Godsmote appeared with Orcir. They hesitated for a second. Behind them lay the bright glint of the looking-glass hallway on Prospero. Ahead of them lay a cramped and gloomy sleepchamber overlooking Terra. At the doorway, where they stood, two realities had been grafted together. Their dismay was understandable.

'Help me!' I yelled. I pointed at the thrashing figure in the corner of the room.

'Kill it!'

Orcir pushed past me, bracing his heavy bolter. There was no hesitation. He fired a sustained burst of shots from the massive weapon, the noise of which was overwhelming in the confines of the tiny room. The bolts shredded the figure. They blew the soft, plump folds of its Bibliotech robes apart and obliterated the body underneath. Blood, sap and fibrous tissue plastered the wall behind it.

But it was not dead.

It rose up, a shattered human skeleton, dripping with gore, and remade itself. It grew. Skin rewove. Organs reassembled or uncooked. The last remnants of the cream Bibliotech robes sloughed off like shedding skin as white-gold armour formed underneath it. Remade, the Warmaster wore a vengeful, insane expression. One of his eyes was blown.

'Get back,' I warned my brothers.

'Hjolda!' Orcir gasped. 'Lupercal? Lord Lupercal?'

'Get back!' I cried.

'Orcir,' Horus whispered, saying the name like a charm. An unseen force propelled Orcir towards the giant.

The Anathame glimmered in Horus's hand. He struck it down into Orcir's chest. Orcir screamed out. His thread already cut, he tried to use his heavy bolter, point-blank, against his killer. Horus spoke Orcir's name again, and once again the name gave Horus power over our wolf-brother. This time, the unseen force lifted Orcir off the killing blade, and threw him like a doll across the bedchamber. His armoured corpse hit the viewing port, and the window shattered.

There was a monstrous bang of decompression. Every stick of furniture, every loose object in the room, every bead of blood, rushed out of the broken port along with the atmosphere and all the tumbling shards of window glass. Orcir's body, limp and spread-eagled, fell away from the window, spinning end over end, and dropped towards Terra, getting smaller and smaller, beginning to burn up like a shooting star.

The decompression did not dislodge Horus. He roared in the failing air. I felt my feet lose purchase. I tried to brace, but the explosive voiding of the chamber would not let me go. The glass shade of a lamp smashed off my shoulder. A book struck my knee. I grabbed the doorframe. A toy horse made of wood flew past my head and went out into the blackness.

I could not hold on. My grip broke, and I shot backwards like a cork. I was suddenly pulled up hard as Godsmote's fist clamped around my arm and anchored it. He had hooked the head of his axe to the door frame, and was clenching the weapon's haft with one hand as he clung on to me. The effort of pulling me in made him roar. As soon as I had a grip too, I added my strength to his.

We pulled ourselves through the doorway, and slammed the door. On the outside, it was just a mirrored surface. We were in the temple precinct again, in the glass hall.

I expected questions from Godsmote, urgent demands for explanation, but he did not even break stride. Driven and single-minded as all Wolves, he knew we were not yet safe. We moved quickly, down the side hall into the main atrium, the space ruined by gunfire.

Horus came behind us. He exploded through the temple's glass wall, bringing sheets of mirror down as though they had been rammed by a Land Raider. He tore his way from one reality to the next, out of my past into my present, out of my memories into my reality. He was running, each great, racing stride ringing out on the polished floor.

'Kasper!' he commanded.

I felt the tug upon me, the power of my name, but Kasper Hawser is only one of the many names I own, and none of them are my true, birth-name, my signifier. Not even I know that. I resisted.

He was gaining on us. Godsmote turned to fight him, Astartes against primarch-thing, Fenrisian Wolf against Luna Wolf.

'Godsmote!' Horus declaimed. Godsmote faltered for a second, and then put his arms into that famous stroke of his, his godsmack. The axe-bite took Horus in the ribcage on the left side, and actually knocked him sideways a few paces. He howled. Godsmote ripped his axe out and did it again, ripping a gash in the Warmaster's left thigh.

'Fith of the Ascommani!' Horus bawled out. He had dug deeper into my memory and found a truer, older

name for my friend and wolf-brother. At the merest
breath of it, Godsmote was picked up and tossed across
the hall. He slammed against the looking-glass wall
four or five metres off the floor, cracked a huge sunburst
pattern in its surface with his impact, and fell onto the
ground beneath.

Horus straightened up and came for me. I shot at him
until my cell was spent, and then threw the pistol aside
and drew my axe. He knocked me down with a slap,
tore off my displacer field unit, and wrenched my axe
from my hands. His titanic hand was around my throat.
My feet left the ground.

'I had grown fond of you,' he hissed in Navid Murza's
voice. 'I even confessed as much. And you repay my
indulgence with this abuse when you should have
accepted the gift of a painless death that I was offering
you. Now it certainly won't be painless.'

'I don't care,' I grunted back.

'Oh, you will,' he promised.

The gleaming, frostblade head of a Fenrisian axe
flashed down between us and parted his arm at the
elbow. I fell onto the floor with his severed forearm still
clutching at my throat. His blood, or whatever foetid
ichor passed for his blood, hosed at me.

'Step back,' said Bear, and put two more axe strokes
into him. Horus bellowed Bear's name, in rage and
pain, but obtained no mastery of him. Bear's axe continued to bite him. Just as had been the case when it
wore the mask of Amon on Nikaea, the Primordial
Annihilator could not subdue Bear with his name.

Bear had done terrible damage to the Horus-thing.
One arm was off, the white-gold armour was rent open
in a dozen bloody places, and there was a grisly cleft
through the side of the Lupercal's head. The brainpan
had split open. The white bone of skull fragments protruded. Part of his cheek had torn away. The blood

streaming out of him was forming a widening pool around his feet.

'Skjald?' Bear growled. 'Run now.'

I got up. Bear settled his grip and prepared to face the next round. Twitching, the Horus-thing advanced, splashing one step after another through its sappy blood, leaving footprints of gore on the glass floor.

'Run now,' Bear urged me.

The Horus-thing accelerated. Bear bent low and put his back into the swing that greeted it. The blow didn't land. Pain and anger seemed to amplify the Horus-thing's power. It smashed Bear aside with a vicious sweep of its remaining arm, and then stooped and tried to rain blows down on the fallen Wolf. Bear rolled wildly to avoid them, escaping a pounding fist that cracked the floor in several places. With no time or opportunity to rise again, Bear slid around on his back, and hacked at the monster again, with his axe, left-handed.

The Horus-thing caught the axe-head this time. It caught it neatly in its huge, armoured paw, and locked its grip. Blood and oily fluid bubbled out of its mouth as it looked down at Bear and uttered some eldritch *unword* of Enuncia.

Balefire, the corposant that lights treetops and mast-heads in the darkest winter nights, swirled down the axe from head to throat, wrapping it in greenish yellow flame, consuming it. The flames spread to Bear's left hand and forearm, burning them away in a wild, incandescent flare. Bear howled. The Horus-thing was exacting punishment for his own missing arm. He was a predator, playing with his prey before the kill.

I snatched up my axe from the floor where it had landed. I did not hesitate. I got between them and struck off Bear's left arm just below the elbow before the maleficarum could spread to the rest of him. He had saved me by severing a limb. I was determined to repay him, and repay him for the constant protection he had offered me, without comment, since our first meeting on the shore of the ice field, when I mistook him for a daemon.

I knew, now, what a daemon really looked like.

Bear rolled clear, clenching his teeth in pain. I tried to drag him back towards the hall's portico. I confess I did not expect to have done much more than delay our ultimate demise.

By then, Aun Helwintr had felt the terrible forces that had been released in the temple precinct. Ominous in his pelt and his long black cloak, his white hair twisted and lacquered into horns, he stepped into the crystal hall behind us, forming with his hands the warding gestures that all rune priests are taught, the gestures of banishment and aversion. The Horus-thing vomited blood and recoiled, but its power dwarfed that of the imposing priest.

For this reason, Helwintr had not come to our aid alone.

One entire glass wall of the temple hall, on the right-hand side, blew in and shattered in a vast cascade of glass. A second later, the same thing happened to the left-hand side. Light and smoke from the killing grounds outside swirled in through the building's ruptured frames. Parts of the roof glazing fell in and smashed.

A huge and heavy shape strode into the hall through the torn down right-hand wall. It was a biped, a construct five metres tall, squat but massive, thickly armoured with adamantium, badged in the colours of the *Vlka Fenryka*. On either side of its bulky main hull, weapon-pods cycled and target-locked.

A second Dreadnought entered through the gap blown in the left-hand side of the hall. It cycled its weapons. The constructs closed the distance a little, vic-ing the Horus-thing between their positions, driving it back towards the end of the hall. Each step they took shook the ground.

They opened fire in unison at some shared, mind-linked command. The tempest wrath of assault cannons and twin-linked lascannons macerated the Horus-thing. Flailing, it was blasted into fragments, into a haze of matter that spattered what little of the hall's mirrored surface remained, and stained it like mould.

Something thrashed at the heart of the blast zone, something that took form as the humanoid figure of Horus was annihilated. Gale force winds and energies screamed out at us. The air filled with swarms of flies.

Something rose up, slowly, out of the molten fireball created by the Dreadnoughts' barrage. It was hard to look at, hard to understand. It defied visual interpreta-tion, like a dream that refuses to let you turn around and see its face.

It was tall and misshapen, a shadow cast by shadows. There was a suggestion of anatomy that was both utterly human and corrupted beyond any organic limit. Every-thing about it had been put together wrong, so that the sight of it dislocated the senses and depraved the mind. It was gristle and rancid meat, blisters and herniated intestines, ulcerated tongues and rotting teeth. It was blinking eyes that were as large as drinking bowls or clustered like the spawn of amphibians. It had horns, two huge, upcurved horns.

Everything in the room suddenly cast too many shad-ows. The clouds of flies grew thicker, trying to invade our eyes, our nostrils, our mouths, our wounds.

A voice said, 'Oh, Aun Helwintr. You do not learn from your mistakes. You have brought mighty warriors to confront me and drive me out, but I know their names and thus have power over them. I name them both. Patrekr the Great Fanged. Cormek Dod.'

'I recognise my failing and will be sure to correct it,'
Helwintr replied. I was astonished to see that he was
smiling. Figures streamed into the shattered hall behind
him, and stepped in through the walls the Dreadnoughts had breached. A dozen Null Maidens. Two
dozen. Their swords were drawn. Their leader, Jenetia
Krole, raised her hand and pointed an accusing finger at
the shadow-shape looming before us.

It let out a long and harrowing cry of anguish as it felt
its power negated. The pariah gene shared by the members of the Silent Sisterhood blocked the puissance of
its sorcery and banished its potent maleficarum. The
wind immediately began to die back. The swarming
flies fell dead, and piled on the ground in black drifts as
thick as the heaps of fragmented glass.

'Knock it down and cut its thread,' ordered Aun Helwintr, and the Dreadnoughts resumed their
conflagration.

They did not stop until every last speck of the deviltry
was obliterated.

FIFTEEN

Threads

I DO NOT believe we killed it, brothers. I do not think the Primordial Annihilator can be harmed in the way that a mortal thing can. But we drove it back, we drove it out. We hurt it for a while at least.

WHEN WE EMERGED, the battle was done. The Wolf King had engaged Magnus in monumental single combat, and broken his spine. Then, at the very moment when we bested the daemon in the temple hall, sorcery boiled loose across the entire, ruined world. Blood rain fell. The Crimson King, and those of his Thousand Sons who had survived, vanished, fleeing by means of their proscribed magic.

Only in this way could they escape total extermination by the Rout.

Let this lesson be remembered.

BLOODY RAIN WAS still falling as we regrouped. The sky was nightfall dark, black as a raven's wing feathers, and underlit by the firestorms engulfing the glass city. With Godsmote, who had recovered from his injuries enough to walk, I stayed with Bear as the wolf priests tended his arm.

Bear's face was impassive. He showed no hint of pain or discomfort as the priests worked at his stump with bone cutters and hooks. An augmetic would be fitted in time. But I saw him grimace slightly as a Dreadnought thumped by our position in the streaming downpour.

Drops of blood rain beaded Bear's face.

'I don't mind the arm,' he grumbled. 'Not when you consider.'

'Consider what?' I asked.

'It's supposed to be an honour,' said Godsmote, nodding towards the Dreadnought as it moved away. 'But who wants to lose so much they end up like that? That's no way to live forever.'

Bear nodded grimly.

'What I don't understand,' I said, 'is how you broke its spell. It knew the names of every one of us, and yet that power had no mastery over you.'

'It's probably because it learned all our names from you, skjald,' Godsmote said. 'And you've never got his name right, not since the first day you came to us.'

I HAVE REMARKED that whatever put the fluency in Juvjk and Wurgen into my mind did a good but imperfect job. Sometimes, at points of stress or when distracted, I lapse, and mis-speak a word, regressing to the Low Gothic of my former life. For reasons I cannot explain, this is especially frequent in the case of terms for birds and animals.

From the outset, my mind had decided that Bear's name was *Bear*. But that was the Low Gothic translation. It was a habit that had stuck, and Bear, forever taciturn, had never seen fit to correct me.

In the language of the *Vlka Fenryka*, his name was *Bjorn*. I recognise my failing and will be sure to correct it.

ONCE PROSPERO HAD burned, I felt great pity for the Wolves. Not for their losses, which were great and lamentable, but for their emptiness. Their anger was spent, and though complete, their victory seemed hollow. They stood around me, silent and hunched, mongrel figures in the blackened ruin, washed by the blood-dark rain. Their fury was exhausted because they had run out of enemies to kill.

They semed lost, as if they did not know what to do next. They would not take part in any rebuilding or recovery. They would not manage the aftermath.

The *Vlka Fenryka* only know how to do one thing.

SPARKS FLY UP. Memory contracts like the flesh on a corpse, tightening on the increasingly pronounced bones pulling the jaws open in a silent scream. In deep lakes of black water, we can watch the reflections of sidereal time pass overhead. I see the Wolves as inheritors, the last guardians of an ancient domain that is so old and crumbling into neglect it has become an incomprehensible ruin. Still, they guard it, like dogs left to guard a house they do not understand.

As long as they endure, their accounts will live on, told and retold by skjalds like me to men like you. A fire will be burning. We will smell the copal resin smoking into the air. Perhaps I will not see the men around me, but I will see their shadows, cast up the cave wall by the spitting fire, like cave art lent the illusion of movement by the inconstant flames.

I will try to listen to what is being said by the men during the long, mumbling conversations, so that I can hear all the secrets of the world, and learn every account from the very first to the very last.

In the coldest, deepest part of the cave, there is a blackness cut by a cold, blue glow. The air smells sterile, like rock in a dry polar highland that lacks any water to form ice. It is far away from the soft warmth and the firelight of the cave, far away from the fraternity of murmuring voices and the smell of smouldering resin. It is there I will be forced to sleep out most of my days. I am too dangerous to keep among the Rout, too compromised. I know too much, and too much knows me. But the *Vlka Fenryka* have grown fond of me, and with that strange, gruff sentimentality of theirs, they cannot bring themselves to quickly and mercifully cut my thread.

So I will be put to sleep in the deep cold of the ice, in stasis far below the Aett, with only Cormek Dod and the other muttering Dreadnoughts as companions. None of us like it there. None of us choose to be there. We miss the firelight. We miss the sunlight. We've dreamed the same dreams a hundred times over, a thousand times. We know them off by heart. We don't choose the dark.

Nevertheless, once in a while, when we are disturbed and revived, we are never content to see the daylight.

If you have to come and wake us, times are not good.

I am standing in the high meadow in Asaheim where I last saw Heoroth Longfang alive, but it is the Wolf King who is towering at my side. The air is as clear as glass. To the west of us, beyond a vast, rolling field of snow and a mighty evergreen forest, mountains rise. They are white, as clean and sharp as carnassials. I know full well that the grey skies behind them aren't storm clouds. They are more mountains, greater mountains,

mountains so immense the sheer scale of them breaks a man's spirit. Where their crags end, buried like thorns in the skin of the sky, the wrath of the winter season Fenrisian storms is gathering and clotting, angry as patriarch gods and malign as trickster daemons.

It is the last hour of the last day before I voluntarily enter stasis.

'You understand why?' asks the Wolf King at my side. His voice is a wet leopard-purr.

'I do,' I say. 'I understand.'

'Ogvai, he speaks highly of your skills as a skjald.'

'The jarl is kind.'

'He's honest. That's why I keep him. But you understand, you can't play out a game with a broken piece on the board.'

'I understand.'

'The accounts, though. We don't want to lose them. Future generations should hear them, and learn from them.'

'I'll conserve them for you, lord,' I say. 'They will be here in my head, ready to tell.'

'Good,' he says. 'Make sure of it. I won't be around to watch over the *Vlka Fenryka* forever. When I'm gone, you'd better make sure they hear the stories.'

I laugh, thinking he's joking.

'You'll never be gone, lord,' I say.

'Never is a long time, skjald,' he replies. 'I'm tough, but I'm not that tough. Just because something's never happened, it doesn't mean it never will.'

'There's a first time for everything.'

'Exactly,' he grunts.

'The unprecedented. Like… Astartes fighting Astartes? Like the Rout being called to sanction another Legion?'

'That?' he answers. He laughs, but it is a sad sound. 'Hjolda, no. *That's* not unprecedented.'

I am lost for a reply. I am never sure when he is

joking. We are looking towards the forest line. The first flakes of snow are fluttering down.

'Are there wolves on Fenris?' I ask.

'Go and look for yourself,' he tells me. 'Go on.'

I look at him. He nods. I start towards the forest line across the snow. I begin to run. I pull my pelt, the one Bercaw gave me, tight around me, like a second skin. In the enormous darkness under the evergreens, I see eyes staring at me: luminous, gold and black-pinned. They are waiting for me, ten thousand pairs of eyes looking out at me from the shadows of the forest. I am not afraid.

I am not afraid of the wolves any more.

Behind me, the Wolf King watches me until I've disappeared into the trees.

'Until next winter,' he says.

Thanks to
Graham McNeill, Jim Swallow, Aaron
Dembski-Bowden, Nick Kyme, Gav Thorpe,
Nik, and Big Steve Bissett, for consults and
suggestions, and the BL staff and readers for
their patience.

ABOUT THE AUTHOR

Dan Abnett is a novelist and award-winning comic book writer. He has written over thirty-five novels, including the acclaimed Gaunt's Ghosts series, the Eisenhorn and Ravenor trilogies and, with Mike Lee, the Darkblade cycle. His novels *Horus Rising* and *Legion* (both for the Black Library) and his Torchwood novel *Border Princes* (for the BBC) were all bestsellers. His novel *Triumff*, for Angry Robot, was published in 2009 and nominated for the British Fantasy Society Award for Best Novel. He lives and works in Maidstone, Kent. Dan's blog and website can be found at *www.danabnett.com*

Follow him on Twitter@VincentAbnett

WARHAMMER
40,000

A SPACE MARINE BATTLES NOVEL

The epic saga that began in A Thousand Sons *and* Prospero Burns *continues in* Battle of the Fang

SINCE THE GENESIS of the Astartes, there has been enmity between the Space Wolves and the Thousand Sons. The brutal and honourable Sons of Fenris and the esoteric Legion of Magnus the Red fought as allies for the Emperor, but all that changed when the Space Wolves attacked Prospero. Magnus and his Thousand Sons were forced to flee their home world to escape annihilation.

The Thousands Sons were defeated, but their hatred only grew in the intervening years. The once-loyal Legion soon fell to Chaos, while the Space Wolves fought bravely in stamping out the Heresy of Horus, proving their loyalty and mettle.

Where once stood brothers now stand the bitterest of enemies.

A thousand years on, the time for vengeance has come. The sorcerous Thousand Sons launch the ultimate attack on their nemesis. Their objective – the Fang, the Space Wolves' fortress on Fenris. Now, a millennia old fury will be unleashed, and destruction and madness will reign. With so many of their brothers chasing Magnus's shadow elsewhere in the galaxy, the Sons of Fenris have never been more vulnerable. The Fang's scant defenders must hold off the overwhelming power of the Thousand Sons, or a proud Chapter will be wiped from the stars forever.

BATTLE OF THE FANG
A SPACE MARINE BATTLES NOVEL
COMING JUNE 2011